A Fine
Retribution

A Fine Retribution

An Alan Lewrie Naval Adventure

Dewey Lambdin

THOMAS DUNNE BOOKS

ST. MARTIN'S PRESS

NEW YORK

THOMAS DUNNE BOOKS.
An imprint of St. Martin's Press.

A FINE RETRIBUTION. Copyright © 2017 by Dewey Lambdin. All rights reserved. Printed in the United States of America. For information, address St. Martin's Press, 175 Fifth Avenue, New York, N.Y. 10010.

www.thomasdunnebooks.com
www.stmartins.com

Maps by Cameron MacLeod Jones

The Library of Congress Cataloging-in-Publication Data is available upon request.

ISBN 978-1-250-10362-8 (hardcover)
ISBN 978-1-250-10363-5 (e-book)

Our books may be purchased in bulk for promotional, educational, or business use. Please contact your local bookseller or the Macmillan Corporate and Premium Sales Department at 1-800-221-7945, extension 5442, or by e-mail at MacmillanSpecialMarkets@macmillan.com.

First Edition: May 2017

10 9 8 7 6 5 4 3 2 1

This one is for "Colonel Johnathon Singleton Mosby," or just plain "Mosby," a spirited little white-furred, ginger-tailed, pink-pawed cat, and a companion for sixteen years. He had one gold eye and one blue eye, and shut them for the last time in late August of 2016. I hope there's a faucet running for you wherever you are, Mosby, and that you're rejoined with your brother, "Forrest," again.

Full-Rigged Ship: Starboard (right) side view

1. Mizen Topgallant
2. Mizen Topsail
3. Spanker
4. Main Royal
5. Main Topgallant
6. Mizen T'gallant Staysail
7. Main Topsail
8. Main Course
9. Main T'gallant Staysail
10. Middle Staysail

11. Main Topmast Staysail
12. Fore Royal
13. Fore Topgallant
14. Fore Topsail
15. Fore Course
16. Fore Topmast Staysail
17. Inner Jib
18. Outer Flying Jib
19. Spritsail

A. Taffrail & Lanterns
B. Stern & Quarter-galleries
C. Poop Deck/Great Cabins Under
D. Rudder & Transom Post
E. Quarterdeck
F. Mizen Chains & Stays
G. Main Chains & Stays
H. Boarding Battens/Entry Port
I. Cargo Loading Skids
J. Shrouds & Ratlines
K. Fore Chains & Stays

L. Waist
M. Gripe & Cutwater
N. Figurehead & Beakhead Rails
O. Bow Sprit
P. Jib Boom
Q. Foc's'le & Anchor Cat-heads
R. Cro'jack Yard (no sail fitted)
S. Top Platforms
T. Cross-Trees
U. Spanker Gaff

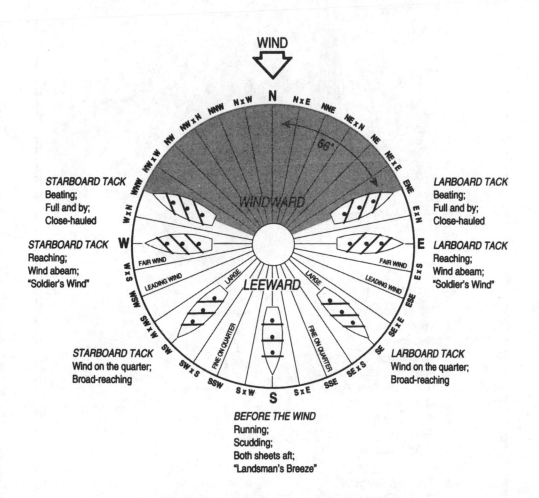

POINTS OF SAIL AND 32-POINT WIND-ROSE

ADRIATIC
SEA

Gaeta

ITALY

Naples

Procida
Ischia *Nisida* Mt. Vesuvius

Capri

BASILICATA

CAMPAGNIA

Taranto

Gallipoli

Golfo di
Taranto

CALABRIA

TYRRHENIAN SEA

Crotone

Catanzaro

Maida Catanzaro
Lido

Tropea *Golfo di Squillace*

Aeolian
Islands *Vibo*
Valentina

Monasterace
Marina

Roccella
Ionica

Milazzo *Scylla* Siderno
Marina di
Gioiosa Ionica

Palermo Locri

Messina Bovalino
Marina

Reggio di
Calabria Brancaleone
Marina

Aspromonte
Mountains *Cape Spartivento*

SICILY *Mt. Etna*

Catania

Syracuse

IONIAN SEA

Mellieha
Bay

MALTA Valletta

N

Mi.   30   60

Haec noster de rege piacula sanguis
sumat et heu cunctae quas misit in aequora gents.

Such be the retribution that my son exacts
from the king, and all the nations, alas! whom the
king has sent to sea.

-VALERIUS FLACCUS,
ARGONAUTICA, BOOK I, LINES 810-811

PROLOGUE

Ships are only hulls, high walls are nothing,
when no life moves in the empty passageways.
—SOPHOCLES, *OEDIPUS REX*, LINE 56

CHAPTER ONE

*T*here was a welcome little breeze cross Algeciras Bay, one that felt re-freshingly cool, enough so to alleviate a stultifying Midsummer day under a blazing Iberian sun. Cooling, aye, but not strong enough to waft away the odours of hot pitch being paid over deck seams that had been re-stuffed with hammered-in oakum. The ship was also being painted to cover the repaired hurts, and the large patches of pale, bare wood where smashed planks of her hull scantlings had been stove in with roundshot. Indeed, in the waist there was an impressive pile of deformed iron shot that had lodged in the ship's timbers but had not penetrated into her vitals. Everything from grapeshot to 24-pounders and even some massive 32-pounders from French carronades; it would all go ashore in dribs and drabs to be sold off to gullible civilians and sailors off other ships as tokens of a signal victory. Or swapped for cheap drink.

HMS *Sapphire*, a weary and battered old two-decked 50-gunner of the Fourth Rate, was almost back to normal since her arrival at Gibraltar a month before, and even *Sapphire*'s Captain had to offer thanks to the dockyard, and the officer in charge of it, Captain William Lobb. Perhaps it was due to the presence of a greater number of warships in Iberian waters since the British Army had opened a campaign over the border into Spain, but His Majesty's Dockyards at Gibraltar were now bung-full of every sort of supplies that had not been available when the ship had based there two years before. There was even a sufficient store of paint; black for the hull, buff for the gunwales, royal blue for the transom, and white for fanciful carvings that decorated her stern, her quarter gallery window frames, and stern gallery posts.

Bless Lobb, he even had sheets of glass, which that very instant were being cut to size and puttied into place to restore the captain's, and wardrooms', starboard quarter gallery sash windows, so if *Sapphire*'s officers "took their ease" with their breeches round their ankles, rain and spray would not come dashing in any longer, much less the risk of sitting on the "thunder box" with a large shot-hole right by one's knee, and the surging ocean close below, as perilous a risk as sailors took when seated on the "heads" in the open air in the bows.

"Chalky, get out of it," Captain Alan Lewrie said to his cat, who was interrupting, as usual. Lewrie was writing a fulsome reccomendation of Acting-Lieutenant Hillhouse in hopes that it might help in the fellow's future promotion. It did not help that Lewrie was not fond of Hillhouse, a bull-headed, sometime sulking lout who, in his late twenties, had yet to pass the oral examinations for an actual promotion. A good sailor, but . . .

Mew! from Chalky, more insistently.

"Oh, here. Chase that," Lewrie griped, balling up one of the early drafts and heaving it cross the great-cabins, but Chalky, now of an age as cats go, had lost his fondness for toys, and stayed atop the desk. *Mrr!* punctuated by a lash of his tail.

"Go find something t'do," Lewrie muttered, almost sweeping the cat off the desk-top. He returned to his letter, but had lost his train of thought, and grunted in frustration.

"'Allo, puss," a sailor from the working-party aft said.

"Chalky, get out o' that, too!" Lewrie snapped, getting to his feet to go retrieve the cat from interfering with the work on his starboard quarter-gallery. He scooped up the cat, who had been poking and pawing at the fresh glass panes before they set, pawing round the empty gaps. There was a newly hung door to the quarter-gallery, and Lewrie shut it. "God, but you're a trial," Lewrie said as he carried the cat in his arms to the starboard side settee and dumped him on the padded seat. "I'll be on deck, Pettus. Keep him out o' trouble, if that's possible."

"I'll try, sir," his cabin steward replied, grinning.

Hatless and coatless, Lewrie went forward to the door to the quarter-deck and stepped out into the full miasma of repair; paint and hot tar and pitch, with only the faintest sweet tang of fresh-sawn lumber, and the louder din of caulking tools, hammers, and the thuds of hot loggerheads as they paid seams.

And there, right at the forward edge of the quarterdeck, stood the reason that HMS *Sapphire* would remain anchored at Gibraltar for some time into the future, and the one item that Captain Lobb could not supply him; the weakened lower mainmast trunk.

French shot had gnawed and chipped it like so many industrious beavers when *Sapphire* had lain herself at the head of the squadron's line of battle to take on the most formidable of the four enemy frigates they had fought a month before. It was a bloody wonder that it hadn't toppled like a storm-lashed tree right then, which would have spelled disaster. Now, though, the lower mast had been re-enforced with spare anchor stocks to vertically span the damage, then woolded with taut-wrapped kedge anchor cable like a splint on a man's broken limb. The topmasts above the fighting top still stood, minus royal or t'gallant yards, but Lewrie could not trust it with any sort of canvas spread above the tops'l.

Whole lower masts, fore, main, or mizen, were not items which lay round loose by the dozens. No, they had to be crafted, scaled to the ship in which they would be installed. Lewrie had discovered that in January of this year when *Sapphire* had been struck by lightning on-passage from Corunna to Portsmouth, and it had taken the Commissioner of Portsmouth Dockyards weeks to come up with a replacement. Just in time, too, for Admiralty could have ordered *Sapphire* de-commissioned and turned her over to the Transport Board to serve out her days as a troop or supply ship. Even after finding a replacement lower mast, Lewrie had had to go up to London to plead, cajole, and make some inventive (and suspiciously optimistic) promises to keep his skilled crew together, and his active commission as her Captain.

Now, here it was again; the same dread of losing her. And how could he explain it away, this time?

You're a cack-handed, clumsy bastard, ain't ya, Lewrie, he imagined Admiralty scolding; *What, you've broken* another*? If you can't play nice with your toys, we'll have to take them away 'til you learn better!* The thought made him smile, if only for an instant.

He went up the larboard ladderway to the poop deck, his usual perch when at sea, but a working-party was just gathering their loggerheads and tar pots after sealing the seams in his cabins' overhead, so a stroll aft to the taffrail lanthorns and flag lockers was out; his shoes would be ruined before the tar cooled. Even his lubberly collapsible wood-and-canvas deck chair, in which he could sprawl high above the bustle of a ship under way, was right out. It was now hung over the iron stanchions which held tight-rolled sailors' hammocks and bedding, like a jack-knife.

With a shrug and a sigh, Lewrie settled for a leisurely stroll forward along the larboard sail-tending gangway, apart from the busy starboard side, acknowledging the sailors or Marines that he met with a nod or a cheery "Good morning" which he most certainly did not feel, dredging up names; after two years, he recognised them as well as he would have all his cousins at a family reunion.

He stopped at the larboard anchor cat-heads and the roundhouse above the forecastle, gave that offending mainmast one more damning glare, then looked out-board at the shore, the high battlements of Gibraltar's fortifi-cations, and the tiers of the town which arose on the steep slopes of The Rock beyond them.

Except on official matters, Lewrie had not taken even a brief run ashore yet, and now that *Sapphire* was finally put to rights, a few hours off the ship would be welcome. There were chop-houses where he could partake in a fresh meal, particularly a seafood house by name of Pescador's, run by a retired Army Sergeant-Major and his Spanish wife and children, that fea-tured a cool cellar full of imported ales and beers from England. There were more taverns and public houses at Gibraltar than there were soldiers in the garrison, it seemed; one in particular, the Ten Tuns, had an awninged outdoor seating area and piles of newspapers where he could idle some hours away with a glass or two of white wine and some Spanish-style *tapas* for appetisers.

Good memories of both places, when his former ship's clerk, Thomas Mountjoy, and he could scheme raids along the Southern Spanish coast a few years back, and Mountjoy, actually an agent with Foreign Office's Secret Branch, could slyly impart the latest doings back in London, or the progress of his plans to subvert the Spanish away from being a French ally to one of theirs.

In his own infuriating "wait for it!" way, Mountjoy had been a fount of inside information, here at Gibraltar, and later in Lisbon, and they had de-veloped a bantering but enjoyable partnership as long as the "skulking set" found him useful.

Now, though, Mountjoy's replacement at Gibraltar was a dour sort of sod who hadn't spared Lewrie two minutes of his time, and had looked askance that some Navy officer had even thought to call upon him at the cover offices of the so-called Falmouth Import & Export Company, Ltd., much less at the top-floor lodgings that Mountjoy had occupied, up near the headquarters of the Army garrison. Lewrie looked up that way briefly, but the awninged outdoor gallery where Mountjoy had set his astronomical telescope to keep an eye on the Spanish Lines was now a blank; even the potted greenery was gone.

Pescador's, perhaps? That memory forced Lewrie to shift his gaze southward to the lower town, and an upper-storey balcony with a set of glazed double doors, where he had lodged his mistress, Maddalena Covilhā. There was no joy from that quarter, either, no joyous waving of glad welcome whenever his ship stood in, or departed. Pescador's was where he had first met her. Would going there be too painful?

Did I do right by her? he asked himself, again.

He'd moved her from Gibraltar to Lisbon when he'd returned to Spanish waters as a Commodore with a small squadron meant to scour the dangerous North coast of Spain to interdict French supply convoys, and Maddalena, being Portuguese, had revelled in becoming a real *Lisboêta* at long last, in the city she'd always longed to see.

But, when General Sir Arthur Wellesley had driven the French from Oporto, Maddalena's birthplace, and Lewrie had thought to shift his squadron there to be days closer to their hunting grounds, she'd balked. She had so many reasons she never wanted to return there; her impoverished, illiterate family the foremost, which she'd fled at the first opportunity, to their great outrage.

It wasn't even a spat, much less an argument, but his suggestion had been the first omen that what relationship they had was exceedingly temporary, after all. War, the Navy, new orders . . . chance?

Lewrie painfully recalled that last night before he had sailed away the final time, and how sad and sombre she had looked as she had whispered, "I will always love you, Alan, *meu amor*," before sweeping up the stairs to her lodgings, leaving him standing in a strong rain.

He had left her an hundred pounds at a Lisbon bank, and left her lodgings paid in full for an entire year, and she had employment with Mountjoy and Secret Branch as a multi-lingual translator; Portuguese, Spanish, English, even French, highly useful in the "war by newsprint" and false information smuggled over the border to infuriate Spanish partisans, and lower the morale of the French who came across the bogus newspapers full of depressing news from home.

Spilled milk, he groaned to himself; *silly, inane . . . call it what you will. If only I'd kept my fool mouth shut!*

For there had been no shift to Oporto; the city's dockyards couldn't support his ships, and there was no guarantee that the French could not come back and re-take the city, with only a small garrison of the Portuguese army to protect it. And now here he was, stuck at Gibraltar with no squadron, no broad pendant, a ship that might be ordered home by the next mail from London, and . . . no mistress.

Lewrie heaved a philosophical sigh as he made his way further forward, right to the beakheads to give the newly re-painted figurehead, a crouching crowned lion with a large gem clutched to its chest, a reassuring pat for good luck. That grinning beast had seen them through to a signal victory, even though at great cost.

Lewrie *could* allow himself a moment of smug satisfaction, even if it was a brief one. It wasn't every day lately that anyone had a Chinaman's chance to bring four French warships to battle and defeat them in such a crushing victory.

They'd been in port long enough for the London papers and *The Naval Chronicle* to catch up with them, along with the copies that his father, Sir Hugo Willoughby, had sent along.

Well, *The Naval Chronicle* re-printed his and his subordinate officers' dry, sufficiently humble action reports, all of which were carefully written to avoid prideful boasting. No, it was the papers, *The Times* and *The Gazette,* that had done the boasting for them, comparing the battle to a miniature Trafalgar, which Lewrie had thought a bit much. The newspaper writers had been positively ghoulish in their descriptions of how many Frenchmen had been slain, mutilated by shot, and surgeons' treatments, revelling in the "butcher's bill" and how a Hearty British Tar was the equal of any five or six cowardly Frogs.

Speeches in Commons and Lord's were re-printed that declared that, after the shameful showing of the Royal Navy under the hapless command of Admiral James Gambier at Aix Roads—"Dismal Jemmy" to the Navy—where a fine victory had been squandered by Gambier's dithering, and French ships that should have been taken or burned to the waterline had been allowed to escape, despite the pluck and daring of Captain Lord Thomas Cochrane's assault with fireships and bombs, it was Captain Sir Alan Lewrie, Bt., and his ships that had revived the "tradition of victory" for the Navy, and had won fresh laurels for it!

There were calls made for commemorative sets of silver plate for all Captains and Commanders present, presentation swords, instant promotions, financial rewards perhaps, coins (not actual medals) for every participant to be minted. Some in the Commons lauded Lewrie as a man just as courageous and daring as Cochrane.

Lewrie had winced at that, for everyone in the Navy knew that Thomas Cochrane was a too-proud, arrogant, and reckless "neck-or-nothing" madman who'd run roughshod over social inferiors, orders, or superior officers if he thought he knew better! Besides, what had the acclaim gotten Cochrane in the end? Gambier's court-martial had white-washed the fool, and it was Cochrane who'd resigned and entered the House of Lords to wrangle for justice for himself.

More personally, Lewrie had gotten yet another packet of newspaper articles, and a welcome letter from his former First Officer, Lieutenant Geoffrey Westcott, who had taken the largest of the prizes home . . . kicking and screaming to avoid the duty, but he'd gone. Now, he was glad that he had, for he was to be promoted to Commander and put in command of a brig-sloop, most-likely, but he would stride his own quarterdeck, at long last. Westcott had gotten assurances that all four prizes would be "bought in" to Royal Navy service, and that meant that soon there would be lashings, umpteen thousands of pounds due to every ship which had participated, a windfall that Westcott was eager to spend on himself, beginning with wine, women, song, and . . . women!

Geoffrey Westcott. Lewrie missed him, too, glad though he was to see a good man advance. Westcott had become the closest friend that Lewrie had allowed himself to have aboard the same ship, in the same crew, slowly abandoning the demanded separation of a Captain from the rest of his ship's people. Lewrie and Westcott had served together nigh six years, though, first in the *Reliant* frigate in 1803, then in *Sapphire* since 1807, and Lewrie had come to rely on Westcott's good sense in all things, sure that Geoffrey would present him with a ship and crew in good order, and in good spirits, and Lewrie had enjoyed the way they had learned to rub together, and . . .

"Just damn my eyes, what do you think you're doing, Twomey?" Acting-Lieutenant Hillhouse screeched. "There's paint all over the bloody deck! Master at Arms, here! Pass word for the Master at Arms!"

Damn, but I miss Westcott! Lewrie thought; *Christ, here we go again!*

CHAPTER TWO

*L*ewrie crossed over the forecastle to the starboard side, then down the ladderway to the waist, where the tirade was continuing, and it had drawn Lieutenant Harcourt, now *Sapphire*'s First Officer, to boot.

"A paint spill, sir?" Lewrie asked, looking at the weedy and wiry of-fending sailor, Twomey, who stood all but trembling under the Second Officer's wrath.

"Should be on charges, sir," Hillhouse growled, "for clumsiness, and making a mess. I've sent for the Master at Arms."

"I heard," Lewrie sternly said. "What happened, Twomey?"

"Can o' buff paint f'r th' gunn'ls, sir," Twomey stuttered, red in the face, "come up empty on a line wif th' ol' brush innit, an' it snagged on th' cap-rails an' spilt a little. Sorry, sir."

There were a couple of splotches of buff paint on the white-sanded deck planks, and another where a stiff, worn-out brush had alit.

"No need for Mister Baggett that I see, Mister Hillhouse," Lewrie told him. "Send for a Bosun's Mate, Nobbs or Plunkett, rather, and some paint thinner to take that up. That, or some of our issue wine, either'd do, hey? See you scrub it all up, Twomey."

"Aye, I will, sir, an' thankee, sir!" Twomey said, head bobbing and grin-ning in relief that he'd escaped an appearance at a Captain's Mast and a threat of punishment. And, the comparison of paint thinner to the quality of "Miss Taylor" or "Blackstrap", the cheapest wines that the Navy supplied, had amused the fellow, too.

"Carry on, all," Lewrie said, turning away.

"Ehm, if I may, though, sir?" Lieutenant Harcourt, the First Officer who had come to the commotion, bade.

"Aye, Mister Harcourt?" Lewrie replied, knowing what was coming. He crooked a finger to lead Harcourt forward to the forecastle belfry and manger where they might not be overheard by the sailors. Noises from the beasts in the manger helped mask their words, and Lewrie had a hope that the farmyard smells from piglets, chickens, nanny goat, and kids might force Harcourt's gripe to be a brief one.

"Discipline, sir," Harcourt began once they were near the manger, and Lewrie *tried* not to roll his eyes as Lieutenant Harcourt mounted his hobby horse once again. "The hands are going slack and truculent. If we were at sea . . ."

"Which we are not, sir," Lewrie was quick to point out. "And most-like we won't be, 'til next Epiphany, at this rate."

"This sitting idle, sir, it isn't doing the people any good," Lieutenant Harcourt said. "We may have to take steps . . ."

"Well, not idle, really," Lewrie countered, striving for a calm tone, instead of grabbing Harcourt by his coat lapels and giving him a good shake. "We've been doing a lot of our own repairs, and that has kept 'em busy."

"For now, sir," Harcourt insisted, "but, now the major work is done, it will be hard to come up with any sort of 'make-work' to keep their minds on their proper duties. Some shore liberty may help after that, but only for so long, and I fear that we may have to resort to the 'cat' or serious stoppages, soon."

"Shore liberty?" Lewrie scoffed. "They'd had one decent run ashore since we got here, and none of our previous prize-money's come in yet. They're as skint as church-mice, with not two pence to rub together, and can't *afford* a good liberty. You know my policy about corporal punishment, sir. I'll not flog our people without a just cause."

But you and Hillhouse would! he thought, a tad angrily.

"Bread and water, no rum, no tobacco . . . those only go so far, sir," Harcourt grumped, stiffening his posture.

"I know," Lewrie replied, growing a bit exasperated. "Come up with activities, contests, watch-against-watch t'keep 'em occupied. We can have 'em row or sail races with the cutters, competing choirs, choose the best dancers. Once the last piddlin' chores are done, I'll declare a 'Make and Mend' day, and 'Splice the Mainbrace'. After that, we'll re-establish cut-lass, pike, and musketry drill, dry practice on the great guns, and those routines should take care of some of their idleness. It's our *job* t'keep the people in good spirits, especially the job of my First Officer. Think what Westcott would've done and emulate his example.

"But, only bring men up on charges that are *deservin'* of the lash, Mister Harcourt," Lewrie sternly cautioned. "They ain't a pack o' raw lubbers, not the sort t'beat and bully into submission."

Harcourt scowled and pursed his lips as if he would say something, ducking his head as if being compared to Lieutenant Westcott was unfair.

Or maybe you don't *compare, and know it,* Lewrie thought.

"You never can tell, Mister Harcourt," Lewrie genially added, smiling in hope that Harcourt might still measure up, "the yards may turn up a new mast for us, and we'll be back at sea, where none o' this matters!"

"A thing devoutly to be wished, sir, aye," Harcourt said, seeming to deflate like a bladder as he realised that his arguments would not avail.

"And don't let the Mids get so bored that they start usin' the crew as objects of cruel amusement, either, sir," Lewrie warned. "Do carry on, Mister Harcourt, and . . . be inventive, hey?"

"Aye, sir."

Lewrie had to admit that he had never really liked either Lieutenant Harcourt, or Hillhouse, who had been a senior Midshipman when he had read himself into command of *Sapphire,* replacing her former Captain.

That sour, dyspeptic Tartar had been a harsh disciplinarian, opposed by a First Officer more like a "Popularity Dick", and the ship had been divided into two factions, with Second Officer Harcourt and Midshipman Hillhouse of the Captain's persuasion. Unfortunately, her Captain and First Officer had despised each other so hotly that they had resorted to a duel with pistols, wounding each other both in body and career.

Westcott! Lewrie and Westcott had found a way to ameliorate the situ-ation, knitting the crew and wardroom into a well-drilled and efficient, happy whole. Lots of action, prize-money, and pride in new-won prowess and the right to swagger when ashore had gone a long way towards ac-complishing that.

Now, though, so long as *Sapphire* sat idle, Lewrie doubted that even the sudden arrival of a whole year's pay *and* prize-money on top of that would lift his sailors' gloom. And Harcourt and Hillhouse were not helping, too set in their ways and dispositions, too eager to resort to corporal punishment before anything else had been tried!

Lewrie thought to return to the larboard sail-tending gangway and make his way aft to the quarterdeck once more, but now Bosun Terrell was barking orders as a work-boat from the dockyards was coming alongside to larboard with fresh casks of water to fill *Sapphire*'s novel iron tanks. And the sight of the Purser, Mr. Cadrick, and his Jack-in-the-Breadroom, Irby, on the gangway with ledger books told Lewrie that there most-like were other boats behind the water hoy, laden with flour sacks, dried fruits for duffs, shore-baked bread, vegetables, and sides of slaughtered beef fetched from the Morrocan port of Tétuan to replace rock-hard salt-meats. Lewrie heaved a sigh and turned to go aft down the main deck.

"'Ware, Cap'm!" a ship's boy cried. "Oh . . . !"

Lewrie was being butted on the shins!

He looked down to discover a kid goat, lowering and shaking its wee head for another go at being a "billy" in training. As the kid launched itself, Lewrie bent and scooped it up, bleating and all four hooves frantically scrambling in sudden indignity, held it to his chest despite the rank odour, and handed it to the "duck fucker" in charge of the manger.

"Sorry, sir, 'e jus' got out, somehow!" the boy spluttered as he took the kid and held it, cradling it like a mis-behaving puppy.

"No matter," Lewrie said. "Leash him if ye have to. Mind, now," Lewrie said in mock severity, "he keeps that up, and I might demand a roast kid for my supper. *Love* roast goat, I surely do!"

The boy gulped and shoved the kid back into the pen with its nanny.

Lewrie went on aft, laughing, and glad to find some amusement in a frustrating day, and went up the ladderway to the quarterdeck, where he was greeted by the ship's mascot, a brown-and-white, black-muzzled dog named Bisquit.

"Well, hallo, Bisquit, and where've you been hidin'?" he asked as he bent and ruffled his fur.

Ship's dog, mine arse! he thought.

Bisquit had been smuggled aboard by the *Reliant* frigate's Midshipmen when anchored at Nassau, New Providence in the Bahamas, an island mutt which had rapidly become the entire crew's pet, but, when *Reliant* had paid off and no one else could take him along to their next ship, it was Lewrie who'd volunteered to take him along to his father's farm at Anglesgreen in Surrey for that long winter to heal up from a wound he'd suffered during a battle with a Spanish frigate off Buenos Aires.

Now, though the dog was still a friend to one and all, especially when there were goodies offered in the messes belowdecks, it was in Lewrie's great-cabins where Bisquit got his main feeding, and a patch of carpet to curl up on. Lewrie's cat, Chalky, was still not too sure of the arrangement, but the two had somewhat adapted to each other's presence.

"Want a sausage, do ye, Bisquit? Thought you would!" Lewrie teased as he headed for his cabins, and the dog frisked alongside him, tail whisking and looking up adoringly. Of *course* he'd like a sausage; he even knew the word! And when Lewrie dug into his stash of wee sausages and jerked meat strips, an entire hundredweight that he kept well-stocked, Chalky came begging for one, too, though he took his atop the dining table where Bisquit would not grab it.

After some petting for both of them, they settled down and he went aft to the doors to his stern gallery, where that little breeze might mitigate the lingering stinks, but there was no shade to be had, and Lewrie merely stood by the doors, looking outwards, again.

Lewrie had allowed himself one of those wee sausages, too, and idly chewed the last of it, pondering a run ashore, after all, though he felt a minor pang of guilt that he could afford to do so when his sailors could not, not 'til *some* prize-money trickled in.

He thought again of the seafood restaurant, and began to yearn for lobster and drawn butter, scallops, shrimp, and mussels in white wine sauce, with piping-hot fresh bread rolls. He tempted himself with an image of a cool ale to begin with, then a whole bottle of some white wine like the *vinho verde* he'd discovered at Lisbon. A green salad with oil and vinegar . . . yum! He thought that there might even be some sparkling white wines from Spain available, now that the trade cross the fortified Lines was so open, and the great expanse of dead ground 'twixt British and Spanish ramparts had been turned into grazing land for Spanish livestock!

Some company during his repast? Pescador's was a favourite of the subaltern officers, the young sparks of the Gibraltar garrison, where they brought the fetching morts "under their protection", most of whom were "no nicer than they had a right to be". An hour or so of harmless flirtation with the ones un-accompanied?

Christ, I show up in full dress, with sash and star, and both my medals, and they learn I'm Sir *Alan Lewrie,* Baronet, *I might have t'beat 'em off with a rope starter!* he thought with a silent laugh.

But, no. There was no real point in it.

He had sadly shed one mistress, and would not be at Gibraltar long enough to take on another. And besides, the older he got, the less he was entranced by the whores, no matter how fetching. That was too anonymous, too commercial, and over the years since his late wife had passed away, he had found himself more in "serial monogamy" than mindless rutting.

Geoffrey Westcott would have laughed such pickiness to scorn! But then, Westcott had never met a mort that he *wouldn't* try to put the leg over.

"Ehm, sir," Pettus, his cabin steward, intruded on his thoughts. "Would you like some cool tea with lemon and sugar, sir?"

"Aye, Pettus, I would at that," Lewrie said, turning his attention back in-board, and espying his desk in the day cabin. He heaved a great, put-upon sigh as he went back to his desk and the un-finished letter of recommendation for Hillhouse.

What can *I say of his good qualities?* he wondered as he sat down; *That he's a skilled seaman, and he can eat with a knife and a fork? I* know, *I've seen him* do *it!*

And if Admiralty lost patience and decided to de-commission his ship, there might be an *host* of Midshipmen and petty officers in need of praise to keep their rates and budding careers alive.

"Where the Devil was I, then?" Lewrie muttered, picking up his pen and dipping it in the ink-well.

CHAPTER THREE

I'll have t'give Yeovill my congratulations," Lewrie said as he polished off the last scrumptious bites of his breakfast.

"Why'z 'at, sir?" Tom Dasher, his new cabin servant, asked as he poured Lewrie a fresh cup of coffee.

"Not a bit of his cooking tasted or smelled like tar or paint thinner," Lewrie japed.

"Well, it's been two days since all that work wuz over, sir," Dasher told him with a puzzled shrug.

"Maybe all the stinks just stuck in my nose, then," Lewrie allowed as he spooned cream and sugar into his coffee and stirred.

"Can't notice nothin', Cap'm," Dasher said after a deep sniff to test the air. "Th' ship smells th' same'z all'ays."

"Aye, doesn't she," Lewrie said with a chuckle. "The nostalgic perfumes of a life at sea, ahh! Farts, sweat, bilges . . ."

Dasher glanced over at Pettus in confusion, looking for guidance, but Pettus could only give him a wee grin and a negative shake of his head. Dasher took Lewrie's empty plate and utensils and went to join the cabin steward.

"What's he goin' on about?" Dasher whispered. "Ain't no perfume that

I kin smell. Th' ship smells right bad, if ya takes time t'notice. Not'z bad as some places I been, but right ripe."

"For me, Dasher, I preferred the tar, paint, and thinner," Pettus said in like manner, winking. "Those odours covered the usual ones."

"Captains is odd, I heard," Dasher grinned. "Perfume, my arse."

"At least you got a good one for your first ship, lad," Pettus assured him. "I'll finish up here, you go make the bed."

There was a sharp rap of a musket butt on the quarterdeck, and a stamp of boots. "Midshipman Holbrooke t'see the Cap'm, SAH!" cried the Marine sentry at the great-cabin door.

"Enter," Lewrie called back, and one of the ship's newest Mids came in with his hat under his arm.

"Beg pardon, sir, but the dockyard has hoisted a Post Boy flag, and a signal, Have Mail," Holbrooke said, almost squirming with delight, in hopes that he might have word from home.

"And you wish to dash off and fetch it, Mister Holbrooke? See if someone's written you?" Lewrie teased. It *had* been a grand breakfast, and he was feeling more chipper than he had in weeks.

"Ehm, *aye*, sir!" Holbrooke agreed.

"Very well," Lewrie told him, "pass word for Crawley's boat crew, and they're to man the second cutter to see you ashore to the Post Office and back. I and my clerk, Mister Faulkes, will sort it all out."

"Aye aye, sir!" Holbrooke said with a beaming grin, and dashed back to the quarterdeck, bawling for Crawley and his gang.

"Hmm," Lewrie mused, sipping his coffee. His chipper mood had vanished, in dread that Admiralty in London might have sent him the bad news of *Sapphire*'s fate, at last. Or, he and Faulkes would have to reject some letters and send them back to their sources, re-opening fresh sorrows. Once in port at Gibraltar, Lewrie had written to the families of those members of the crew who had been killed in battle, or had succumbed to their wounds, but it was good odds that before news of their battle had reached England, wives, sweethearts, parents, or children of the dead had written their loved ones, all un-knowing; before the paper accounts, before Lewrie's condolences had reached them.

Damn the uncertainty of postal deliveries, he thought.

"More coffee, sir?" Pettus asked.

"Ah, no, Pettus," Lewrie decided, getting to his feet. "I think I'll go sit on the poop deck and await the mail." Before leaving his cabins, he picked up an un-finished novel from the settee, in hopes he could use that as a carefree prop to disguise his worries.

Lewrie plunked himself down in his collapsible deck chair and tried to lose himself in the book, but it was hard going amid all the bustle of manning the second cutter and the boat crew shoving off, the stamp of feet both shod and bare, and the clash of steel on steel as the crew began an hour of cutlass drill, and the calls for First Position . . . Third in Two Motions . . . Balance Step . . . Extension, Slash co-mingled with the seduction of the dairy maid in the milking barn.

It was even noisy enough that Bisquit came to the poop deck to lay his head in Lewrie's lap for a second or two, get some reassuring pats, then curled up on the deck in his shadow. Lewrie found himself taking peeks at his pocket watch and watching the slow progress of the cutter to the landing stage by the dockyards, its long idleness, then its slow return to the ship.

Finally, as the cutter thumped against the hull below the larboard entry-port, Lewrie dog-eared his place in the book, rose, and went down to the quarterdeck to re-enter his cabins where he could pose as dis-interested on the starboard side settee.

"Midshipman Holbrooke, with a mail sack, SAH!" the Marine sentry called out, with a note of wistful longing in his voice that one of the letters might be for him.

"Enter!" Lewrie bade, and got to his feet as Holbrooke came in, making a show of dog-earing his book once more and setting it aside. "Much of it, is there, Mister Holbrooke?"

"A fair amount I would judge, sir, though not all that heavy," the Mid told him, making a *moue* of dis-appointment that the mail sack was not bulging, or almost too heavy to carry in one hand.

"Well, we'll see to it, nonetheless," Lewrie told him, taking charge of the sack and dropping it on his desk in the day-cabin. "You may go, Mister Holbrooke, and thankee. We'll have it sorted and ready for dispersing by Noon. Pass word for Mister Faulkes to come aft."

"Aye, sir," Holbrooke replied, obviously wishing that he could help tear into it and snatch out anything addressed to him instanter.

Whilst waiting for Faulkes to turn up, Lewrie opened the sack and pored through the loose pile of letters, looking for anything that seemed official. The Marine sentry announced Faulkes, at last, and Lewrie snapped his "Enter!" almost-absentmindedly, intent on his own search.

"Sorry, sir," Faulkes said, "I was forward, in the galley, with Yeovill, when you called."

"No matter," Lewrie told him. "Here, help sort, will you?"

"Aye, sir. Oh dear. Oh dear, again," Faulkes said as he began to make a small stack off to one side. "Mister Yelland . . . Mister Roe, Midshipman Ward . . . one for Kibworth. One for Lieutenant Elmes?"

Dead men's letters, handled as if they were infectious, 'twixt forefinger and thumb pinched to the smallest corners. The Sailing Master, the junior Marine Lieutenant, two fallen Midshipmen, and the former Third Officer, then an host of sailors or private Marines.

"Send them back to the Post Office, sir?" Faulkes asked.

"Aye, I'd suppose," Lewrie glumly agreed, "though what they do with 'em's anyone's guess. Who'd pay the post for returned letters? Faulkes . . . have you been drinking?" Lewrie asked, making the connexion of his clerk and the galley, where the Ship's Cook, Tanner, always kept a secret stash of brandy, rum, or wine, and by the time that the evening mess was served up, Tanner would be reeling, bawling drunk, to the detriment of the rations, happily "three sheets to the wind".

"Only a wee, convivial nip, sir," Faulkes tried to laugh off, though having trouble with "convivial".

"We've *spoken* about that, sir," Lewrie sternly pointed out. "I trust you are not so deep in your cups that you can manage to fulfill your duties. Hmm?"

Lewrie had discovered long ago that Faulkes had a problem with drink, more so than the average sailor aboard, but as long as he kept a taut leash on it, he had tolerated his fault. Lately, though, the fellow seemed *always* to be "cherry merry".

"I'll be fine, sir, honest," Faulkes vowed, though he seemed a tad unsteady on his feet.

"You had better be, Mister Faulkes," Lewrie warned. "Sort out everything for the wardroom, the Midshipmen's mess, then handle the issue of the rest to the hands before the Noon mess. *Minus* the rum issue at Seven Bells, hmm?"

"Aye, sir," Faulkes said, taut-lipped and abashed.

As for Lewrie, there was, thankfully, nothing from Admiralty, nor anything official; it was all personal letters from friends in the Navy or from London. Sir Malcolm Shockley, in the House of Commons, sent his congratulations, and an account of the praise he had said in a speech. There was his old school friend, with whom he had been expelled from Harrow, Peter Rushton, now Viscount Draywick, who uttered the same sentiments, and bragged about his speech in Lord's.

There was one from Lady Eudoxia Stangbourne, wife of Percy, Viscount Stangbourne, whose self-raised light dragoon regiment was now in Spain as part of General Sir Arthur Wellesley's army. Her English was much improved, probably with the help of a full-time secretary, from her native Russian. The former trick rider, trick shooter, and *ingenue* actress with Daniel Wigmore's travelling circus and theatrical troupe wrote happy congratulations for his victory, along with snippets of news from Percy, and what he was doing, and her hopes that they all could be together again in happier times.

There was a quick note from his youngest son, Hugh, boasting of what Lewrie's former squadron was doing on the North coast of Spain, and how many more prizes they had taken, how many French ships they'd burned, and of the addition of a third frigate and two more brig-sloops to Captain Chalmers's command; Commodore, rather, since Admiralty had granted him permission to hoist his own broad pendant so long as Lewrie and *Sapphire* were un-available.

Glad tidings t'make my teeth grind, Lewrie thought of that!

And, wonder of wonders, there was a letter from his elder son, Sewallis, who hadn't written or responded to Lewrie's letters in ages!

"Damn my eyes, my boy's a Passed Midshipman!" Lewrie crowed.

"Ehm, which one, sir?" Pettus asked perking up from polishing silver in the dining coach.

"Sewallis, my older," Lewrie happily told him. "His ship put into Portsmouth for provisions, Channel Fleet held an Examining Board whilst she was there, and he passed on his first go!"

"Why, that's grand, sir!" Pettus congratulated. "Even though I can't recall ever meeting your elder, sir, I'm sure you're that proud of him. A credit to the family name."

"He writes that the Post-Captains on the Board told him that he was the best-prepared Mid they'd seen . . . that his answers were clear as a bell," Lewrie happily related. "Damn! Just damn my eyes. Well!"

Sewallis, though, also wrote that while he was now rated as a Passed Midshipman, he had yet to hear anything regarding a promotion to Lieutenant, so he was still aboard the same plodding two-decker 74 he had been in the last two years. In point of fact, Sewallis's congratulations anent his father's victory seemed insincere. He seemed bitter that grand things, honour and glory, and adventures, fell so easily on Lewrie, and his younger brother, Hugh, who could not help but write him gloating letters of derring-do and lashings of prize-money. Sewallis, Lewrie recalled, had been aboard ships of the line since running away to sea and practically forging his way into a ship in 1803. Most of his time at sea was spent on the blockade of the French naval port of Brest, standing off-and-on the same marks day after day, week after week, hoping that the French would come out, though they never did. And when the seas in the Bay of Biscay churned up, it would be days or weeks far from land, clawing far out to deep waters for safety, and a brutal sort of seamanship. In Lisbon, when Lewrie and Hugh had time for a brief hour or two together ashore, Hugh had japed, rather snidely, that he doubted if Sewallis had ever heard a shot fired in anger since he'd first gone to sea, and no wonder his rare letters to his brother had prompted Hugh to imagine that Sewallis was "losing interest", more into drink, flirting, and dancing on his rare times ashore!

I dearly wish he'd have spent some time in frigates or sloops, Lewrie thought as he set Sewallis's letter aside, at last; *There's the real school for sailors. Well, maybe when he gets his promotion he'll get off the "liners" at last, and* find *some excitement.*

Lewrie had left the old *Ariadne,* a 64, early in his own career, when she'd been hulked at Antigua, and felt that his *real* training came in the *Parrot* schooner, the *Desperate* sloop, then the hired-in brig of war *Shrike* during the American Revolution. Those ships had been his schools, and filled with fond memories of action and adventures. Hugh had escaped the Third Rate ships of the line and had already been aboard two frigates; at least *he* was having fun.

"Good God," Lewrie muttered in surprise, for the last letter was from Miss Jessica Chenery, sister of one of his Midshipmen. He broke the wax seal with eagerness and spread the pages on the desk to read.

> *Dear Captain Lewrie,*
>
> *When first the Accounts of your Battle with four enemy Ships appeared in the newspapers, I felt, as any Patriotic Englishwoman, great Pride in the Prowess of our Navy, though I was Aghast at the papers' descriptions of how many of the French were slain. It was only after we received Charley's letter and his description of how Horrid it was, that I and my family were steeped in Dread at how much Risk that my youngest Brother was in, and how shocking it was to him to lose two fellow Midshipmen who had become Dear Friends, and put personal anecdotal characterisations to the Officers and Sailors lost, making them even more Human and too Precious to perish.*

Father suspects that what Charley wrote of the Horror is not a
Tithe on the grim Reality, as a way to assure us that his new
profession is not quite as Dangerous as it now seems.
    I knew in my heart that, despite your kindly Assurances about a
Naval Career for him, as he dearly wished, it would be fraught with
Peril, and now I am wracked with constant worry for him, and for
you, sir.

The young lady had not been shy about taking Lewrie to task when he'd collected young Charles Chenery at the family's manse to bear him off to Portsmouth, and *Sapphire*. She'd been quite outspoken about her worries, then, though her later letters had been much cheerier. Lewrie felt a qualm that he had so distressed her.

From the first Accounts, I prayed that you would have not been
Injured, and trust that my letter finds you Well and in good Health.
Your ship is now at Gibraltar undergoing Repairs, Charley says, and
may not return to sea for some time, I gather? For my part, I count
that a Blessing, removing you and my brother from immediate risk of
Harm.

"You can call it that," Lewrie muttered. "I don't."

Still, she meant well, and Lewrie felt a twinge of gratitude that Jessica Chenery would pray for his well-being, and a respite from whatever perils she imagined that seafarers faced.

At least she's too intelligent to believe in sea monsters, he thought with a wee grin; *Intelligent, creative . . . damned fetching.*

He leaned back in his chair, recalling the too-brief meeting at the Reverend Chenery's manse that cold February pre-dawn morning. It had only been half an hour, perhaps less, before he had to depart so his coach might reach Portsmouth Dockyards before the gates were closed at Midnight, but Jessica Chenery had made quite an impression on him. Much like her younger brother, Midshipman Charles Chenery, she had hair so dark brown that it had appeared black in some lights, and the oddest shade of dark blue eyes. Yawn-inducing early morning, perhaps not half an hour risen from bed, and dressed for warmth, not to impress, in a drab wool gown and grey wool shawl with her hair down and bound loose at the nape of her neck, still . . . she had been stunning. Clear-complexioned, quite creamy and flawless, in fact, and as she had taken him to task with her fears for her brother in his new career, Jessica Chenery's warm concerns had made her seem animated; even more animated when she had been urged to display some of her artwork, portraits staggeringly realistic and true-to-life, or amusing prints for children she'd sold. She had even offered to paint him in the future, and had stated her going rate, much to Reverend Chenery's discomfort. And when they had stood together to admire a portrait of her sister and newborn baby, even a drab brown wool gown could not disguise what Lewrie took to be a slim and girlish form.

Over the course of the Spring and Summer, he had been surprised to receive several letters from her, some enquiring about a member of her church family at St. Anselm's, an Army Lieutenant who had not survived the grisly retreat to Corunna with Sir John Moore's army, and a young fellow who *might* have become her fiancé, if he'd lived. Then, in another letter, Jessica had included a pen-and-ink sketch of Lewrie, one very detailed and declared by his officers to be a spitting image, and that gleaned from that half an hour in her father's house!

Chatty, cheerful letters asking of her brother's progress, and whose portraits she had painted, the offer to do the illustrations for a children's book, of meeting his old cabin steward, John Aspinall, who had become a publisher and author of several nautical guides for young fellows wishing to go to sea, after he'd "swallowed the anchor".

Aye, talented, creative, well-spoken, and with a gift of expression in her writing . . . and damned fetching she was. Though, what had Pettus said, his smirk well-concealed, after the portrait had arrived? That "it appears that the young lady has set her cap for you, sir"?

"Oh, pshaw," Lewrie muttered again, then sat back upright and returned to her letter. It had turned to breezy news of what Summer in London was like; how she, her father, and their long-time lodger, the widowed *émigré* French painter, Madame Berenice Pellatan, had gone to the annual flower show, and to the display of the Royal Academy's art show of this year's winners and runners-up, and how Jessica felt tempted to submit a piece of her own next Summer, under a pseudonym, of *course,* and what a jape it would be for a woman to even place, much less win!

Lewrie imagined the sly "cat that ate the canary" look on her face as she created her submission, and wondered how she would reveal her identity to the staid Royal Academy's senior members if she did win. He strongly suspected that it would be something dramatic, and a Nine Day Wonder.

Her father would be mortified, of course, though Lewrie suspected that

that worthy was not above sharing in the monetary prize, The Reverend Chenery—vicar or rector, Lewrie wasn't sure which—had a well-to-do parish, but seemed as miserly and "skint" as an Irish crofter, and none too happy with his daughter's choice of even *daring* to have a career, much less the fact that she had made nigh an hundred pounds income the year before. If she was a man, she would qualify to be a *voter* in her parish. If Jessica found herself a husband Lewrie doubted if her father could scrounge up fifty or sixty pounds per annum for her dowry! Antiquarianism, ancient books, maps, relics from the Greeks, Romans, or Phoenicians that might prove that America had been visited long before Columbus; what *rot*!

It was a given, therefore, that Jessica Chenery would *not* be attracting a suitable mate anytime soon, when most young bachelors would expect double that "dot", or more, and most "respectable men" would be as aghast as her father with her artistry! Young women who "de-sexed" themselves by dabbling in proper men's pursuits would be an embarrassment that eligible bachelors' parents would do anything to avoid!

And that would be a waste, Lewrie thought, a hellish waste of a fine young lady. Such forward ladies ended up as nannies, spinster housekeepers, or some wealthier lady's maid!

Dammit, Lewrie was coming to like her, her good humour and her spirit, her courage to make her own way. And, the fact that she was very fetching and a remarkable beauty was a bonus. Well, "*like*" wasn't quite the word for his feelings by then; he was becoming enamoured in a way, enough so that a return to England to pay *Sapphire* off could almost be said to be a brief blessing.

I could get my portrait done, he thought with a fond smile; *a chance to spend some time with her . . . before my next ship, of course . . . and get to know her better.*

To what end, though? he had to ask himself. She was in her late twenties, he was in his mid-fourties; well, forty-six to be accurate, and he doubted that a young lady of a family with *every* brother and brother-in-law but for her youngest brother in Holy Orders, would be amenable to sinful tumbles.

Just a portrait, then, he decided as he finished her letter, then reached for his pen to reply that instant.

CHAPTER FOUR

*T*here is always the off-chance that a laminate replacement mast could be fashioned, Sir Alan," Captain William Lobb told him as they stood in the bustle of the Gibraltar Dockyards. Lobb had taken up his predecessor's task of building 36-foot gunboats for the defense of the vast anchorage, even though the many larger and better-armed Spanish gunboats that had lurked over at Algeciras and up the rivers were no longer a threat, and if a French army showed up to lay siege it was a given that the Spanish would burn them before surrendering.

"Laminated," Lewrie repeated. "I am not familiar . . ."

"One constructs several courses of vertical timbers round some much lighter and slimmer core, sir," Lobb expounded, "much like the Romans formed their *fasces* . . . the bundles of axes on long shafts as a symbol of power, and justice. One shaft would snap when put under strain, but a bundle would be as rigid as a single thick mast or spar. It *could* be made, but, as you can see, suitable planking long enough to reach from the keelson and partner timbers to the height of the main top are simply not readily available, even less so than a one-piece replacement mainmast, unfortunately."

"And all those pieces would have to be nailed together, toed I suppose, then bound with iron hoops?" Lewrie asked.

"Exactly so, Sir Alan," Lobb sadly agreed, "and, as you can see, most of the lumber here in the yards run about twelve feet long, so it would require a special order from a home yard for pieces of the proper length."

"So, I'm stuck here 'til the bottom rots out of her, is that what you're saying, Captain Lobb?" Lewrie despaired, even allowing himself a slight audible groan, and a tooth-baring wince.

"I fear so, sir," Lobb said with a sad shrug of his shoulders. "In my last report to Admiralty, I expressed my frustration, and I do trust, your frustration as well, that I do not see a timely solution. You might have better luck sailing her home and placing yourself at the mercy of Portsmouth's artificers."

"Mercy, sir?" Lewrie scoffed. "They *have* none!"

"We've done the best we could . . . ," Lobb began.

"I know you have, sir, and I'm grateful," Lewrie told him.

"We've scarfed in and bound . . . plugs, as it were, to stiffen your lower mainmast," Lobb said, taking off his hat to mop himself with a pocket handkerchief for a moment, "and I daresay that they, along with your bracing anchor stocks and rope woolding, will hold up well enough, so long as you don't put too much sail pressure aloft. It would be a slow passage home, but . . ."

"Oh, *believe* me, Captain Lobb, we're *used* to slow in *Sapphire*," Lewrie hooted without much mirth. "I doubt we've logged nine knots the last two years, and that with a *clean* bottom! The best I could expect would be a thrice-reefed tops'l, bare upper masts, and a stays'l or two . . . perhaps *no* tops'l and a thrice-reefed main course."

"Ehm, perhaps stays'ls only, sir," Lobb suggested. "I share your feelings, Sir Alan. I would much prefer a sea-going command, not this stint of shore duty. My predecessor, Captain Middleton, I believe, has a ship, after his term here was done. I bitterly envy the man."

"Well, I suppose I should write Admiralty of my intentions to return home, then do it," Lewrie said, feeling as if he was giving it all up, trapped into doing so. "My Purser will be ashore to prevail upon you for stores in a day or two. Then, wind and weather permitting, I'll be out of your hair, at last."

"Whatever you need, Sir Alan . . . within reason that Admiralty will allow," Lobb said with a light touch, to make a jape of it.

"Good day, then, sir," Lewrie bade him, doffing his hat.

"And a good day to you, Sir Alan," Lobb responded in kind.

God-dammit! Lewrie fumed on his way to his waiting boat; *Just dammit to bloody-fucking Hell! Bloody damned French gunners, as blind as so many bats . . . couldn't hit a beer keg with a bloody sledgehammer but their* wild *shots've done for us! The cack-handed, cunny-thumbed . . . snail-eatin' sonso'bitches!*

He reached the top of the floating landing stage ramp, paused to take a deep breath and try to calm himself so that he could face his boat crew with the proper equanimity required of Post-Captains in the Royal Navy. He found that the fingers of his left hand had a death grip on the hilt of his hanger, and he let go to flex his fingers back to life.

And there was his ship, anchored fore-and-aft about half a mile off, with the morning sun gleaming upon her fresh-painted hull, upper works, and gunn'ls, as bright and fresh as a new-minted shilling. The sun and some-what still harbour waters in-shore of her reflected her on the bay, spar-kled winking flashes of sun dapples all down her length, and made a rippling mirror image like something seen through a rain-streaked pane of glass. *Sapphire* was as pretty, and as trig, as her namesake gem, and even the lack of gasketed sails on her mainmast yards could not, at that distance, detract from her perfection.

Her gun-ports were open for welcome ventilation on her lower decks, and every now and then, in unison, the black iron muzzles of her guns jerked into sight as the crew practiced play-loading, running out, then sim-ulated recoil; three pretend rounds every two minutes, as they had since he'd taken command of her in 1807, even the lower deck 24-pounders. His exacting standards, which his crew had learned to perform, and the cut-ting of crude sights on the upmost breeching rings and muzzles, had pro-duced the smashing broadsides, and a fair amount of accuracy, that had turned *Sapphire* from a lumbering ugly duckling to a killer, a world-striding conqueror manned by proud, skilled men as invincible as an armada of ancient Vikings.

And she would limp home to become a dray waggon, and all that ex-perience would be strewn to the wind like chaff to man other ships in need of hands—twenty there, a dozen here? It was disgusting!

Lewrie went on down the ramp to the floating stage and into his wait-ing cutter, one long stride over the gunn'l to a thwart with a hand on an oarsman's shoulder for a moment, then aft to take a seat by his Cox'n, the "Black Irishman", Liam Desmond, who'd been with him since the Nore Mutiny in '97, and the *Proteus* frigate.

"Back to the ship, Desmond," Lewrie growled.

"Aye, sor," Desmond replied. "No help from the yards, sor?"

"No, not a damned bit," Lewrie told him.

"Pity, for she's lookin' like th' belle o' th' fair, today," Desmond commented with a jerk of his chin towards *Sapphire*. "Hoist oars, lads. Out oars, larb'd, cast off lines, shove off, bowman an' starb'd stroke oar . . . out oars, starb'd, and . . . stroke."

The cutter surged forward, bows lifting as eight oarsmen put their backs into it, then a second stroke, a third, and seawater began to hiss and burble, with a chuckling sound under the stern transom, and a slight judder to the tiller bar under Desmond's arm.

Once aboard in the privacy of his great-cabins, Lewrie stripped off his coat and waist-coat, rolled up his shirt sleeves, and loosened his neck stock and sat down at his desk, ready for a long afternoon of ink smudges and finger cramp as he wrote letters to prepare people in England for his ignoble return. Lewrie wondered if a letter for Admiralty would really be necessary, for it was good odds that he and his ship might arrive at Portsmouth days before, if not the day of, the letter's reception; there was not a mail packet in port at the moment, and he might as well carry it himself, post it once moored in the Solent, a surprise to everyone.

The necessities, really, was a much shorter list; his father, his sons, his sneering brother-in-law, Governour Chiswick at Anglesgreen, his solicitor, Mr. Matthew Mountjoy (in hopes that some prize-money might have been sent on from Lisbon in the meantime), and . . . Miss Jessica Chenery. That one would be the most enjoyable, the one left for last like a sweet dessert after an indifferent supper. And he would see if she could work him into her schedule to paint him that promised portrait!

"Cool tea, sir?" Pettus asked as he began to write the one to Admiralty. Long ago, Lewrie had developed a taste for at least one quart of tea to be brewed for him each morning, allowed to cool, and served with sugar pared off a cone kept in his locking caddy, and if available, a generous squeeze of lemon juice, and those who thought it daft could go to the Devil.

"Aye, Pettus," Lewrie said, not even looking up. "Have we any lemons?"

"Yes, sir, a fresh dozen came off shore yesterday morning, and Dasher's already sliced one into quarters," Pettus replied.

Lewrie looked up to see Dasher making a puckery face as if he had sucked one.

"Tangy, sir," Dasher commented, "wif a dash o' sugar, or salt."

"Salt? My word," Lewrie commented, with a pucker and a shiver.

"Never would've thought o' *that* combination. Something closer to lemonade's best."

"Never had lemonade, sir," Dasher said with a shrug.

"Then we'll see to it that you try some," Lewrie promised, and the imp's face lit up in anticipation.

So much like Jessop, Lewrie's former cabin servant, who had been killed in the boarding action with the big 40-gun French frigate, one more street waif who had signed aboard as a volunteer ship's boy for eight pounds pay a year, shoes and slop clothing, three meals a day, and a safe place to sleep instead of wherever one could doss for the night without harm.

Jessop had been sixteen or seventeen when he'd fallen, dirty-blond, sharp-eyed, and wiry, aspiring to be more than a servant, who had learned his knots, had become a hand on one of the carronades, and had been learning how to go aloft as a budding topman. Jessop had also learned how to drink, chew tobacco, gotten tattooed, and taken runs at the whores when the ship was put out of Discipline.

Perhaps Dasher won't go that way, Lewrie thought, giving the lad a closer look as he fetched a tall china mug of cool tea.

Tom Dasher—which couldn't be his real name—was darker-haired with odd green eyes, only thirteen or fourteen, and, until he came to the great-cabins, was as dirty and smudge-streaked as the "duck fucker" who tended the forecastle manger, or the usual Midshipmen's mess steward, the filthiest to be found aboard any man-o'-war. A good hosing down, new slops, an attempt at a haircut, and iron-buckled shoes with stockings (for once) had spruced Dasher up considerably, but he was still learning his trade, after a shiftless life on the streets of London, or so he said, and when pressed, the details of what he'd done to survive were damned thin.

"Oh, one other thing, Dasher," Lewrie told him.

"Aye, sir?"

"I wish you to go forrud and find my cook, Yeovill," Lewrie bade him, "and tell him I intend to dine in the First and Second Officers, Marine Officer, Purser, Acting-Sailing Master Mister Stubbs, and the senior Mid this evening at Seven P.M."

"First Officer, Second, Mister Keane, an' . . ." Dasher said with a frown of concentration, ticking them off on the fingers of one hand.

"Six guests plus myself," Lewrie supplied. "Seven, in all."

"Seven t'eat, at Seven in th' ev'nin', aye sir." Dasher said, then, emulating his name, dashed off, slamming the door to the quarterdeck on his way.

"Early days, sir," Pettus commented.

"He'll come round . . . I hope," Lewrie said with a shrug and a lift of his eyebrows.

Aye, dine 'em in, and tell 'em we're sailin' for home, Lewrie told himself; *with our tails 'twixt our legs.*

BOOK ONE

What comes next you never know,
Lady Luck runs the show,
So pass the Falernian, lad.

-PETRONIUS, THE SATYRICON,
"DINNER WITH TRIMALCHIO"

BOOK ONE

CHAPTER FIVE

You should have taken more mousers aboard, Captain Lewrie," Mr. Posey, the Surveyor of Portsmouth Dockyards, japed after taking a long look at *Sapphire*'s damaged lower mainmast. "Large and fierce terriers, perhaps? For it seems your ship is infested with a particularly large species of wood-eating *rats*, hah hah hah!"

"I thought it more the work of beavers, but . . ." Lewrie tried to play along, though his jaws were clenched.

"Pity, for there's money in beaver pelts," Posey went on in gay amusement, "even the inferior *French* breed!"

Mr. Posey whipped out a colourful calico handkerchief, making Lewrie fear that the man had not gotten over his gargling, sneezing fits of January, when first he'd come aboard to survey the lightning-struck mainmast, but it was only to wipe his eyes of humour tears.

"Yes, well . . . ," Lewrie began, but Posey was nowhere through.

"Egads, Captain Lewrie, but you keep breaking things aboard your ship, and the Navy may start making you *pay* for their replacement, ha ha!"

Knew that *was coming,* Lewrie thought with a wince; *Damme, ye think you're bloody hilarious, don't ye?*

"Even if I do end up payin' for it," Lewrie asked, growing a tad impatient, "do you think the yard can put her to rights?"

"Are you under orders at the moment, sir?" Posey asked, more seriously.

"No, I only wrote Admiralty of our arrival from a foreign station yesterday morning, soon as we anchored," Lewrie told him. "They already knew of her state of repair. I'm waiting to hear."

"Oh," Mr. Posey said with a sorrowful suck at his teeth. "In that case, Captain Lewrie, I fear that 'til the Commissioner of the yards hears from London, there's little he, or I, can do for you. An official authorisation to justify the expense of a new lower mainmast, and the dockyard's labour, will be necessary."

"The last time, I went up to London to plead my case," Lewrie said. "Perhaps I should go again."

"One never knows, sir, a personal appeal *may* avail," Posey said.

Lewrie took Posey's diffident response to that course of action as a bad omen; the man shrugged and looked away cutty-eyed for a second as if he had other incoming ships and their hurts to deal with, and was merely being polite 'til he could make a dignified escape.

"Let us pray that Our Lords Commissioners at Admiralty will send word soon, then, Mister Posey," Lewrie told him. " 'Til then, I'm sure you have other pressing concerns."

"I will advert to you what they order us to do, the very first instant, Captain Lewrie," Posey replied, all outwardly solicitous, but making steps towards the entry-port and his waiting boat, eager to get off *Sapphire* as if she was a plague ship sporting the yellow Quarantine pendant!

Damn their eyes, everyone's a wit! Lewrie fumed after he saw him off with as much false *bonhomie* as he could muster at that dour moment. He stalked off to the quarterdeck and up a ladderway to the poop in a foul mood, knowing that he *couldn't* go up to London. His letter that announced his arrival had gone off the day before, soon as the anchors had bitten the harbour grounds, and unless the "flying coach" carrying the mail had vanished off the face of the Earth, his letter had been opened and read this very morning. A reply could come as early as the next morning; if it was urgent, word of *Sapphire*'s fate could come down the line of semaphore towers even earlier. He was "anchored" as firmly as the ship!

He leaned against the hammock-filled cross-deck iron stanchion racks at the forward end of the poop deck, looking down at the quarterdeck, the waist, and the sail-tending gangways, where hundreds of his crew performed minor ship-keeping tasks, or lazed about to enjoy yet another "Make and Mend" day of idleness. Lewrie dearly wished that he could order the ship be put Out of Discipline to allow the bum-boats alongside with their gew-gaws, fancy foods, and the doxies, but that wasn't possible at the moment. The men's pay had yet to arrive, and they could not afford even a *sniff* of a whore's perfume in passing.

One of the last letters he had posted at Gibraltar had been to the Prize Court at Lisbon, informing them that should they *ever* decide how much *Sapphire* was due, the money should be sent on to Portsmouth.

Those four prize frigates, though, had been turned over to the Prize Court here at Portsmouth—Lieutenant Geoffrey Westcott had seen to that, he'd assured him—and such an ado was made of their capture and arrival that the Court *might* yield to public and political pressure and render their decisions. Lewrie had shot them a short note as well, and with any luck, money in the form of chits might come aboard for the men to spend. They'd be cheated badly, of course, for those chits could only be turned in for real money and full value when presented to the Councillor of the Cheque in London. Bum-boat vendors and jobbers would buy them up, sometimes for as little as *half* the value, sure that sailors were rarely thinking in the long-term, and too eager to have coins, or war-issue Bank of England paper notes, in hand to squander as quick as they could spend it. If paid in bank notes, they would spend even quicker, for no one, sailors most especially, thought that paper money was *real* money!

Admittedly, even Lewrie had his doubts about bank notes, sure that someday someone in government would cry "April Fool's!", and he'd much prefer a pile of guineas to run his hands through like water!

After weeks at Gibraltar, his announcement that they would be sailing for Portsmouth was more than welcome to one and all aboard, for it meant an end to enforced idleness and doubt, a chance to see their home country, again, and *could* result in the dispersal of back-pay *and* prize-money. Though many looked upwards cautiously, after a few days at sea, and in fine weather, few feared that the mainmast would fail, so *Sapphire* had been a happy ship, filled with comfortable and expected at-sea routine, and the Dog Watches thumping with music and dance, and, no matter how closely Lieutenant Harcourt and Acting-Lieutenant Hillhouse had overseen the crew, they had found few defaulters to bring to Lewrie's attention, and certainly no one worthy of the cat-of-nine-tails at the hatch gratings.

It couldn't last, though, Lewrie knew, just a brief interlude between spells of boredom and uncertainty, and here they were, again, broke, idle, and up in the air in a *new* harbour!

Now, *what the Devil can you do, clown?* he chid himself; think *of something t'keep 'em engaged. For how long?*

Lewrie heaved a sigh, shrugged, and promised himself a rare bout of drink. A good supper fetched from shore, a bottle of wine or two, and more than several brandies or some of his American whisky, then—was God just—a good, lazy, and overlong night's sleep!

CHAPTER SIX

A substantial sack of mail for all hands arrived aboard three days later, and with it, several pieces for Captain Sir Alan Lewrie, one, most ominously, from Admiralty.

Lewrie was loath to open it, at first, busying himself with a fresh cup of creamed and sugared coffee, but at last, he picked it up and broke the seal to spread it atop his desk.

"Oh no, no no no *no!*" he muttered, his voice rising as he read its contents, perking the attention of his cabin steward and servant.

Dasher opened his mouth to blurt out a question, but Pettus shushed him with a shake of his head and a finger to his lips.

> *The Lords Commissioners for the Execution of the High Office of Admiralty have determined that the current material Condition of His Majesty's Ship Sapphire, now lying at Portsmouth, renders the said Ship Redundant to the Needs of the Royal Navy.*
>
> *The financial Cost, and the Time required to return the said Ship to full Active Duty, and the Inability of any Ship of the Fourth Rate to render useful Service in these times requires her immediate De-Commissioning. To that end, you are directed to turn the said Ship over to the Commissioner of His Majesty's Dockyards, Portsmouth,*

*to be placed In-Ordinary, pending any Use which could be made of
the said Ship in future.*

They did it, Lewrie groaned to himself; *they've gone and done it! Half-
pay for me, is it? Thank Christ I've no debts owing. For only a month or so . . .
I hope! . . . before I get new orders, and a new ship.*

*The Port Admiral, Portsmouth, Admiral Lord Gardner, is directed
and authorised to assist you in all Respects anent in so doing, and
with the Distribution of the said Ship's Pay and any Prize-Moneys
owing, pending the final Accounting and Arrival of Funds.*

My people can finally get drunk and put the leg over, Lewrie was relieved
to think.

He should have had the word passed to summon his officers to give
them the bad news that moment so plans could be implemented, but, truc-
ulently, he delayed, setting the orders aside so he could read the rest of his
mail as if it was just another idle day at anchor, and, if he ignored it, it might
yet go away.

There was one from his solicitor in London, Mr. Matthew Mountjoy, a
man who served both as his shore business agent and his prize agent, and
Lewrie turned to that one in hopes of badly needed better news.

My Dear Sir Alan;
 *What a windfall is come your way! Shortly after I was in receipt
of your letter informing me of your arrival in England, a substantial
packet arrived from the Lisbon Prize-Court, enumerating the results
of their determinations of your captures since the start of this year.*
 *For the value of sixteen prizes, all told, and especially the
value of the war material found as cargo, cargo of the utmost use
to the armies of our allies, the Portuguese and Spanish, and of
use by our own forces as well it goes without saying, the Court
declares the sum total owing is £192,000, of which your two-
eighths share, less my humble fee, is £46,800!*
 *We are assured that Admiralty Prize-Court here in England is
also informed of the results, and that, if your ship may pay off, as
you feared in your most recent letter, that the sum total will be due to
you and your ship and will be dispersed in full in either case.*

"Yes, by Christ!" Lewrie shouted, loud enough to startle his cat. "And come in pudding time, at that!"

"Some . . . good news, sir, might I ask?" Pettus cautiously said, after clearing his throat.

"Damned right, Pettus!" Lewrie hooted. "There's prize-money from Spain coming. There's t'be a share-out within a fortnight!"

"A *lot* will it be, sir?" Dasher asked, mouth and eyes agape in anticipation.

"Lashings of it, Dasher," Lewrie assured him. "A perfect *rain* storm of prize-money!"

"Huzzah!" Dasher cried. "Whoo!" and began a frantic attempt at a celebratory dance/prance about the cabins.

That'll *soften the blow for one and all*, Lewrie thought as the boy tried to turn a Catherine wheel, and even the well-behaved Pettus looked ready to assay a hornpipe. Lewrie was sure that once he sent Dasher forward to summon the officers, the boy would blurt his good news to every hand he passed. Both Lewrie and Pettus had warned the lad that what he heard aft was not to be passed on as scuttlebutt but in this instance, that caution could be ignored.

Good God, though, Lewrie marvelled; *a bloody windfall, is it? A bloody* fortune's *more like it! I've never made that much in prize-money my entire career . . . and that's sayin' something!*

A few pounds from captures now and then, his paltry share when a Midshipman in the American Revolution, next to nothing 'tween the wars in the Far East fighting native pirates, for all that was secret work. Well, there was that stash of gold British guineas he'd come across hidden behind a false panel in the quarter gallery of a French prize taken off the Danish Virgins—£2,000 it had been, on its way to the Yankee Congress as bribes to expand French territory. Nothing from his first time in the Bahamas enforcing the Navigation Acts, chasing slave-stealing pirates like Calico Jack Finney who took British ships then flogged the cargoes in his emporium at Nassau.

There had been some when he'd taken the French *corvette*, the *Sans Culottes*, after evacuating Toulon, the ship that had become his first post as a Commander, the sloop *Jester*. Some from captures in the Mediterranean when the French marched into Italy, a bit more from the Adriatic during Napoleon Bonaparte's first Italian Campaign, and there were so many ships present at the Battle of Cape St. Vincent that his share for being "in sight" was barely a year's pay.

Taking the *L'Uranie* frigate in the South Atlantic, captures during the American Quasi-War with France, the Battle of Camperdown, the Battle of Copenhagen, his share of the fight off the Chandeleur Islands of Spanish Louisiana, even the fight two years before against two big Spanish frigates off Andalusia . . . none of it altogether even came close to this sum!

If he put the lion's share of what was due him into the Three Percents, say £40,000, that would guarantee him an annual income of £1,200, which was a princely sum for a single gentleman in its own right, and in addition to what was already there it would be even more! He'd also be able to keep a *goodly* sum with Coutts' Bank for spending money.

And, what a home Prize Court would award for his recent taking of four French frigates, even shared with all five of the ships "in sight" and participants in the fight would be an extra ladle-full of gravy!

The Devil with a spell of half-pay, he gleefully thought; *I'm as rich as Croesus . . . maybe up there with my father after he came home from India with all* his *loot!*

Suddenly, the idea of a month or so "on the beach" seemed like a Lotus Eater's idyll!

Why, with any luck at all, he could now dowry his maddeningly spiteful and willful daughter, Charlotte, with £200 a year and allow her the London Season that she and his former brother-in-law, Governour Chiswick, had been pestering him for! Aye, let her find herself a gullible husband and be shot of her! And God pity the fool who'd have her for a wife, for she was certain to become a termagant, a tongue-lashing and demanding shrew!

Letters to write about this! he thought. He must tell his sons, his father, Geoffrey Westcott to let his friend know that when he took command of his ship as a Commander, he could do it in style.

For now, though . . .

"Ah, Dasher," Lewrie said, "do you go forward and pass word for the First and Second Officers, and the Purser, Mister Cadrick."

"Ehm, aye, sir!" Dasher replied, looking as eager as a race horse at the start line to be off with his "golden" news, and most-likely wondering just how much would fall his way even as a ship's boy.

Lewrie let out a contented sigh, even as he contemplated that there would be even more letters to write. He had, at last, found a way to praise Acting-Lieutenant Hillhouse, and recommend him for a promotion to a real commission. Now, with *Sapphire* just days away from the knacker's yard, all the surviving Midshipmen must be found new ships, and would need letters of recommendation, as well.

Even the dull ones.

CHAPTER SEVEN

*L*ewrie and Bosun Terrell took one last tour of the ship, from the cable tiers up forward to the "lady's hole" right aft down below the orlop; into the empty powder magazines, the fish room, the tiller flat, the yawning wardroom, Midshipmen's cockpit, and down the lower and upper gundecks that now seemed vast and echoing with no guns or carriages fitted, no mess tables lowered, and not one sailor still aboard, but for the few people who made up the Standing Officers, who would live aboard her in-ordinary 'til she was hulked and broken up, became a floating prison for enemy sailors, or was made into a receiving ship—which would be a prison, of a sort—for new-come volunteer British sailors, or the unfortunates dredged up by the Press.

Everything useful for a ship at sea had been landed ashore with the store houses, every spare block and tackle, sand-glass, miles of rope, and all manner of Bosun's Stores but for what Terrell and the men of the Standing Officer party might need. Even the Ship's Cook's, Mr. Tanner's, galley had been reduced to what implements, pots, and steep tubs were necessary to feed no more than a dozen, not hundreds; though it was a surety that the Standing Officers would move their wives and children aboard to be maintained on Navy largesse.

"Lanthorns, oil, and candles, sir," Terrell said, checking off the last items on his massive sheaf of lists. "And that's the lot, at last. Poor old cow. Beg pardon for sayin, Cap'm sir, but she was a fine ship, and we had a grand time in her."

"That we did, Mister Terrell," Lewrie said in equal gloom. "I still think she could've rendered good service, but the Navy thought otherwise. It's all Third Rate seventy-fours or thirty-eight-gun frigates these days. Even the sixty-four-gun two-deckers are being laid up . . . like there's still another Trafalgar or two the Fleet has to be ready for."

"With who, sir?" Terrell growled as they made their way up to the weather deck and waist. "The Roosians, the Chinese? The French've had it, at sea. Gawd, but this'll be damned dull duty!"

How right you are, Terrell, Lewrie thought as they emerged into sunshine, gave that damned lower mainmast yet another scathing glare, a mast now struck "to a gantline" with all topmasts and yards stored under the sail-tending gangways, no long, lazy-whipping commissioning pendant flying, no Union Jack waving over her taffrails, and only the lone harbour jack showing on her bowsprit.

He, Terrell, and *Sapphire*'s people *might* have fought the last great squadron fight, unless the French, England's last remaining foe, suddenly became much better sailors than they had been in the past, and sallied forth all the ships they had built over the years. What would it be like for Terrell and the rest of the watch-tending crew in harbour, seemingly forever, serving their boresome duties 'til the war ended, or *Sapphire*'s bottom rotted out of her? Even sailing on the equally boresome blockades would beat that all hollow!

"All's in order, Sir Alan?" a clerk from the Dockyard Commissioner enquired at the foot of the starboard ladderway to the quarterdeck, where he had set up a tall desk.

"Aye, and her rats are now bold enough to romp free," Lewrie sourly japed. "They're holding Fiddler's Green on the orlop."

"Then if you will sign here, Sir Alan, and initial here . . . and here . . . and here," the clerk said, opening a ledger which accounted for every jot and tittle of Navy Issue goods either landed ashore or retained aboard. Within two minutes of pen-scratching, it was done, and *Sapphire* belonged to someone else. Copies for Admiralty, for the Dockyards, for Lewrie, and for Terrell to keep up with now that he was the master of a lifeless hulk, were proof that her former Captain owed not one penny for any item lost or un-accounted for.

The clerk packed up his traps, folded up his desk, and he and his assistant fussily prepared to depart.

"Well, that's it, then, Mister Terrell," Lewrie said as he made his way up to the gangway and the open entry-port. "I sincerely wish that the Navy finds some use for her, and you can get back to sea. It would be a sorry waste of a good man to leave you here swingin' idle."

"Thankee for sayin' so, Cap'm sir," Terrell replied, doffing his hat in parting salute. "Same could be said for you, as well, sir, for a good Captain, and a fightin' Captain, is too rare to waste, either, and when ya get a new command, I'd admire did ya send for me and Nobbs and Plunkett."

"Wish I could, Mister Terrell," Lewrie earnestly told him. "Now, mind the water and sand buckets round the galley. If Tanner gets into his cups, he'll burn more than the rations."

"Aye, I will, Cap'm sir!" Terrell said with a laugh, then stood to one side of the entry-port as Lewrie swung out to take hold of the man-ropes. Terrell brought his silver call to his lips to pipe Lewrie over the side one last time as he descended the boarding battens to a waiting civilian boat.

"King's Stairs, sir?" the head waterman asked.

"Aye, King's Stairs," Lewrie gruffly told him.

A boat boy, perhaps the boatman's son, hoisted and trimmed the lugs'l and the boat set off for shore. Once under way, Lewrie looked back at his ship for a long, longing minute or two, then shrugged his shoulders and stared without really seeing at the landing.

Now what the Devil do I do? he asked himself.

He would have to coach to London, of course, report to Admiralty and turn in the last paperwork, see the Councillor of the Cheque and receive his own back-pay, then list himself as a half-pay officer, but also lay a strong case for another active commission. He *should* make a brief detour to Anglesgreen and his father's country house for a day or so to collect his chest of civilian clothing. That, though, would force him to confront his daughter, Charlotte, who still lived with Governour Chiswick, his wife Millicent, and their children, delaying his search for London lodgings.

Lodging, my God! he thought.

When he and his late wife, Caroline, had been estranged, and since she had passed over, he could, in past, find lodgings for himself and his small entourage at the Madeira Club, founded by his father Sir Hugo and Sir Malcolm Shockley years before, but the last few times he had been up to London, the club was over-full, with single gentlemen two to a set of rooms, and the best he could do was dine in there, and partake of the club's delightfully toothsome suppers, and their vast wine cellars. Lewrie doubted if the Madeira Club would have any more room for him than it had before.

The last time up, he had spent a few testy days at his father's grand house in Upper Grosvenor Street, where even a Prodigal Son's welcome was *damned* thin, and it had only been him and Pettus who'd needed a place to stay.

Now, he had Pettus, Dasher, Yeovill his cook, Liam Desmond his Cox'n, a new stroke oar, Michael Deavers, who'd taken poor old Patrick Furfy's place after Furfy had died when taking the big French frigate, Chalky, and Bisquit, and what his father would make of them didn't bear imagining. Plus, he had a dray waggon filled with his shipboard furnishings, personal stores, chests, weapons, and wine stores to deal with. Sir Hugo *might* allow him only a day or two at most before demanding that he find a place of his own.

And what, in the name o' God, do I do with takin' a whole house? he asked himself; *And for how bloody long?*

He'd written his father, giving him fair warning, and he hadn't heard back so far, so . . . would he be allowed at least *one* night before being shooed off? At least his father's wine and spirit stocks would be safe from Faulkes's pilfering; the fellow had gone ashore with some of the paperwork and had returned, saying that he had found a position with the Dockyard Commissioner's staff, a nice, safe shore billet with an increase in pay.

The boat came ghosting up alongside the wet, slimy green stone landing, as the boat's boy handed the lugs'l and leaped ashore with a bow line, as the older boatman reached out to seize a rusted ring-bolt for the stern line. Lewrie dug into his wash-leather coin-purse and paid the fare, then gingerly made his way up the slime-slick stairs to solid ground, and his waiting entourage.

"A damned shame, sor," Desmond said, spitting into the harbour waters. "There was life in th' old girl, yet."

"Aye, Desmond," Lewrie said, turning for one last look at his former ship. "We ready to go?"

"Aye, sor," Desmond told him. "Deavers an' Dasher will go with the dray, all loaded an' lashed proper, an' th' hired coach is ready."

"We most-like won't make London tonight," Lewrie said, looking at his pocket watch for a moment, "but with any luck, we can find some posting house 'twixt here and Guildford. Not with the dray waggon to slow us down. And that's if it don't bog down halfway up Portdown Hill. Let's get aboard, then, and be off."

"Aye, sor," Desmond said, but continued standing, looking out at *Sapphire* for another long moment, as if to fix her in his memory. "Ye know, sor, ships have souls, after a time. An' all th' people who ever serve 'em . . . the souls of all who . . . remain with 'em, d'ye see. Well . . ."

"Pat Furfy," Lewrie realised what he was driving at.

"Aye, sor . . . poor old Pat," Desmond gravelled. "Best place for him, I s'pose, th' great lummox. Swore t'his Mam when we ran away to sea that I'd do me best t'keep him outta mischief . . . and Pat was one t'be led astray *so* easy. God knows what'd happen to him did he ever swallow th' anchor an' turn a farmer or somethin'."

"He would have loved my father's farm," Lewrie said, growing sad at losing the fellow after all those years. "He was so good with the beasts and all. He would have been more than welcome to live out his days there. We owed him that. I owed him that, and more."

"An' he woulda been at Will Cony's tavern, drinkin' more than his share o' th' Old Ploughman's beer," Desmond said, smiling and chuckling without real mirth. "Lord, Pat was strong t'take a drink!"

"When we do get to Anglesgreen, we'll drink some in his name," Lewrie suggested. "Soon as we get settled in London, we'll coach down."

"Aye, a grand, peaceful place, that, sor," Desmond sighed.

"Thinking of swallowing the anchor yourself, Desmond?" Lewrie asked, fearing that he would lose his long-time Cox'n, too, one more in a long line of departed shipmates, no matter the vast difference in their stations.

"Ah, no, sor," Desmond said with another long sigh. "Though that girl, Abigail, who waits tables for Mister Cony? When the time comes, it'd be pleasant t'think o' settlin' down, at last, with someone like her. By th' time th' war's done, though, sor, I expect t'be way too old for much more than tendin' a sheep or two, an' nappin' in a corner o' th' barn! Looks like I'm t'be a sailor 'til Kingdom Come, iff'n ye'll still have need o' me."

"Then let's get you up to London, then down to Anglesgreen and see what Mistress Abigail is up to!" Lewrie said to cheer him up. "Ye never can tell . . . she might still be free."

"Aye, sor, she might be, at that!" Desmond said with a real grin.

He took off his flat-brimmed straw hat, crossed himself, and whispered, "G'bye Pat . . . g'bye, *Sapphire*. God rest, th' both o' ya."

CHAPTER EIGHT

*N*ight had found their little convoy, forcing a halt overnight at a cozy posting house short of Guildford, near the juncture of the Petersfield road. An early dawn rising and departure, unfortunately, coincided with the early market traffic into London, so it was an hour short of Noon before the coach and dray rattled up to Sir Hugo Saint George Willoughby's front doors in Upper Grosvenor Street. Lewrie jumped out of the hired coach and went up the entry steps to rap on the door, and to be answered by the frostily stand-offish butler, who at least recognised him this time.

"Ah, Sir Alan," the butler intoned, "you are arrived. I shall announce you to Sir Hugo."

"Thankee, Harwell," Lewrie said, motioning over his shoulder at the laden waggon. "Is there a back entrance, a coach house, where my goods can be stored for a few days?"

Harwell coolly looked him up and down in seeming dis-belief that he'd even ask such a question, gave it a long, hard thought, and only then said, "Goods, Sir Alan?" as he might to an un-wanted pedlar.

"My great-cabins furnishings and such," Lewrie said.

"There is a coach house, but Sir Hugo's equipage occupies it at the moment, Sir Alan," Harwell said, frowning. "You would be stabling the horses and storing the waggon as well, would you, sir?"

"No, they're hired. I just need a place to unload," Lewrie told him, growing a bit irked. Though it was a fine summer day for London, standing outside without immediate admittance was mildly insulting.

"I will have a footman direct your waggoner, sir," Mr. Harwell decided. "Come in, if you will, sir."

Lewrie turned and whistled to his fellow passengers in the coach, and Desmond, Pettus, and Yeovill emerged, along with several sea-chests, travelling luggage from the boot, Bisquit on a leash, and Chalky in his wicker cage, along with their personal sea bags and belongings. Up the steps they came, to mill about in the entrance foyer.

"An entourage, is it, Sir Alan?" Harwell asked with one eyebrow most accusingly up. "One would *suppose* we will be able to sort it all out. I will annouce you to Sir Hugo, who is abovestairs."

"Grand place, it is," Desmond muttered to Yeovill and Pettus.

"Yes, it is," Pettus agreed in a similar hushed tone. "I forget that you two didn't come up to London with the Captain the last time."

"Good kitchens?" Yeovill wondered. "Be a treat, someone else doing the cooking for a day or two."

A footman lad dashed past, dressed in black "ditto" suitings, white shirt and neck-stock, and a red waist-coat, a miniature version of the butler, out to direct Deavers and Dasher and the waggoner to an alley entrance round the corner. His passage excited the dog, who began whining and yelping, straining at his leash.

Lewrie's father, Sir Hugo, appeared at the top of the stairs and began his descent with his butler in tow, and both of them looking perturbed.

"Well!" Sir Hugo said in a chary bark of a welcome. "You've come at last, have you? And brought a circus?"

"Good to see you, too, Father," Lewrie said in greeting, used to Sir Hugo's thin hospitality by then.

"How many of you are there, then?" Sir Hugo asked as he reached the foyer, and offered a brief handshake to his son. "And how long are you expecting to stay?"

"Myself and five others, Father," Lewrie told him, "and I hope to find other lodgings right after I settle things at Admiralty."

"You've brought your bloody *cat*?" Sir Hugo scoffed, peering at the cage. "I see you're sensible enough to get yourself a *proper* pet. But, I'll not have your dog piddling or scatting on my good carpets.

"*Five* others, is it?" Sir Hugo said with a scowl. "I see only three."

"My cabin steward, Pettus, I believe you know from earlier, but allow me to name to you my Cox'n, Liam Desmond, and my cook, James Yeovill," Lewrie said. "Men, my Father, Sir Hugo St. George Willoughby. There are two more with my dray waggon, unloading its content into your coach house, temporarily, a man from my boat crew, Michael Deavers, and my cabin servant, Tom Dasher."

"Unloading . . . ?" Sir Hugo said with a start. "Did ye loot some prize and fetch it all here? Anything the Customs men or the Police will come asking about?"

"My cabin furnishings, wine store, things like that," Lewrie shrugged off. "Some of it might have to come inside for safekeeping, but . . ."

"If it's only, as you say, for a few days, I'd suppose," Sir Hugo harrumphed. "Might you be able to deal with it, Harwell?"

"After training Guards recruits, I am used to chaos, Sir Hugo," the butler said with a smug expression on his stern phyz. "Though, perhaps for the few days Sir Alan's entourage might assist the running of the house, to ease the burden on the staff?"

"But of course, Mister Harwell," Lewrie offered.

"Your room is prepared, Sir Alan," Harwell said, "and your man can see to you. Spare rooms belowstairs are available for your men, though they may have to share two, or three, to a room."

"Let's be about it, then," Sir Hugo declared, as if that particular burden on his household was solved. "Come up to the drawing room, my boy, and take your ease."

"After I've paid my coachman and waggoner," Lewrie said, pulling out his coin-purse. "Be up in a moment."

Finally shed of his hat and sword belt, Lewrie trotted up the stairs to the parlour and joined his father, who was seated on a settee near the book cases on the far end of the spacious and richly appointed room. Someone had let Bisquit off his leash (after a judicious allowance outside to void his bowels and bladder) and Sir Hugo was making a fuss over him, making Bisquit's tail whip. Chalky was hunkered up on a deep windowsill cushion, tail wrapped round his forelegs. Like all cats, he did not deal well with new and strange surroundings.

"Anything good in your wine store?" Sir Hugo asked. Perhaps he was mellowed by Bisquit's presence and affectionate response to being petted, but the old man almost seemed pleasant for a rare once.

"There's two ankers of good port, some Spanish or Portuguese sparkling wines," Lewrie ticked off as he took a seat in a wing-back chair across from his father, "but the bulk of it's un-distinguished . . . drinkable and pleasant, but nothing grand. I've a crock or two of American corn whisky, some 'liberated' French brandy, quite decent . . ."

"What sort of corn?" Sir Hugo asked, looking up from the dog.

"Indian corn, what we'd call maize," Lewrie told him. "Aged in oak barrels several years. They call it bourbon whisky."

"Like Scottish whisky, or Irish?" Sir Hugo frowned.

"Different grains, different flavour," Lewrie said. "You ought try it."

"I'll stick to brandy, thankee," Sir Hugo dismissively scoffed. "The whiskys I've tasted leave me in mind of sucking on wood chips. So . . . you've lost your ship, have you?"

Lewrie explained how and why, and how much he regretted the loss, even though *Sapphire* had less than a year, at best, left in her active commission before he would have had to leave her, anyway.

"The thing that irks the most, though," Lewrie said, sounding wistful, "is seeing all my skilled gunners scattered to the wide like so much chaff. God, they were good, and accurate, too! We took that big French frigate we faced to *pieces* with aimed fire . . . her quarterdeck and helm, her carronades, lower masts, and roundshot and grape right into her gun-ports, at long musket shot, *double* long musket shot, not hull-to-hull." Lewrie explained his experiments with crude sights cut into muzzles and breeching rings.

Perhaps the reassuring sound of Lewrie's voice at last calmed Chalky, for he slunk off the cushioned window seat and came to Lewrie's knee to mew for a snug place in his lap, and some comforting pets.

"What? Using cannons like those Baker rifles they're issuing to the Rifle regiments?" Sir Hugo said with a dubious snort. "Never *heard* the like. And they *didn't* charge you with defacing the King's artillery?"

"It can be done, we proved it," Lewrie declared. "Oh, not at any great range, or with a high sea runnin', but it can work."

"Well, if you say so," Sir Hugo finally allowed. "That . . . cat of yours, there. Black and white, as I recall?"

"That was Toulon," Lewrie said, stroking the cat, "this'un is Chalky. Toulon passed away on the way to Cape Town, years ago, and Chalky came off a French prize during the Quasi-War the Yankee Doodles had with the French. He's of an age, now, too."

"The dog can be let out into the walled back garden, but what will *it* do when caught short?" Sir Hugo asked, giving the cat a dubious glance.

"I brought a barrel of sand, and his litter box," Lewrie said, knowing that his father disliked cats, and secretly enjoying the man's discomfort. "He's used to it, ain't ye, puss'ums?"

"And that will be in *your* room, hear me?" Sir Hugo snapped. "So you can spare me, and the rest of the house, the smells."

"Of course," Lewrie agreed with a chuckle.

"So, Admiralty tomorrow, then . . . what?" Sir Hugo asked as the dog at last padded away to explore the parlour, giving everything some good sniffs.

"Well, I hear that I'm to be dined in at the Madeira Club, to celebrate," Lewrie speculated aloud, "and, I expect that I might get about town to look up old friends, do some shopping . . ."

"Pity about the club," Sir Hugo said, "we've bought up the two houses either side for expansion, but you may have brick dust in your soup. Workmen knocking out walls, connecting hallways, plasterers and painters in from dawn to dusk, carpenters hammering and sawing away to refurbish the new rooms. At least the wine cellar is still good. But, the question is, how long might it be 'twixt your old ship and a new one?"

"Impossible t'say," Lewrie said with a confident shrug. "Can't be *too* long, after all the folderol the papers made of our fight. They can't keep a successful Captain ashore more than a month or so."

"About that," Sir Hugo said, squirming about to cross his legs. "Soon as I got your letter from Gibraltar, I spoke with my solicitor, and he's spoken with a reputable land agent about finding you a place t'hang your hat 'til the Navy sends you back to sea. At first I thought a set of rooms would do, but now, with your menagerie and all, perhaps a house might be necessary. Something to let for a time, and not too dear?"

"A house?" Lewrie gawped. The idea of taking an entire house had never occurred to him. Between ships, he'd had his rented house and small farm at Anglesgreen, a set of rooms for himself and one man-servant early on, the Madeira Club, or short stays in public lodging like Willis's Rooms or some other hotel. But, to let a whole house, and for how long month-to-month, and all the furniture necessary to make it even comfortable for ancient Spartans or Catholic monks would be an expensive undertaking, and a huge commitment. To maintain a house, one needed servants, chamber maids, a scullery maid to assist Yeovill in the kitchens, a maid-of-all-work, a footman or two, even a butler? Good Lord!

"Hadn't *thought* of a house," Lewrie all but croaked in alarm. "Oh, if I eventually *retired*, or . . ."

"You can afford it, surely," Sir Hugo tossed off, rising to go to a side table to pour himself a glass of Rhenish. "I read that the Navy's bought in the ships your squadron took at prizes."

"Aye, they did," Lewrie agreed. "I've £3,900 due me, and from our other captures . . . well, all told, I'm almost £50,000 to the good."

"Egad!" Sir Hugo barked. "You've come home a 'chicken *nabob*'! John Company *wallahs* leave India with *that* much."

"Nowhere as well as you, but . . ." Lewrie said, ready to preen his fingernails on his coat lapels.

I never did learn how much you *made away with,* he thought with amusement. His father would never reveal what his time with the East India Company army had earned him, but Sir Hugo had cleared all of his debtors once back in England, had dangled so much gold under the late Uncle Phineas Chiswick's nose to purchase his country estate of three hundred and twenty acres at Anglesgreen (uncomfortably close to his son, wife, and family!), had run up his odd one-level house more like an Indian *bungalow* than a proper country house, and bought this grand house in one of London's most fashionable districts, even grander than his old place in St. James's Square (though that'un had *not* been on the good side).

"Hah!" his father hooted in wicked mirth. "Not even close! A glass, would you?" he offered with a wave of the cut-glass decanter.

"Aye," Lewrie said, getting to his feet, still numbed by the thought of taking an actual house. Why, it was almost like admitting that he would *never* go back to sea!

"You'll have this place once I'm gone, and you'd have to spend money to maintain it properly, at any rate," Sir Hugo said as he poured Lewrie a glass. "Can't spend your whole life like a vagabond or a Gypsy tinker. Oh, you'll have my money, my sums in the Three Percents, and my investments, to help keep this place, and the farm, up to snuff, but . . . now you can afford it, you might as well get used to being a homeowner. Or someone's renter, anyway,"

"Grow up, d'ye mean?" Lewrie sourly asked.

"Something like that, hee hee," Sir Hugo agreed.

"Seems a shame," Lewrie told him, "to furnish a place, hire on house staff, for only two months or so."

"Well, there's always second-hand goods a'plenty available," his father brushed off, "half London's in the process of selling up and moving in or out. Perhaps the land agent can find a place that's already furnished. As for staff, I use a good agent for that, and with half the better houses closed for the Summer, and so many people laid off, I'm sure that maids and such would be grateful for a few months of employment, with room and board all found."

"Excuse me, Sir Hugo," the butler, Harwell, said as he entered the parlour, "but dinner is ready."

"Ah, excellent!" Sir Hugo said, tossing off his glass of wine. "My son's people are settled in?"

"Their rooms assigned, and sitting down to dinner with the rest of the staff, this moment, sir," Harwell assured him.

"There will be roast beef, the 'Fatted Calf' as it were, this evening," Sir Hugo promised as they headed for the dining room, "but for now, I trust that roast chicken will suffice, my boy?"

"Topping!" Lewrie said. One thing could be counted upon; his father's hospitality might be lacking, but he always set a good table!

CHAPTER NINE

Damme, but this feels good! Lewrie told himself after he entered the courtyard behind the curtain wall at Admiralty, and for a rare once feeling welcome. Admittedly it helped that he wore his medals for St. Vincent and Camperdown, and the star and sash of his knighthood, so that may have helped the other officers in the courtyard take notice, wonder among themselves just who he was, and then, aided by one or two of his acquaintance, realise who he was and break into smiles of recognition, doffing their hats in salute as he neared the entry.

What respectful acknowledgement and hero-worship there may have been ended there, as he was greeted by the tiler on duty, typically an older pensioner who might have attained Bosun's rank and who might have been impressed by a Nelson, but few others.

"Ah, Cap'um sir, you've an appointment?" a grizzled old fellow enquired with a wary squint. "If you don't, you'll have a long wait today, for it's arseholes and elbows in the Waiting Room, and even the queue at the tea cart's long as a main course yard."

"I do, for Ten," Lewrie informed him as the tiler held the door for him.

"That's no guarantee, busy as they are today, sir," the oldster almost whinnied, "but go on in if you've a mind."

It never changed, Lewrie bemusedly thought as he went inside and gave the infamous Waiting Room a quick once-over in search of a chair; *There'll not be a single man I know here t'yarn with, and I'll lay any odds there'll be that Midshipman drooling a rope o' snot, lookin' for a berth the last five years!*

"You've an appointment, sir?" one of the assistant clerks asked.

"Captain Sir Alan Lewrie, for Ten this morning," Lewrie said.

"Oh! Captain Lewrie, sir!" the clerk perked up, sounding louder than the usual hushed tone required, and perking the interest of the officers and Mids already seated in the Waiting Room. "Of course, sir. I shall convey your presence to the First Secretary, Mister Pole. Do make yourself comfortable, sir, the wait should not be too long."

A Midshipman in his late twenties sprang from a leather-padded chair (which he should not have occupied if he had any sense) and gave it to Lewrie, with a grin, a bob of his head, and a cheery "congratulations on your victory, sir!" There was even the latest copy of *The Naval Chronicle* to thumb through. Lewrie shammed extreme interest in the publication, and plastered his best "stoic hero" expression on his phyz, but secretly enjoyed the humm-umm of conversation that his arrival caused, wishing that his chary father could witness the show, and realise that the only son he claimed as his was *not* a total pest!

The wait was, indeed, a short one, for another assistant clerk, the one that Lewrie had dubbed the "bad news boy" long before, as opposed to the other one he'd called the "happy-making clerk", announced his name, and that Mr. Pole would see him.

"My dear Captain Lewrie," Pole said as he entered that worthy's offices abovestairs, "Sir Alan if I may, my heartiest congratulations on your defeat of four French frigates at one go, sir!"

"Well, I had the assistance of my squadron's captains," Lewrie said with the expected modesty, "though I will own that it was a rough-and-tumble fight, a better one than one can expect from the French."

"A *splendid* action, Sir Alan, simply splendid," Mr. Pole gushed, and went so far as to shake Lewrie's hand before waving him to a seat. "A battle that, I gather from the latest reports from Captain Chalmers, completely dissuaded the French from sortying a second squadron to interfere with his operations against their supplying their forces in Spain by sea."

"I trust my replacement is still reaping a grand harvest along the North coast of Spain?" Lewrie asked as he crossed his legs and laid his hat in his lap.

"I fear that your previous success *has* daunted the French investment in the endeavour, Sir Alan," Pole told him as he took a seat behind his desk, "with your previous squadron's numbers expanded, and no warships to protect them, but . . . still a decent harvest. There are plans in mind, to be implemented later, for an even greater naval presence in those waters, and even staging some raids ashore to draw more of the French army in Spain away from Sir Arthur Welleseley's operations."

"Wish I was there t'see *that*!" Lewrie said with some heat. "When I worked off the Andalusian coast two years, ago, I had the use of two companies of soldiers, my Marines and an armed landing party of sailors to raise merry Hell."

"Ah, and so I do now recall, Sir Alan," Pole said with a knowing nod. "Pity about your ship, the ah . . . *Sapphire*, though. But, you *must* take care not to go about *breaking* things, what?"

Christ, are you a comedian, too? Lewrie thought, willing himself to keep his face straight.

"The real pity was losing my highly experienced gunners, Mister Pole," Lewrie said, instead. "Has anyone determined what use might be made of her? She might've been a slow'un, but she was a good ship."

"I do believe there is talk of turning her over to the Transport Board, once her lower mainmast is replaced," Pole said with an uncaring shrug. "The fifty-gun ship has had her day, if she ever had one, that is. There were never more than a dozen of them in active commission at one time. No, the sixty-four is more suitable for overseas duties, and as convoy escorts. Eighteen-pounders on the upper gun-decks, instead of twelves, and with more twenty-four-pounders on the lower gun-decks, as well. And, the longer hull needed to mount more guns on each deck translates to a longer, finer waterline; hence more speed."

"I must admit, though, Mister Pole, that I dearly miss my days in fast frigates," Lewrie said, wondering if a hint in that direction might get him back aboard a Fifth Rate 38.

"Oh, I fear there are an hundred Captains junior to you wishing the same thing, Sir Alan," the First Secretary said with what passed for a chuckle. "You may be too senior for frigates, by now. And, your experience commanding . . . ehm, *two* squadrons by this point would preclude a frigate command," he added, referring to a file on his desk.

"Ah, well," Lewrie said, only a trifle dis-appointed by that sad fact. "A squadron command, in a two-decker sixty-four will be my fate, is your meaning, Mister Pole? And, soon, I hope. Even with a small entourage here in London with me, finding a suitable apartment, as the French call 'em, is difficult, and it's not sensible to take a house, when my time ashore 'tween commissions might not be longer than a month or so."

"Oh, I am certain that some suitable commission worthy of your experience will turn up, Sir Alan," Pole assured him, but not with any real promise. Or so it seemed to Lewrie; Pole gave him the impression of cutty-eyed shiftiness. "I see that all the certificates and paperwork for the paying off of your ship are in order, settled at the Port Admiral's offices at Portsmouth? Everything properly accounted for? Ah, good. Nothing for it, then, but for your appointment with the Office of the Cheque to collect your back-pay, and list yourself on half-pay."

"Not for too long, I trust," Lewrie replied, trying to be subtle with his hint for immediate employment.

"Well, I think that about covers it, Sir Alan," Mr. Pole said, rising from behind his desk to bring the interview to an end. "Enjoy your brief time ashore, and the accolades of a grateful and admiring public."

Damn my eyes, that *was quick!* Lewrie thought, irked that Pole had not offered more assurance that he would be back at sea anytime soon.

"Thankee for that, Mister Pole," Lewrie said, instead. "I do intend to visit old friends for as long as I'm allowed. I believe you have my father's house listed as my current address? Once I find suitable lodgings, I will inform you of the address, to ah . . . speed the reception of future orders."

"Once again, Sir Alan, my heartiest congratulations upon your accomplishments, and the thanks of the Royal Navy," Pole said as he saw Lewrie to the door.

It took little over an hour to wrangle with the clerks to settle his back-pay to the last farthing, and to list him on the half-pay roll, leaving him with bags of time on his hands, and a note-of-hand which he intended to deposit at Coutts' Bank, right after his mid-day dinner. He even had time to swing by the Bank of England to make a healthy contribution into the Three Percent Funds, then go home to his father's house, write a note to his solicitor, Mr. Mountjoy, informing him of his financial doings, and then . . . what?

Good Christ, I'm really *on half-pay!* he told himself, wondering what else there was to do with his days, with the rest of this day. He considered finding a good tailor, for he could not go round London in his best-dress uniform forever. All his civilian togs were at Sir Hugo's country estate at

Anglesgreen, so he *must* go there, soon, but first he had to meet with that estate agent his father had whistled up and take lodgings somewhere, and how much a month might that cost he wondered.

From what he'd seen fashionable gentlemen of London wearing, he might have real need of a tailor, an entire new wardrobe of civilian suitings. The trip to Admiralty had been enlightening in that respect. Or, were they really fashionable, or cast-offs from three years previous, or last year's fad? Lewrie was certain that he could afford it, but . . . did he *want* to, and which tailor could he trust in that regard?

Becoming a temporary civilian was daunting in the extreme, offering an host of courses of action, all necessary, but all of seeming equal importance of a sudden. He found himself standing in front of the carriage gates to the Admiralty's courtyard, fingers flexing on the hilt of his rarely worn fifty-guinea presentation sword, dithering like a fart in a trance!

What to do first, then secondly, then . . . !

"Food," he muttered to himself. Of a sudden, he felt peckish, and recalled that there was a perfectly suitable two-penny ordinary nearby which served a hearty dinner, a place a cut above the usual, which, to his memory, had never sickened anybody, or laid them in a coffin. He would eat, first, and let the day take care of itself.

CHAPTER TEN

*U*nfortunately, the decision as to how he would spend his time, and in what order, was decided for him at supper that evening, though it was a rather good repast, it must be noted.

"So, you've completed your dealings with Admiralty, I take it?" his father, Sir Hugo, surmised over the lamb chops course. "Been to the bank and all, as well? My my, how industrious of you. Speaking of . . . I've arranged for you to meet that estate agent tomorrow morning, no no don't thank me. He'll come round to fetch you at Ten, and I'm assured that he has several choice properties for you to see."

"Tomorrow morning?" Lewrie gawped, with a forkful of asparagus halfway to his mouth. "Mean t'say . . ."

"No time like the present," Sir Hugo heartily chortled, "or in this case, the morrow. No sense in wasting your days, gadding about, what? Coffee houses, clubbing, associating with your old friends, of both high and low degree? Plenty of time for that after you're properly settled."

"And out from under your feet," Lewrie sourly responded, reaching for a fresh bread roll.

"You know my ways by now," Sir Hugo said, striving for an air of philosophical indifference, "I *am* capable of hospitality and generosity, especially to my kin, but even they cramp my style after a time, and intrude

60

'pon my desire for privacy. Strike whilst the iron is hot, me lad. Strike whilst the iron is hot!"

Accordingly, the estate agent, one Mr. George Penneworth, came knocking at the appointed hour and was shown up abovestairs to the drawing room. He came in a handsome coach-and-four, an equipage that Lewrie suspected was his own, not hired on, and a sign that the letting and selling of properties was a most lucrative occupation, one which might end up costing Lewrie rather more than he'd bargained for.

"I know next to nothing 'bout kitchens and such," Lewrie objected from the first after being introduced, "so you don't mind if I bring along my cook, Mister Yeovill, to advise me?"

"Certainly not, Sir Alan!" the effusive Mr. Penneworth gushed in total agreement. "Wise of you, I must say, to prepare yourself as much as you may. Most discerning," he smarmily went on.

Mr. Penneworth was dressed in the very best Beau Brummell fashion, though his bulk stretched it taut; dark green suitings, the trousers strapped under shiny black half-boots, a gold watch chain and fob cross his waistcoat, also stretched by what Lewrie suspected was extra-fine dining that his line of work, and the great profits that he derived from it, allowed him.

Once in the man's coach, and rattling off to the first house he had arranged to show, Lewrie explained his circumstances, how many he had in his entourage, and his expectations that he could only take a short-term lease should the Navy offer him a new active commission.

Mr. Penneworth pursed his full lips at that news, surely expecting, from what Sir Hugo had told him prior to the appointment, that a longer-term lease would be forthcoming. Not to be daunted, the man put a glad face back on. "I am certain that I can find you a suitable place, at satisfactory terms, though you may have to pay the initial three months up front, with no refund should you be called back to sea.

"Now, then!" Penneworth went on, "For a gentleman of your standing, and fame," he said with a slight bow from the waist, "nought but a First Rate dwelling will do."

"What, like a First Rate ship of the line?" Lewrie asked, completely at sea. "Don't know if I rate a flagship. Wouldn't that be . . . ?"

With un-quenched enthusiasm, Mr. Penneworth launched into a very brief explanation of the arcane builders' trade, and a series of Acts which governed them over the last century, entire.

"There have been many requirements decreed over the years, going back to the Great London Fire, sir," Penneworth happily prosed on, "In short, a First Rate house in London is one worth at least eight hundred and fifty pounds at the time of its construction, and consisting of at least nine squares of room on a lot, the out-buildings extra."

"Squares," Lewrie said, most dubiously.

"Oh, my pardons, sir," Penneworth said, laughing off Lewrie's ignorance of the contractors' argot, "but a square is a building measurement of one hundred square feet, ten by ten. A nine-square house would be nine hundred square feet on its foundation, thence the same footage upwards to the ground floor, the first storey, and et cetera."

"Thirty feet cross the front, and thirty feet deep, I'd think," Lewrie said with a nod of understanding. "Ah!"

Not so bad, he thought; *a manageable size, nowhere near as big as my father's place. How much did the old fart pay for his?*

"About that, sir, though most building lots in London are only twenty-four feet wide, making the overall depth rather tricky to measure out," Penneworth told him. "Second, Third, and Fourth Rate houses are, of course, smaller, and I doubt you'd wish to waste your time seeing any of *those.* Why, one would not have enough space in *any* room to swing the proverbial cat, ha ha! And some of the lesser houses are on much shorter lots, with no back garden, or stabling worth speaking of. No, no, I assure you that what you seek is a First Rate dwelling, one constructed to the highest standards of crafsmanship and materials. All else are little more than shoddily built . . . *hovels!*"

Mr. Penneworth at this point launched into a brief lecture upon the differences between superior grey brick for the outer walls, and red brick which was used behind the laths and plaster to make parti-walls and partitions; solid Portland stone for foundation footings, the window dressings, porches, eaves, and cornices, even fireplaces, and why Bath stone did not hold up well in London; how Reigate stone was best for hearths, basement floors and areas, and how handsome upper floors were when halls were paved Purbeck stone; how excellent Welsh slate was to tiles or pantiles for rooves; and Crown glass, not sheet, was better though on their tour they might encounter the newer Plate glass.

"And, here we are!" Penneworth exclaimed as they got to the first house, which turned out to be an *eighteen*-square grey brick monstrosity available for only fifty pounds a month, and big enough to house an army battalion, if they didn't much care for bathing, and would tolerate an hourly parade of rats.

On the way to the second to be shown, Mr. Penneworth expressed his belief that such an older place would be better than one of newer construction. "Things settle, d'ye see, after a time, and once settled, they're sound as the pound, a place that's been lived in for a decade or so," he said with a sagacious tap on the side of his nose, which did *not* go very far towards easing Lewrie's sudden feeling that a "settled" house, like the one they had just seen, sounded suspiciously like an old ship whose bottom was about to drop right off!

They saw two more places before dinner, then broke their search off to dine at a chop-house of Penneworth's recommendation; quite good but costlier than most, and Lewrie footed the whole bill, watching Mr. Penneworth put away enough for two!

They saw one more that afternoon, also too damned big to be managed, before turning off the rich expanse of Hay Hill Street into Dover Street for the last of the day, by which time Lewrie's reticence had stifled Mr. Penneworth's "helpful" enthusiasm.

"Quite nicely situated, this one, Sir Alan," Penneworth told him, "Dover Street runs down to Piccadilly, and a short stroll to the various gentlemen's clubs. Green Park is quite close by. To the West by a few streets is Park Lane and Hyde Park. Open expanses, fresher air, all that, what? Much less in the way of carting traffic with Green Park on the other side of Piccadilly, too. A quieter street than most, and this one has a roomy stable and coach house I think you'll like."

"Don't have a coach," Lewrie told him, feeling rather truculent and uncooperative by then, having tramped up too many flights of stairs, and more in the mood for a comfortable chair, bootless feet, and a glass of whisky.

"Mmm, a saddle horse . . . ," Penneworth said, a bit surprised.

"I depend on hackneys," Lewrie said, "or what sort of prad they have in the hired stables at Hyde Park. A trot down Rotten Row, wind and weather permittin', is the most I can hope for."

"Ah, sir," Penneworth said, subdued again, wondering just how a fashionable gentleman could do without either coach or horses. "Ehm, this one should suit a Navy man, Sir Alan. Admiral Lord Nelson resided at Number Seventeen for a time."

"With his wife, or the Hamiltons?" Lewrie asked with one wry brow up.

"During the Peace of Amiens, after Copenhagen, I believe it was, Sir Alan, so it was surely with Sir William and Lady Emma," Penneworth said, sniggering. "By which time the lady was quite . . . rotund. And, here we are!" he suddenly announced, sounding relieved. "Number Twenty-two Dover Street!"

The coach pulled to a stop and they alit on the east side of the street, giving them a wider look to the opposite side where the residence in question sat. Lewrie took a good look round, noting how all the houses seemed to be of a piece, one yellowish-brown brick expanse down each side of the street, punctuated with white-ish foundations, upper parapets, eaves, and cornices, and white-ish stone window treatments and stone courses to delineate each upper floor.

"The tradesmen's entrance down there, below the wrought-iron ornamental," Penneworth pointed out the steps leading down to a door in the basement, and the windows set just a bit below the street level. "The entrance is Doric in style," he said, indicating the stone-framed doorway, with a shallow inverted stone V above it.

"Doors *should* be Dor-ic, hey, Mister Penneworth?" Lewrie japed.

"Number Twenty-two is a twelve-square residence, Sir Alan," that worthy said, ignoring the wee witticism, "the lot thirty feet wide, so the main house should be fourty deep." He produced his large ring of keys, flicked through them, and found the one needed. "Shall we go in, sir?"

They crossed the cobbled street, Lewrie noting the two windows to the left of the entry, and the glossily black-painted door, trying to recall how high the Window Tax was these days.

"Four levels, altogether," Penneworth said as he opened the door into a foyer laid with the usual black and white chequered tile. The woodwork was painted white, as were the risers of the stair to the right-hand side, though the treads were polished oak. The stairs were about four feet wide, and a long hall stretched all the way to the back of the house, also done in black and white chequer, painted a pale cerulean sky blue.

"The front parlour, here," Penneworth said, indicating a large room to the left, entered through a wide double door, a spacious room about twenty feet long and perhaps fifteen wide, with a stone fireplace at the far end, and book cases either side. The walls above the white wainscoting were painted a very pale canary yellow, set off by white crown mouldings, and narrow Doric columns rising from the wainscotting.

"Let's stamp about, Yeovill," Lewrie said as he took heavy steps cross the oak-planked floor, and looking for wear. But the floor and its supports seemed as solid as a frigate's timbers. The plaster all round showed no cracks, or damp, either.

Penneworth showed them through another Doric-style wooden door into a dining room behind the parlour, which could also be entered by a hall door in the same style; this room repeated the white mouldings and wainscot work, but its walls were done in a darker blue paint.

And behind the dining room, about equal in size to the parlour, was a morning room at the very back, a smaller dining room where one might breakfast, or dine *en famille*, if no supper guests were in. It had a pair of windows overlooking the back garden area, and it was repeated in pale canary yellow, about ten feet wide, and only fifteen feet long, with a pair of large pantries along the outer wall. There was another door to the hall-way, and a landing which led down to the basement and kitchens, so Penne-worth led them down.

There was a solid and stout back door to the garden area, then a pair of rooms before they got to the kitchen, one for the butler's pantry, and one for the housekeeper's office and still room, though both were quite empty but for some shelving.

"There's a bath space, here," Penneworth said, opening a door into a stone-lined room with a drain hole in the centre. "You are connected to the city drains, and there's more than enough room for a hip bath tub. Much closer to the kitchen, so the task of fetching water abovestairs in volume is not necessary. And, there's a small fireplace to keep the bath room warm in winter. And in the kitchen . . ."

"Your territory, I think, Yeovill," Lewrie said, waving his cook to be first to enter.

"Larder there, wine cellar . . . aha, an amply sized Franklin oven!" Yeovill marvelled, opening the oven door to peek in, and lift the various round plates atop where his pots and such would rest. He then crossed to the massive fireplace on the outer wall to look over the iron rods to sup-port large pots or cauldrons over a fire, and the rotating spit above.

"What the Devil's that contraption, Yeovill?" Lewrie asked as he caught sight of a large, round metal cage wheel, and the chains that led to the spit.

"Oh, sir, that's what turns the spit," Yeovill said with a laugh. "You can raise or lower it, depending, and when you wish to do a roast, you put a small dog in the cage to walk the wheel to keep the spit at a steady turn.

A terrier would be best for that, so when I don't do a roast, he can double as a ratter."

"There are servants' quarters beyond," Penneworth pointed out, showing them several small rooms either side of the front passageway that led to the stout door of the front tradesmen's entrance, all of them thankfully somewhat furnished with single wooden bed-steads, a night table with a drawer each, and small chests of drawers.

"All I'd need, then, are new mattresses and bed linen," Lewrie said. "Good!"

"Well, there's pots, cauldrons, pitchers, stone crocks, and implements to be bought, too, sir," Yeovill informed him, "along with all the flour, sugar, and staples."

Well-off at last or not, Lewrie pictured growing stacks of silver shillings in his head.

"Here in the front, sir, under the street, actually, there is a large space for fuel," Penneworth told them. "Coal, wood, and such?"

They took a look at that, then, as long as they were on the basement level, they went out into the back garden to take a look at that, and the stables and coach house.

There was a stone area, then stone steps up to the garden proper, which might have been well-tended in the past, though was now over-grown with scraggly grass several inches long, and some wilting ornamentals. There was a pump lever, a match to the one in the kitchen, to draw water from the company that supplied water to the district.

The stable and coach house had room for two coaches, and at least six horses, plus tack room, hay and grain bins. Above, there was the sparse lodgings for a coachman, groom, and stable boy, if Lewrie was ever of a mind to hire such people on.

"First floor, sir?" Penneworth suggested once they were back inside, and the rear door locked with a loud clank. They went up the back stairs to the ground-floor hallway, then up the front stairs to the first storey, Penneworth describing the curved mahoghany railings on the way up.

The upper hall was also done in sky blue; six feet wide, they were told, more than sufficient for servants with trays, the moving of furniture, and a sense of spaciousness.

There was a front drawing room overlooking the street, with a set of three large windows, this time, equal in size to the parlour below on the ground gloor, done in the same white woodwork and trim, but painted almost a teal blue.

"And not a bit of wallpaper in sight so far, thank the Good Lord," Lewrie said, for he'd never been big on florals, reproductions of ancient Rome or Greece, or whimsical Chinese gardens and birds.

Off to the right of the drawing room, above the foyer, was a smaller room with only one of the windows, what Penneworth termed a library or study. The rest of the first storey was made up of bed-chambers with dressing rooms, four of them all told, and at the very back, just off the stairs that led to the second storey, was the "necessary closet" which, thankfully, had its own window for ventilation. Chamber pots in each bed-chamber could take care of night-time urination, but the "necessary closet" was for serious work, one with two wooden seats of ease with a shoulder-high partition between, and doors in front of both so the night soil could be taken down the back stairs by the servants each morning without disturbing the "air" of the house.

The second storey proved to be the highest, with a decent-sized nursery and bed-chamber for any children of the house, and servants' rooms behind, with their own "necessary closet", all thankfully furnished in some fashion. Penneworth told them that there was a chamber for the female housekeeper up there, so she could keep an eye on the female servants who'd sleep under the roof. And, there was an exit to the roof itself, and a walkway inside the slate roof proper, and the parapet, so tile workers or chimney swifts could access the many chimneys. Penneworth assured Lewrie that the landlord had had the swifts in just after the last family had moved on to larger lodgings, and that there had been no complaints on how the chimneys drew, just a month before.

"How much per month, sir?" Lewrie asked once they were all in the ground-floor parlour for a last look-about.

"Twenty pounds the month, Sir Alan," Penneworth told him, making a "pooh-poohing" expression, as if it was a grand bargain, "with three months in advance, as I said before, and month-to-month after, if you find it necessary, given the uncertainty of your circumstances."

"Hmm, I'll have to purchase some furnishings," Lewrie speculated, "enough for two bed-chambers, for the drawing room, things which I have no need for at sea, or Yeovill'd need in a ship's galley. What if, when I do get orders, and a new ship, the rent might be reduced if I leave all that behind for the new tenants?"

"Hmm, I would have to discuss it with the principal, Sir Alan," Penneworth said, obviously not used to haggling with his sort of customers, who were wont to spend more freely, especially for a house in the Mayfair area. "A *few* pounds less per month, perhaps, but *after* the first three-month advance at the stated rate, I fear."

"That would be alright," Lewrie told him. "What d'ye think, Yeovill? Just big enough t'be roomy, but not so big I'd need a small army of help t'manage it."

"Bags of room for all of us belowstairs, sir," Yeovill agreed, "with Desmond promoted to 'Bosun' of the house, Dasher to serve as a footman, Pettus to tend to you, and Deavers to help in the kitchen? We could still use a scullery maid, a pair of chamber maids, but we'd get by handsomely."

"Right, then," Lewrie decided, "I'll take it, sir. If you will come by my father's house in the morning, I'll have a note-of-hand on Coutts' Bank for you for the first three months, and you can negotiate with your principal owner for a longer stay at your leisure."

"Excellent, Sir Alan, simply excellent!" Penneworth exclaimed, "I am certain that you shall be pleased with your selection, and most comfortable for as long as you stay!"

"In point of fact, if you will come in once we reach my father's place, you'll have my note-of-hand at once!" Lewrie assured the man.

And I can get off my screamin' bloody feet! he told himself.

CHAPTER ELEVEN

Oh, Christ, what've I gotten myself into? was the thought that struck Lewrie several times a day over the next week, along with the apt analogy between fitting out a house and bringing a warship out of de-commissioned Ordinary to a state ready to go to sea.

It did not help that breakfast conversations with his father pretty-much consisted of irritated scowls, dubious "harrumphs", and pointed questions as to Lewrie's progress, his plans for that day, and some much put-upon sighs of stretched-beyond-measure tolerance.

"And just what is that you do with your privacy, that you have to have me out instanter?" Lewrie finally protested. "Havin' whores in, chasin' after your chamber maids in the nude?"

It here must be noted that, whilst Sir Hugo was undisputedly "of an age", the females of his house staff were young, quite comely, and all were perkily, cheerfully nigh-flirtatious, which was a trial for Lewrie's men, and even for Tom Dasher, who came away from all of his interactions with them with a red face and burning ears, barely able to stutter.

"What I do in my private moments is none of your God-damned business!" Sir Hugo snapped, though looking a tad cutty-eyed and smug as he leered over the rim of his coffee cup. "What is it today, hey? Bedding, settees, two gross of candles? Well, you'd best be at it!"

⚓

It was a lot more than candles that Lewrie needed, as he was learning to his dismay. Need small-clothes, shirts, bed linens, and tablecloths washed? That required copper cauldrons for the boiling, the rinsing, clotheslines both within and without the house where they could dry, depending on London's weather, and the amount of coalsmoke smut in the air, with a gross of cloths pins, to boot, and a goodly supply of lye soap, several irons to heat on the stovetop, and a place to put a clothes press!

It wasn't just Lewrie's glassware and tableware needed, either, for the house staff needed plates, bowls, knives, forks, and spoons, and glasses and mugs to eat with, and more pots and pans than Yeovill had to prepare the victuals, then the staples themselves . . . !

Furnishings, well . . . half London was continually in the process of selling up and moving, and the city had used goods on sale nigh on every street corner, with more shops dealing in cheap and shoddy used goods, piled into cavernous warehouse-like stores, with decent pieces lost in a jumble. Lewrie could have spent a week picking over the discards, but he did have one old school chum who might be able to "steer him a fair course" . . . even if that old school chum might soak him dearly. After all, the fellow was a former "Captain Sharp" who'd supported himself by playing a man of taste and refinement to "country-puts" just come to town with inheritances, looking for fashionable advice on just about everything, and more than happy to pay for all that guidance to such a "helpful" fellow, who also got a cut from tailors, dressmakers, milliners, bootmakers, landlords, and furniture dealers to which he steered the gullible.

Lewrie decided that he needed to see Clotworthy Chute! With a firm grasp upon his coin-purse, even so.

Clotworthy had come up in the world from those old, bad days, and his expulsion from Harrow for helping Lewrie and Peter Rushton, now Viscount Draywick, burn down the governor's coach house in youthful emulation of the Gunpowder Plot. He had, to all accounts, become an honest dealer in fine new furnishings, genuine antiques, and all sorts of artworks, from paintings to statuary, some reputed to be ancient Greco-Roman obtained during aristocratic Grand Tours of the Continent.

Of course, acid washes and a month in seawater could age a week-old copy of a Roman bronze most marvellously well, as Clotworthy had proven in the past.

Lewrie found Chute's expansive shops in New Bond Street, and Clotworthy himself, in fine, and gladsome, fig.

"Alan, me old!" Clotworthy enthused as he came to greet him. "Gad, the conquerin' hero returns with the gilded laurel wreath of glory 'pon his locks, what?"

"Good t'see ye, Clotworthy," Lewrie said in response, shaking hands with him. "I see you've prospered."

Always a fellow fonder than most of a good table, Clotworthy had, over the years, packed on more than his share of pounds, and was now quite elegantly, fashionably rotund, his bulk garbed in fine suitings, the very picture of a wealthy and successful man of business.

"Oh, I do well enough," Chute admitted, sweeping a hand over the vastness of his shops, and the goods on display. "Ran into Peter t'other day, and heard that you're back. The three of us *must* dine together, have a caterwaulin' carouse or two if you're long in town, for old times' sake, hey?"

"Just so long as it don't involve settin' something afire," Lewrie agreed.

"D'ye know, Alan, that Harrow has invited Peter to give a speech to the student body?" Chute said with a laugh, and a shake of his head. "Why, they'll be dinin' you and me in, and all's forgiven, do they keep that up, ha ha! Mean t'say, no horses were hurt in the fire!"

"For the moment, though, Clotworthy, I've come to shop," Lewrie told him. "Necessity's forced me to take a house."

"And you thought of me, first," Chute marvelled. "How grand! Where'd you light, and what do you need?"

After Lewrie explained why he needed to take a house, for a *very* short term, he told him, how little he had from his great-cabins, and what he expected to need to make the place the slightest bit presentable, Clotworthy frowned for a time, pursed his lips, and placed both hands under his chin, fingers spread to touch right and left counterparts.

"A drawing room . . . at least one bed-chamber to furnish, perhaps the front parlour on the ground floor, hmm?" Chute posed, humming to himself. "Colours? Paint, wallpaper that's already there?"

"Thought I'd leave the parlour almost bare, with nothing but my shipboard settee and such," Lewrie told him. "The drawing room abovestairs is paint, only, in a greenish-blue. Teal, they call it?"

"And you'd be leaving it all behind when you get a new ship?"

Clotworthy further supposed. "Well, then . . . good antiques are right out. Even some of my, ah . . . diligenty crafted reproductions, hah! But, see here, Alan. You've a *cheval* mirror for your dressing room so you can primp properly? No? Sufficient side-tables for your parlour, so you can have enough candle holders? Enough Turkey carpets?"

"Ah, no," Lewrie had to confess.

"My dear fellow, you need more than you realise," Clotworthy said with a sad shake of his head. "Never fear, though. You've come to the right place, and I'll see what I can do for you, and for a *most* reasonable price. Mean t'say . . . I'd never rook an old friend, what?"

First I heard o' that from you! Lewrie warily told himself.

"Dash it all," Chute said, "it'd be best did we coach over to your new digs and let me decide what'd suit it, make some notes . . ."

"Dine somewhere along Piccadilly?" Lewrie offered, hoping that a fine feed at his expense would help keep the cost low.

"That's sounds topping, Alan, me old!" Clotworthy replied. "Let us go whistle up a hackney and be about it. I must say, though . . . what *are* you wearing? I don't recall . . ."

"My father's gone all Beau Brummell on me," Lewrie said with a frown. "With all my civilian clothes down at the country estate, I had to borrow some of his older suitings."

"I'd recommend a good tailor, instanter, but . . . no fear, I no longer get a share of his fees," Chute vowed. "Well, only if a customer is simply too gullible to live, ha ha!" he quibbled.

A quick jaunt to Dover Street, a rapid tour of the house with Clotworthy cocking his head, squinting, and scribbling notes in a thin ledger, and now and then making "Aha" and "Hmm" noises, and they were off to dinner at a chop-house conveniently near the Reverend Chenery's church, Saint Anselm's, in Piccadilly Street, where Chute put away a steak, a dozen oysters, a salad, baked potato adrip with butter, some pease pudding, followed by a large dollop of figgy-dowdy pudding with port, and they were back in New Bond Street, where Clotworthy showed Lewrie round, pointing out items he thought would do, all of which were bustled away by workmen that instant to be packed aboard a dray waggon for immediate delivery the very next morning.

It all only came to £28/10/8, a sum Lewrie deemed was more than reasonable, and they parted with a promise that Chute would be asked to supper at the Madeira Club when they threw Lewrie his celebratory supper, once he was completely settled.

⚓

"Made progress today, have you?" Sir Hugo grumpily asked at supper that evening.

"Quite a lot, actually," Lewrie told him. "Furniture shows up in the morning, and I'll have another dray remove my stuff from your coach house. I'll still have to hire on some staff, but I believe I can move in, and be out from underfoot, by the next day after. Went to Clotworthy Chute's, and found everything I need."

"Chute? That scamp expelled with you at Harrow?" Sir Hugo asked with a bark of a laugh. "Did he leave ha'pence in your purse, haw haw?"

"All at a very reasonable price," Lewrie told his father.

"A leopard don't change his spots, my boy," Sir Hugo sniggered, "though I must confess he's put me in the way of a good investment or two, especially the Portuguese Brazil trade. Damn my eyes, but it's a sellers' market, that."

"What about the Brazil trade?" Lewrie just had to ask.

"Hah!" Sir Hugo enthused. "When the Portuguese royal court had to flee when Napoleon invaded their country two years ago, Admiral Sir Sydney Smith, and our Foreign Minister, Lord Castlereagh, presented 'em with a treaty heavily in our favour, opening their ports and their markets to British ships and goods, which had been closed to us for ages. The *worst* sort of mercantilism, the Spanish and the Portuguese, practiced. Their Ambassador to England, de Soussa Coutinho, held a meeting with over an hundred English merchants, who formed the Society of English Merchants Trading in Brazil, and the scramble for profits was on!

"What we'd usually sell in Europe, that Napoleon's idiotic Continental System blockades, goes to Brazil, and at low prices, to boot, and those poor, benighted devils never saw the like! Not one backward Latin colony can manufacture anything worth having, so Brazil snatched up everything shipped over," Sir Hugo chortled. "Wool shawls, and wool blankets, for God's sake. In such a hot country? Warming pans for their beds? They most-like use 'em to *flambé* snake and monkey meat! Coffin furniture, when they bury people in winding sheets? And *ice skates,* haw haw! What they use 'em for, only Heaven knows. The best part is what we get in return," Sir Hugo said, cutting himself a bite and chewing in seeming bliss.

"Ehm, what *do* we get in return?" Lewrie just had to ask.

"Brazil's simply riddled with gold and silver mines, emerald and diamond, and topaz mines," Sir Hugo went on quite rapturously between sips of claret, "and we get access to their vast tropical forests for log wood, dye wood, and timber for new ships, for furniture, I don't know what-all. All in exchange for shovels, axes, saws, cheap shoes, and kegs of nails! It's such a one-sided trade that everyone invested is raking in profits. Normally, I'd take anything that your old chum says with a huge *pile* of salt, but in this instance, Clotworthy Chute is a seer on par with Old Testament prophets, ha ha!"

"Which means you've made yourself a tidy sum, hey?" Lewrie said with a sly grin.

"That's for me to know, and you to discover when my will's read!" Sir Hugo snapped, turning waspishly grumpy, just as the fish course came from the kitchens.

"I didn't know you'd become a devotee of the Exchange," Lewrie saw fit to tease further, which jibe made Sir Hugo's upper lip twitch.

"Investin' through a broker's a deal different than engaging in direct . . . trade, I'll have ye know!" his father all but snarled back in sudden heat to be demeaned as someone who bought and sold like any grubbing shopkeeper, but the nicely lemoned crispy-skinned sole course seemed to mollify him. After a moment he tossed in, "Profits off my Three Percents allow me to dabble, here and there . . . nothing beyond a flutter or two. Nothing larger than what I'd wager in the Long Rooms at the Cocoa Tree, or Boodle's. My days of gambling deep are long past. I only trust that you learned *your* lesson, hmm?"

Ouch! Lewrie thought with a wee wince; *He just* won't *forgive me for my gamblin' in the early days, and what I cost him payin' my debts off! Hell, I haven't risked more than a shilling on* any *game in ages!*

"Move tomorrow, is it?" Sir Hugo asked after a long silence.

"Aye," Lewrie agreed, "then, once settled, I thought I'd ride down to the country . . . fetch back a few things. Try to settle things with Charlotte."

"Hmphf!" Sir Hugo said with a snort. "That should be amusing to see. Will you give in to Governour's idea of givin' the little minx a London Season?"

"'Fraid I'll have to," Lewrie told him. "Next year, perhaps . . . and increase her dowry, too. Maybe 'dot' her with two hundred pounds per annum . . . and a decent allowance for hats and dresses so she can make a good show. Then, she might stop accusin' me of gettin' her mother murdered by the French."

"Haw!" Sir Hugo barked. "That may prove t'be a task worthy of

Hercules, my lad. There's been too much bile spilled in her ears by Governour, the late Phineas Chiswick . . . the ill-tempered miser, and, all those anonymous letters her mother got about your overseas dalliances . . . even the sly poison I expect that Harry Embleton invented for spite, for Charlotte to be mollified. Come to think on it, your repute in Anglesgreen ain't of the best. There's quite a few there who despise you worse than cold, boiled mutton."

After a long moment with his head cocked over, Sir Hugo's face lit up in a rather evil grin as he announced, "By God, for what it's worth, I might coach down with you . . . just to see the show, haw haw! God knows I've tried to talk the girl out of her pets, but . . . in for the penny, in for the pound, what?"

"Oh," Lewrie coolly commented at that offer, assured once again that his only daughter would *always* be the bane of his existence, and a spiteful one at that. "How . . . jolly."

CHAPTER TWELVE

A h, welcome back, sor!" Cox'n Liam Desmond gladly said after a knock or two on the house door. "Good trip to the country, was it, sor?"

"Not bad, considerin'," Lewrie answered as he entered his new foyer, shedding his wide-brimmed country hat, walking-stick, and light summer overcoat. The weather at Anglesgreen had been all that anyone could ask for, though a sullen, misty rain had set in round Guildford on the return journey. "Will Cony at the Old Ploughman sends his best respects to you, by the way. And so does Mistress Abigail."

"Oh, did she, sor?" Desmond said, beaming. In past visits, Liam Desmond and the perky brunette waitress at Will Cony's establishment had struck up a pleasing, flirtatious relationship. "Sorry I missed going down with you this time."

"Everything in order here, Desmond?" Lewrie asked as his father came in, so Lewrie got a brief report as Desmond went to take Sir Hugo's things and hang them up.

"Been nice and quiet, sor," Desmond told him, "and Yeovill's had us fed right to the gills."

"Speaking of," Lewrie told him, "we fetched back a brace of cured hams, and a barrel of the Old Ploughman's best summer ale. Oh, and I've a chest to be brought in from the coach."

"I'll send Deavers and Dasher for all of it, sor," Desmond promised.

"Well, come in and let me show you round, Father," Lewrie bade. "Here's the front parlour."

"You could use some better furnishings than your old ship-board things," Sir Hugo said with a deprecating sniff as he paced round the room, "and some books either side of the hearth'd not go amiss. What is this tile in the fireplace?"

"Glazed tile throws back more heat than bare brick," Lewrie assured him, "or so I was informed. Dining room through here."

His side-board, wine cabinet, and eight-place table and chairs did go a long way to make a presentable showing, though years of use aboard ship, and being struck below to the orlop when Quarters was announced had taken its toll by way of dents and scars.

The morning room in back now had a four-place table, another side-board, and not much else, and Sir Hugo was more interested in the view of the back garden and stables. "Ye need drapes," he decided.

"Tell me about it," Lewrie said with a groan. "Yet another expense. The drawing room abovestairs is much nicer," he promised.

It was, and Sir Hugo even sounded impressed. The teal paint scheme was now nicely set off with mahoghany settees, chairs, and side-tables, upholstered in black, gold, and pale tan striped cloth, with a Turkey carpet in buff, blue, and gold. There were a pair of wing-back chairs and a padded bench in front of the fireplace, and along the window side of the room there were more tables, and some white-painted side-chairs upholstered in gold-tinted cloth.

"Yonder, there's room for an office and study, library, whatever," Lewrie pointed out. "I've nothing t'put in there at the moment, but . . ."

"Quite presentable, I must say," Sir Hugo said in scant praise. "That scamp, Chute, did you proud. Seems a shame you'd leave it all behind, do you get a new ship."

"I might keep a piece or two," Lewrie said with a shrug. "Will you take some tea?"

"Yes, I will," his father agreed, quite amiably. "Tea, with a dollop of brandy. What's back yonder?" he asked, going to the hall and looking "aft". And Lewrie had to show him the bed-chamber that he had furnished, and the others that remained bare. For his own sleeping space, Lewrie had opted for one of the back rooms with a window looking down at the garden and stables, which Sir Hugo thought a good choice, away from the rattle and clatter of coaches and cart traffic from the street, though once again suggesting that some good, thick, and sound-deadening drapes were needed, the sooner the better, especially if the seasons lapsed into Fall, and its coolness.

They settled into the wing-back chairs either side of the fireplace as the requested tea service arrived, along with a bottle of brandy, Lewrie apologising that it was Spanish, not French.

"Hmm, red and gold stripes aren't that much amiss," Sir Hugo said, thumping one upholstered arm of his chair once he had creamed, sugared, and laced his tea with a large dollop of the brandy. "Sets the room off, in a way."

"None o' my doin', I'll admit," Lewrie said with a laugh. "I let Clotworthy do the choosin' and matchin'. He has an eye."

"Ye'll be needin' maids." Sir Hugo owlishly peered about, and ran a finger along the top of the tea table, finding a fine film of dust in the short time that the furniture had arrived.

"Aye, I know," Lewrie said with a sigh. "I'm thinking of hiring old and ugly ones."

"Whyever'd ye do a thing like *that*?" Sir Hugo gasped.

"Four sailors and a boy, fresh from the sea, who haven't even *sniffed* a fetchin' young woman in a month o' Sundays?" Lewrie scowled, "I take on pretty ones, and it'd be an Out of Discipline orgy, and I'd be out twenty, thirty pounds for every girl who turns up pregnant."

"Well, there is that," Sir Hugo gruffly admitted. "Damn my eyes, ye cost *me* enough for the ones you topped, before you went to sea, hah!"

"It was only the two," Lewrie grumbled, crossing his legs.

"At least twenty-odd pounds went a lot further then than it does now," Sir Hugo said, slightly amused. "Twenty pounds, and up the road to the next parish, so the mort don't end up on the local Poor's Rate, haw!"

"How much does it cost you, now, hey?" Lewrie teased, unable to resist doing so.

"For your information, my maids are decorative, and amusing," Sir Hugo insisted, "but taboo. If I feel risible, which I still *do*, damn yer eyes, there are ladies of the commercial persuasion *outside* my house upon whom I may call. King's Place, for instance, just round the corner near Saint James's Palace . . . there are at least five very fine brothels in one short street. Fifteen guineas for 'all night in', with wine and supper extra.

Quiet, most discreet, and elegantly furnished. The Duke of Queensbury goes there, even if he is pushing eighty years or more. Hah! Lord Q of Piccadilly, better known as 'Lord Fumble', the poor, old lecher. I ain't in his condition, yet, thankee very much!"

"Quite handy, too," Lewrie sniggered. "Why, you could *stroll* there, hire an anonymous hackney driver. Feelin' peckish?" Lewrie asked of a sudden as he felt the first pangs of hunger. "Would you care to stay for supper? Your cooks, here or at Anglesgreen, never allowed my man, Yeovill, to show his skills. He sets a toothsome table."

"Hmm, tempting, but no," Sir Hugo declined after a long moment, and poured himself another heavily-laced cup of tea. "Some other time, perhaps. Our long coach rides has rattled me about so badly that all I wish is a nap at my house, and a late collation."

And, after a third cup of brandied tea, Lewrie's father creaked to his feet to take his leave, off-handedly congratulated him, again, on the house and its decor as he donned his own light duster coat, hat, and gathered up his walking-stick. A last reminder about draperies and a suggestion about the best hiring agency for chamber maids, and he was off in his coach, all but setting Lewrie fresh tasks for the morrow.

"Another pot o' tea, sor?" Desmond asked once Lewrie was back in the drawing room.

"I think not, Desmond," Lewrie decided. "I've had enough."

"Gettin' on for ev'nin', sor," Desmond said, gathering up the tea service and tray. "I'll see t'lightin' some candles. And with this steady drizzle, d'ye think we should light some fires t'take the damp off the air?"

"Aye, good idea," Lewrie agreed, "and we'll find out if the landlord *did* have the swifts clean 'em, and if they draw well, as Mister Penneworth swore they do."

"Aye, sor," Desmond said. "I'll see t'that, directly."

"Desmond?" Lewrie asked before he left the room. "How does it feel, turnin' butler for a time, 'stead o' Cox'n?"

"Oh, tolerable, sor," Desmond said with a grin, " 'til we can get back t'sea, that is. Don't know as I'd much care for it, if it lasts too long, though, sor. Seems . . . un-natural like."

"Well, pray God that we hear from Admiralty before the Summer's out," Lewrie told him, sharing his father's weariness and making his way to his bed-chamber to pull off his boots and don a comfortable old pair of shoes as Deavers and Dasher tramped about with buckets of coal, kindling, and tinder, and sparking flint starters to light candles, all of which put Lewrie in mind of how much several hundredweight of coal had cost, and how many gross of beeswax candles he had had to purchase, even for the servants' quarters, instead of cheaper tallow candles that smoked and stank of sheep fat. Next day, he'd be at the mercy of some mercer or draper with their fat books of fabric samples, drapery rods, and their workmen underfoot to hang it all, all that *and* a parade of applicants from a domestic registry seeking employment as maids in all their various stations, from scullery maid to maid-of-all-work to chamber maids, and at Mid-summer rates, their pay would be anywhere from five to twelve pounds a year, with food, lodging, shoes, and clothing all provided, and . . .

Life at sea is so *much cheaper,* he despondently thought; and, *the Navy paid me to live it! I need a drink, a stiff one!*

He watched dusk settle over Dover Street, and a light, misting rain turn into a depressingly steady downpour, from one of the deep window seats of the upper drawing room, which window seat he discovered badly needed some sort of upholstering pad. At least the fireplaces in the rooms where fires had been laid did draw well with no smoke rolling back inside, and the tiles reflected warmth better than naked brick, though he added brass reflector plates to his growing shopping list.

Glum, glum, glum, Lewrie thought; *the day, and our jaunt down to the country.*

To Lewrie's lights, time spent at his father's rambling estate at Anglesgreen was splendid, and in Summer the most enjoyable, but . . .

Oh, it had started grandly, with the customary stop at the Old Ploughman, where his ex-Bosun, Will Cony, his wife, Maggie, and their brood of boys made them feel welcome with a sumptuous country feast and lashings of fine ale. Sir Hugo's housekeeper and cook, Mrs. Furlough, with enough warning of their coming, always had the best of the season on the table, and the bounty of the estate cooked to perfection. Then there was the stables the next morning, and Lewrie's favourite mount, Anson, tossing his head and mane, prancing, pawing, and whickering his delight to see an old friend, and impatient to go for a good, long ride about the property, cross the pastureland, up into the wood lots and the wild forest trails, eager for a brisk canter, and at last a full gallop down to the flatter lands, as if showing off.

His kin, though, and his dealings with them the next day . . .

His brother-in-law, Governour Chiswick, had once been a lean and hungry panther of a fellow when he'd met him and his younger brother, Burgess, during the American Revolution, but those days were long gone, and Governour had grown stouter and more top-lofty every time Lewrie had seen him since. He'd become estate manager for their late uncle Phineas Chiswick, a grueling, shit-eating job, biding his time 'til the old miser had finally died, and he could inherit. Now, Governour, a man who had been sure that his way was the only way, was the parish Magistrate, and to all accounts was a quick-tongued scold and a hard man in love of his power, and his hard-applied version of Law.

Sadly, Governour's two boys and two girls, once cheerful scamps and playmates with Lewrie's own children, seemed to have taken lessons from Governour, not his long-suffering and meek wife, Millicent, and had turned just as arrogant and top-lofty as their father, which Lewrie thought was a sorry turn of events, and the ruin of their potential. It would have helped if any of them had shown the slightest curiosity and interest in Lewrie's recent victory, or how he thought the war was going in Spain and Portugal, but no . . . they showed more interest in how much that victory had *earned* him, and what the latest scandalous gossip was going round in London!

For the boys, it was all local horse racing, and questions about the Ascot, the Derby, and the exploits of a horse named Eclipse. With the girls, it was fashion, fashion, fashion, balls and who wore what to church or the local fair, and pity one of the neighbour girls (fill in the blank) who did not show as well as they!

That was tiresome, but not nearly as bad as having to listen to Governour opine on this, opine on that, boast of what punishment he'd awarded some miscreant, his *excellent* administration of the Law, just as harsh as the parish needed, and why it had taken Lewrie so long to come round to his own way of thinking as to what was to be done with his daughter, Charlotte, and the right way (Governour's, of course) to brighten the girl's prospects.

And Charlotte, at last. After Lewrie's wife, Caroline, had been murdered on that beach near Calais as they'd fled France, and his return to service in early 1803, Charlotte had had nowhere else to go but Governour's house to live with her cousins. After being steeped so long in spiteful comments, being tutored in how to comport herself and speak a cut above country ways, Lewrie wasn't sure what to expect from her, but what he got was dis-appointing.

How heart-breaking it was, to clap eyes on her, now almost come to her majority, the spitting image of his dear Caroline, with the same light brown hair, the amber eyes, the same slim and erect form and grace of movement. Even her smile, though rarely seen when in the presence of her father, was Caroline's! Yet, Charlotte struck him as a stranger who'd deigned to come down to the country from London's West End for a bit of amusement but had found none worth speaking of.

A snob, aping a peer's offspring, was who she seemed, and even reminiscing about her brothers' recent doings, Sewallis's advance to Passed Midshipman, or Hugh's adventures and growing naval renown, struck no familial chord, only a sly and arch "I am sure it is to their credit, though it is sad they were led to emulate your career so far from the greater doings of the times, and in such a *bleak* milieu."

And, when Lewrie had announced his plans for her future, and the Season she desired to seek a suitable mate, with a dowry increased to two hundred pounds per annum, there was not even a squeal of delight from her, no arms flung round his neck in gratitude, no jouncing on her toes, no.

Charlotte had inclined her head in thanks, with a secret smile more triumphant than glad, as if she and her uncle Governour had won the argument at long last, and she'd cast *him* the breathless wide grin of thanks that should have been Lewrie's! Next Summer, Lewrie cautioned, not this year, late as the Season was, and that was fine with her, for that would give her time to prepare a winning *trousseau*. She'd played the coy minx when prevailing upon her grandfather, Sir Hugo, for a place to lodge, and her thanks for his grudging agreement was more fulsome by far than any emotion she showed Lewrie!

"Ehm, Cap'm sir?" Tom Dasher said with a clearing of his throat as he entered the drawing room. "Yeovill says yer supper's ready."

"Ah?" Lewrie harumphed, glad to be drawn from his bleak study. "Good. I'll be right down. What's he prepared?"

"Nice breaded an' fried fish, sir, haddock, I thinks," Dasher said with a grin, and a lick of his lips, "could be cod, I don't know. Green salad, fat chips, an' a beef steak."

"Then we'll all eat well tonight," Lewrie said with a grin of his own, knowing that Yeovill would have cooked the same for all.

"Ehm, Pettus says the country was nice, sir," Dasher went on. "Never been, meself, but he was goin' on about it. Ya have a good time, beg pardon fer askin', sir?"

"Oh, just bloody *jolly*, Dasher," Lewrie gravelled, "Just *damned* jolly!"

CHAPTER THIRTEEN

*L*ewrie got his "high ramble" with Clotworthy Chute and his other old school chum, Viscount Peter Rushton, treating them to a fine supper at his favourite restaurant in Savoy Street just off the Strand by Somerset House and an evening of high-cockalorum at the Cocoa Tree to dabble at the gaming tables in the Long Rooms.

Peter had been an Honourable at Harrow, and after expulsion he had done his younger-son stint in the 17th Light Dragoons, inheriting his Barony when his elder brother had been carried off by a made dish that his affianced had prepared to show that she could cook as good as any hired cook, though her Frenchified sauce had sat too long and gone bad. Peter had become Viscount when his father passed over, and was now in Lord's, where his rare speeches now and then even made sense!

When Lewrie's celebratory supper at the Madeira Club finally came to pass, he invited those two rowdies to attend with him and his father, Sir Hugo. Though the Madeira Club did not have the *ton* of his own gentlemen's club, Peter had been most impressed by the supper, and the expansive wine cellar, along with the conviviality of the company.

Upon those outings, and upon his shopping trips round the town, Lewrie was delighted to learn that not everyone in London had succumbed to

Beau Brummell fashion, and that his civilian suitings could still be thought stylish, and better yet, still fitted him well, too.

Finally, with a full house staff engaged, a fourteen-year-old scullery wench no bigger than a "hop-o'-my-thumb", a maid-of-all-work named Agnes, a chubby nondescript of eighteen or so, and a brace of chamber maids as fearsome in appearance as bull-baiting mastiffs, one Martha and a Margaret, and frankly, hard to tell apart without different-coloured bib aprons, Lewrie was free to consider having that portrait done.

He sent Dasher in the role of footman/page to bear a note to the Chenery manse, and not without a precautionary protection letter declaring the lad as a member of his retinue, so the Impress Service didn't snatch up a likely young fellow in sailor's togs and carry him down to Deptford or the Nore as a "volunteer" for King's Service! The lad swore he was London born, but definitely in the East End, and was unsure if he could find Piccadilly, right at the end of the street!

Happily, he was back in less than three-quarters of an hour with a response. Miss Jessica Chenery's note said that she was not engaged with a project at the moment, and would be delighted to see him, again, and equally pleased to do his portrait!

It was such a nice day that he walked the relatively short distance to the manse at St. Anselm's church, enjoying the sight of Green Park cross the way, and the idlers and strollers out in a dry and warm morning after a rainy night.

A mob-capped maid whom he recalled as Betty opened the door for him and showed him into the front parlour, taking his hat and walking-stick. A moment later, and Miss Jessica Chenery swept into the room.

My God, she's more stunning than I remember! he told himself in awe as she sketched a brief curtsy with a glad smile on her face.

"Captain Lewrie, how glad I am to see you well," she said as she rose, "after such a grievously won fight."

Damme, she has a pleasant voice! he thought as he bowed in reply.

"Miss Chenery, how delightful to re-make your acquaintance," he said. "I must confess that your cheerful letters buoyed my spirits up since sailing for Spain."

"Do, sit, Captain Lewrie," Jessica said, waving him towards the nearest settee. "Would you take tea?"

"That would be grand, thankee," Lewrie told her.

Jessica's ringing of a wee china bell, though, brought more than a maid servant, for Reverend Chenery's long-time boarder, Madame Berenice Pellatan, an overly dressed and overly made up French *émigré* artist, glided in, a hand already extended to be kissed, forcing Lewrie to his feet once again to perform another bow.

"*Capitaine Chevalier* Lewrie, *enchanté*!" Madame Pellatan trilled.

"Madame Berenice, how grand to see you, again," Lewrie replied, taking that hand and giving it a peck. "You do well, Madame?"

"Ah la, *Capitaine,* the *dreads* we have suffered over you, young *M'sieur* Charles, and your ship, out on the *vast* and *dangerous* sea . . . !"

What expressions of dread were interrupted by a rapid series of clumps down the stairs, and the bursting in of Midshipman Charles Chenery, still in his naval uniform.

"Captain, sir!" the lad said in glad takings. "Good to see you!"

"What, Mister Chenery, still ashore are you?" Lewrie pretended to be astonished, and shaking his hand, man-to-man. "I'd've thought you would be back to sea before me!"

"Well, sir, not for want of trying," Chenery explained with a rueful expression. "I practically *haunt* Admiralty, but so far, no luck. In truth, sir, but for you I have no patrons, and so little time in the Navy that I'm a complete nobody."

"Well, as soon as I get orders to a new ship, Mister Chenery, you may rest assured there'll be a place in her cockpit for you!" Lewrie promised.

"Oh Lord, my pardons," Jessica said, grinning widely and trying to stifle an outright laugh, "but to hear my little brother called by any other name but Charley . . . !"

"He's more than earned it, Miss Chenery," Lewrie told her with a stab at sternness, "though he's not yet a 'scaly fish', your brother's done a man's work since joining *Sapphire*. Come a long way."

"Ah, Betty, tea for all if you please," Jessica said once the maid showed up, and they all took their seats.

"Your note said that you now reside in Dover Street, Captain Lewrie?" Jessica asked.

"Good enough for Nelson for a time, so I s'pose it's good enough for me, 'til I hear from Admiralty," Lewrie said.

"Why, you're practically just round the corner, almost next-door neighbours to us," the girl marvelled, prompting Lewrie to tell them the amusing tale of how he'd been forced to take a house instead of "bachelor" lodgings, and the many frustrations of establishing a household with all the appurtenances after years of ship-board living.

"Why, I've even had to find a terrier, to turn the roasting spit!" he declared with a laugh. "Rather a good ratter, too, name o' Bully!"

The tea service arrived, a rather ornate one in plate silver, and Jessica poured cups for all, apologising for the lack of tea cakes, and only her brother sounded dis-appointed.

The first and only time that Lewrie had been face-to-face with Miss Jessica Chenery had been little more than half an hour, a damned early in the foggy, cold pre-dawn when collecting her brother to coach down to Portsmouth to the ship. Even then, despite the gloom of the parlour and the young lady's drab winter wool gown and shawl, Lewrie had been most impressed by her, and *rencontre* after so long was not a let-down, nor did his memory play tricks on his recollections of her.

This morning, her hair was done up instead of maidenly long, and appeared more brown than black in the light, though her eyes, under a pair of thick, dark, and arched brows, were still the most mystifyingly dark blue. Jessica's face was a lean long oval, with a firm little chin and attractive cheekbones, and her only mar was a nose just a tad too large, rendering her only slightly less than beautiful, but still . . . striking, and remarkable.

Lewrie had thought her slim, in the short time they had stood together admiring one of her most-realistic portraits, and today, she appeared even more so, lithe and almost willowy. Drab wool had given way to a light muslin summer gown of dark coral with white lace trim, with puffed quarter-sleeves that bared very slim arms. Her hands with long, fine, talented fingers . . . !

Damme, what a fetchin' girl! he thought as he stirred cream and sugar into his tea, striving not to leer too obviously, and keep up with the conversation.

"Your father, Reverend Chenery, is well, Miss Chenery?" Lewrie asked.

"He is, Captain Lewrie," she replied, beaming at him, "thank you for asking. He would be with us, but he is working on this Sunday's sermon, and wished me to express his regrets that he could not greet you."

"La, now that you reside in the parish, you will of course wish to attend Divine Services at Saint Anselm's, *M'sieur?*" Madame Pellatan gushed.

"Well . . . of course, Madame," Lewrie said, taken aback. "At sea, with no Chaplain aboard, me and Sundays don't get together that often, sorry t'say. The last time I was in a church proper, it must've been a Christmas, and I confess I drowsed off a bit during the choir's cantata, and da uh . . . came close to applauding when it ended."

Keep a civil tongue in yer head, ye twit! he chid himself; *You're not aboard ship any longer!*

His home parish? That would be St. George's at Anglesgreen, but he hadn't been there since the war began again in 1803. Then, he had to explain where Anglesgreen was in Surrey, what sort of village that it was, and why he'd ended up there.

"You will be welcome in our box, Captain Lewrie," Jessica told him, with almost a shy look.

"And I would appreciate that more than you know, Miss Chenery," Lewrie told her, causing another smile to spread on her features.

"So," she said, getting down to business at last and setting aside her cup and saucer on a side-table. "You wish me to do your portrait, sir?"

"Aye, I do," Lewrie replied. "I haven't sat for anyone since I was a Lieutenant, longer ago than I'd care to admit. Your kind offer the last time I was here set me to thinking that I should have a new'un done before I go toothless, wrinkled, and bald as an egg, so people remember me how I looked in my *late* prime, ha ha."

"With your scar, a smile, and . . . how did you put it, sir, warts and all?" Jessica prompted with a tinkling laugh.

"Surely a scar nobly earned in battle," Madame Pellatan cooed.

"More a silly duel over a young lady's reputation," Lewrie corrected. "The honourable marks are in places better left imagined!"

"My calendar is clear at the moment, sir," Jessica told him. "I could begin my sketches almost at once. Where, though . . ." She paused to think. "There's really very little room here, and the light isn't of the best our side of the street."

"Well, the front parlour at my house faces East, Sou'east, and there's plenty of morning light, most days," Lewrie offered. "If that would not compromise your reputation, Miss Chenery."

"I could be her chaperone, *M'sieur*," Madame Pellatan leaped to suggest.

"Or I, sir," Charles Chenery offered. "After all, I only have to call at Admiralty once the week, and would have bags of time on my hands."

"And, you could visit with my Cox'n, Deavers, and the other lads," Lewrie was quick to say, in dread of Madame Berenice's ogling longer than a Dog Watch. "I've Bisquit and Chalky with me, too. I *had* to take a house. My father took one look at us, swore we resembled an itinerant circus, and wished us out of his place before the beasts wrecked it."

"Since you live so close by, that would serve admirably, sir," Jessica enthused, then turned more thoughtful. "Ehm, would it be too much of an imposition to ah, go see how suitable it might be, Captain Lewrie?"

"Of course not!" Lewrie declared. "How about this instant?"

"In case it is, I can carry your easel and such," Midshipman Chenery volunteered, "and all you need to make an early start."

"Yes, let's go!" Jessica happily agreed. "Though if I do not yet know the size of the portrait that would do Captain Lewrie justice, let us leave the easel, canvas, and such for later. I'll get my bonnet . . ."

Their preparations to rise and depart were suddenly interrupted by the arrival of an energetic dog, a floppy-eared black-and-white cocker spaniel with brown eyebrows, which dashed to Jessica, frantically waggling its butt in an attempt to clamber into her lap.

"Oh, Rembrandt . . . snookums!" Jessica cried in delight, cupping the dog's head in both hands. "Been in the back garden, have you? Mud on your paws? No? Alright, then."

"Come here, pest," her brother coaxed. "Father thinks him more of a trial worthy of Job. He is amusing, though."

"And we love you, don't we, Rembrandt?" Jessica cooed, bending down to give the dog a hug.

"He could meet Bisquit," Lewrie suggested. "My dog."

"He does need exercise," Charles Chenery allowed. "Should I fetch his leash?"

"If Captain Lewrie truly does not mind him?" Jessica asked with a fetching incline of her head. "We try to walk him in Green Park as often as the weather allows, but . . ."

"Aye, bring him along," Lewrie urged.

"Apologies for the sparesness," Lewrie said minutes later after the short stroll to his house. "This is all from my great-cabins," he explained, then had to tell them when and where he'd gotten the low, brass Hindoo tray-table before the settee, and the small arsenal of firearms; the fusil musket, his Ferguson rifled breech-loader, the Girandoni air-rifle and the unique over-under fowling piece that Viscount Percy Stangbourne had given him, a fifty-guinea presentation sword from the East India Company for saving one of their convoys in the South Atlantic, his preferred everyday hanger, and the older one that he'd surrendered to Napoleon Bonaparte at Toulon in '94.

"Bonaparte, himself?" Madame Pellatan gasped, a bit too theatrically. "*Mon Dieu*, you *met* the Corsican Ogre?"

And Lewrie, trying not to appear *too* smug, explained how he'd ended up on a beach with the survivors of the *razeed* mortar bomb after she'd been blown sky-high and sunk, and what a drowned rat he'd looked, with his breeches draining gallons of water, and his stockings round his ankles, and why he could not give his parole and keep his sword yet abandon his men.

"During the Peace of Amiens, my wife and I travelled to Paris," Lewrie went on, "since *everybody* was doin' it, and I was of a mind to get it back. I had several French Captain's swords, with notes as to whom they belonged, and hoped t'trade. Next thing I knew, we're at the Tuileries Palace, face-to-face with Bonaparte himself, and him in a powerful snit, but I got it back. They said we might even take wine with him and his wife, Josephine, but that was right out."

Then, he had to relate how he and his wife had been warned that they should flee, soonest, and how they had done so, right to the cove near Calais where a boat waited, and how Caroline had been shot in the back and died.

After expressions of awe and words of sympathy, Lewrie lightened the mood with the tale of how one Pulteney Plumb and his French wife, he a master of quick-change comedic sketches, and she formerly one of the chorus at the *Comédie Française*, had spirited them away with an un-ending series of disguises and *faux personae*, as they had done to rescue French aristocrats during the bloody days of the Terror, and Lewrie mostly playing the role of a mute, an unfortunate kicked in the head by a horse, or a drooling lunatick.

"He called himself the 'Yellow Tansy'," Lewrie said with a laugh. "God knows why. They own a small theatre near Covent Garden, and they do put on a fine, amusin' show, some of the routines quite topical, as if they base 'em on the latest caricatures by Gillray or Rowlandson, but I wouldn't recommend the neighbourhood after dark."

"La, how *tragique*, how *formidable*, how . . . !" Madame Berenice marvelled, all but blubbing up in awe of his tale.

"What an adventurous life you have led, Captain Lewrie!" Miss

Jessica said in wonder, and what Lewrie happily took as a fair dash of hero-worship.

Woof? came from the hall, a tentative introduction by Bisquit with his head round the edge of the doors. Rembrandt strained at his leash to go greet him, and Jessica stepped closer to allow him. The dogs did what dogs usually did, sniffing noses, sniffing rumps, then Bisquit was head down, front paws dancing and whining in invitation to play. A moment later and they were off, dashing down the hallway and back again in a headlong gallop. Their return for a quick dash about the front parlour chased Chalky from wherever he had been lurking, and ran him to the top of one book case and atop the mantel, bottled up and spitting in annoyance.

"So, would this room suit, Miss Chenery?" Lewrie asked, amused by the creatures' antics.

"Oh, wondrously well, sir!" Jessica told him, looking about one more time. "And the light yellow colour of the walls brightens the ambient light. Perhaps I can only work from early morning to mid-day, but it will be almost perfect. If you do not mind starting so early?" she asked with a pleased, expectant expression.

"I am completely at your disposal, Miss Chenery," Lewrie told her. "My time is yours."

"Hmm, then let us say . . . from the waist up, and a canvas about two feet by three?" she said, raising both hands to frame him in a box.

"Are hands extra?" Lewrie joshed. "I'm told that the Spanish painter, Goya, charges more for hands."

"*Mon Dieu,* where would you learn that, *M'sieur?*" Madame Berenice gasped.

"One of our spies that I landed ashore in Andalusia wrote back that he'd met the fellow once he got to Madrid," Lewrie boasted.

"*Espionage.* Yet another tale of adventure you must tell us, someday, *M'sieur!*" she gushed.

"Like t'see the rest of the house?" Lewrie asked, and, following the dogs' progress, he showed them the dining room, then upstairs to the drawing room, which they thought most tastefully furnished, and what a shame it would be to leave most of it for the next tenants should he get orders, and a new ship, before he had time to enjoy it.

"I fear I must obtain a canvas and stretch it before I can begin," Jessica told him as they strolled side-by-side back to the church manse, with the dogs roving back and forth before them. "Would Wednesday be a good day to start, Captain Lewrie?"

"Sounds good to me," Lewrie happily agreed. "Damn, Bisquit!"

His dog had rarely been on a leash, simply *would not* heel, and was torn 'twixt the distractions of busy Piccadilly Street, and his new companion, Rembrandt. Leashes tangled, and Lewrie almost went arse-over-tit several times as he walked on the kerb side, outboard of the girl.

His curse made Jessica shyly giggle.

"Pardons," Lewrie said, embarrassed that he'd been too long away from proper company and the mores of Society.

"Believe me, sir, I've heard worse from Charley since he's been back," Jessica said, much amused. "He's gotten quite . . . salty, to my father's distress. Though it's fun to watch him go red in the face!"

"Aye, one goes to sea, and learns a lot more than how to hand, reef, and steer," Lewrie apologised, looking over at her with a grin, and reckoning that Jessica Chenery stood about three or four inches below his own five feet nine in sensible low-heeled shoes.

"I trust that, during our sessions, you will explain what that means, Captain Lewrie," Jessica teased. "Charley's new-learned argot is a complete mystery to all of us."

"I'll have you boxing the compass, doing long splices, and taking Noon Sights, by the time you're done with me," Lewrie said, laughing.

At last, they reached the door to the manse, and Lewrie tipped his hat to one and all, bidding them adieu 'til the day of the appointed first session. "And do feel free to bring Rembrandt along. He and Bisquit seem t'have become fast friends."

"Then I shall, Captain Lewrie," Jessica promised, "though I fear for your furniture do they become *too* exuberant."

"No matter," Lewrie shrugged off. "'Til Wednesday morning, then. I'll shove myself into full dress, shave close, and try to sit patient."

"Warts and all, with a smile, sir," Jessica replied impishly, "and I'll not charge more do you show a hand."

It was difficult drawing the dogs apart, but Lewrie at last got Bisquit back to his side, doffed his hat one last time, and strolled back down Piccadilly with a jaunty step, letting his dog have a sniff at everything that took his fancy on the way.

Damme, a well-spent morning! he told himself; *And what a fine way t' fritter away my time ashore, in daily company of such a grand young woman! So long as I can keep my hands to myself!*

CHAPTER FOURTEEN

*L*ewrie paid off the driver of his hired hackney and went up the steps to his father's front door, lifting the highly-polished brass pineapple door knocker to rap for admission, thinking it hypocritical of the old fart to display the sign of generous hospitality yet be such a grim and begrudging host.

"Ah, Sir Alan, sir!" Sir Hugo's butler, Harwell, said as he saw Lewrie into the entry hall. He sounded a tad too chipper and genial for Lewrie's taste, given his usual cold and aloof welcomes. "Sir Hugo is abovestairs, sir. Shall I see you up?"

"No need t'bother him, Harwell," Lewrie said, tucking his fore-and-aft bicorne hat under his arm instead of handing it over. "I gave Admiralty my new address last week, but I was wondering if any letters were delivered here before . . . the last few days and such."

"Hmm," Harwell replied, mulling that for a long moment. "I do recall that some mail did come for you, Sir Alan." Harwell went to the sideboard, sorted through a thin stack of letters, and found two made out to him. "Here you are, Sir Alan. Been to Admiralty this morning, have you, sir?"

That much was obvious; Lewrie was in full uniform, right down to his sash and star of knighthood, with the fifty-guinea sword at his hip. Indeed there were two letters for him, both from naval friends, but nothing from Admiralty.

"Admiralty, aye, Harwell," Lewrie said off-handedly as he read the senders' names and addresses. "Pretty-much a good morning wasted. Well. I'll be going on."

"Should I whistle up a hackney for you, Sir Alan?" Harwell offered.

"No, thankee," Lewrie told him, somewhat despondently, "I think I'll walk home. Give Father my regards."

"But of course, Sir Alan," Harwell said as he saw him out the door to the street.

What's takin' the bastards so long? Lewrie sourly thought as he set out down Park Lane; *Don't they know I'm a fuckin' hero?*

It was much too nice a late Summer day to fret, but fret he did, almost oblivious to the delightful aspect of Hyde Park just cross the way, the richness of the terrace houses along Park Lane, and the grand spectacle of expensive coach traffic, most of them open-topped so the occupants could enjoy the day, and show themselves off. Fine, blooded saddle horses cantered or trotted by, with well-to-do men astride them, or elegantly garbed ladies perched side-saddle, and each passing equipage seemed to jingle in tune with the tinkling laughter of the people in them. Birds sang, there were snatches of music from the park, and even the calls from strolling flower vendors, piemen, and itinerant street merchants were as gay as anything offered in a music hall, yet . . . it was lost on Lewrie. He might as well have been slogging through a driving downpour, with mud to his ankles.

Five, almost six weeks had gone by since he'd turned in his last paperwork for paying off *Sapphire,* and so far his visits to Admiralty had been fruitless, his hours sitting on hard chairs in the infamous Waiting Room a complete and boring waste of time, ended only by a curt note from the First or Second Secretary which said that neither of them had time to see him, and delivered with a sketchy bow and nod from the clerk whom Lewrie had dubbed "the get ye gone clerk" long before.

Twenty-nine years in "King's Coat", and I can't remember bein' on half-pay this *long 'tween ships!* he groused to himself, though he knew that was an exaggeration.

There had been a spell just after the formal end of the American Revolution when he'd been at sixes and sevens, but back then, he'd been *eager* for shore living, and high-cockalorum, revisiting his wastrel and rakehell pre-Navy youth in his London haunts. From 1789 when he'd paid off little

Alacrity and come home with Caroline and his increasing brood from the Bahamas, 'til the French declaration of war in early 1793, he'd not been unduly bothered by so long a period ashore, since there was peace, a new and unfamiliar life as a farmer on rented land, and no reason that he could have imagined that would ever recall him back to sea.

There were a few months spent at Anglesgreen between the *Jester* sloop and his appointment as Post-Captain into the *Proteus* frigate, of course, but those months had breezed by.

No, the longest he'd spent ashore was after paying off *Reliant* in 1806, a whole winter healing up from the leg wound he got off Buenos Aires, and that had nothing to do with his competence, or his value to the Navy. Now, though . . . what was the delay? Lewrie could not imagine why he was not offered a new command and active commission. It was not a prideful boast for him to admit that he was *somewhat* famous.

His initial welcome at Portsmouth to pay off *Sapphire*, his first appearance at Admiralty afterwards, and the acclaim he'd gotten from fellow officers present, his reception at the Madeira Club, the Cocoa Tree, and invitations to dine at several gentlemen's clubs since, and the praiseful newspaper accounts, had been most gratifying. When he'd first attended St. Anselm's with the Chenerys, Jessica's father, Reverend Chenery, had announced his presence among the congregation, to their gladsome, nigh hero-worshipping applause, and they'd all but mobbed him outside right after, as if Admiral Nelson had risen from his tomb at Westminster Abbey and made his appearance!

Gratifying, aye, all of it, a mark of honour, success at his profession (even if, in his idle youth, he'd never have put one foot aboard a ship if given the choice!), and the gilded laurel leaves of glory upon his brows after which every gentleman officer strove!

That most recent acclaim had felt especially pleasing, since he stood close to Jessica Chenery as he was mobbed, noting how glowing she was, even as he "pshawed", deflected some of it to her brother Charley, and *tried* to be suitably modest. And, as the elders of the parish had drifted off, younger people of Jessica's closer circle had come forth to meet him, a blizzard of names and faces; girlhood friends and their husbands, for all were now married but for Jessica and one rather drab spinster. Sly glances 'twixt the young ladies and Jessica seemed to question if "He was the One", or so Lewrie imagined by their squeals.

Don't get smug, he chid himself, recalling the day, though he'd enjoyed it immensely. *Damme, is* all *London full o' whores?* he asked himself a moment later as he finally took better note of his surroundings, for there were over-done, tawdry young women strolling along either side of Park Lane, flirtatiously twirling their parasols, tossing their hair, and making a swishing show of their fine gowns, even in early afternoon.

He nodded to passersby, touching the front of his hat in reply to the gentlemen who made a like gesture, flashing brief smiles to the ladies with them, all of which put him in a slightly better mood. When he'd left his father's house, he'd intended to walk the whole way home, as if donning a hair shirt like some rabid monk who'd flog himself, but he began to reflect how very *far* a walk it would be, and regretted his choice. He stopped at the corner of Pitt's Head Mews to look about and take a deep breath of the fresher air from Hyde Park, cocking an ear to sounds of birds, children playing criquet, rounders, or tag close by.

Well, he admitted to himself; *maybe some time ashore, with no responsibilities, ain't all that bad. For a while, anyway. Summer in England, in London . . . ah!*

"Well, hallo sir," a roughed and made-up strumpet gaily said, "by yourself, are you? Want some comp'ny, do you?"

He gave her a quick looking-over and decided to laugh her off.

"No, thankee, not today, girl," he told her, "but the best of luck to ye. Hoy, cabman!" he shouted to a passing hackney that held no passengers.

"Dare I ask how things went at Admiralty, sir?" Pettus enquired as he took Lewrie's hat and sword.

"Nothing worth speakin' of, Pettus," Lewrie told him, going into the front parlour for a quick look-see at the canvas on the easel where Jessica Chenery had made her first pencil outlines. Chalky awoke, did himself a long stretch or two, yawned, and meowed a welcome, then came off the now-padded window seat for a more personal greeting. Lewrie quickly peeled off his uniform coat and handed that to Pettus before it got coated with fur, and scooped his cat up for some pets, which the cat quickly grew tired of; he hated being carried about.

"Want something, sir?" Pettus asked.

"A tall, cool ale, I think," Lewrie decided. "I'll be in the drawing room, irritating Chalky."

"Yes, sir, coming right up," Pettus said with a rueful grin, for whenever Lewrie's ships had drummed Quarters for battle or live-firing practice, it had been he who had carried Chalky down to the quiet and safety of the orlop, and still bore a few scratchmarks.

Upstairs, Lewrie plumped himself down on the settee and put the cat aside so he could tug off his boots, then slouch into a comfortable sprawl, quite unlike the edge-of-the-seating, erect posture expected in proper company. Wiggling fingers tempted the cat back into his lap to be stroked and jaw-rubbed.

Lewrie looked about the formal drawing room, which no longer struck him as alien and new as it had been when the furnishings had been delivered. Even the damned drapes of heavy, pattern-embroidered chintz in pale blue-grey, which Jessica and Madame Pellatan had helped him select, seemed fitting, a natural choice, and . . . nice. Even homey!

It really is a pleasant house, Lewrie admitted to himself; *and it don't* stink *like a ship. I* should *be satisfied.*

Most unlike ship-board living, he could bathe in hot water three days a week (no need to get too carried away!) and could shave daily without balancing himself against rolls and plunges, could dress in underclothes and shirts free of salt crystals, washed with soap that would foam, fresh-smelling from a drying line. He could sleep on bed linens just as fresh, changed and laundered weekly, upon a deep feather mattress just soft and yielding enough.

Sleep! He could sit up with a good book and a flask of brandy or aged American corn whisky 'til ten or so, and retire for a *complete* night's rest, with never a thud of a sentry's musket, a bellow that Midshipman Hen-Head reports Lieutenant Jingle-Brain's duty, and a request for him to come to the quarterdeck after a haggard two hours' slumber.

Then, there was food. No salt-meat junk touched his plate, no rock-hard ship's bisquit graced his bread barge, with or without the proverbial wee-vils that some chewed up regardless, claiming that "a man can't get enough meat!" Did he wish fruit, fresh vegetables, or salad greens, there was always someone crying his goods in the street right outside, and his fish course was always fresh from the Billingsgate market (well, fresh-ish!), not salt-cured and stored right aft in the fish room where rats and roaches dined as well as the crew.

I could *stand this . . . for a while, at any rate,* he assured himself as Pettus arrived with his ale.

CHAPTER FIFTEEN

"adame Pellatan does not chaperone you today, Miss Jessica?"
Lewrie asked as he saw Jessica and her brother, Charley, into the front
parlour the next morning, along with their cocker spaniel.

"Not today, Sir Alan," Jessica replied, removing her gloves and bonnet. "She and other French *émigrés* breakfast together at least once a fortnight, and spend the day, really, reliving better times."

"What a shame," Lewrie said, not meaning a word of it. The woman
got up his nose with her affectedly elegant airs.

"I hope Charley will not be too bored, watching me work, and you . . .
play-act a plaster figure," Jessica said with a winsome smile and a glint of
amusement in her eyes.

"There's the dogs," Charles Chenery said with a shrug of duty to be
borne. "And there's some books . . . if you do not mind, sir?"

"Mostly educational, nautical, all that," Lewrie told him. He'd unpacked
some of his books and placed them either side of the fireplace in the parlour. There were other books still in chests, but not the sort he imagined
would go over well; novels for the most part, and all of them of a prurient
nature. *Not* the reading matter to show off to a young lady, or a minister's
son! They really would have best been left at his father's house, to join that
lecher's lacivious collection.

Rembrandt and Bisquit re-introduced each other with sniffs, yips, and a gallop down the hall, and Chalky decided that the top of the table in the dining room would be quieter.

"Now, Sir Alan," Jessica instructed as she took a seat behind her easel with dark chalk in hand. "Turn your head a bit more to the right . . . there. A slight smile, as you requested. Ehm, perhaps a wee bit less? Fine," she said, sticking out her left hand with her thumb up.

"Artists really do that?" Lewrie japed. "I thought that was an exaggeration."

"Yes, we really do that, for scale," Jessica replied with a gay laugh. "Rule of thumb, all that?"

"Fine ship models, sir," Charley said from the mantel. "May I?"

"Of course," Lewrie allowed. "The first'un is the *Jester* sloop, my first posting as a Commander. I got her when we evacuated Toulon."

And as Jessica firmed up her initial sketches, Lewrie told the tale of how she'd been a French *corvette* named the *Sans Culottes*, and the embarrassing jape he'd made to Admiral Sir Samuel Hood at supper, which had resulted in her re-naming. Bung-full of royalist evacuees and British soldiers, Lawrie had fled Toulon in temporary command of a shoddy frigate, the *Radicale*, but had been pursued and overhauled by two *corvettes*, one of which had been driven off, and *Sans Culottes* boarded and taken by the motley men he'd had at his disposal, all fighting for their lives and the lives of their wives and children, who would have been taken back to Toulon and guillotined had they failed.

"Better *Jester* . . . meaning I was a poor comic, than HMS 'Bare-Ar . . . ehm, Bottomed'," Lewrie joked, damning his loose, salty tongue once more. "My wife and I fulfilled my promise to a dying French navy officer, Charles de Crillart, to see his family safe, but only his cousin, Sophie, survived, and became our ward. She would have been *Comtesse* de Maubeuge, but for the revolution, but now she's married to one of my former First Officers, Anthony Langlie, and living with his parents in Kent. Three children, now, I believe.

"And, I got my first cat out of it," Lewrie added, describing his black-and-white little clumsy, Toulon. "How he got his name, for he was a disaster, too, haw haw!"

As for his first mistress, Phoebe, who had come away with him on that sortie was best left un-said!

"Madame Berenice has told us such horrific tales of what life was like during the revolution," Jessica said, setting aside her chalk for a moment and swiping a loose strand of hair from her face, which left a smudge of chalk on her forehead, to her brother's amusement. "How *monstrous* the French are! Everywhere they go, they leave nothing but death and slaughter. Look at Spain, Portugal, Austria, and what crimes they committed to make their empire. What they did to you, Sir Alan, and your wife, on a casual whim because you angered Bonaparte in what was likely the most *trivial* way!"

"We're right t'hate 'em, I've always been told," Lewrie agreed, "like the Devil hates Holy Water."

"This other one, sir?" Charles Chenery asked, lifting down the model of *Proteus* that Lewrie had just received after a meeting quite by chance with his former barrister, Andrew MacDougall, who'd defended him at his trial for "stealing" a dozen slaves on Jamaica to man his fever-ravaged ship, at a shop in New Bond Street. "And why is there a little Chinaman figure on the quarterdeck?"

"That's the *Proteus* frigate," Lewrie told him, explaining why he had been put on trial, and why William Wilberforce and members of his society to eliminate slavery in the British Empire had engaged MacDougall. "And that model would have been used in court to prove the witnesses against me were lying like Blazes."

That took a more-lengthy tale; of the long-standing dislike 'twixt Lewrie and the Beauman family on Jamaica, and their hatred of Lewrie's old friend, Christopher Cashman, whom he'd met on an expedition into Spanish Florida to meet with the Muskogee Indians to persuade them to take up arms against the American Rebels on the frontiers; and how Cashman's settlement on Jamaica next to the Beauman plantations, and service in an island-raised regiment to fight the slave rebellion on the French colony of Saint Domingue, now Haiti, had resulted in a duel, and Lewrie's role as Cashman's second.

"Once the Beaumans' followers had testified that they could see me, plain as day, on a dark night and on a quarterdeck of a ship night one mile offshore," Lewrie told them, "with no lights lit, well . . . Mister Mac-Dougall was going t'step off a scaled distance from the jurors, and dare them t'say who, or what, was on the quarterdeck, then show them that wee mandarin figure, proving their testimony an utter load of . . . ah, rot. Fortunately, Beauman, his wife, and his minions fled the country before that happened, when they realised that they could be tried for perjury, and MacDougall never had t'use it. It's a quite nice model, almost as good as Admiralty models."

"My Lord!" Jessica said at the end, her jaw agape in sheer awe. "When I said you'd lived a most adventurous life, I spoke too soon, for we did not know a *tenth*, an *hundredth*, of it. Red Indians, liberating slaves from their chains . . . you must tell us all, Sir Alan! Why, you must publish your memoirs!"

"Aye, sir!" her brother heartily agreed. "The . . . Muskogees, you called them? What was it like, to live in an Indian village?"

"Should I call for some tea whilst I do?" Lewrie offered, thinking that this portrait session was done for the morning.

Aye, give a dog like me a chance t'boast! he smugly thought, and told them of *chickees* and *hutis*, animal and bird calls from outlying scouts on the march, the long palavers with tribal elders and the perils of the "black drink", why Spanish Moss was a most un-trustworthy bedding, unless one liked being infested with wee red "chiggers"; how foul skunks reeked, and why one must take care not to waken "Water Cougar" in any stream, and what bathing in a lake full of alligators was like.

"And, long before I wed my late wife, Caroline, I was married in Florida, most un-officially," Lewrie related. "I had to, else their war chief, Man Killer, did me in. She was a slave one of their hunting expeditions had taken from the Cherokees, name of Soft Rabbit, a sweet girl, really," and went on to tell them how their "marriage" most-like had been dissolved at the next Green Corn ceremony in the Spring.

"After I got stabbed in the left thigh by a Spanish bayonet on the beach right before we departed," Lewrie said, "she put a poultice of some kind on the wound, and damn . . . uh, it was amazing that it healed me up better than anything! Better than a blue-mould bread poultice would should one apply it to a horse's leg. Once back aboard *Shrike*, our Surgeon's Mate ripped it off in disgust, but even he had to admit that it worked, and I should remain a biped, ha ha!"

The fact that he and Soft Rabbit had wed because he had gotten her pregnant, and that there was a by-blow, now a member of a prominent Charleston, South Carolina, Indian-trading family, was better left un-said!

By then, what tea was left in the pot had gone cold, and both of the dogs were making wee whines of distress, so Lewrie suggested a trip to the back garden before his carpets were piddled on. Down to the basement they went, out to the area, and up the stone steps to the garden proper, with the dogs scampering in haste for relief.

"It's quite spacious, Sir Alan," Jessica said in delight as she took it all in. "Over-grown, of course, but a lot could be made of it."

"Well, I did have some workers in to scythe the grass, rake, and tidy up," Lewrie said with a shrug, "but, if I hear from Admiralty anytime soon, that'd be best left to the next tenants."

"Hmm, a trellis at the top of the steps, where flowering vines could thrive," Jessica said, walking about the garden. "These bushes do need more watering than London's usual rain, and some trimming, but in time they would bloom out and make a most attractive display."

"You have a green thumb, do you, Miss Jessica?" Lewrie asked. "My late wife did, though I couldn't tell one type of flower from the next. Some red, some yellow, some blue, and the 'what-ye-call-'ems' come up in April, haw!"

"Oh, I do my poor best with our own garden, small as it is," she replied, looking rueful for a second. "I more admire what our kin have done with theirs, since my brothers' parish manses are out in the country . . . and all their wives, and my sister, do wonders with their gardens, Sir Alan. Even my uncle Milton, at Oxford."

"Allow me," Lewrie said, pulling out a handkerchief to offer her, "but you have some chalk on your forehead."

"Oh! Do I? How clumsy of me!" she said, reddening slightly, and dabbing the smudge. "All gone?"

"Think you got it," Lewrie told her.

Their fingers brushed as she handed the handkerchief back, and she reddened once more, looking shyly away, turning her face up to the sky. "Ah, well. It must be past Ten, and the clouds are rolling in. I fear we've lost the light."

"My fault," Lewrie assured her. "Me and my . . . tales."

"But tales of a most fascinating nature, Sir Alan!" she declared.

"Oh, well," Lewrie said with a shrug, as if her compliment was welcome, but he was not worthy of it. "I fear you've taken on a task that might take up the rest of the summer, do I yarn on as I have."

"Which only makes my work on your portrait all the more enjoyable, Sir Alan," she was quick to assure him.

"And, after so many months in nought but male company, being in yours is enjoyable to me, as well, Miss Jessica," Lewrie said in truth, though trying hard not to leer.

The dogs had finished their business, with many swipes of their hind paws, before dashing back to their people, to frisk about for attention, coos, and "wubbies", before setting off on another round of boisterous play.

"At one end of the garden, hmm, round here," Jessica said with her hands out as if to frame it in her mind, "a gazebo of some kind, or a bricked, or stone-flagged area for taking tea in the open air would be nice. Somewhere to sit in good weather, and contemplate the serenity of your garden."

"At Canton, in China, there was an island pleasure garden just cross the river," Lewrie recalled. "They had these open-sided shelters a bit off the ground, where they'd take tea, and bring baskets of food. Willow trees swayin' in the breezes, flowers everywhere you'd look."

"You've been to China?" she exclaimed in delight. "You *must* tell me all about *that*, Sir Alan! Charley, Sir Alan's been to China!"

"Well, they didn't allow 'round-eyed foreign devils' to see much of the city, or the countryside, but aye, I did see Canton, Macau, and what lay along the banks of the Pearl River, and the foreign trading strip at Jack Ass Point," Lewrie told them. "Couldn't go beyond the walls, lest we pollute their people. Arrogant, the Chinese officials are, as if their Celestial Kingdom is the only empire on Earth, and everyone else is barbarian, only alive to pay tribute to 'em."

"You must tell all to us, next time we come, Sir Alan," she gaily insisted. "Yours will be the most delightful, and amusing, commission I've ever undertaken, and I look forward to our next session!"

"As do I, Miss Jessica," Lewrie told her. "Hmm, I'd imagine my dog needs the exercise. Might I escort you home, Miss Chenery?"

"That would be wonderful, Sir Alan, yes," she assured him.

"Here, Bisquit!" Lewrie called to his dog. "Want to go get some 'walkies'?"

Back in the parlour, leashing Bisquit and gathering up their hats and such, Lewrie recalled what he'd thought of when he'd looked forward to Jessica's letters far away off the coast of North Spain; he'd wondered whether he'd been besotted.

Am I? he asked himself as they stepped out into Dover Street; *Yes, I do believe that I am!*

BOOK TWO

I say therefore to the unmarried and widows,
"It is good for them if they abide" even as I.
But if they cannot contain, let them marry;
for it is better to marry than to burn.

~SAINT PAUL, 1 CORINTHIANS, VERSE 7:7 8-9

CHAPTER SIXTEEN

*O*ne must be meticulous, sir," Jessica said more than once to Lewrie's queries as to when the portrait might be done, partially teasing with a puckish grin on her face, or partially aloof and authoritative, with a brush held aloft like like a teacher's cane, in threat. Each query resulted in a laugh. "Perfection, for which I strive, can't be achieved in an hour, don't you know!"

A whole morning was spent just on the scar on his cheek, and if it should be too prominent, or merely hinted at. The tone and colour of his skin, would he prefer a ruddier hue representative of exposure to far-off tropic sunlight, or how he now appeared after months in the airs of London? The gilt buttons of his dress uniform coat she wished to sketch so she could get the details right, later; the enamelled star of the Order of the Bath, which she had never seen, Jessica wished to limn as well, perhaps with a one-haired brush to get it absolutely correct to the tiniest detail.

All of which, Lewrie didn't *really* mind, for all her fussiness prolonged their sessions together. Of course, she, her brother, or Madame Berenice Pellatan were full of questions about his career and adventures, which slowed her work to a crawl, but that was welcome, too. And, when pleading that he should shut himself up and pose, for God's sake, Lewrie would get Jessica to talk, about her family, about herself, or merely the latest news in the morning's papers, and after a couple of hours of that, a pot of coffee or tea would be necessary, replete with sweet bisquits or one of Yeovill's dainty treats, over which Lewrie was delighted to learn that Jessica Chenery had a merry, tongue-in-cheek and wry wit, along with a most intelligent grasp of what went on in the world, and had firm opinions of her own, a fact which Lewrie suspected would have appalled her father, the Reverend Chenery, a most staid fellow, who most-like firmly believed that women should keep to their sewing and such.

Did she ride? Alas, Jessica had little exposure to horses in London, and her father's city manse did not have a glebe, a home farm, where horses could be pastured. She had learned when visiting country parishes as a child, bareback on led ponies, or astride on a borrowed man's saddle 'til the day that her parents insisted that, should their daughters continue, they should learn the proper ladies' side-saddle.

"Oh, Sir Alan, I always felt it so precarious that I should go over the right side and backwards at anything more than a slow walk!" she declared, laughing out loud, to the amusement of all.

"Well, perhaps we might go riding in Hyde Park," Lewrie idly suggested, "and we find you a very gentle, old mare."

"I would like that, though I'm sure to prove an embarrassment to you, sir," Jessica hesitantly agreed. "Or, I could borrow a pair of breeches from Charley, and wear them under a loose skirt, and ride more securely."

"What a scandalous idea!" her brother barked, and Madame Berenice spluttered that she would make a laughingstock of herself, and "de-sex" herself. "Oh la, *non non, ma chérie*! It is not ladylike, it it not done!"

"And why not?" Jessica replied with a daring toss of her head.

"A gentle one for the lady," Lewrie requested of the stabler a day or two later. "*Very* gentle."

An older mare was led out, a patient roan of only thirteen hands, and saddled for Jessica. Lewrie had brought a cloth feed bag full of treats; some cauliflower florets, carrot chunks, sugar lumps, and apple quarters, and by the time Jessica had offered the horse some of the goodies, stroking the rented prad as she did so, she'd made her mount a fond friend. At last she mounted from the lady's block, rested one leg in the crook with her left foot in the stirrup, looking game but nervous. Lewrie had been befriending himself to a grey gelding, also of an age, and swung up astride after giving his mount the rest of the treats.

"Shall we?" he asked, clucking and urging his horse forwards.

"A slow pace, I beg you," Jessica said after a deep breath to resolve herself. Her horse stepped off in trail of Lewrie's, though it did look back at her as if wondering where the rest of the apples were. The mare, long used to the bridle path along Rotten Row, came up alongside Lewrie's gelding as if they had been paired together on a regular basis, or were long-time stable mates as close as cater-cousins, or got along together as well as Bisquit and Rembrandt.

"I doubt she'll be bolting on you," Lewrie commented, noting how stiffly Jessica held herself. "If anything does spook her, I am right here t'grab her reins. Relax, Miss Chenery, and enjoy the day."

And a very nice day it was, with rarely seen clear blue skies, for London, just warm enough to be comfortable, and Hyde Park was redolent of decorative beds of late-season flowers, and many blooming bushes. After some time, Jessica did ease her stiffness, began to look about beyond her plodding horse's head, gathering courage enough to talk with growing ease.

Lewrie told her about riding over his father's country estate at Anglesgreen, about his favourite saddle horse, Anson, and what the house looked like, explaining Sir Hugo's poor jape when naming it *Dun Roman,* for "Done Roamin' ".

"I should admire to see it, Sir Alan," Jessica said with one quizzical brow up. "It's of only one storey? How odd, though."

"Well, there is a partial basement," Lewrie allowed. "It's like the houses he saw or lived in in India, with deep, wide galleries out front and back, against the harsh sunshine. At least here in England, he has no need for *pankah* fans for cool breezes, or half-naked servants stirrin' 'em all day and night."

"India!" Jessica marvelled. "Your entire family is well-travelled, sir! How did he end up there?"

Lewrie explained how his father had gone "smash", had spent some time in Portugal free of creditors' demands, then had wangled an appointment in the East India Company Army, as Colonel of the 19th Native Infantry at Calcutta, and how they had been thrown together years later in a military expedition in the Far East, because the 19th was a low-caste regiment, able to cross the *Khali Pani*, the "black water", without breaking their caste. He went on about nefarious French finagling with blood-thirsty native pirates aimed to ruin "John Company" trade should there be another war, fights at Canton, the South China Seas, Borneo, and in the Spanish Philippines, and disguised warships, when he'd been only a Lieutenant.

"He came home a full *nabob*," Lewrie said, "good looting, I think, cleared his debts, bought his house in Upper Grosvenor, the estate at Anglesgreen, right next to where my late wife and I were renting, near her kinfolk, and has been living well ever since."

And in that cheery, conversational way, they spent nearly two hours, that first day, plodding along at a sedate pace, brushed aside by the younger gallants and "sparks" showing off their blooded horses and their equitation skills. At last, they assayed a trot, then an easy canter back to the hired stableyard, as Jessica felt more and more comfortable on a lady's saddle. She even looked happily triumphant when they at last drew reins and dismounted.

"Thank you for a *most* enjoyable morning, Sir Alan!" she gushed after he had reached up to take her by her waist to ease her down, and let his hands linger for a moment. "Would it be too much of an imposition to wish that we might do this again? But only if I get the same, sweet horse the next time," she added, stroking her mount's neck and muzzle before it was led away.

"Your wish is my command, Miss Jessica," Lewrie assured her. "How's the mare called?" he asked one of the ostlers. "Nancy, is it? Next time, then, the lady must have Nancy to ride. And it's no imposition at all, my dear. I enjoyed it immensely, too."

From then on, they rode together at least once a week, depending on the weather, sometimes with her brother along.

A morning session was going right well, with Jessica humming to herself, so pleased was she with the results, even allowing Lewrie a peek after an hour or so, just at the arrival of the tea service.

"I do believe that I resemble myself, to the Tee!" Lewrie said, now that his face, the trickiest part, was completed at last. "A hint of a smile, a hint of teeth, hmm. I'm all there, warts and all, as I requested. It's marvellous."

"Quite remarkably realistic," Madame Berenice judged it. "Most fitting, especially for male subjects, though if Jessica painted for a lady client, a touch of the wispiness, the idealised gauziness, an air of the flattering ephemeral would be required, *n'est-ce pas?* Women *must* be flattered, especiallly if they are not blessed with natural beauty. Such did I do recently for the wife of a coal merchant, oh *là*, the poor dear."

"Shall I pour, Sir Alan?" Jessica offered.

"If ye'd be so kind, Miss Jessica," Lewrie said, "for I'm fair-parched.

No, Bisquit, no, dogs. Wait your turn, humans first," he chid the dogs, who whined, licked their chops, frisked about, or sat with their tails whipping the carpet, eager for their share of ginger snaps. "Oh, here then, have one. You, too, Rembrandt."

"I do hope the weather is good, tomorrow, else we shall miss the showing at Ackermann's," Madame Berenice said with a put-upon sigh as she bit off part of a snap, then took a sip of tea. She cast a wary glance out the front parlour windows with another theatrical sigh.

"I thought we'd both attend, right after tomorrow's morning session," Jessica said, stirring cream and sugar into her cup. "That would indeed depend upon whether it's raining, and upon Charley, though if I cannot entice him into chaperoning us, we may have to miss it. He has no patience for gazing at art, unless it's scandalous caricatures," she said with a laugh.

"What's Ackermann's?" Lewrie asked over the rim of his tea cup.

"Ackermann's Repository of Arts," Jessica told him, "is a large gallery which displays and sells paintings," she said, feeding her dog another ginger snap. "There's to be an exhibition of works submitted to the Royal Academy for this year's competition, the ones that didn't make the final rounds' selections, but might be rather good, anyway."

"So you can see what your competition's up to?" Lewrie teased, making Jessica blush nicely as she grinned back.

"Quite the coup for Ackermann's to arrange it," Madame Berenice said, "given the shop's prior reputation for dealing in bawdy satirics and outright . . . *pornographie*," she said with a false shudder. "It has improved its repute, but the Good Lord only knows what sort of idle clientele still goes there, looking for prints of a scandalous nature. And, it is not in the best neighbourhood. Number One oh one, in the Strand. Not the safest environ for two ladies, un-escorted," Madame Pellatan said with another put-on shudder.

"If it rains, or Charley's more interested in something else, we can't go," Jessica said.

"Perhaps the bawdy prints would entice him," Lewrie japed.

"Hah!" Jessica barked in sudden humour. "Let *that* reach Father's ears, and we'd never hear the end of it!"

"Well, perhaps I could escort you, if my doin' so isn't an equal scandal to your father, Miss Jessica," Lewrie offered. "Now that my portrait is all but done, but for the uniform details, or nearabouts, let's say that we skip tomorrow's session. I could hire a hackney or a coach, come collect you round mid-day, and make an afternoon of it. And, there's one of my favourite chop-houses nearby in Savoy Street, just off the start of the Strand. It's like an 'all nations' dram shop, with cuisine from half of Europe on their menu. My treat."

"Oh, Sir Alan, that would be simply grand of you!" Jessica enthused, "Though . . . are you sure we would not be imposing on your time?"

"*Mais oui,* the gesture *magnifique,*" Madame Pellatan cooed, "one worthy of *le chevalier grand*!"

"Then it's settled? Excellent!" Lewrie declared.

"We'll bring umbrellas, just in case, though," Jessica wisely suggested. "Then, rain or no, at least we will be in Sir Alan's capable hands."

CHAPTER SEVENTEEN

Hmm, maybe we should've picked a better day, Lewrie thought as their two-horse hackney fell into the queue of other carriages and grander private coaches bringing attendees to Ackermann's Repository of Arts the next day. It was only at the last minute that he learned that this would the opening day of the exhibition, which would attract not only the idle *hoi polloi* out for any free entertainment, but the Quality, members of the Peerage, the famous, rich, and infamous. One peek out the window of the hackney revealed a press of people on the sidewalks from storefronts to the kerb-sides, with barely room for coach passengers to alight, and the lines in front of the shop's doors looked to be daunting, too. At least the weather was not *too* threatening, the usual grey overcast, part clouds and part coalsmoke, which might end in a misty drizzle after all. Lewrie stuck his head out again to take a deep sniff, but his nose, trained to the smell of fresh water and rain on the wind at sea, failed him; all he could sense was horse manure.

After several minutes of slowly creeping forward as the queue of equipages dropped their passengers and wheeled away, Lewrie decided that there was nothing more for it.

"I fear we might as well debark here, ladies," Lewrie told them, gathering up his walking-stick and furled umbrella. "Mind your possessions, your reticules. There's sure t'be more than a few 'three-handed Jennies' about. Pickpockets," he added, explaining how his pocket watch, chain, and fob had been lifted by an expert, right in the lobby of the Old Bailey just after his acquittal in 1801. Once on the sidewalk, he paid off the cab-man, telling him that he was free to hustle up other fares, and they would hail another when they were done.

Then, they spent at least a quarter-hour standing in line before gaining admittance, shoulder-to-shoulder with people, some of whom complained of sharing a sidewalk with the working or idle poor, barely a cut above "Captain Tom of the Mob, begad!"

Lewrie was in a civilian suiting, a black coat, buff breeches, top-boots, and a maroon waist-coat, with a matching neck-stock, and a low-crowned, narrow-brimmed black hat. Madame Pellatan had gone all-in, in pink and white, a white silk shawl, a young mountain-sized powdered wig sprigged with wee birds and butterflies, with her face and neck an inch deep in powder and rouge. Thank God that Jessica had dressed so much simpler in a mid-blue gown trimmed with white lace, with an ivory satin shawl draped over her arms, with a perky visored bonnet on her head, though her hair had been done up with a royal blue and gilt rope of some kind woven into her formal updo.

Ackermann's must have hired some toughs to keep an eye on the crowd, steering away curious urchins and the poorly dressed, giving any suspicious-looking idlers and pickpockets ferocious warning squints. At last, they gained admittance, squeezing through the doors against an out-rush of previous gawkers, and into a buzzing, guffawing, tittering mob of sightseers, some of them smelling no better than they had a right to, and the air, with so many candles lit, suddenly seemed much warmer than it had been outside.

"Where do we start?" Jessica asked, frowning as she peered from one side to the other, and sidling up closer to Lewrie, out of dread, or sheer necessity to avoid being jostled. Framed paintings rose to the ceilings in a jumble, whilst the works to be exhibited stood about on easels, or braced atop the counters.

"If this is a way to show the works, it's not workin'," Lewrie said. "Who thought this arrangement up?" There were also some bins where un-framed canvases stood to be leafed through, held up for inspection, then jammed back in. There were also open-top boxes where shifty sorts of men pawed through, laughing and nudging their compatriots.

"I almost regret coming," Madame Pellatan bemoaned, at her most the-atrical, drawing out a Chinese fan to whisk before her face.

"I think I see some sense to all this," Lewrie said at last, and pointed to the left. "It looks as if people are startin' over yonder, and workin' their way round to the right. Let's see if we can sidle over, even if we have to queue up again."

That was the key to finding the exhibition pieces in all of that crush, though it did not allow them the space to take in any of the artworks. Step back far enough to contemplate one, and half a dozen others would step in front of them. To snake their way beyond those viewers, they would be too close to appreciate much more than the brush strokes and the col-ours.

Crowded, and *boring,* Lewrie thought, who had never had much appre-ciation for fine art, though he had once owned a tittilating scene of an Ottoman Turkish *hareem,* with tits and thighs aplenty hung in his old rented rooms on Panton Street, just after the American Revolution, but his late wife had taken one shocked look at it, given him the evil eye, and sold it off to a street monger, instanter.

There were pastorals, featuring grist mills, trees, and cattle; ruined ab-beys and churches abandoned since Henry the Eighth's years; grand and vast country estates with horses and dogs; more horses held by jockeys or stablemen, thoroughbreds and Arabians with heads too tiny to be real; hunt scenes with more hounds; the tumble-down, ivy-covered ruins of an-cient Greece and Rome, though those had intriguing sunset clouds and colours; and there were ships in battle, done by artists who had only the vaguest grasp of what ships looked like, what ocean waves looked like, rows of curly-cued or saw-toothed waves marching in tidy rows, at which he scoffed.

"Alan, old son," someone called out. "Is that you?"

"Who?" Lewrie asked, turning to look about, finding his old school chum, Peter Rushton, Viscount Draywick. "Peter, you old scamp. Damn my eyes!" he cried, forgetting his vow to keep close watch over his salty tongue, and leading his small party through the crush to shake hands. "Good t'see you, again! How d'ye keep?"

"Main-well, considering," Rushton replied, "question is, how do *you* keep, now you're a householder?"

"Just temporary," Lewrie told him. "Oh, Peter, allow me to name you to the ladies. Madame Pellatan, Miss Chenery, this is Peter Rushton, Viscount

Draywick, a schoolmate of mine from my brief time at Harrow. Peter, this is Madame Berenice Pellatan, a noted artist who fled the Terror with her husband from Paris."

"Madame, pleased to make your acquaintance," Rushton said with a brief bow from the waist.

"*M'sieur le Vicomte enchanté*," Madame Pellatan intoned with a deep curtsy, and a hand out to be kissed, which Peter did peckingly, keeping a straight face though amused by her airs.

"Allow me to further name to you Miss Jessica Chenery, another artist of rising renown, who is doing my portrait," Lewrie said, "Miss Chenery, Peter Rushton, Viscount Draywick."

"Miss Chenery, happy to make your acquaintance," Peter replied. "Ah, and here is Lady Draywick. Come, my dear, and greet one of my old school friends," he said as his wife emerged from the crowd, repeating the introduction ritual afresh.

No wonder ye took Tess on for yer mistress, Lewrie thought; *for your "lawful blanket's" a fubsy Tartar.*

Though there was no accounting for a man's taste, Lewrie knew Peter Rushton of old, and had always ranked him as a fellow of a most discriminating taste when it came to women, so . . . how to explain his choice of wife? Surely, she *must* have been attractive at one time; either that, or possessed of one Hell of a dowry. Peter's own wealth notwithstanding, Lady Draywick looked like a dowdy, older housemaid out on the town her one free day a week, dressed in her mistress's finery. She also had a permanent frown on her phyz, which deepened upon introduction to Lewrie, and Jessica, giving Lewrie the impression that Lady Draywick suspected her husband, and all of his so-called old friends, of being so many lechering, adulterous wallowing swine, and any fetching younger mort of being a whore, or one of her husband's kept women.

"Alan . . . Sir Alan, Baronet now . . . got sent down with me from Harrow when we set the governor's coach house on fire, ha ha," Peter boasted. "Hadn't seen him in ages after he went off to the Navy, but whilst Clotworthy Chute and I were in Venice, just before Bonaparte threatened to take it, there Alan was, and we sailed out of danger on his ship. You recall Clotworthy, dear? He was in on our fiery cabal, too. Think we're all still banned from Harrow for life, ha ha!"

"Thought they asked you back t'speak to the students," Lewrie said. "Clotworthy mentioned it whilst helping me furnish my place."

"Then they're getting hellish-desperate for exemplary speakers," Rushton hooted in mirth. "Why, they'll be having highwaymen in, next!"

"Why did you set the coach house on fire?" Jessica asked, halfway 'twixt glee and a show of alarm.

"Oh, because the school governor was a tyrant," Rushton said.

"The food was pig swill," Lewrie stuck in.

"The coach house was . . . there," Rushton sniggered.

"But we let the horses out before we lit it," Lewrie assured her. "Just our luck t'be caught still holdin' the torches."

"Hmmph!" from Lady Draywick. "*Some* wit never improves with age."

"You're doing Alan's portrait, d'ye say, Miss Chenery?" Peter asked. "That'd be a trial, making him appear human, haw haw."

"I am, milord," Jessica answered gladly, "and we're almost done, though I fear Sir Alan finds posing too long a trial, but our sessions have proved most amusing and exciting. He's lived a most adventurous life."

"I daresay," Lady Draywick drawled, sure that "sessions" with Jessica Chenery were done stark-naked.

"*Mademoiselle* Jessica has the ability to render her subjects more true-to-life and realistic than anyone I have ever seen, *m'sieur vicomte*," Madame Pellatan stuck in, feeling ignored. "Her likeness of the Baronet simply *leaps* off the canvas."

"It'll be done soon," Lewrie told them, "and you and Lady Draywick should come over for an un-veiling. Your brother, Harold, too, if he's of a mind. My cook is a marvel, and is sure t'lay on a fine feast, in celebration."

"I say, that's sounds jolly, what, m'dear?" Rushton said to his wife. "Clotworthy, too, since he said he furnished your place in such a grand manner. I wonder, Miss Chenery . . . have you any paintings in this exhibition?"

"None submitted to the Royal Academy, milord, though I have been tempted to try, under an assumed name, of course," Jessica replied, in an impish way, "I *have* left several pieces at Ackermann's on consignment, but I fear you'd find them un-suitable, unless you wish fanciful paintings done for children." She looked all round, up to the rafters, and could only spot one of hers still hanging, of a squirming puppy in a young girl's lap, trying to lick the girl's face.

"Ah, yes . . . pretty," Rushton said, sounding let down. "A pity my children are mostly grown. Amusing, though."

"Miss Chenery has been very successful with her fanciful art," Lewrie boasted. "Even illustrated a children's book, right?"

"For money?" Lady Draywick sniffed.

"Yes, milady, for money," Jessica shot back, her dander up.

"And why not?" Lewrie felt compelled to defend her. "Anyone with great talent, even a woman, should never hide it under a bushel basket, or be expected to sketch relatives for free."

"Well, I . . . !" Lady Draywick began.

"Hah! Modern outlook, Alan. Quite right, too!" Peter rushed to intervene. "More show to see. You will excuse us, Sir Alan, Madame . . . Miss Chenery. Send me a note when you're ready to display your portrait, Alan. Good day," he said, bowing his way from them, and dragging his dis-approving mate with him, still clucking in irritation.

"Thank you, Sir Alan," Jessica said, bestowing upon him a warm smile. "For defending me, and for your sentiment."

"Meant every word of it, Miss Jessica," Lewrie replied, feeling as if he'd done something noble, for a rare once. "What a fubsy . . ."

"Yes, Lady Draywick is a . . . well, whatever one *wishes* to call her can't be said in public," Jessica stammered, on the verge of some foul language.

"Ah, but in private, now!" Lewrie teased, returning the impish smile on her face, and delighting that he could amuse her. "Ye know, for all the years I've known Peter, this was the first time I ever met his wife?"

"Well, perhaps some rocks are better left un-turned," Jessica slyly japed. "One never knows what lurks beneath them."

"Oh, well said!" Lewrie encouraged. "You're gettin' the hang of it. I don't know whether I've corrupted you, or wakened a talent long un-used." And that was rewarded with another smile on her face, this one warmer and fonder, and Lewrie was surprised by the flood of warmth that that awakened in his chest.

"Oh, is that a David?" Madame Pellatan exclaimed, pointing to the far side of the gallery. "He was a dear friend of ours, before we had to flee Paris. I'd know his work anywhere! But, how can it be here, in England? His *Belisarius* is so well known. We must see it, Jessica!"

"Who?" Lewrie asked as he was dragged along in Madame Pellatan's wake as she ploughed through the crowd like a charging bull.

"Jacques-Louis David," the older lady said over her shoulder, "a most famous painter! Oh," she sniffed, crestfallen as she got a better look at it. "*Quel dommage*, it is only a copy, and done much smaller than the original. An exceptionally good one, but . . . pity the buyer who is taken in. How dare they sell it as the original!"

Madame Berenice droned on, despite it being a copy, about the composition, the musculature depicted, so much blah-blah to Lewrie that he lifted his gaze to other works hung high above, hoping for a promising nude or two, but no such luck.

"The dynamic nature of it," Madame Berenice went on, "and the lifelike character. It is an example of ingratitude to those who serve the state. *Belisarius* depicts a successful Roman general who has suffered the ingratitude of a heartless emperor, reduced to begging on the streets to support himself and his daughter. Jessica, see how dramatically the faces, the bodies are rendered? The human form must be studied in detail, what lies under the skin, else all will appear stilted and forced. The Italian, DaVinci, did just as meticulous studies for his paintings, his sculptures."

"And medical books help," Jessica commented. "Yes, anatomy books," she added, to answer Lewrie's quizzical look. "I have a set that I found in a used-book dealer's bin. Skeleton, sinews, muscles, and veins . . . some illustrations done in colour. Almost as good as attending medical school anatomies, which of course I could *never* do! I've found them most useful."

"Then I'll never let you near a surgeon's scalpel, or even the steak knives," Lewrie japed. "Talk about stayin' on your good side!"

"Oh, Sir Alan, you are so droll!" Jessica replied, touching him on the sleeve for a second. "You could never get on my bad side!"

There was a gap in the crowd in front of the David, allowing Madame Pellatan and Jessica to get closer, prating of brush strokes, whilst Lewrie was cut off by several fancily dressed couples swanning in between. Before he could sidle through to rejoin them, a young fellow in high Beau Brummell fashion leaned over Jessica's shoulder and made a comment, using the press of the crowd as an excuse to put himself against her bottom, chuckling and leering.

"*Excuse* me, sir!" Jessica snapped, whirling to face the man.

"I said there's better muscles to be seen in the flesh, my dear," the fop repeated.

"You groped me, sir!" Jessica hotly accused.

"Pushed 'gainst you," the fop shrugged off. "Quite by accident. Perhaps you'll like me better, after you get a chance to know me. A guinea, shall we say, sweet'un?"

"You'll like *me* a lot *less,* after I knock your damned teeth out," Lewrie growled as he got up to them, and Jessica was quick to come to Lewrie's side, a bit behind his left shoulder.

"Beg pardon, you . . . !" the young fellow began to bristle up.

"You will leave the young *lady* alone . . . sir!" Lewrie warned him. "Get ye gone, now, before it costs you more than you can spare."

"I was only making idle conversation, most innocently," the young man glibly crooned, shamming sweet reason. "I was jostled, and meant no offence."

"You were not!" Jessica retorted. "You groped me, and made improper advances, and prop . . . propositioned me!" she stammered.

"I'm sure that you're mistaken, girl," the young man sniggered.

"Bugger off," Lewrie snarled.

"Or what, sir?" the fellow shot back, full of confidence, even seeming to enjoy the confrontation.

"*Boy,*" Lewrie sneered, "I've probably killed more men than you've had hot dinners, and one more, especially one like you, makes no significance. Now, bugger off before I rip your head off and shit down your neck!"

The young fellow lost his confident, cocky smile. His face twitched in alarm, and he finally noticed the scar on Lewrie's cheek, taking it for the mark of a successful duellist, the sort that sought out reasons to cross blades or blaze with pistols. And those eyes glaring into his, they were so cold and Arctic grey!

"Here now, no need to . . . ," he gulped.

"You will apologise for your boorishness," Lewrie demanded, "then get yourself gone. Now, while I'm still feelin' charitable."

"Sorry, Miss, my mistake, apologies," the fop stammered, doffing his hat, stumbling back into the crowd, under Lewrie's glare all the way to the door and the street outside.

"Oh, sorry," Lewrie said, letting Jessica go, for in defence of her, he'd put a possessive arm round her waist, as she had put a hand on his shoulder.

"Oh, no, do not be sorry, Sir Alan!" Jessica insisted, "That was wondrously done, and I am so very grateful for your assistance, and your defence of my honour."

"Well, sorry 'bout the language," Lewrie said with a shrug, and a sheepish smile.

"What a despicable cad!" Madame Berenice spat.

Hope she don't mean me, Lewrie thought.

"Rip his head off, and . . . oh, my *word*!" Jessica tittered, put a hand to her mouth, but could not help breaking into laughter, as if in sudden relief.

"Such despicable manners in the younger people in these times," Madame Pellatan declared, sweeping her hands over her gown, her wig, re-settling her shawl, and checking her reticule fussily, as if she had been the one groped and propositioned. She looked red in the face, as if *she* had found Lewrie's threat beyond the pale, if no one else did.

After several hours at Ackermann's gazing at pictures and discussing their merits (two hours longer than Lewrie would have liked!) they left the gallery and flagged down an empty hackney to take them to the chop-house in Savoy Street that Lewrie had recommended.

Jessica was most pleased with their outing, for upon enquiring about the pictures she had left with Ackermann's, she'd been told that two of them had sold, and that her share of the proceeds was £8/7/4! So it was a joyful, bubbling early supper conversation that they had.

The restaurant did not dis-appoint, either, with lobster and seafood crepes drizzled with a creamy lemon sauce for Jessica; veal medallions with pasta in sour-cream gravy with loads of paprika, and asparagus for Lewrie; and for Madame Pellatan, succulent sliced duck in a brandy-orange sauce, with goose liver pâté, and dribbles of salty dark fish roe in imitation of caviar that she declared was almost as tasty as any repast she'd enjoyed in Paris in the good old days.

It all was washed down with lashings of Rhenish, claret, or *sauvignon blanc,* and a sparkling Portuguese wine in lieu of champagne with dessert, which was hot apple pie and cheddar, drizzled with sweet cream, and port or brandy to linger over, Lewrie could not help himself from expounding on cuisines he'd experienced; Chinese, West Indian, Creole in Spanish New Orleans, Hindoo, Portuguese and Spanish, Neapolitan and Genoese cooking, and the tasty things, some exceedingly humble, that he'd discovered along the coasts of the Carolinas.

"We must thank you, again, Sir Alan," Madame Pellatan said as their hackney drew up in front of St. Anselm's manse later that evening, "for a . . . *pardon!*" She paused to stifle a weary, drink-sodden yawn. "For a most delightful outing. *Merci, merci beaucoup!*"

"My pleasure, Madame," Lewrie told her, "I had an enjoyable time, too." He opened the coach doors, hopped down, and folded down the metal step, ready to assist her down.

"*Merci,*" Madame Pellatan said once on the sidewalk, though a tad unsteady on her feet, using her furled umbrella as a prop.

He turned to assist Jessica, and she took his offered hand as she gingerly stepped down, holding on longer than really necessary, even giving his hand a squeeze.

"Yes indeed, thank you, Sir Alan," Jessica said with a warm smile. "For your generosity, your company, your gallant defence, and for a marvellous supper, and . . . for everything!"

"You're most welcome, Miss Jessica," Lewrie replied, daring to lift her hand to his lips to bestow a lingering kiss upon it. "For my part, I had a grand time today, as well."

"Shall we come by tomorrow morning, to finish your portrait?" she asked, gazing up at him with her eyes alight.

"Looking forward to it," Lewrie told her, "though at this point, I could hang my uniform coat on a mop-stick and let it stand in for me. Buttons, medals, epaulets, and all, hah?"

"Oh, no, you must still wear it, Sir Alan," she said with a wee laugh. "Remember what we discussed today, about the shape of the human form, clothed or not. Your image would end up looking lop-sided, else," she teased.

"Well then, I and my coat will be at your complete disposal," he assured her. "Good night, Miss Jessica, Madame Pellatan," he said, doffing his hat to both, with a slight bow from the waist.

Of a sudden, Jessica got up on tiptoe and kissed him on the cheek, laying a hand on his shoulder. "Good night, then, Sir Alan," she cooed, "and thank you, again, for a wondrous day."

He saw them safely to their door, made sure that they gained entry, then went back to the hackney, chest swelling with . . . *what?*

It was all he could do not to have returned her kiss, swept her into his arms and kissed her properly. Her light scent of clean hair and lavender water had almost made him giddy!

"Where to now, sir?" the cabman asked.

"Twenty-two Dover Street," Lewrie said as he got back in, savouring the memory of his arm round her slim waist for a moment.

"Ah, same street where th' widow Nelson lives, then?"

"Hmm, what?" Lewrie asked.

"Th' Admiral's widow moved there, sir," the cabman said as he flicked reins and clucked to his horse. "Poor old lady."

"I was told Nelson himself lived there for a time," Lewrie said.

"Never did, sir," the cabman insisted. "He set his poor wife up in Dover Street, but moved himself in with the Hamiltons, and that Emma, somewhere in Grosvenor Street. Someone told ya wrong, sir."

That Penneworth sold me a bill o' goods, the shit, Lewrie told himself. He sat back against the hard, leather-covered bench, his mind returning to his pleasant reveries of the day, and images of Jessica; oohing over one painting, frowning in dislike at another, how animated and lively she was, how daintily she'd dined.

Great, she can eat with a knife and fork! he thought, ready to burst out laughing; *Hell of a recommendation!*

He wished that his portrait was *never* finished, that he could continue his delightful daily association with her for as long as he could, even beyond the day that Admiralty recalled him to service.

How to propose a continuation . . . ?

Propose? He thought with a start; *My God! Brr!*

He found himself touching his cheek where she'd given him that peck, wondering if there was something more to that gesture than mere gratitude, or a mild fondness. Did he dare find out, and what would he do if she laughed him off as a generous, amusing old colt's tooth, but a colt's tooth after all?

It's madness, it's daft but then, I s'pose I am as daft as a March hare, he confessed to himself; *over her!*

CHAPTER EIGHTEEN

"So, that's you, is it?" his father, Sir Hugo, commented after he'd been relieved of his hat, overcoat, and walking-stick in the entry hall of Lewrie's house, and had gotten a snifter with a large dollop of brandy in his hand. "Quite a remarkable likeness, I must say. You to a Tee," he said, pacing the front parlour to inspect the painting.

"Not framed yet, but . . . ," Lewrie said with a shrug.

"How much ye pay for it?" Sir Hugo asked.

"Twenty pounds," Lewrie told him. "You need a new one?"

"Me?" Sir Hugo scoffed. "No, the last I had done was just after I came home from India, when I was still passably decent-looking, and I'll be damned if I care to look as bad as I do now to history. Cost me fifty pounds, back then, so you got yourself a bargain. A damned good artist."

"Yes, she is," Lewrie said with pride.

"She? Well, damme. Top her into the bargain, did ye?" his father sniggered, going to the cheery warmth of the fireplace to thaw his chilled backside. "Hellish-cool day, getting on for Autumn, and today's misty rain does me no good. Ahh!"

"Miss Jessica Chenery is a proper young lady," Lewrie informed him a bit stiffly, "not the sort t'put the leg over."

"Jessica, ye say?" Sir Hugo asked, "Jessica? Damned if I can recall ever hearing anyone named Jessica. What sort of name is that?"

"Shakespeare coined the name," Lewrie told him, "it's from *The Merchant of Venice*. Shylock's daughter was named Jessica."

"What? Ye mean t'say the girl's Jewish?" Sir Hugo barked.

"What?" Lewrie gawped. "*What?* Have ya drunk so much you've flushed away the *last* o' your wits? She's Church of England, and her whole family's in Holy Orders, her brothers but for the youngest, who was one of my Midshipmen, her sisters are married to ministers, and her uncle's a Senior Fellow at Oxford. Her father's rector of Saint Anselm's down the road in Piccadilly. Where I've been attending. *Jewish*, my Christ, how you still manage *t'think* is beyond me!"

"You? In church?" Sir Hugo sniffed. "By God, I *know* London is dead boresome of a Sunday, as dead as cold mutton for lack of amusements, but . . . you, in church? Haw haw haw!"

"Miss Jessica and Reverend Chenery invited me. I sit in their box," Lewrie told him.

"Oh, sweet on her, are ye? She fetching?" his father asked, as if he enjoyed bantering with his son.

"Fetching, aye," Lewrie told him, "remarkably, unforgettably so, sweet, lively, intelligent, artistic, and highly skilled," he said, sweeping a hand to point at his portrait on the easel. "A delightful young lady, in all. And sweet on her? I find myself enchanted," he confessed, feeling the heat rising in his face, and a lurch in his innards as he spoke of her. "Smitten . . . besotted."

"Oh, my sweet Lord!" Sir Hugo gasped. "Wasn't one wife enough for ye? Talk about hope over reality. Where's the brandy decanter? Unfair, ye know. Poor soldiers' or sailors' wives, left on their own to manage, years on end. You mark my words, ye'll be called back to the Navy and break her heart. And a minister's daughter? Not much by way of dowry, ye know."

"*Hang* dowry!" Lewrie exclaimed. "And I'm beginning to doubt I'll *ever* be recalled. I've put out feelers with some people I know, and it don't sound good."

He refilled his father's glass and threw himself into one of the wing-back chairs before the fire, explaining his visits to Lord Draywick's brother, Harold, who worked for Lord Castlereagh, the Secretary of State for War, and his friend in the Foreign Office Secret Branch, James Peel.

"I don't have the right sort of patrons," Lewrie said, trying not to sound too sorry for himself, or bitter. "And, along the way, I've made some enemies in the Navy, with officers who *do* have powerful patrons, in very senior positions. Envy, spite, God only knows, but, here I sit, still waitin' t'hear from Admiralty, months after I beat that French squadron, and paid *Sapphire* off. I took this house for three months, with an option to go month-to-month after, and here it is, five months later, and I'm *still* drawin' half-pay, and odd looks when I show up at Admiralty, beggin' for an interview!"

"But, you *do* have patrons?" Sir Hugo wondered.

"Oh, some," Lewrie sulkily agreed, "there was Samuel Hood, and 'Old Jarvey', but Hood's long retired, and Admiral Jervis got kicked to the kerb when he was First Sea Lord and tried to cut out all the corruption in the dockyards and victualling. Any who'd say a good word for me are former Post-Captains I served under, most of whom have made Rear-Admiral by now, but these days, Rear-Admirals are two-a-penny, and don't have all that much clout. I just may be in as bad odour as Captain Lord Thomas Cochrane! Look at how they treated him after Aix Roads, and how Admiral Gambier got off with a pat on the cheek. I may as well be a *pariah* dog!"

"Ye do have friends in the Commons, in Lord's," his father pointed out. "That Peter Rushton, Sir Malcolm Schockley. They might be able to bring some influence to bear.

"Or," Sir Hugo went on, "if all comes to nought, you've done a dozen men's duty, won some prominent battles, raked in a vast pile of 'tin' in prize-money, and been knighted and made baronet, to boot. It might not be all that bad, t'sit on your laurels."

"Wouldn't sittin' on your laurels be painful?" Lewrie japed in spite of his fretful mood. "Wear 'em, aye, but sit on 'em? Ow!"

"Ye know what I mean," Sir Hugo said, scowling. "There's many a man'd envy you the chance for an honourable retirement, and take a well-deserved rest. It ain't like you ever *loved* the Navy, haw!"

"Aye, and thank you so much for shoving me into it," Lewrie shot back. "Sorry Granny Lewrie didn't conveniently die and leave you my inheritance t'squander."

"Well, I did need the money perishing-bad at the time," Sir Hugo baldly admitted. "But we're both jingling with 'chink', now, and it'd be a shame did ye not enjoy spending some of it on things that give pleasure, after all your time at sea. You've two fine sons to take your place in the Navy. Sewallis is a Passed Midshipman, and Hugh's sure to be one, soon. If the Navy don't love ye anymore, why not enjoy the rest of your life?"

"It's just . . . ," Lewrie said, scowling as he rose to fetch himself a glass of brandy, and refill his father's glass again. "The war ain't over, there're things still to do," he said, sitting down once more and crossing his legs. "Sooner or later, Bonaparte'll figure out what t'do with that huge fleet he's been building, and . . . I feel as if I'd be lettin' the side down if I was ashore, havin' a grand time."

"I knew when to quit," Sir Hugo snorted.

"You quit when you came home a full *nabob* and paid off all your creditors!" Lewrie scoffed. "You've barely dabbled at soldierin', since!"

"So, if ye can't play 'pulley-hauley' and longer, ye'll make a young lady miserable? Ye do recall, we ain't the *finest* sort of rakes in England? Sooner or later . . . God, you, with a minister's daughter, and the poor thing related to *me*? The more they get to know our sort, the sooner they tie us to the stakes, and pile up the firewood!"

"Well, there is that," Lewrie confessed, almost wincing at the idea of his sins and scandals coming to light, as they had when those scathing, accusatory letters had reached his late wife from a spurned lover who'd borne one of his bastards. "I don't know if she'd have me, anyway. She *seems* fond, but now the portrait's done, there may be no reason for her to socialize with me beyond that. Her talents are in demand, and someone else'll want a portrait, some children's book that needs illustrating," he gloomed. "She may say thanks, but no thanks, lookin' for a younger man."

"Jewish, and she *works* for a living?" Sir Hugo pretended to gasp.

"I *told* you . . . !" Lewrie snapped, 'til he realized that his father was sniggering at him, and grinning like an American 'possum.

"At the fear of driving her off, screaming, I must meet this young lady," Sir Hugo said after a deep sip of brandy. "See if your taste in women has gotten worse after all those depriving years at sea. A *woman*, in *business*, well! Who'd have ever imagined a thing like that? Illustrating books, for *money*, haw! Making a decent living at it, does she?"

"Cleared over an hundred pounds, last year, she told me. Good enough to qualify for the vote," Lewrie said, a tad boastful.

"Oh, God, don't get started on *that* idea!" his father cried.

"You'll stay for dinner?" Lewrie offered.

"Yays, I believe I will," Sir Hugo drawled, "for it's becoming too raw to coach home to eat. You've been bragging on your cook, that Yeovill fellow. I might as well see if he's as good as you claim."

"There's to be a party to unveil the painting, too," Lewrie said. "I've invited Peter Rushton, Clotworthy Chute, Peter's brother Harold, Reverend

Chenery, Charles the Midshipman, Jessica, and a Madame Berenice Pellatan, a French artist *émigré* who lodges with the family at the manse. You could meet her, then. Interested?"

"Hmm, that sounds intriguing," his father allowed. "Is the Berenice mort fetching?"

"Only if you prefer blowsy, overdone French women," Lewrie told him, which made his father fake a shiver, and swig down more brandy.

"It's gilt, of course," Jessica explained as she showed him the final, framed results. "Not so wide, or baroque, or rococo to detract from the subject matter. It's all a matter of the proper scale."

Lewrie, standing back to take it all in, raised a hand with his thumb extended upwards in imitation of her gestures when making her initial sketches, and Jessica grinned and bowed her head to acknowledge the teasing.

"The band between I had them paint blue, somewhere 'twixt the blue of your sash, and a royal blue," Jessica went on, pointing to a smooth, rounded gap between the ornate carvings. "Just a touch of grey, which, I think, will draw observers to the colour of your eyes."

"I see what ye mean," Lewrie said, appreciative.

"So, Sir Alan, are you happy with my humble work?" Jessica asked, looking confident that he would be.

"Absolutely, Miss Jessica," he told her, casting a glance over to Madame Pellatan who had accompanied Jessica, and wishing that the old mort could drop through a hole in the floor.

Courage to the stickin' post, he chid himself, readying to say what had been on his mind for some time, feeling his chest, his face, flushing with boyish nervousness.

"I am dis-appointed, though, Miss Jessica," he began.

"Oh?" Jessica reacted, startled, frowning and looking hurt.

"Oh, Sir Alan, how can you say such a thing?" Madame Pellatan interrupted.

"I mean t'say . . . now the portrait's done, we will not be required to see each other on an almost daily, ah . . . association, and I, ah . . . ," Lewrie stammered, feeling like the largest, calf-head cully, "and I must own that I will miss that a great deal, the ah . . . laughing and joking over tea, while I was posing, which must have been a trial to you, 'stead o' sittin' mute, and hindered your work?"

Lewrie cast a quick glance over at Madame Pellatan, again, who was now sitting bolt upright with her eyes blared wide in surprise.

"I have come, over our short time together, in your presence," Lewrie bulled on, wondering if he was *capable* of making sense. "Ah, to have delighted in your company, enjoyed gettin' t'know you, Miss Jessica, and . . ."

"The dogs need to visit the back gardens, I think," Madame Pellatan said, springing to her feet, sweeping out of the front parlour to the hallway, and coaxing Bisquit and Rembrandt to follow her.

Thank bloody Christ for that! Lewrie thought.

"Ah," he began again, "I'm sure that your talents are in great demand, Miss Jessica, new clients for portraits, your own paintings, another book t'be illustrated, but ah . . . I would think it a shame do we not, can we not, continue to enjoy each other's company, which has been . . . hang it!" He stumbled to a halt, phrases tangling in his head, and she was looking at him with a wide smile on her face, her dark blue eyes glittering, taking deep breaths, and he was sure that she was only being polite as she patiently listened to a capering lunatick in full rave in Bedlam.

"I have come to like being with you, Miss Jessica, and I'd not wish to stop," Lewrie baldly summed up. "Our rides in the park, walking the dogs, exhibitions, suppers, even taking a cup of tea or two."

Now she'll laugh at me! he thought, visibly wincing; *Go ahead, get it over with!*

"You cannot imagine how happy I am to hear you say that, Sir Alan," Jessica said, instead, seeming to melt from trepidation to elation as she took a tentative step closer to him. "From the moment you came to collect Charley to take him to your ship, you have occupied my mind. And, as we began to exchange letters . . . such wonderful letters . . . you were always in my thoughts. And, when you asked me to do your portrait, I was over the *Moon* with joy.

"I, too, have come to enjoy our time together, and would think it an honour, and a joy, to continue our merry and pleasing relationship!" Jessica declared, almost shuddering with emotion.

"Thank God!" Lewrie breathed out in relief. "Even do I stumble and stammer like an un-prepared schoolboy unready to recite?"

"Only if you do not expect me to become an expert horsewoman, Sir Alan!" she teased, stepping even closer, and Lewrie extended both hands to take hold of hers which were offered to him eagerly.

"Ehm, I wonder, then," Lewrie said, sure that he was grinning like the village idiot but at that moment didn't care a damn whether he was, "if you would allow me to be less formal, and just call you Jessica. And, 'Sir' Alan sounds awfully stiff. If you could . . ."

"Alan," she replied with a sweet, fond coo.

"Jessica," he said in like fondness.

"Oh, Lord, what must Madame Berenice imagine?" Jessica laughed as they swung hands. "She might think that you were proposing on the spot, without speaking to my father first!"

Am I ready t'go that far, right now? Lewrie asked himself.

"Well, it might help did we get to know each other a *bit* more, first," he allowed. "Never can tell, I might change into 'Wolf Head' or 'Bloody Bones' after dark, and scare you and the dogs! Suppers, some balls, attending the theatre, riding in the park of course, just . . . being together."

"But of course!" Jessica exclaimed in delight. "And, properly chaperoned," she added, remembering Society's strict rules.

"I'd never do a thing to harm your good name, Jessica," Lewrie promised.

"I know you won't, Alan," she replied, experimenting with the easy use of his Christian name and liking the sound of it, the taste of it. "Now, where shall we hang your portrait?"

She looked happily playful, which gave Lewrie's heart a lurch as he imagined what life might be like with her.

"Hmm, since it's the only artwork in the whole house at the moment, maybe over the mantel in the drawing room, I'd think," Lewrie decided. "Can't hang it in the dining room, that'd make supper guests think I'm boasting, or something. Like dronin' on and borin' 'em to death with my tales."

"But, what adventurous tales you have to tell, Alan," Jessica assured him with a fond smile as they got the portrait down off the easel, as Lewrie called for Desmond and Deavers to come help with a hammer and nails.

"Oh, believe me, you'd tire of 'em sooner or later," Lewrie was quick to say. " 'What, that 'un, *again*?' and you'd be rollin' your eyes in embarrassment."

"I cannot imagine that ever happening, Alan," she insisted.

"Never can tell, five or ten years on," he said, realising at once the implications of that statement.

"Oh! And do you imagine that we will be together that far into the future, Alan?" Jessica said with an expectant hitch of breath.

Oh, shit! he thought; *I think I do! In for the penny, in for the pound.*

"Aye, I think we will," he said in a sudden daze. "I *hope* we will, if you will have me, that is." He sat the portrait down against his leg to prop it up, and took her hands, again. "I s'pose what I've been stammering round is . . . I've come to adore you, Jessica, and I'd be honoured beyond all measure if you'd . . ."

"Yes!" Jessica exclaimed. "Oh, yes, Alan, yes! I will be honoured, and elated beyond all measure to be your wife!"

For the first time they embraced properly, clinging to each other tightly, and Lewrie lifted her off her feet for a long moment, delighting in how light, how slim she felt, his head aswim with emotion.

Did it, did it, anyway, and why the Devil not? he thought.

"I love you," he murmured into her hair, "I've been be-sotted since the moment I met you!"

"Oh, that was the moment for me, as well, from the instant that you smiled, without even saying a word, Alan!" Jessica whispered harshly as she bestowed a kiss upon his cheek, and he could feel wetness on her face.

"Oh, don't cry, Jessica, I ain't *that* bad!" he said.

"I can't help it," she confessed, stepping back long enough to draw a handkerchief from a sleeve of her gown. "I *love* you, and you've made me the happiest . . . !"

"Need some nails, sor?" Liam Desmond said as he and Deavers came into the parlour. "Oh, oops."

"We need help hanging my picture over the mantel in the drawing room, Desmond," Lewrie told him. "Miss Jessica and I . . . we have just become, ah . . . engaged."

"Oh, good for you, sor! That's grand, that is!" Desmond said.

"Amen to that, Cap'm sir!" Deavers chimed in. "Aye, we'll get it hung for you, straightaway, sir!"

And Desmond and Deavers took charge of the painting to heft it upstairs for them, leaving them alone for a moment.

"I suppose I now *must* speak with your father," Lawrie said with a nervous laugh. "Ask my estate agent what this house may cost to buy outright . . . no sense in leasing. If you think it's suitable to your tastes, my dear?"

My dear! he thought; *So easy a thing to say to one and all, with no meaning to it, but now . . . !*

"It's a lovely house, Alan," Jessica agreed with a vigourous nod of her head, still dabbing at her eyes, "a *perfect* house, where I trust we shall be immensely happy. Yes, do you speak with my father tonight, he could post the first reading of the banns this Sunday!"

"Unless you'd prefer we coach to Gretna Green and wed instanter," Lewrie teased, laughing, feeling happy and relieved at the same time.

"Hah!" Jessica cried, throwing her head back, "Highly romantic, but most impractical. Father would die of apoplexy did we do *that*! No, I have always imagined that I'd be wed at Saint Anselm's, with my father presiding. Ehm, when you do speak with him, he'll try to get you to promise to bring my painting to an end, what he's always regarded as foolishness, most improper for a woman."

"And I'll tell him I have no intentions to do so," Lewrie vowed. "I'll not be his instrument for breaking your dear heart, Jessica."

"Oh, Alan, you are the dearest, dearest man!" she cried, throwing her arms round him once more. "You make me so happy I could die!" And this time they kissed, at first tentatively, then with growing passion, one that made Lewrie's head reel again. At last they stepped back, and she smoothed her hair, looking shy.

"I suppose we must see to the hanging of the portrait," she said, cocking her head in an endearingly impish way. "We must behave proper for the household staff."

"For a few more weeks, anyway," Lewrie rejoined, leering a bit.

Minutes later, Desmond and Deavers trooped back down to the kitchens, where Yeovill was chopping salad greens, Pettus was folding fresh-pressed shirts, and Tom Dasher was blacking Lewrie's boots.

"What's all that commotion?" Pettus asked, looking aloft where some womanly shrieks could be heard.

"I owe ya a pound, Pettus me boyo," Desmond said gruffly as he scooped up the spit-turning terrier. "Ya won yer wager, damn yer eyes."

"What wager?" Pettus asked, with a quizzical cock of his head.

"Ya *said* Miss Chenery'd set her cap for th' Captain, an' I was of th' opposite opinion," Desmond replied. "Well, th' Captain's just proposed to her, an' ya can hear how she took *that*!"

"Th' Cap'm's t'marry?" Dasher marvelled. "Wot kinda cake will ya bake, Mister Yeovill?"

"Well, well, well," Pettus said, breaking into a wide smile. "I *knew* it. Anyone could see it coming from a league off. Good for him, and good for her! And if you don't have a pound to spare, Liam, I'll settle for a bottle of dark rum!"

CHAPTER NINETEEN

So, who hates me that much?" Lewrie asked James Peel after a rather good meal at a chop-house conveniently near the Foreign Office.

"Good Lord, Lewrie, who doesn't?" Peel wryly rejoined as he had a last forkful of his figgy-dowdy pudding. "You could write your own list, I'd imagine. The people who've blighted your career most-like are the people you despise already."

"Well, hmm," Lewrie grunted, mulling that over. "The first to spring to mind'd be Francis Forrester, the fubsy shit. A horrible mess-mate when we were Mids together in the old *Ariadne,* and a pompous ass, but he's been 'Yellow-Squadroned' for years after he hared off to look for the French fleet, left his command at Nassau, then grounded his ship at English Harbour, Antigua."

"But still possessed of influential patrons," Peel, the old spy, told him, "and all sure that he was done wrong. Go on."

Lewrie ticked off people he suspected; Captain Grierson, also from a spell in Bahamian waters, whom he'd embarrassed, and spoiled the man's poor joke of sailing up to Nassau showing no colours, to be deliberately mistaken for the French. There had been a "grass widow" involved, too, that Lewrie was topping, and Grierson wanted.

There was his son Hugh's present Captain Richard Chalmers, a man who took his religion almost as seriously as the unfortunate Admiral "Dismal Jemmy" Gambier, who thought that Lewrie was such a sinner that he'd piss in the holy water font, and try to put the leg over the Virgin Mary.

William Fillebrowne came to mind at once. He was from a very wealthy family, and had tried to emulate their Grand Tours of the Continent by using his ship as a store house for treasures bought off needy French *émigrés* for a shilling to the pound, a clench-jawed Oxonian "Mumbletonian" more interested in quim than duty, and with a curious penchant for pursuing Lewrie's cast-off women; first his mistress Phoebe Aretino, then even one of his "cream pot" loves from his Midshipman days, Lucy Shockley *née* Beauman, the young wife of older Sir Malcolm Shockley, in Venice. Their last *rencontre* at Gibraltar had been so testy and insulting that it could have been a reason for a duel!

There were a few other fellow officers that sprang to mind, but Lewrie could easily dismiss them for lack of rank and seniority, and he hadn't thought that they had powerful patrons during the times he had worked with them. He tossed off a hopeless shrug, at last.

"You forgot Admiral Tobias Treghues," Peel said with that air of "I know something you don't!" common to everyone Lewrie had ever met in the skulking-spying trade.

"Christ, is he even still alive?" Lewrie gawped. "Last I heard, he was somewhere in the Far East, achievin' very little, and makin' everyone else miserable, Got his wits scrambled by a French gunner's rammer during the American Revolution, and hasn't been in his right mind, since, and you never knew whether he'd praise ye one day, then have ye mast-headed the next! *He* was a Bible-thumper, too, now that I recall. And he's made Rear-Admiral? Gawd!"

"Being out of one's wits just might be a prerequisite for flag rank," Peel said with a hearty chuckle. "Yes, he's still alive, with his shrew of a wife carried aboard his flagship, and between them, they have lots of influence. Believe it or not, he *prefers* the East Indies, while most people will throw up their commissions to avoid it, so Admiralty lets him be."

"Anybody else to surprise me with, Jemmy?" Lewrie asked.

"Your former Commodore, Blanding, who's also a Rear-Admiral, now," Peel said.

"Blanding?" Lewrie exclaimed. "I pestered him half to death with suggestions when we were chasin' that French squadron bound for New Orleans when Bonaparte got it back from Spain, but that's of little reason t'hate me!"

"I gather it's more to do with your knighthood and being made baronet," Peel told him.

"But, that was King George havin' a bad day!" Lewrie exclaimed. "And I still suspect that my knighthood wasn't for beatin' the French at the Chandeleur Islands, but some cruel reward for Caroline, my late wife, bein' murdered by Napoleon's police, and them tryin' t'kill me . . . t'drum up patriotic rage to justify goin' back to war with 'em.

"Blanding wants to blame anyone, he'd best lay it at the feet of King George, and William Pitt," Lewrie went on, "and the King getting 'knight and baronet' stuck in his head from the people in line before me. He almost took my *ear* off, swingin' that sword about!"

"He commanded your victory, and he was made Knight of the Bath, but you received what he imagines was *his* due, and he's never forgiven you for it," Peel said with a sad shake of his head.

"D'ye think it'd made any difference if I wrote him and apologised?" Lewrie speculated.

"I rather doubt it, at this point," Peel brusquely said. "He's festered on it far too long. Ehm, there's another name that arose in my queries."

"Who?" Lewrie demanded.

"Rear-Admiral Keith Ashburn," Peel told him.

"Keith Ashburn?" Lewrie almost yelped in shock. "But . . . he and I were friends, about the only friend I had in the Midshipmen's mess back in 1780. In old *Ariadne*, he was practically my 'sea daddy' who taught me just about everything I didn't know! *Why*, for God's sake?"

"I gather that he remembers how much you disliked the Navy in the beginning, how idle and arrogant you were, or seemed to be, about being completely ignorant, as a defence," Peel said with a shrug. "I think the gist of what one of my listeners heard was that he thought you've been damned lucky, so far, too idle and . . . insouciant was the word . . . to be trusted with command of a rowboat, much less a warship, or a squadron, and that sooner or later you'd come a cropper and take a lot of good men with you when you fail. Sorry, but that's what he said of you."

"Everybody else just envies me, or thinks me a sinful heretic?" Lewrie said with a dis-believing scowl.

"Envy, yes, for certain," Peel said with a faint grin. "You're too damned lucky at prize-money, being in the right place at the right time, when they go years without firing a shot in anger, and winning your battles, winning fame and glory that should have been theirs, if God was truly just. It don't look good. With so many pitted against you, getting a new active commission will be nigh impossible."

"Oh, my God," Lewrie slowly breathed out, visibly sagging as he slouched deeper against his dining chair. "My father suggested that I enjoy my temporary retirement, rest on my laurels, but . . . dammit! I suppose I'll have to, now."

"Oh, and there's that fellow you relieved for illness just before the Battle of Copenhagen, Captain Speakes?" Peel added.

"Dammit, I *paid* him for those Franklin stoves!" Lewrie growled. "Just 'cause his Purser sold 'em off when *Thermopylae* was laid up in-ordinary wasn't my fault."

"And, his grand scheme to recoup his own career with those torpedoes failed," Peel reminded him. "Daft idea to begin with, depending on tides and currents to float explosives with shoddy timers and detonators into enemy harbours. Speakes is a Second Class Commodore with a small squadron off Scotland, and the weather doesn't suit his damned parrot. You let him down, didn't believe in the project, and didn't carry it through. He's still a true believer."

"Bugger him," Lewrie spat. "The damned things'd never work."

Oh, but that had been a dangerous Summer of 1805, experimenting with cask torpedoes and the later catamaran torpedoes jam-packed with black powder in vast quantities, with clock timers that wound trigger lines to flintlock pistol strikers that *might* work, if the powder did not get soaked from shoddy workmanship, *if* wind and tide wafted them in the right direction, *if* the damned devices went off at all, and if the enemy didn't spot them. For all the work spent on developing them, only one wee French guard ship at Boulogne had been destroyed out of all the hundreds of invasion vessels, and only because her crew got curious and hauled it alongside for a looking-over.

"So, are you enjoying your forced retirement?" Peel asked as he leaned back in his chair, and waved to their waiter for more coffee.

"Most of the time, aye," Lewrie had to admit.

"And how is married life?" Peel enquired with a brow up.

That erased the scowl from Lewrie's face, and put him in better takings. "Utterly delightful," he said with a pleased smile. "I am a completely happy man . . . even if some of my kin think me daft for re-marrying."

"Then you're a bloody wonder among men, and still a very lucky one," Peel said with a wry laugh. "I understand that Dame Lewrie still paints?"

"She did my portrait in my front parlour, and the morning light there is so good that it's become her studio," Lewrie told him. "What is the expression, 'happy wife, happy life'? My old cabin steward, Aspinall, is in publishing, and he's offered her a book to be illustrated. A novel, written by a woman, of all things! We've a rough galley of it, but it's all rather lurid . . . West Country moors, ghosts, ruined manors, earnest hearts beating as one, and I don't know what-all. I've not been able to make much sense of it, except that there's love and a rich marriage at the end. Jessica intends to continue under her maiden name, for now . . . J. A. Chenery."

" 'Happy wife, happy life'," Peel sniggered.

"But, does she ever submit anything to the Royal Academy, it'll be under J. A. Lewrie," Lewrie told his old compatriot. "How's the spy game?"

"Rather boring," Peel confessed as their fresh coffee came to the table. "Hush-hush, but lots of paperwork and reports submitted by people still out on the sharp end. The most I risk now is paper cuts, but at least I can go home to my wife and children each evening without having my *throat* cut. I must allow that I rather miss my active, old days out upon a hostile world under old Zachariah Twigg, working with you in the West Indies, or dodging round the Germanies before the French gobbled them all up. I just may be too stout and short of wind for such activities, but, at least I'm senior enough to have a say on what government, or military policies might be. Thomas Mountjoy down at Lisbon is in the same pickle. His pack of agents has expanded, but all he does is read reports and write summaries. And complain about the Spanish and their slack-wit generals. Not so much going on now that General Sir Arthur Wellesley is in winter Quarters at Elvas just over the Portuguese border, but he'll be back into Spain come Spring. He's initiated a corps of Exploring Officers to scout out the French, the roads, the terrain, and liaise with the Spanish partisan bands . . . in full British uniform, so they can't be shot as spies. Wellesley will *not* be caught without information."

"It was grand how he beat the French at Talavera," Lewrie said. "About the same way he won at Vimeiro, which I was fortunate enough to witness. Hide most of his troops on the back slope 'til the French come stumbling up in their tight column blocks, then surprise them at close range before they can deploy into line. Talavera was a slaughter."

"Yes, and then the Spanish looted his baggage trains and ate all his soldiers' food," Peel gravelled. "God, what a country! Only Romney Marsh seems to enjoy it, galloping from one partisan force to the next, relishing the ambushes and massacres. What a blood-thirsty sod!"

"He's more than welcome to it," Lewrie heartily agreed, for he had been forced to endure that lunatick who played at war and skull-duggery as if it was a grand costume party, with the opportunity to cut throats, emasculate and torture French prisoners, skin them alive and nail them to trees or barn doors. And he was a Cambridge man, and Etonian!

"My treat, I believe?" James Peel said as the waiter brought the tab. They rose, reclaimed their hats, top coats, gloves, and walking-sticks. Once outside the frowsty warmth of the chop-house, Lewrie whistled for a hackney, whilst Peel prepared to trudge back to his offices through the new-fallen snow. "It's not *all* gloom and doom, old fellow. You still have allies in the Navy, most now of flag rank like Benjamin Rodgers, Thomas Charlton, and your wily old Scot swashbuckler, Andrew Ayscough. If one of them asks for you, and justifies the why, Admiralty mayn't be able to refuse him."

"I count on that, Mister Peel," Lewrie told him. "Though I won't hold my breath waitin' for that to happen."

"Well, good luck anyway, and give my regards to your lady wife."

A hackney slithered to a stop by the kerb at Lewrie's waving, wheels and hooves skidding on slush and ice. Lewrie climbed aboard and gave his address.

"Have you a lap-robe handy?" he asked the cabman.

"No, sir, sorry, but ya kin put th' winders up," the driver shouted down.

Should've worn my boat-cloak, Lewrie glumly thought as he tried to wrap his heavy overcoat over his knees and booted shins. Once comfortable, he mused upon "retirement" and marriage being delightful.

Well, the retirement part still irked, but the joys of marriage to Jessica almost made up for it, despite the reactions from his kin. His father had groaned, "Oh, Gawd, you're really going to do it? Well, on your head be it, ye damned fool!" and even meeting Jessica had not mollified Sir Hugo's opinion all that much.

The banns had been posted and the wedding celebrated before he heard from his far-off sons. Hugh had been bemused but supportive, but he had already been of the opinion that his father could not be expected to live a monk's life, and had seemed appreciative of Lewrie's mistress at Gibraltar and Lisbon. Sewallis's letter in reply was not as congratulatory, but he'd always been a prim young sod. His older son even cautioned him about taking a much younger lady to wife, as if he was so much wiser!

Lewrie's former brothers-in-law were split on it, Burgess now in Spain with Wellesley's army sounded delighted, and his wife, Theodora, and her parents had actually attended. Governour, who could have come to London, had pled bad roads and bad weather at the last moment, and came just a quim-hair short of denouncing a re-marriage that did not honour the memory of his dead sister and how vexed Lewrie's daughter, Charlotte, had taken the news. From Charlotte herself had come her own letter, a tearful accusation of his foolishness and heartlessness, and "how dare you sully the sainted memory of my mother, or imagine that anyone could replace her!"

But of course, Charlotte would have no qualms over her increased dowry, and use her father's wealth to prepare herself for her London Season, most-like cursing his name in the process. But then, what else had Lewrie come to expect from her?

At least no one in either parish had leaped to their feet to deny the match when the banns were read the required three times. Weddings by banns, Lewrie learned, were going out of fashion, with most couples obtaining an ecclesiastical license, but Jessica was traditional in that regard, something she'd looked forward to all her life, and Lewrie was not fool enough to object. Lawyers, and her father, the Reverend Chenery, got involved to settle the marriage contract, to determine how much "pin money" he would allow her each month to manage his household, agreeing that her father would settle £60 on Jessica for her dowry, and startling the fellow when Lewrie stipulated that he would *not* demand that she give up her art career, and that whatever she earned would be hers, not under his coverture!

The *next* thing that got up Reverend Chenery's nose was Jessica's wish that their wedding would be a double-ring ceremony, and that Lewrie wear a matching wedding band! Lewrie had never heard of such, either; even the happiest of married men in England, or anywhere else, for that matter, did not wear a ring to announce their status. He went along with it, though, if only to please her, and it created quite a stir in church, especially among the ladies present, who sighed and went for their handkerchiefs, thinking it most romantic, whilst the married men shifted uneasily in their seats, wondering what the Hell *that* was all about!

Of course, Lewrie had worn his best-dress uniform with star and sash and both his medals, again at Jessica's insistence, though there were no other Navy officers present to form the arch of swords that she had read about (bad luck, that!) to see them out the doors. Only her brother, Charley, showed up in his Midshipman uniform.

Charley had come to Lewrie at the last moment with yet another of Jessica's innovations, pinning a sprig of rosemary on his coat lapel.

"Whatever's this for?" Lewrie had asked, He had heard of grooms wearing a flower that matched the bride's bouquet, but rosemary?

"It's to represent Fidelity, sir," Midshipman Chenery had said.

Fidelity? Lewrie had thought at that moment, rolling the word round in his head like a sharp-edged rock; *Really? Gawd, I love her dear, but . . . ! Well, I s'pose, if I must!*

So far, though, it was early days, and Lewrie had no trouble with the concept, for Jessica was deliriously happy, which made him equally happy, and when it came to their physical expressions of that happiness . . .

He felt a tightness in his crutch as he recalled the evenings after the wedding, and the wedding breakfast. They had coached to Anglesgreen and his father's country house for a week or so of "honeymoon" togetherness . . . well, as alone as they could get with Pettus along to do for him, and a rather pretty young girl named Lucy to see to Jessica's needs, and with Mr. and Mrs. Furlough in charge of the house, with grooms, stablemen, and chamber maids of the house staff there.

The wedding breakfast had stretched into a wedding brunch before they had hit the road, and the roads *had* been winter-bad, making the going so slow that they had not gotten to the village before full dark.

Through a fine country supper, Lewrie could sense Jessica's mounting nervousness, despite the good cheer of the Furloughs, and the tour of the house to show off Sir Hugo's relics brought back from the Far East, tigerskin rug and all, and Lewrie's amusing banter did not ease that nervousness. His new wife was about to be introduced to the mystery of the utmost intimacy, about which no "good girl" was told a mere iota, even by her mother or sisters!

Had Jessica and her long-time girlhood friends, most now married and already mothers, ever dare share "war stories" about sexual love and pleasure, or the lack of it? Lewrie rather doubted it! And he did not wish to be dreaded as a brute!

As the house staff prepared to retire, yawning and wishing them good night, Lewrie led her to their bed-chamber where their nightgowns and nightshirts were laid out, the bed heated with a pair of warming pans and turned down. Lewrie shammed a yawn, complained of all the drink they'd "taken aboard" at the wedding breakfast, the journey, and his lack of sleep the night before, and had suggested that their first night, they just go to *sleep*!

They had un-dressed separately, then slid into bed, leaving one candle burning for a while, now chastely garbed in flannel bed clothes. During their brief courtship, there had been kisses, first virginally shy, then more passionate, tentative embraces that had turned to close, suggestive hugs of longer duration. That night, they had kissed, had giggled, had pressed close together, and Lewrie's hands had stroked, but he had not groped, 'til they had snuffed the candle, spooned close on their sides, and had actually slumbered.

Then, after an active day about the property, the next evening did not find Jessica quite so fearful, and Lewrie patiently took his time to stoke her passion, casting off his nightshirt and coaxing her out of hers, working his way with gentle kisses from her neck and ears to her navel and hips and back, worshipping sensitive wee breasts 'til she was moaning and whimpering with want, and her cry of momentary pain from losing her maidenhead was lost in gasps of wonder.

The third night, Jessica had even rolled close to him after a half-hour of afterglow, endearments, and silliness, and had coyly asked if they could do that a second time! And when they woke to the wintry sun streaming through a window, the morning of the fourth day, she had not been shy when tossing back the bed covers and rising to fetch her discarded nightgown, allowing him his first full look at how lovely she was, laughing deep in her throat as he told her how beautiful she was. He meant every word of it, declaring, "Do ye think it sacrilegious, if I say that I worship you?"

Slim arms and shoulders, a lean, straight back, a slim waist, wee bottom, and long, slender legs, with small but deliciously firm breasts, wide and close-set together with her long, un-pinned hair tumbling down to half-cover them; that image of her would stick in his head forever! Elfin, willowy, lithe . . . ! He thought that he'd need an entire dictionary of words to describe how flawless she was, and how Jessica fulfilled every fantasy of his ideal image of female beauty!

They had mostly had a grand time at Anglesgreen, riding down to the village to dine at the Old Ploughman, where Will Cony, Lewrie's old cabin servant and Cox'n, his wife, Maggie, who had worked for the Lewries when they'd rented their farm, and their brood of sons and daughters made Jessica as welcome as a visiting royal. She'd ridden side-saddle for that jaunt, but about the farm she'd borrowed a pair of Lewrie's corduroy breeches to wear under her gown, and Sir Hugo's saddle, to ride, feeling so much more secure of her seat, and declaring that she just might do the same back in London, no matter what anyone said of it!

Of course, they had had to call upon Governour Chiswick, his wife, Millicent, their children, and Lewrie's daughter, Charlotte, and that had been a stiff affair, a dinner and afternoon of rather formal, icy civility, and, despite Lewrie's fears, Charlotte did not make a scene or catty comments, remaining aloof and stand-offish no matter how Jessica tried to warm to her. Lewrie had explained before they'd coached over how Caroline's murder had affected her, and how most had laid the blame on him.

"Step-mothers," Jessica had moodily mused once home, "in all of the children's books, all the folk tales, they are always the ogres, are they not, Alan? I fear that Charlotte and I will never become close, even does she find a husband and form a household of her own. A pity, really, for I feel she could be a sweet girl."

"She was . . . once," Lewrie had told her.

"Well, I shall pray for her future happiness, and try to make the best of it," Jessica concluded. "Oh, the winter cattle, huddled up so! I must sketch that!"

"'Ere ye goes, sir," the cabman called down at last. "Twenny-two Dover Street," and Lewrie alit, paid the fare, and, frozen to the bone, but aflame inside, dashed through the door of his house.

"Oh, there you are, darling, home at last!" Jessica called out with delight as Deavers took Lewrie's things. "How did your meeting with your friend at the Foreign Office go?"

"Not very promising, I'm afraid," he told her as he entered the front parlour, where Jessica was standing before two paintings on easels, side-by-side, with a palette board in one hand and a brush in the other, dressed in winter woolens and shawl, with a mob-cap on her head, and her hair down and long, pulled to the nape of her neck, at perfect "at home" ease. She set her tools aside and came to embrace him.

"Hallo to you, my love," Lewrie said, beaming as he gave her a strong hug and a lingering kiss.

"Why, you're half-frozen!" she exclaimed.

"Aye, but you're so warm," Lewrie purred as he nuzzled her neck.

"Go sit by the fire and warm yourself," she instructed. "Shall I ring for tea, or brandy?"

"Both!" Lewrie declared as he went to the fireplace to lift the skirts of his coat to thaw his backside. "Still working on those?"

"Trying to," Jessica said, taking a moment to regard her paintings.

"Dim and gloomy as it is this morning, I haven't accomplished much, and the light's gone for the day, so I suppose I should quit. They'll be finished, eventually," she said, dipping her brush in turpentine to clean it.

"Thought you'd catch your death when you did the sketches," he said, sitting in one of the wing-back chairs with his hands extended to warm them.

Jessica had been entranced with the vista from his father's house, and with the house itself, spending a good part of one day sitting out on the front gallery in warm clothing, one of Lewrie's over-coats and a blanket, to draw the distant village and the farmland and forest between, with lots of hot coffee, tea, or beef broth to sustain her 'til she was satisfied. The next clear day, she had set up her easel in the lane and rendered the house and the stub of the old Roman, or Saxon, or Norman tower that had been incorporated into the house, no one was sure when, or why, it had been erected atop the hillside. Now, she was working on them at the same time, adding details such as sheep, cattle, or farm workers, though keeping a winter aspect. That activity had given her a case of the sniffles that had alarmed everyone.

Lewrie especially liked the painting of the house, for she had it look trimmed for Christmas, with holly and pine wreaths in the windows, and welcoming, glowing amber light spilling from all the windows, reflected on the thin snowfall and the icicles on the cherub fountain in the middle of the gravel coach drive.

"Oh, there are some letters that have come for you," Jessica said, "none addressed to the both of us, yet," she added with a mock rueful grin and a cock of her head, and Lewrie went to fetch them off the entry hall sideboard, himself.

"Aha! Percy Stangbourne," he said with glee as he read the sender. "You remember his wife, Eudoxia, who came to our wedding?"

"Oh, yes, what a remarkable woman!" Jessica declared, "And her father, that . . . how do you say it, Arslan Artomovich?" She giggled. "What a romantic match, a Russian actress, horsewoman, marksman, and circus performer, married to a Viscount, no matter what anyone thinks of it. Her father, though . . . hmm!"

Arslan Artomovich Durschenko had done what he had done at his daughter's marriage; gotten "cherry merry" drunk and taught anyone who dared to dance like a Cossack, and Lewrie thought he'd sprained every muscle in his legs and lamed himself trying to compete with him!

"Percy says he's utterly delighted to hear that I've married, and Eudoxia's written him to describe you, all good of course, and he sends you his very best regards and good wishes," Lewrie related, and read Percy's account of his part in the Battle of Talavera, and how much he had come to despise his Spanish allies.

There were other letters from fellow officers, a sarcastic one from Geoffrey Westcott, a perennial bachelor too busy wenching to ever wed; Anthony Langlie, who had married his French ward, Sophie; and one from Rear-Admiral Thomas Charlton.

"Hmm, Thom Charlton says he's in London, between commissions," Lewrie related, "and his mail just caught up with him. He's staying at Nerot's Hotel in Saint James's, in Knight's Street. I should write and invite him to dine with us," further explaining how they had met in the Adriatic, what they had accomplished, and how Thomas Charlton had given one of his sons his first berth as a Midshipman in 1803.

"But of course, darling," Jessica agreed. "It would be grand to meet him."

"Hmm, something about a proposal he wants to discuss with me," Lewrie read on aloud.

"A proposal?" Jessica asked, swiping a loose lock of hair back under her mob-cap, with a quizzical brow up. "What sort of proposal?"

"Don't know," Lewrie replied, "he doesn't say. Maybe I should call on him at his lodgings, first, find out what he means, *then* invite him to dine."

"Something concerning the Navy, Alan? Oh, dear," Jessica said, hugging her shawl closer round her.

"It may be," Lewrie said, feeling a *frisson* of excitement that it might pull him out of his forced retirement, even as he sensed his wife's alarm, which he tried to calm. "Who knows? He might wish to ask if I know a promising fellow to be his Flag-Lieutenant or his Flag-Captain, if he's gettin' a new command. Or, he might ask how I managed t'raise all those rabbits and quail aboard my last ship, and how they fare at sea, ha ha!"

He gave her a dis-arming smile and a shrug to reassure her, then could not help allowing his gaze to stray to where his great-cabin furnishing had stood in the parlour, but saw the new settee, matching chairs, and side-tables that Jessica had bought after they'd returned to London from their honeymoon. His old things, she'd complained, had reeked of salt, tar, gunpowder, and mildew, and hints of the orlop and rotting salt-meats too long in brine casks. All had been relegated to the servants' flat above the un-used stables.

"So, you might not be called back to sea anytime soon?" she asked, sounding a touch fearful.

"I rather doubt it, my love," Lewrie shrugged off, but at heart he wondered. If Charlton asked, would he actually leave his sweet wife and this happy life with her? As dear as he adored her, as loath as he was to be apart from her for even a single night, he feared that he might!

BOOK THREE

Fire is the test of gold; adversity, of strong men.
  -Lucius Annaeus Seneca, "*on Providence*"

CHAPTER TWENTY

"My stars, Lewrie, I do believe that you must live inside some faery ring," Rear-Admiral of the Blue Thomas Charlton exclaimed after they had settled down at a table at a coffee house a short walk from Nerot's Hotel the next morning. "How many years since our time in the Adriatic, how long since we've seen each other, and you don't look as if you've aged a single day!"

"Ehm, clean livin', early retirin', and no drink?" Lewrie japed away the compliment. "You look fit and trim, I must say."

"Oh, tosh," Charlton replied with a fake scowl.

Did one picture a mental image of a typical English gentleman, Thom Charlton was your man. He had a long, rectangular head and face, a high brow, and a long nose, and features rather un-remarkable, with a head of hair which at one time had been thick and brown, but had gone completely salt-and-pepper, far beyond the faint brushes of grey along his temples that Lewrie recalled from their last meeting. He was still tall, slim, but substantial, a full three inches taller than Lewrie's five feet nine. This morning, Charlton was dressed in civilian suitings; even when in uniform, unless he wore the medal, no one would have guessed that he was one of the "Trafalgar Captains".

They ordered coffee and brandy, stipulating that it should be hot, not

the usual tepid found in most coffee houses, then caught up on their doings
for a genial half-hour, with Charlton enquiring about Lewrie's youngest
son, Hugh, who had been in his first two years of service when Charlton
had sailed his ship into the combined Franco-Spanish fleet.

"Ah, the North coast of Spain," Charlton said, "a grand place for the
lad to be, right now. I've heard that our ships there are to be strongly re-
enforced, and become a proper Admiral's command."

"Yours, sir?" Lewrie asked with a sly grin. If it was given to Charlton,
he might need an officer already familiar with the coast and its dangers.

"Oh, no, I fear not, Lewrie," Charlton said with another deprecating
shrug and scowl. "In point of fact, the rumour round Admiralty is that it
may be given to Rear-Admiral Sir Home Popham."

"Popham?" Lewrie gawped. "Good God, *that* idiot? Didn't his repri-
mand over Buenos Aires mean *anything*? I was with him at Cape Town
and Buenos Aires, and thank Christ I was able t'sail away before that turned
t'shit."

"Ah, but unlike Lord Cochrane, say, Popham is a very cool and smooth
fellow, glib as anything," Charlton rejoined with a sly laugh, "and he's
made a point during his career to make friends, left, right, and centre. Popham is possessed of powerful patrons, too, all of whom can easily dismiss
his . . . odder moments. He could be barking mad and hot on an expedition to the Moon, but he could convince one to not only sponsor it, but
come along with him for the fun of it.

"What's Cochrane done since Aix Roads, after all?" Charlton went on.
"Tossed over his naval career, taken his seat in Lord's, and become a pest
over his slighted honour, so much so that his patrons are embarrassed to
speak up for him. No, Popham will succeed, I expect, because he *needs*
to . . . in his usual ambitious way. He might even envision an invasion or
two, to lure French troops away from Wellesley when he goes back into
Spain in the Spring."

"Well, good luck to him, then," Lewrie decided, "so long as he doesn't
bite off more than he can chew . . . again."

"Speaking of invasions . . . ," Charlton said, idly twiddling with his
spoon. "Recall, I wrote of a proposal to discuss with you."

"Who do ye want crushed, sir?" Lewrie asked with a grin, which much
amused the older man for a moment.

"Ah, that's the Lewrie I remember from the Adriatic," Charlton mused.
"And, the officer who raised so much Hell along the Andalusian coast a
few years back."

"Well, not too much Hell, sir," Lewrie countered, "with only one troop transport and two companies of soldiers. And, once we barely hit our stride, General Dalrymple at Gibraltar limited our usefulness, fearful that we might convince the Spanish *t'stay* allied with France, if we nipped 'em *too* sore. There were secret negotiations goin' on, behind the scenes, to get 'em to switch sides, and when they did, and we could have done the same against the French, our little enterprise'd been put out of business."

"But what if such an enterprise could be put back together again, in a much larger way, Lewrie?" Charlton cagily asked. "We've already seen something like that in Italy, with at least a brigade of troops. Fought a battle against the French, bloodied their noses, then got off quite handily."

"Well, d'ye mean an actual, hold-the-ground invasion, sir, or a series of raids?" Lewrie wondered aloud, head cocked to one side with a frown on his face, "It's one thing t'burn semaphore towers, scandalise gun batteries, or even take and blow up small forts, but it's quite another thing to seize port towns and hold them long enough for a real army to follow up."

"Hmm, let's say raids, in the beginning," Charlton decided. "I recall the early days of the American Revolution, when I was a lowly Lieutenant round New York, and how cleverly General Howe used large barges to winkle Washington's rag-tag army about. Howe managed to move from his camps on Staten Island cross the Hudson River to Manhattan, then cross the East River, cavalry, artillery, and all."

"A bit before my Midshipman days, sir," Lewrie confessed, "and I only saw New York long afterwards, anchored off Sandy Hook, or sent ashore for supplies after Yorktown, and rejoining my ship. I do remember the busy barge traffic, but, I also recall that the barges that you remember were flat-bottomed, slab-sided scows, totally useless in any offshore landings. Outside the Hudson or the East River, they'd turn turtle in a heartbeat. And, they were built to carry whole goods waggons and horse teams, like ferries, which is why Howe could move his whole army so quickly. I fear that we couldn't get much more than infantry ashore, not without specially-designed rowing barges with bow ramps of some kind, but whenever I asked about such boats at any dockyard, everyone swore they were impossible."

"Hmm, how did you do it, then, even with only infantry?" Thom Charlton asked, stirring sugar into a fresh cup, and dribbling a dram of brandy into it from the half-pint flask.

That prompted Lewrie to relate how it had been necessary to use sailors from the vast naval hospital at Gibraltar, separated from their ships by sickness or injuries, to supplement the few merchant sailors who manned the ships hired on by the Transport Board. He'd managed to round up six 29-foot rowing/sailing barges, a common Royal Navy pattern, with eight sailors and a coxswain to man each, and stand guard over their charges at the beach 'til the troops had accomplished their mission and returned to be borne back to the transport. The two companies of soldiers he'd been allotted, about one hundred twenty-five all told, would enter and leave the transport via anti-boarding nets slung over the ship's side by the chain platforms of the fore, main, and mizen masts.

"Troops from Light Companies are best," Lewrie told Charlton, "they're trained t'think on their feet better than soldiers from Line or Battalion Companies, even Grenadier Companies. And of course, I sent my fifty Marines ashore, too, with an equal number of armed sailors, to strengthen the raids. But, as I said, sir, everyone landed with only their muskets, hangers, bayonets, their cartridge boxes and a rucksack with gun tools and spare flints, and canteens. Any sort of artillery, even dis-mounted boat bow guns, were out of the question."

"Perhaps something bigger?" Charlton posed. "There are thirty-six-foot gunboats with bow platforms to bear twelve-pounder guns. If they could be obtained, and modified with some sort of wood ramp that could be shoved over the bows, perhaps a light six-pounder gun could be wheeled ashore."

"On Army field carriages with high wheels, though, sir," Lewrie countered, "and what does one do about the caissons to carry the shot and powder charges? And how many men would be necessary to man-haul the guns? Even six-pounders of the old pattern weigh too much to get over a soft sand beach onto the rough ground behind the shore. And, there's the problem of hoisting such heavy boats to be stored on the cross-deck beams, then hoisted off and put in the water before the soldiers could embark. We *towed* ours, at all times, else it took so long to prepare the troops to land that the enemy would be alerted to our presence and march an entire brigade against us, sittin' on their arses above the beach and cheerin' on the show."

"Hmm, there is that," Charlton rather grumpily realised. "So, infantry only, and limited objectives, with standard barges."

"Unless some genius naval architect can come up with some sort of really big transport ships that can run up on the beach and open a set of bow doors, that's the only way I can see it bein' done, sir," Lewrie assured him. "Now, how ye get 'em *off* again's a puzzler."

"But, could we land a regiment, a battalion, at once?" Charlton wondered. "How many soldiers per each transport?"

"Whoof, sir!" Lewrie exclaimed, sitting back in his chair in surprise. "What's a battalion? Six, eight hundred men? They might start *out* nigh a thousand men in ten companies, but, after sickness, desertion, and wounds, a battalion might average six or eight hundred. To send a battalion overseas, the usual is about one hundred fifty troops per each transport ship, but, with room aboard required for the Navy sailors who'll man the barges, and work the ships, I doubt if we could carry two companies aboard each, with water and rations enough for at least a month at a time. Hmm, an hundred and twenty soldiers, maybe one hundred and sixty? That'd take at least five transports, and . . ." He paused, drawing numbers with a finger on the table top, and trying to do sums in his head. "Boggles my poor mind, it does, sir. A rather ambitious enterprise, in all, which I doubt the Navy would invest in, or the Army would spare a whole battalion for. Sure to be an expensive thing, too, and a rather iffy . . . experiment."

"That is indeed true, Captain Lewrie," Charlton said, obviously disappointed that there was not a quick solution to be had. "I still wish that you could, ah . . . toy with the idea, and write me up what you imagine would be needed. Dream big, sir, and do not let any worries about money, or the availability of soldiers or sailors, daunt you."

"Well, I suppose I could, sir," Lewrie allowed, "after all, it's not as if the Navy has much need of me any longer," he added, letting his grievance see the light of day. "Is this proposal for something specific you have in mind, sir?"

"No *need* for you, after your battle off Galicia? I'd have imagined Admiralty wouldn't have allowed you a *Dog Watch* ashore before they gave you a fresh command!"

"It seems I made the mistake of bein' *too* successful, too lucky, for *some* people, sir," Lewrie almost spat, though trying to make light of his situation. "I'm as in demand as smallpox, or the bloody flux."

"Well, I never heard the like!" Charlton primly replied, with as much outrage as he would allow himself in public. "That smells very much like the petty jealousy of small-minded men. Your patrons?"

"You just may be the most influential of them, sir, among the few I have," Lewrie confessed. "That's why I asked whether this study was leading to something substantial."

"Well, I must admit that I am between active commissions myself at the moment," Charlton told him, "but I've only been on half-pay for six weeks, and fully expect to be called back. To something substantial, as you put it? Not really, not yet, but . . . ," he said, lifting both hands as he shrugged. "If it does lead Admiralty, or Horse Guards, to consider the proposal feasible, you may of course rely on me to demand your services, Captain Lewrie. Who would know more about raiding, and landings from the sea, and assembling an . . . oh, what's the term for it?"

"Amphibious operations, sir?" Lewrie supplied.

"Hah! Exactly!" Charlton exclaimed, slapping a hand on the top of the table. " 'Amphibious' is the word . . . though a damned odd one."

"And how soon might you need it, sir?" Lewrie asked, feeling as if this might actually lead to something.

"Oh, no real rush," Charlton pooh-poohed, "take your time, and put a shiny buff on it, listing how many ships, barges, sailors, and soldiers you think best . . . how many Lieutenants, Mids, and such would be necessary to man the transports with Navy crews, and such."

"Right down to the extra fourty cartridges per man, and the two canteens needed, sir," Lewrie promised, brightening. "By the way, sir, will Mistress Charlton be dining with us tonight?"

"No, I fear not," Charlton said, "she's at our country place at Little Waltham, near Chelmsford, happily preparing a family Christmas, the likes of which we haven't been able to celebrate in some time, with children home from their schools, and all. I do, however, look forward to meeting Dame Lewrie this evening. Some sort of artist, is she not?"

"Quite successful at it, too," Lewrie proudly told him. "If I include some diagrams and drawings of the details, I might prevail upon Jessica to help me in that regard. Shall we say seven this evening?"

"Done, and done!" Admiral Charlton said with another firm slap of the table top.

Lewrie got home, yet again badly in need of a warm-up, shivering as Deavers took his things in the entry hall. A most unfamiliar sound came from the floor above; tinkling, laughing, a feminine shriek or two.

"What the Devil's that?" Lewrie asked.

"Oh, that's your wife and her lady friends, sir," Deavers told him. "They're having themselves a 'cat-lapping'. Tea, scones and such, and some sherry."

Bisquit came trotting down the hall to greet his master, closely followed by his wife's cocker spaniel, both prancing about to welcome him home and get some attention, and Lewrie bent down to pet them and tease.

"'Ey sent down fer some o' yer American whisky, too, sir, then some o' that ginger beer from Jamaica," Tom Dasher imparted with a wink.

"High and merry times," Lewrie commented, feeling a bit irked. He had been looking forward to some warming and affectionate hugs in private, but the company in the drawing room precluded those; he felt proprietary about his limited stash of Kentucky whisky, which Jessica had sampled, once, and thought too powerful; and, lastly, once he had gotten the aforementioned hugs, he was aflame to snatch up paper, pen, and ink, to begin sketching out the proposal that Thomas Charlton had requested, but with company in the house, that was right out, too, and he would have to go abovestairs to make a brief appearance and partake in their silly civilian prattle. He heaved a put-upon sigh and began to trot upstairs, with the dogs at his heels.

"Ah, you're back, my dear!" Jessica gladly exclaimed, extending an arm to draw him to her as he entered the drawing room. "And how was your meeting with your Admiral Charlton?"

"It was wonderful to see him, again, after all these years," he replied, taking her hand and bending down to bestow a cheek kiss. "I told him to come by at seven for supper with us."

"Oh, good," Jessica agreed, "not too late in the evening. And, does his wife come, too?"

"In the country, preparing for Christmas, and a family reunion," Lewrie told her. "Good afternoon, ladies," he said to Jessica's guests, "having a good visit, are you?"

"We are, Sir Alan," one Mrs. Stansfield, and next to Jessica the prettiest of the lot, said. "Join us, do!"

Lewrie was getting used to civilian company, and a distinguished lot they were, Jessica's girlhood friends from St. Anselm's and a private grammar school that the parish ran. Mrs. Stansfield was the wife of a young physician in practice with his father; Mrs. Merton was wed to a mid-level clerk at a private bank; Mrs. Pryor's husband was into steam engines, and perky Mrs. Eaton's husband was a barrister and son of a silk-robed King's Bench practitioner. Lewrie was surprised that he liked them all, though the physician and the barrister could be a tad full of themselves. The fellow he liked the best was Mr. Heiliger, and his round, blonde wife, for the Heiliger family had emigrated from Hamburg ages before and was in the brewery business, with their manufactury up the Thames past Windsor;

their German-style pilseners and pale ales were spritely and delightful, and a nice change from stouts, porters, and dark ales. The Heiligers also had a small contract with the Navy Victualling Board to supply Deptford Dock-yards with small beer.

"I fear we have been making free with some of your exotic American corn whisky, Sir Alan," Mrs. Merton giggled. "So fearsome!"

"A dollop of it in your tea, dearest?" Jessica asked as she poured him a fragile Meissen china cup. "You must be freezing."

"Please do, thankee, love," Lewrie replied, adding sugar and cream to his cup, stirring it up, then finding a seat on one of their delicate side-chairs.

"It is so much more palatable when mixed with ginger beer," Mrs. Pryor commented.

"I'd imagine that almost anything *would* be improved," Lewrie japed, which raised a polite laugh. "Rooski vodka, raw gin . . . paint thinner?"

"My husband and his father are partial to Scottish whisky now and then," Mrs. Eaton told them all, with her glass held close to her cheek, "which I do not find agreeable at all. But, did I dare lace it with ginger beer, or even water, I think they would throw me out of the house, ha ha!"

"A good brandy is heady enough for me, thank you!" Mrs. Merton asserted.

"Ah, but you've never had a Chinese *mao tai* brandy, which makes even fine Franch brandies taste like soapy water," Lewrie imparted, happy to prattle along with them. "It is so alcoholic that one can see the fumes condense inside a snifter, and run back down to the bottom. It has what they call 'legs'. Very tasty, though, for all that."

"Alan was in Calcutta, and Canton, 'tween the wars," Jessica proudly related with a fond smile in his direction, which drew some impressed and curious breaths. "Though I believe you have nothing good to say of Hindoo spirits, do you, dear?"

"They do have something akin to rum," Lewrie said with a grin, "with an admixture of cholera. India has sugar cane, and lots of fermented fruit drinks, but the water there makes most of 'em deadly."

"Cholera!" Mrs. Stansfield tittered. "Jessica has told us of your rather wicked sense of humour, Sir Alan, which, along with your other sterling qualities, makes you the most agreeable of men to whom she could be wed."

Lewrie nodded his thanks for the compliment, casting a beamish look at his wife in silent thanks, but thinking, *The mort hasn't had enough t'drink yet . . . she can still form compound phrases and not tangle her prepositions! Either that, or she's a practiced toper!*

"Your Admiral . . . Charlton, is it?" Mrs, Heiliger asked. "Is he a naval hero like yourself, Sir Alan?"

"He was my son Hugh's Captain at Trafalgar, ma'am," Lewrie told her. "That makes him one of the 'Immortals' as far as I'm concerned. A hero, aye!"

"And were you there, too, Sir Alan?" Mistress Kensington, the lone un-wed spinster of their set, asked. She was a rather mousy and drab young woman whose parents ran the grammar school where she also now taught.

"Ah no, Miss Kensington," Lewrie replied. "I was escorting a pair of horse transports to Cape Town, and only heard about it when we put into Funchal on Madeira for water."

"Is Admiral Charlton in London to accept a new commission?" Jessica asked with the slightest of frown lines in her forehead. "Should we serve champagne tonight?"

"On half-pay like me, darling," Lewrie was quick to assure her, "and looking forward to some time with his wife and children."

"Yet, Jessica told us that the man said something to you about some sort of proposal, Sir Alan," Mrs. Merton enquired, making all of them look at their girlhood friend almost in sympathy. "Dare we ask if it is some plan which might discomfit the French, sir?"

Lewrie put on a deep frown and hunched forward in his chair, then looked right and left as if searching for enemy spies. "I conjure you all, ladies, that what I say will not leave this room."

That caused a rustle of dress material, and some deep breaths.

"His proposal is . . ." Lewrie said in a conspiratorial whisper, "that we lift a frigate with hot-air balloons, sail it to Paris, and crash it on Napoleon's head."

God, they took me seriously! he thought, taking in their looks. He popped his mouth open and struck a clown's pose to assure them that it was a jape, and they broke out in most un-ladylike laughter.

"Oh, Sir Alan," Mrs. Stansfield giggled, "you are such a wag!"

"So, what *was* Admiral Charlton's proposal, love?" Jessica asked after the tea party guests had departed, and they were alone in the drawing room.

"He wanted t'pick my brains about how I managed raids and troop landings in Southern Spain a few years back," Lewrie said, drawing her closer so she could lean her head on his shoulder. "How it might be done with a whole regiment, what it'd take, how many transports, and such. Don't worry, darling, it's all a flummery, all stuff and nonsense. The Navy'd never spare the ships, the Army'd never give up a *good* regiment, and it'd cost far too much money wasted on an experiment. And believe me, dear, 'experiment' is a nasty, scary word to the people who run the Admiralty."

"But, if it isn't in the cards, then why would he ask you to draw it up for him?" Jessica pressed, fretting and burrowing closer to him. "Does he contemplate gaining a command where he would try it . . . and, would he ask for you to help him with it?"

"Far as I know, Charlton's on the beach, the same as me," he explained, his mouth against her fragrant hair. "He's no idea where he's goin' next, and his next commission might take him somewhere he has no chance, or need, for such an expedition. It's all moonshine, but . . . writin' it, and cajolin' *you* to do some illustrations for me to include," he said with a squeeze round her shoulders, "even if I have t'ask pretty please, with sugar on it, hey? Well, it'll keep me occupied through the winter, I expect."

"You are *sure*, Alan," she muttered into his coat.

"As sure as I am of anything, dearest," he told her. "I'm not goin' anywhere. My foes and their patrons'll see to that. The only thing I'm sure of is that I should run downstairs and see Yeovill and ask what we're servin' for supper."

"But, I've already spoken to him, and made all the arrangements, Alan," Jessica objected, wriggling a little in his embrace. "Supper is already planned. Unless you think I can't manage our household," she said with a bit of heat.

"Oh, God, no!" Lewrie hooted. "I'd never say that!"

Not if I know what's good for me, I wouldn't! he thought.

He was rewarded with a poke in the ribs.

"Think I'll go down, anyway," Lewrie said, giving her one last kiss on her forehead before getting to his feet. "The kitchens are the warmest place in the house, and I could still use a thawing out."

"You just want to yarn with your sailors," Jessica accused, but in a playful way as she rose with him.

"Well, there is that," Lewrie cheerfully admitted. "Come on, dogs . . . kitchen treats!"

CHAPTER TWENTY-ONE

s Lewrie made a beginning on Charlton's requested proposal, he found many other things arising to draw him from the endeavour; for it was approaching the Christmas Season, his first with his new wife, in his own house in what seemed ages, and ashore for the first time in his memory. There were letters to be written to people on both sides of the family, to people at sea or who resided too far off to visit, and Lewrie and Jessica occupied each end of the dining table in the warm morning room after breakfasts, scribbling, folding, and sealing with wax and Lewrie's rarely used stamp of his knighthood, and Jessica took secret delight each time she used it.

There was the house to decorate with holly, ivy, pine boughs, and coloured wax candles, gifts to be purchased for immediate family and the Boxing Day gifts for their household servants, the obtaining of which kept Lewrie out on shopping errands that prevented him from doing anything about the proposal.

There were parties to plan, wine and spirits to be laid by for their guests, and a continual round of supper parties at the homes of Jessica's friends to attend, as well as outings to enjoy the holiday festivities. Dramas at the Theatres Royal, the obligatory attendance at a performance of Handel's *Messiah* with Reverend Chenery along, and other symphonies which that

worthy begged off as a bit too scandalous (thank God!). Lewrie even cajoled all the younger couples to cram into several hackney coaches and go
see the quick-change sketch comedies at Pulteney Plumb's theatre, which
all agreed was most amusing.

There were family suppers at Saint Anselm's manse, at Lewrie's, and
even at Sir Hugo's house, where Charley Chenery secretly goggled over
Sir Hugo's vast collection of *risqué* novels and satiric caricatures. And, of
course, there were the requisite Divine Services, to mark the season,
gloomy as they could be, the joy of Twelfth Night parties followed by a
heavy-handed Epiphany service. All that was missing was a really rowdy
Frost Fair on the Thames, which did not ice over quite thick enough to
support the booths, or skating.

At last, round the start of January, Lewrie finally got serious about scribbling his ideas down, feeling happily satisfied that Christmas as a married
man had gone about as sweetly as could be expected, even allowing for
Jessica being "under her moon" for a week before Christmas Eve, and in-
sisting on sleeping in the second furnished bed-chamber.

She had put aside her art work for the holidays, too joyously busy with
all the preparations, and the celebrations that went with it, but was now
intent on a new series of Christmas-inspired paintings involving dogs making off with the goose or the turkey, or children going wide-eyed over a
steaming pudding, and was best left to her own devices whilst inspired,
leaving Lewrie time at the morning room table with paper, pen, ink, and
his rough, first draughts.

The basics were easy enough to explain; barges alongside both beams
of all three masts at once, anti-boarding nets slung down which the soldiers would scramble; equipment lists necessary for a quick raid, not for
camping ashore, or cooking rations. He did some rough and crude sketches
of boats going ashore in line-abreast so all the troops could debark at once,
the transport ships aligned as close to shore as possible and parallel to the
beach, anchored by bow and stern to make a passably useful breakwater
should the seas be up.

But, for the life of him, Lewrie still could not fathom how to land artillery. It would take too long to hoist out of the holds of the transports, too
long to ferry ashore in the barges, and would be almost impossible to land
from the barges, over their bows, without the entire raiding party, soldiers
and sailors, carrying them carriage by carriage, then barrel by barrel, to
be assembled. It might take an entire day!

He dabbled in wild speculation, sketching improbable designs of barges with bow ramps, but never could figure out how sailors could even ply their oars with a fully-assembled field piece sitting amidships of a barge, and the span of the axles, and the wheels, taking up most of the inside beam. Did he include a caisson for powder and shot, it would take *two* barges to land one gun, and half the battalion to man-haul both together, unless there was a way to sling draught horses over the side to swim ashore, and that would take even more transport ships just for them and their fodder, and . . . !

Now I'm sure this'll never be tried! he groaned to himself.

Despite his misgivings, and with Jessica's help with the illustrations, no matter how reluctant she was to further the inanity that, should it look too good it might be deemed feasible, Lewrie ended up with a full proposal to mail to Charlton, and a copy for himself, if even as a folly to be stowed deep out of sight. Besides, there were more important things occupying his time, social obligations that he and Jessica had to attend, and a "hop-master" to visit. It had been years since Lewrie had had reason to tax his dancing skills, but he'd always enjoyed dances, and had secretly thought himself a graceful and practiced man who was quick on his feet, but feared that there was a lot to re-learn of the older figures, and some newer trends to study before he dared take the floor without embarrassing himself, or his new wife!

Roughly a week after Candlemas, Lewrie came home from a local book-seller's with several novels, an assortment of newspapers, and a copy of *The Naval Chronicle*, intending to read the day away in front of the drawing room fire, when Liam Desmond pointed his attention to some mail on the shiny pewter tray on the entrance hall side-board.

"Somthin' from Admiralty, sor," Desmond said with a wink.

"Oh, is there?" Lewrie asked, glancing into the front parlour where Jessica was sketching, hopefully too intent to note the arrival of any let-ters, yet. "Hmm, thankee, Desmond. I'll be abovestairs."

He scooped up the letter from Admiralty, and once relieved of his over-coat, hat, gloves, and walking-stick, hid it between two newspapers, and went upstairs as quickly, and as quietly, as he could.

Ain't even Lady Day yet, so what's this about? he asked himself, thinking that he would have no reason to go to Whitehall to collect his quarterly half-pay 'til the next Quarter Day, which wasn't 'til the 25th of March. Once in the drawing room, he dumped everything on the settee and took a moment to warm his backside before the fire, then fetched the letter, threw himself into a wing-back chair close to the fire, and tore it open.

Good Lord, they really want t'do *it?* he gawped, a quim-hair shy of shouting his reaction out loud. "Please inform the First Secretary of your availability to discuss the proposal you recently submitted to Rear-Admiral Thomas Charlton anent the creation of a landing force suitable for raids against hostile coasts . . . " he read aloud in slowly increasing volume. "Mine arse on a *band-box*! They're really thinkin' of it? Just damn my *eyes*! Whoo!"

"Summat, sir?" Tom Dasher asked from the doorway. "Ya call fer hot coffee?"

"Hot coffee, aye, Dasher, with cream and sugar," Lewrie happily agreed, "and a tot o' rum t'boot!"

He *couldn't* sit still, and had to spring to his feet and pace about the drawing room to re-read the short letter, feeling a rising excitement that it meant that Admiralty would offer him an active commission to implement the plan, hopefully as a Commodore, First Class at last, with a Post-Captain under him to run his new ship, leaving him free to devote all his efforts elsewhere; might it mean a return to a large frigate, or something larger, a Third Rate 74 at last? A Fourth Rate might serve, but there were damned few of those left, and . . . *Get hold of yourself, ye damned fool,* he had to temper himself; *it may only mean the* plan's *approved, and I'm still stuck ashore. Maybe they'll give it to someone in good favour, like Popham. Charlton said that Popham was plannin' t'carry the fight ashore on the North Spanish coast. Someone else'll get all the credit, and I'll still linger about like a beggar in the streets? Just about what I've come to expect, damn their blood! Yet?*

Lewrie had good reason to feel aggrieved, and unfairly, spitefully illused, so much so that he almost dreaded getting his hopes up, only to have them dashed once more, like a stray mutt kicked or shooed off too often to dare lick a hand that offered a beef steak. He took a deep, calming breath and sat back down in front of the fire, waiting on his coffee, and giving the idea a long think. Oh, he could rush to pen a letter in reply at once and whistle up an urchin to deliver it with the promise of a whole shilling . . . but that would look too needy, too desperate, and he had his pride, and his honour to consider. No, he thought; it would be best did he set Admiralty's letter aside for a day, read his papers and *The Naval Chronicle,* perhaps even delve into several first chapters of one of the novels before writing them back a day or two later. Admiralty officials *knew* that he was re-

married, he was mortal-certain, and taking his time to reply might gar-
ner the impression that he was now too busy, or too engaged in civilian
doings and pleasures, to quiver and leap at the possibly-offered bone,
with his tail wagging and many a hungry begging whine!

Aloof but willin', Lewrie determined in his mind, even as he wondered
how he'd inform Jessica of the letter, and calm her fears of his returning
to service with a dismissive laugh or two of how someone else would most-
like get the duty, only using his ideas. *That'd work,* he told himself; *She'd
buy that, I'm sure. After supper tonight, after a bottle of wine or two.*

"Yer coffee, sir," Dasher said as he entered the drawing room with a
tray and the shiny pewter service.

"Ah, thankee, Dasher," Lewrie said, perking up as if nothing was amiss,
and tucking the letter into a breast pocket of his coat. Just as he was spoon-
ing sugar into his coffee, though, Jessica came into the drawing room to
join him, garbed in a paint-spattered smock over her warm winter gown,
with her hair pinned up under a mob-cap.

"Alan, you came in without telling me?" she teased. "Thank you,
Dasher," she added as the lad offered her a cup.

"You looked so intent on what you were doing that I didn't wish t'disturb
you, dearest," Lewrie replied with a dis-arming smile, and a reach cross
the wee table between them to fondly take her hand.

"We've several letters," Jessica said after she'd gotten her coffee to her
taste, and withdrawing several from a pocket of her smock, sorting through
them and naming the writers. "One or two for you, from your son Hugh,
and one from Commander Westcott."

"Didn't notice when I came in," Lewrie lied, "I was too eager to warm
my bones in front of a good fire, and find out what's happening in the
world," he said, gesturing to the papers and books on the settee.

Jessica handed him his letters, then opened one addressed to her and
laughed aloud. "Oh, Lord, my sister-in-law up at Windsor is *enceinte* with
her *third* child, ehm . . . hoping for another boy, and we're invited to come
up some time after Midsummer Day."

"To make goo-goo eyes over the sprout's spit-up, I suppose?" Lewrie
teased.

"You're awful," Jessica said back, chuckling, turning to another of her
letters.

"Mine arse on . . . ahem," Lewrie cried, censoring himself, "old Geoffrey
Westcott's captured himself a brace of Yankee Doodles, filled to the
gunn'ls with grain, tryin' t'sneak into L'Orient! *There's* your pretty penny

or two, aha! Two full-rigged ships, too, sure t'be worth a lot after the Prize Courts get through with 'em."

"American ships, dear?" Jessica asked.

"Their loss for tryin' to smuggle goods into France without clearing their cargoes with England," Lewrie explained. "They sell to us, or else."

"You miss it, don't you, Alan?" Jessica asked him, looking pensive. "The excitement, *and* the prize-money."

"Hmm, I can't pretend that I don't, love," Lewrie confessed. "I made my pile, though, enough so that if I came home from Indian service they'd call me a 'chicken *nabob*'. But, as shy of battle as the French have become, there's little excitement of the chase, or the fight, available any longer. It's all gruelling blockade work for the most part, standin' off-and-on the coast in dirty weather, and a boresome routine, weeks and months on end. Like my eldest, Sewallis, endures, much to his dis-appointment."

"So, you're not tempted to . . . ?" Jessica pressed.

"I may be like an old, worn-out fox hound, my dear," Lewrie said with a wry laugh. "When he hears the master's horn, he may bark and pace the pen, but . . . ," he ended with a wistful shrug.

"Oh, you're not anywhere *close* to old, my love!" Jessica said with a teasing laugh. "And thank God for it," she added with a glance that was nigh lascivious.

Christ, explainin' that letter to her tonight's goin' t'be a bit harder than I thought! Lewrie told himself.

Three mornings later, though, and Lewrie was at Admiralty, in his best dress uniform, For the first time in his memory, he didn't have to bide in the Waiting Room very long, no more than ten minutes, before being summoned upstairs, and not to the offices of the First Secretary as he usually would be received, but down the hall into the Board Room.

They must be considerin' this damned *seriously!* he told himself, awed by the oaken grandeur of the large room, its huge maps of the world on one inner wall, the ornateness of the carved fireplace surround, and the wind vane indicator dial connected to the instrument on the roof. On the long, highly polished board room table a silver coffee service awaited, and a brace of men, one in uniform, sat together at the far end, who rose as he was shown in.

"Aha, Captain Sir Alan Lewrie, welcome, sir," the man in civilian suitings said, "allow me to name myself to you . . . John Croker, the new

First Secretary, and of course you know Captain Robert Middleton, from your time together at Gibraltar. Captain Middleton is now the Commissioner Without Special Functions. Sit you down, Sir Alan. Will you take coffee?"

"Indeed I would, Mister Croker," Lewrie replied, taking a seat near them. "Hallo, Captain Middleton. Good to see you, again."

"Most fortuitously, Captain Middleton was in charge of His Majesty's Dockyards at Gibraltar when you first outfitted a transport and staged your first raids along the Andalusian coast of Spain," Croker said as he "played mother" with the coffee pot and a china cup.

"On the smallest scale allowed, that," Lewrie told Croker, "but Captain Middleton was most helpful at obtaining all I requred, and then some. I take it, sir, that Mistress Middleton is having more luck with her gardens here in England than she did at Gibraltar?"

"We are both amazed at what a sufficient supply of fertiliser will do, Sir Alan," Middleton said with a laugh. "I doubt that there were less than fifty horses, cattle, or sheep at Gibraltar, and the only manure available came with the livestock imported from Tétuan. Oh, aye, her garden and vegetable crops now thrive."

Some more pleasantries were exchanged before they got down to the root of the matter. Folios were spread out, and copies of Lewrie's proposal were gone over, point by point for several hours, requiring food to be sent for, cold sliced beef, mustard, bread and pickles, and some chicken broth, along with a bottle of claret, and more coffee.

There were objections, of course; where would a man-starved Navy get the large crews for the transports' management and the hands needed to row the barges ashore? From a ship of the Third or Fourth Rate just paying off? The Lieutenants from that ship could be appointed as the transports' commanding officers, and senior Midshipmen could be given the temporary rank of Sub-Lieutenant to aid them, with Master's Mates promoted as Sailing Masters, and less-experienced Midshipmen put aboard in their usual subordinate roles.

"And, of course, is a Third Rate sixty-four made the flagship of the force," Lewrie threw in, "she would have a Marine complement that could re-enforce the landings. Seventy private Marines, plus officers, Sergeants, and Corporals, and the flagship given twenty-nine-foot Admiralty pattern barges and cutters, instead of gigs and jolly-boats?"

Two companies of infantry in each transport, about one hundred to one hundred and fifty troops in all, in three-masted ships of over three hundred and fifty tons burthen, their hulls coppered, even if the rate paid per ton for such ships was dearer than that for un-coppered hulls.

"Five of them, sirs, for a full regiment, if such is available," Lewrie told them. "Ten companies. Has anyone asked Horse Guards yet?"

"The ah, proposal has been presented to them," Croker replied with a shrug, "but as of yet we have not heard anything back. They've not given us a flat 'no', so we must assume that your scheme is still being studied. Where did you get the troops the first time round?"

"General Dalrymple offered two companies sent out to fill the gaps in a regiment on Sicily," Lewrie said. "And none too keen on it they were, in the beginning. Their officers, all young'uns fresh from their tailors, had to leave all their luxury goods behind, and subsist on ship's rations . . . though the twice-daily rum issue was welcomed by their troops."

"I doubt you'd get a crack regiment," Captain Middleton said with a sour expression. "One would suppose that our Army regards this as a rather iffy experiment that may come to nothing, or fail outright, so . . . Horse Guards may suggest that we fill the transports with Royal Marines, instead."

"Now that would be a delightful result!" Lewrie enthused. "A Marine has twice the wits of a soldier, and they're used to life at sea to begin with. Do we use Marines, we could place only one hundred aboard each transport, since they come in much smaller complements of fourty, fifty aboard frigates, and give everyone more elbow room, less men per ton."

"Ahem," Croker said, moistening a finger to turn a page. "You included a section about intelligence, Sir Alan. Spies, do you mean?"

"Aye, Mister Croker . . . spies," Lewrie said with a wide smile of delight, thinking that proper English gentlemen shied like frightened horses when anything covert or cloak-and-dagger arose. "At Gibraltar, I had the able assistance of Foreign Office's Secret Branch. A Mister Thomas Mountjoy had cultivated a whole coven of informers among the dis-affected Spanish along the whole coast, from Gibraltar to the French border, with disguised British agents posing as humble fishermen and coastal traders to collect their intelligence, and determine what my targets were."

"Thomas Mountjoy?" Captain Middleton exclaimed in surprise. "I *knew* the fellow, just in passing, mind, but . . . I thought he was just a tradesman with some import and export company! Grew magnificent flowers on his balcony, God only knew how. My wife envied him his 'green thumb'!"

"The very fellow, sir," Lewrie said with a laugh, "and living a public *persona* so mild and in-offensive that everyone was fooled, especially the

French and Spanish spies on Gibraltar . . . the ones that old General Dal-rymple imagined were under every bed, ha ha! His brief was to swing Spain from their allegiance to France, and become *our* allies, and a grand job he did of that.

"There *must* be an intelligence network of spies, informers, and informal scouts," Lewrie insisted, "who can keep track of what the foe is up to, where their troops are garrisoned, what sort of troops, and how well armed they are . . . what sort of things can we raid and burn that'll hurt them the most, with us running the least risk of meeting too much opposition for the few hours we're ashore. We need someone like Mountjoy and his agents to guide us, or we're just thrashing about blind."

"Aha, hmm," Croker mused. "Well."

"And," Lewrie enquired in the sudden silence, "just where would we be using this proposed raiding force, sirs? One would assume that we'd be hitting the French somewhere in Spain, to draw troops away from General Wellesley's army, or . . . the French coasts, either in the Mediterranean or along the Bay of Biscay? In the Baltic? Somewhere in the bloody Balkans?"

"We are not absolutely sure *where* such a force might be used, at the moment, Sir Alan," Croker admitted with spread hands as if to encompass a world map on the table top. "We are met today to discuss the plausibility of forming such a force, only. Where it will go and how big an endeavour it turns out to be . . . and how much it will cost . . . is still to be determined."

Shit! Lewrie thought; *At least they laid on dinner!*

"I for one think it most feasible," Middleton declared. "We've seen the havoc that Sir Alan caused with only one transport, and the upset he gave the Spanish before they changed sides."

"Havoc, chaos, and mayhem," Lewrie japed. "I'm your man for that!"

"I, too, am of a mind to recommend it to the First Lord, Henry Lord Mulgrave," Croker announced with a firm nod. "It's novel, it is daring . . ."

Oh, don't say that! Lewrie thought with a wince; *Those are bad words, sure t'get the plan strangled in its cradle!*

". . . and promises to achieve results far beyond the modest investment made to try it out," Croker concluded.

"Ain't Mulgrave on his way out, though, sir?" Middleton pointed out. "I heard a vague rumour that his health was failing, and that the front-runner for the office might be the Right Honourable Charles Yorke."

"Hmm, that would be bad," Croker opined. "Lord Mulgrave's done good things as First Lord, and he'll be missed if he goes. Yorke may do just as well, but . . . there's nothing official, yet."

"And if Lord Mulgrave steps down, any plan he approves might be shelved 'til the new First Lord finds his feet," Middleton said with a grunt of impatience.

"So it might be months, if ever?" Lewrie wearily asked. "I must confess that I had hopes that my proposal would gain approval *sometime* soon, and that I might be allowed to put it into motion. But, if I must wait . . . well."

"As the author of the plan, and the one officer most familiar with its implementation, you would, of course, be the first choice . . . *if* the experiment is approved, Sir Alan," Croker assured him, a bit too quickly to be taken at face value, or a firm promise.

There's that other *bad word*, Lewrie gloomed; *"experiment"! Mine arse on a* band-box*!*

"Are there any other details we need to thrash out today, sirs?" Lewrie asked, forcing himself to keep a good face on. "If not, then I suppose I should run along home." After a glance out the windows that faced the courtyard and the curtain wall, he added, "Before the evening fog gets so thick a cabman can't find his arse with a lanthorn."

They all rose and shook hands in parting, chuckling mildly over Lewrie's wee witticism, and making vague promises of future meetings as soon as someone in authority gave the plan the go-ahead.

The evening fog was indeed thickening by the time he got home, swirling lazily round the few streetlights along Dover Street, and the lanthorns by the doorways of the houses either side of the street. He was joyously greeted by the dogs, up on their hind legs and pawing at his breeches for pets, and by Chalky, who stood on the entry hall side-board, arching his back, yawning and stretching, and mewing for attention, too. Oddly, there was only one candle lit in the front parlour, and a low fire in need of stoking in the hearth, with Jessica nowhere to be seen.

"Dame Lewrie?" he asked after handing over his hat, boat cloak, and sword.

"She's in the drawing room, sir," Pettus told him.

"Ah, good," Lewrie said, rubbing his chilled hands.

"How did things go at Admiralty, pardon for asking, sir?" Pettus simply had to enquire.

"Still early days, Pettus," Lewrie told him before heading for the stairs. "We're bound ashore awhile longer, it seems."

"Oh, well, sir," Pettus shrugged, though he sounded oddly glad of the news, and Lewrie took note that his wife's pretty young maid, Lucy, and Pettus shared a secret smile as she passed by.

Damme, has he topped her, yet? Lewrie wondered; *They sure look like they're both in cream-pot love! Have t'keep an eye on that.*

Abovestairs, the drawing room was much brighter lit with many candles, and the fire was crackling nicely. Jessica was seated on the settee near a side-table where a four-prong candelabra glowed, reading a novel. She set the book aside as he entered and rose to come embrace him with warmth, and gladly shared a long kiss with him.

"How did it go?" she asked, looking concerned.

"Oh, they loved the plan," Lewrie told her as they walked to the fire and the pair of wing-back chairs. "It's novel, it's daring, and most-like as dead as mutton, 'cause it's still being mulled over by various and sundry, and probably will be 'til *next* Epiphany, with no clue where it'd be sent, *if* it's approved," he wryly carped, telling her of meeting the new First Secretary, and his old acquaintance, Captain Middleton, and whether any decision would have to wait 'til a new First Lord of the Admiralty took up his post.

"So I should not fear that you will be torn away from me anytime soon, Alan?" Jessica said with a fond look, and in evident relief.

"I'm here 'til the cows come home, as the Yankee Doodles say," Lewrie assured her. "If they do approve the plan, there's no guarantee that they'll let the likes of *me* have anything t'do with it, either, so . . . I suppose you're stuck with me."

"Oh, good!" Jessica exclaimed with a laugh. "Exactly what I wanted! Though, I must allow that you do look dashing in your uniform, dear. Forgive me if I say that I hope that you wear it only on special occasions."

"At least it still fits," Lewrie replied, and tossing her a kiss, and thinking that the fit was the only good virtue he'd found.

CHAPTER TWENTY-TWO

*R*iding in the park was a welcome break from winter-bound domesticity, for the February skies had cleared, the temperatures had risen a tad, and there had been no rain or snow three days running, making for a brilliant sunshine day, so bright that the remaining piles of snowfall could barely be looked upon. There was just one snag.

"Jess, my Lord! That's scandalous!" her brother Charley said as her favourite livery stable prad was led out for mounting, saddled with a man's saddle, and she swung up astride!

"And I thank you for your oldest pair of breeches, Charley," she said with a delighted giggle as she flicked the deep skirts of her long, wool riding coat over her boots. "They fit me ever so much better than Alan's. And I won't even mind the tar stains, since no one will ever see them!"

"Ah, Captain, sir?" Charley Chenery pled, looking for aid from that direction. "Can you not do something to spare Jess the embarrassment? The family? Mean to say!"

"Oh, don't ask me, Mister Chenery," Lewrie rejoined with a laugh. "We should know by now that Jessica will go her own way."

"See?" Jessica said, tossing back her head to laugh as well. "*One* man understands me. Let's do the Lady's Mile, and spare all of the prudes on Rotten Row their outrage."

Off they went, first at a sedate walk, then at an easy trot as Jessica felt
more comfortable and sure of herself, her favourite gentle mare tossing
her head as if in on the prank. When Jessica urged them to a canter, her
younger brother lagged back as if to say that he was definitely *not* with
them, and had no part in it. Yet, even on the Lady's Mile through Hyde
Park, they left many slack-jawed people in their wake, and a chorus of,
"Well, I nevers". Young girls getting used to side-saddles craned their
necks to watch, making pleas that they could ride that way, too.

"They say, Alan, that a young lady must have two saddles. One for her
right leg, one for her left," Jessica teased.

"Why? What for?" Lewrie asked, sure he was being twitted.

"So one half of one's fundament doesn't grow too muscular!" she said
with a straight face, then broke out a wide grin and a laugh. "Do imagine
how lop-sided one could look if one didn't!"

"Catch up, Charley," Lewrie called back. "Your sister has a joke to tell
you!"

"I'd rather not," her brother replied, rather snippishly. "Hear it, that is."

"Then you won't get dinner," Jessica threatened, "and Yeovill's prepared all your favourites!"

"Oh, that was glorious!" Jessica exclaimed as they removed hats, coats,
gloves, and mittens in the entry hall. "I cannot wait 'til the Spring, when
we can coach to Anglesgreen and go riding like that every morning."

"Where no one from our parish can see," Charley glumly carped.

"Poor Charley," Jessica cooed, giving her brother a hug. "I've no wish
to shame you, but riding astride is so . . . exhilarating, and so much safer.
Why, I almost dreaded horses after Mother and Father insisted that I ride
the properly expected way. You wouldn't wish me to fall off backwards and
break my neck, would you?" She ruffled his hair to tease him from his pet.

Lewrie left them to it, ready for a warm-up in front of the parlour fire,
but a letter on the side-board caught his eye; blue wax seal, and stamped
with a crowned anchor in a bead wreath. He sucked in an expectant breath,
snatched it off the salver, and went into the front parlour, to the windows
where the light was better.

*Sir, you are Required and Directed to Call upon the First Secretary
at your earliest Convenience tomorrow to discuss the Implementation
of the Plan previously evaluated earlier this month. Admiralty, and*

Horse Guards, have seen fit to grant tentative Approval for a Test Deployment . . .

He would have roared a hearty "Hell, yes!", thrust the letter into the air, and even essayed a gleeful hornpipe dance, but realised how upset he'd make his wife, and that before a good dinner.

Time enough, later, he chid himself, and stuck the letter deep into a breast pocket of his coat before going to the fireplace to warm his hands and backside. *Now, if they'll only let* me *be the one that commands it, please Jesus!* he wished most fervently, looking out to the entry hall where Jessica and her brother were making their amends with some familial joshing. He locked eyes with Jessica and bestowed a wide grin on her, as if amused by their little tiff, but approving of her *outré* riding style. That reassurance lit up her face and made her look as if she would giggle out loud, so pleased with the morning, seemingly so pleased with her life with him.

We'll see how long that lasts, Lewrie thought; *when I tell her that I might be goin' back t'sea.*

He was at Admiralty, suffering the hectoring tones of the old Greenwich Pensioner tiler, just a bit before Eight, and was summoned up barely after checking his boat-cloak, hat, and sword with an usher, with no need to hunt up a seat in the already crowded Waiting Room.

"Ah, good morning, Sir Alan," First Secretary Croker welcomed as Lewrie entered that worthy's offices. "Captain Middleton will be with us in a moment. Coffee, or tea, sir?"

"Coffee, if ye please," Lewrie said, taking a seat before the desk. He had barely sugared and creamed his cup to his taste when they were joined by Middleton who bustled in, yawning.

"Well, then," Crocker began, "we're going to try it on, sirs . . . but, with only three transports, for now. That will still give you six companies of troops. And, if the initial raids prove to be fruitful, then we will expand to the full five transports, and the full battalion of troops. Since Captain Middleton has so much experience lately with the dockyards at Gibraltar, he will be seconded to you, with the authority of a Commissioner of the Admiralty, to smooth the path in fitting out the transports with all the needfuls, and the boats, and crews. You gentlemen will have your choice of such ships as you find suitable to the endeavour."

"Where, sir?" Lewrie asked.

"Portsmouth, to begin with," Croker told him. "There is an old Sixth Rate frigate, the ah . . . *Boston,* returning from the West Indies to pay off and be scrapped for her fittings. Her very name reveals how old she is, what? First in commission in 1762, before the American Revolution. Her Captain will be getting a new command, but her three Lieutenants and her Midshipmen will be available to man the transports you select, and her Master's Mates can serve as Sailing Masters, as we discussed. There will be a welcome rash of promotions for several of *Boston*'s people."

"And the owners and ship husbands will continue to be recompensed monthly, Mister Croker?" Middleton asked. "What, then, will be done with the hired civilian crews, masters, and mates?"

"They will move on to other merchant ships," Croker told him in a sly way. "It is thought necessary to purchase the transports into naval service, outright, much like hired-in merchantmen used as armed auxiliaries. The cost for that necessity is why you are limited to only three, for now, Sir Alan. You, Captain Middleton, are to negotiate the purchase prices, so long as you are not spend-thrift. Keep around nine or ten thousand pounds, with as much of the necessary fittings all found, and Portsmouth Dockyards will make up the needful."

"Armed?" Middleton posed with one brow up.

"Oh, swivels, perhaps, but no carriage guns," Croker allowed. "Muskets, pistols, cutlasses, boarding pikes, and hatchets, that sort of weapons. With troops aboard, there'd be no room for guns, or working them."

"And where after they're ready, Mister Croker?" Lewrie asked.

"Malta and Sicily, though you should keep that under your hats for now," Croker cautioned them. "Admiralty envisions that Southern Italy, round the old Kingdom of Naples and the Two Sicilies, is to be a good proving ground. Our Army has already made some temporary forays there with good results, to the great embarrassment of the French, and with no fears of our losing either Sicily or Malta to *them,* our Army deemed it feasible to free up some garrison troops for your use."

"And is there a strong intelligence network in place there?" Lewrie pressed on. "Can't succeed without one, as I mentioned."

"I *gather* that there is," Croker allowed, though not sounding all too sure upon that head. "The French ruler Napoleon put in place, Marshal Murat, is a perfectly brutal tyrant, quite unlike his predecessor, Joseph Bonaparte, as cruel as a Turkish *satrap,* if I may style him so, and his heavy-handedness has created a great and growing resistance to occupation . . . though there are few reports that the Neapolitans emulate the ferocious activities of the Spanish or Portuguese partisan fighters, yet. Murat's forces are made up mostly of soldiers dragooned into French service from the Germanies, Holland, Piedmont, Savoia, Genoa, Naples, and other Italian duchies, who may not enjoy being conscripted to fight to expand the French Empire, either, so it may be that some of them may be dis-affected, as well."

"Sounds as if they may not be too much of a threat to our raids, then," Middleton commented with a dismissive grunt, more concerned at stirring up a cup of coffee for himself.

"Don't know about that, sir," Lewrie told him. "It never pays t'take the French too lightly. Murat may have just enough Frenchmen on hand to keep the rest in line. Death by firin' squad if they fail, or go sullen? Besides, they may be gettin' their pay regularly, have plenty of food, cheap wine, and biddable peasant girls to lord it over. They may be as happy as clams with their lot. Even the Italian conscripts . . . they're far from home, no one they know can see what devilment they're up to, the locals ain't *their* people, so they can be as beastly as they, and Marshal Murat, want, and get away with it. They just might fight to stay top dogs."

"Hmm, perhaps the intelligence gathered by our, ah . . . people who do such things, would know more about that when the expedition arrives on the scene, Sir Alan," Croker said with an air of distaste.

Turd in your punch-bowl, Lewrie thought, wondering how many other ideal assumptions had been made about this enterprise.

"Ehm, I would suppose, Mister Croker, that the transports represent a squadron, no matter how small," Lewrie went on, hoping that he didn't sound too desperate. "So, might a flagship of some kind be necessary? If so, what kind? You make it sound as if I will be offered the command of the experiment, so . . . ?"

Croker just stared at him.

"I, or any other officer assigned, needs a warship from which to command, plan, direct . . . ," Lewrie added, wondering how grovelling he appeared.

"The transports, and the troops aboard them, are to be considered an adjunct to a larger squadron with the frigates and brig-sloops diverted from their blockading duties, from time to time, to protect and support the landing force whenever it sets out on a raid," Croker patiently laid out as if setting Lewrie up for dis-appointment. "There were no plans to provide a flagship—."

"Whoever it is, sir, can't run the training of the transports' crews from a hotel room at Portsmouth," Lewrie interrupted, "nor can an officer senior enough to command this plan be expected to sail them into action from a corner of a transport's ward room."

"Pursers, sir," Middleton said, making both Lewrie and Croker turn to gawp at him and his *non sequitur.* "It seems to me that Purser's Mates aboard the transports must be supervised by a senior man, aboard a flagship. Then, there's the Army to consider. One would suppose that a Colonel of some sort will be appointed over the troop contingent, and he and his staff will need berthing and planning space, close to the naval officer in command of the raids, 'til the moment that he goes ashore with his men. And, did we not factor in the use of a larger warship's Marines, along with armed seamen, to re-enforce the army? Lewrie is right . . . the officer in charge needs a flagship."

"Well . . . hmm," Croker said, nettled but determined not to let the others see it, drumming fingers atop his desk.

It was rare in Lewrie's naval career that he'd ever stood on his dignity and sense of honour, for the good reason that he doubted if he *had* any, but he'd seen many officers demanding their rights, their due place in a pending action, their claim for a shot at fame and glory, or merely a higher seat above the salt. He reckoned that if he balked at running the operations from the back of a dram shop, Croker would appoint someone else in his place, but, dammit, it was *his* plan, *his* past experiences that another officer didn't possess, and *damned* if he would do it "on the cheap". He would go with the due honours he had earned, or he would turn truculent. Life on half-pay with Jessica was too sweet to leave if he sailed off slighted.

He sat, legs crossed, arms crossed, as Croker delved into some papers on the side of his desk, ready to fume in high dudgeon.

"I think, ah . . . ," Croker slowly said. "Perhaps a sixty-four of the Third Rate *might* be coming available. I've a request here from a Captain Nunnelly of the *Vigilance* asking to be relieved for some medical reason. She's been allowed to quit the Brest blockade, and will be in Portsmouth within a fortnight, as soon as my communication reaches her. Would a sixty-four suit, Sir Alan?"

"Admirably, Mister Croker," Lewrie said, almost letting out a sigh of relief, a breath held too long. "She'd have bags of room for a small army staff, at least seventy Marines aboard, and her eighteen- and twenty-four-pounder guns could provide fire support for the troops sent ashore."

Now, let the other shoe drop, Lewrie thought; *will I have her, or some other senior son of a bitch?*

"Room enough for me, temporarily?" Captain Middleton stuck in. "Hunting up suitable transports and fitting them out, for as long as I am there, is better done from a ship with available rowing boats, than from a room at an inn. Save me the costs of lodging, meals, and boatman's fees."

"Of course, sir," Croker agreed. "Now, Sir Alan, do forgive me for giving you a false impression."

Oh, shit, it'll be someone else! Lewrie thought, appalled.

"It is, after all, your plan in all respects, based upon your own previous experience, and the officer now in command of the squadron to which the endeavour shall be attached requested you to command it. Of course, the duty will be yours."

"Well, alright, then!" Lewrie rejoiced.

"In point of fact, you will serve under Rear Admiral of the Blue, Thomas Charlton," Croker went on. "What is that odd word, serendipity? The odd, co-inciding stroke of fortune? Admiral Charlton was promised a new active commission when we spoke with him before Christmas, and a suggestion was made of several areas of operation, though nothing definite was promised. Then, when he was given his orders to sail for the Mediterranean, and Malta, he broached the subject of your proposal as a way to discomfit the French, which set the study of it in motion. When we recently informed him that the plan would be tentatively approved, he wrote back, saying that he'd trust no one else with putting it into operation. When you coach down to Portsmouth, Sir Alan, make sure you fetch your cabin furnishings along."

"I will, sir, and thank you," Lewrie said, then added, "May I name to you, sir, Midshipman Charles Chenery. He served under me when I had *Sapphire,* and is currently available. I'll be needing someone to clerk for us 'til *Vigilance* comes in, a staff of one 'twixt me and the transport squadron, after."

"You wish him, then you have him, Sir Alan," Croker agreed. "I will have your formal orders written up and sent you by tomorrow's post, both your command of the transports to be selected, and for the *Vigilance,* so you can relieve her present Captain."

"Excellent, Mister Croker!" Lewrie exclaimed, now in much finer takings, now that things were settled.

"Now, let us hope that this . . . experiment in amphibious expeditionary operations proves fruitful, and successful," Croker replied.

"If that's it, I suppose we should bid you good morning, sir," Captain Middleton said, rising.

"And a good morning to you as well, gentlemen," Croker replied, coming from behind his desk to see them to the door, and shake hands. "There is really no tearing rush, but it would be nice if you could be at Portsmouth before the next fortnight's out."

"Within ten days, I'd think, right, Lewrie?" Middleton supposed.

"About that," Lewrie agreed.

"Coach down together, take rooms at the George Inn for a day or two?" Middleton went on.

"'Til our ship comes in, aye," Lewrie agreed.

Will Jessica forgive me for takin' her brother away, too? Lewrie asked himself once ensconced in a hackney on the way home.

She had turned tearful once he'd revealed the letter to her after supper, even with his assurances that it was bad odds that Admiralty would give him the assignment beyond organising it, and once they had retired she had clung to him fiercely, and they had made love as desperately as if that night would be their last. Their earlier-than-usual breakfast had been a frosty affair, though Jessica had tried to put a brave face on it.

What would she make of it, though, now that his orders were official? How dis-appointed, how heartbroken, would he make her? There was so much to do to prepare for his own departure, so much to do to prepare her and their household for his absence; solicitor, bank, and house staff, for he'd be taking Desmond, Deavers, Pettus, Dasher, and Yeovill with him, of course, and new people must be vetted and hired at very short notice.

Lewrie devoutly hoped that it would not prove to be too much for her. For the most part, the wives of naval officers or army officers that he had met over the years had given him the impression that they were capable of continuing life without their husbands, despite their fears, and the unfair burdens placed upon them. His late wife, Caroline, had been self-sufficient, whether in their cottage at Nassau in their early years, or when they'd rented their farm from her uncle Phineas Chiswick at Anglesgreen; there was always too much to see to, whether it was livestock, children, pantry or still room, or the farm workers, to keep her engaged.

Would Jessica find the same engagements, the strength to be that same sort of self-sufficient? he wondered. She was certainly not one of those silly shrinking violets who had nothing to do with her days but read ghastly novels, make idle rounds of tea, cards, and gossip sessions, as Lewrie secretly supposed of her girlhood set of friends. She had her career, her paintings, commissions for portraits and illustrating books, her family, and charitable and social events held at St. Anselm's. And, in the short time she'd had as mistress of their house, Jessica had not been blithely above how it was managed, what would be served at meals, how it was cleaned, how the beds were made, how the fires must be laid, or let even Yeovill be the only one to do the shopping! Surely, she would cope! He was sure of it . . . mostly.

He cautioned himself, though, to not act *too* glad to be going back to sea, 'til his coach at last drove away, at least.

CHAPTER TWENTY-THREE

*I*n the next few days, Lewrie longed for his bachelor days, his years as a widower, for preparing to go to sea as a husband, a homeowner with a domestic staff, was a great deal harder and more complicated!

There was a great deal of bustle, morning to night, long trips to shops and purveyors to stock his wine-cabinet and spirits stores, fresh bed linens to be bought after Jessica declared his old ones too shameful to see the light of day in decent company. New cushions and durable fabric coverings for them had to be obtained and sewn up, for the mice in the stables where his collapsible settee and side-chairs had been stored had dined extremely well. He would have to leave his dining room furnishings in London, for the use of the house, and would have to buy new, or slightly used, in Portsmouth. Yeovill's lists for spices, sauces, and staples was a long one; at least Yeovill would sail with him, since cooking for a small household was too small a stage for him to display his talents.

Pettus, his man for what seemed ages, would not!

"Hey, what? Not goin'?" Lewrie yelped. "Come again?"

"Me and Lucy, sir, Dame Lewrie's maid?" Pettus squirmed in embarrassment. "Her and I, well . . . we love each other, sir, and I'd not leave her now for all the tea in China. Dame Lewrie says, if I can keep your life in order, then I can do the same for the house, and we can stay on as a married couple, so . . ."

"Do Liam's job, like a butler, or major-domo?" Lewrie gawped.

"Liam swears he isn't cut out for it, sir," Pettus told him, "and he'll be happy to be back at sea as your Cox'n. Do you allow me to suggest Deavers as my replacement, sir. He's been asking, since I told him why I'd like to stay, and I've been tutoring him on all that he'd need to know. Before his family went smash in the corn trade, he lived in a middling-fine house, and he thinks you can always find another sailor to be your stroke-oar. If you'll allow me, sir?"

Long before, Pettus had become his cabin steward as an escape from being a lubberly Landsman caught up in the Impress, a gentleman's gentleman thwarted in love and very ill-suited to a rough sailor's life.

What could Lewrie say, but "yes", wish him and Lucy the best, promise a wedding gift, and swear that his house, his household, and his wife's safety would be in the very best of hands, and leave it to Jessica's good sense, and a helping hand from his father, Sir Hugo, and his butler, Harwell, to choose a new cook and a footman, and drop in to make sure that Jessica's way was well-paved as she made the adjustment to living without him.

Jessica . . . well, she put as good a face on it as she could, helping him pack, making sure that he had both sets of keys to all of his sea-chests, that he had enough shirts and underdrawers, both wool, cotton, and silk stockings, saw to his glassware, dinner ware, serving bowls, mugs, cups, tea or coffee service, and shiny pewter articles for his side-board and desk, the candle holders and lanthorns to be hung from the overhead beams were all in good order. During the day, at least.

At night, though, with the servants gone to bed and she and Alan alone, Jessica would allow herself to weep into the pillows, or on his shoulder, tearfully confessing her fears for his safety, the wracking loneliness she'd feel after he was gone, and worrying whether she could cope, after all. Those nights ended in frantic, hotly passionate lovemaking which left them both too spent to fret, or cry.

Lastly, Lewrie suffered yet another defection from his retinue.

"Bisquit is getting rather old, Alan," Jessica said one morning after breakfast, as they took a stroll through the back garden, and gave the dogs their morning romp. Bisquit, Rembrandt, and the wee kitchen ratter/spit turner yelped, postured, dashed, and tousled from one end of the garden to the other, with the terrier, Bully, leaping over both.

"Aye, I suppose he is," Lewrie idly agreed, tossing a stick to see which would grab it first. "I've no idea how old he was when the Mids snuck him aboard."

"He gets along so well with Rembrandt, and Bully," Jessica said, "and you said that he always had to hide below when you held gun drill, or went into action, poor thing. Trembling in fear for hours after?"

"Well, he always seemed to get over it," Lewrie said. "When I got *Sapphire,* he was eager enough t'go back t'sea with us. Couldn't keep him from jumpin' up on the dray waggon, or runnin' along beside the coach. We gave him a chance t'be a farm dog, but . . ."

"I'd think it cruel to take him to sea with you this time, love," Jessica told him. "You may not have noticed, but Bisquit spends more of his time with Bully and Rembrandt than he does us. Yeovill and Dasher tell me that the three of them sleep close together in the kitchens at night, as snug as a litter of puppies. I'd lay you a wager that did he have a voice, he'd ask you to let him stay with his friends."

"Hoy, Bisquit!" Lewrie shouted, and the dog paused in his play for a moment, looked at him, then returned to tail-chasing. "Hmmm . . . you may be right, darling. A new ship, a sixty-four with over five hundred strangers in her crew, and only a few long-time mates, all of them aft . . . I couldn't declare him the *ship's* mascot. *Vigilance* might be teemin' with mascots already, and might not be ready to accept a Johnny Newcome. It may be kinder, though I'll miss him dearly."

"And you are a kind man, dear Alan," Jessica praised, hugging him in thanks, and rewarding him with a peck of a kiss from winter-cold lips.

There was a send-off supper at the Madeira Club which his father attended, along with Sir Malcolm Shockley, the other club founder, then a last night of carousing with Clotworthy Chute and Viscount Draywick, Peter Rushton, during which Lewrie expressed how loath he was to part from his wife after such a short time together.

"Alan, old fellow," Clotworthy had drawled, well into his cups, "I fear you're taking this married thing entirely too seriously!"

"Egads, man!" Peter Rushton had exclaimed, "It may be for the best. Does a fellow stay yoked to his wife too long, the shine wears off, and one becomes a plodding dray horse. A year or two apart, and when you come back, it's honeymoon all over again! The Navy just may be saving your marriage! Then, after that, when she *does* turn lumpish and dull, there's always time for a fresh, young mistress!"

"Mistresses, yes!" Clotworthy had roared. "God bless 'em, they're worth every guinea they screw from us!"

His goods waggon was loaded with all his things, and the chests for Yeovill, Deavers, Liam Desmond, and Tom Dasher, and those worthies would coach down to Portsmouth on their own, but for Deavers who would coach with Lewrie, Captain Middleton, and his manservant. A new cook prepared Lewrie's last breakfast, and a strange new footman served it, very early before dawn, if Lewrie hoped to reach Portsmouth before the dock-yard gates were shut at midnight. It was a glumly quiet and cool affair, a frightened silence broken only by the scrape and tinkle of knives and forks on china, of spoons in cups, as if neither Jessica nor Lewrie dared speak, lest the dam on their emotions give way. They sat close together, close enough to touch hands and twine fingers after the plates had been removed, and a last cup of coffee was poured.

"I would suppose . . . ," Lewrie began to say.

"Captain Middleton's coach is not here, yet, my dear love," his wife said, squeezing his free hand tighter for a moment, then gave out a star-tled, stricken gasp as someone rapped on the front door.

"Speak of the Devil?" Lewrie tried to jape, but it was only her brother, Charles Chenery, who came clumping into the dining room in his best, new Midshipman's uniform with a rather cheerful "Good morrow, all. Is there time for a cup of coffee? It's rather cold and foggy this morning."

"Ready to go to sea, Mister Chenery?" Lewrie asked, as affably as he could, trying to avoid seeing Jessica's shivery frowns.

"Like a race horse, sir, waiting for the starter's gun," Chenery replied, heading for the side-board to serve himself, and snatch up a slice of toast from the bread barge. "Before I forget, sir, I fetched along Jessica's por-trait. Madame Pellatan had it crated up for you."

"Oh, that's grand!" Lewrie exclaimed.

"It's too misty, too romantic to . . . ," Jessica said before raising her nap-kin to her face.

"Now, Jess, don't take on so," her brother tried to cosset her. "As the old saying goes, 'growl we may, but go we must', and it's our duty."

"Oh, just . . . !" Jessica almost spat.

"Your sea-chest is here, Mister Chenery?" Lewrie asked, giving his wife's hand another, reassuring squeeze.

"Aye, sir, in the entry hall," Chenery said, round bites of his toast and sips of coffee. "I brought away a light sea bag with all my essentials 'til we get aboard ship."

"You may just have time to go see Desmond and the lads so they can stow it on the goods waggon, then," Lewrie directed in the formal way of an order. "If you'd be so good."

God, for a loving brother, he's a clueless arse! Lewrie thought.

"Ehm, aye aye, sir," Charley said, catching the hint, and went out to the hallway, still chewing and slurping.

Lewrie tossed his napkin aside and slid his chair back, preparing to rise. "I would suppose it is time, darling. Sorry, but there it is. Half past Five, when Middleton promised to arrive, so . . ."

"Oh, God, Alan, this is hellish!" Jessica declared, her voice breaking, as she sprang to her feet, almost knocking over her chair, and threw herself on him. "Damn the war, damn Napoleon, damn the Navy and . . . I will miss you so horribly, dearest love. Oh, Alan!"

He held her close as if to press his entire length against her, lifting her an inch off her toes, and whispered endearments into her hair, between kisses. "I will miss you painfully, longingly . . . achingly. The last few months of being your husband has been the most wondrous . . . oh, don't weep, darling. Sshh, now. I *will* be back, I swear it. And while I'm gone, I will cherish your memory every moment, the feel of you, your perfume, your laugh, your smile, your teasing."

Damned if I don't mean every word of it, too! he thought.

"Stiff upper lip, now, Jessica," he coaxed. "Let my last image of you be as cheerful as you can manage."

"*That'd* be asking a lot," she said with a wry note to her voice, a brief bark of dry laughter, "but, I'll try." She picked up her discarded napkin to wipe her eyes. "There, better?" she asked, smiling, or trying to.

"Much better," Lewrie whispered. "Did you weep, it'd break my heart. Well," he said, holding her in a looser embrace, "I suppose I should dress, and be ready to greet Captain Middleton."

A last, long and lingering passionate kiss, and they went out arm-in-arm to the entry hall so he could belt on his hanger, swaddle himself in his boat-cloak, clap on his bicorne, and don his gloves. Almost immediately, a coach could be heard rattling to a stop before the stoop, followed a moment later by the rap of the heavy brass door knocker. Jessica took a deep breath and smoothed her fingers over her cheeks, then plastered a smile on her face as Pettus, in his new civilian suitings, opened the door to admit Captain Middleton.

"Ah, ready to go are we, Sir Alan?" Middleton said, right brightly at that ungodly hour. "And Dame Lewrie, my pleasure to make your acquaintance, ma'am, given the unfortunate circumstances, and may I say that Sir Alan is a most fortunate man, to marry such an attractive lady."

"Why, thank you for the compliment, Captain Middleton, even at such an hour," Jessica replied, dipping him a curtsy and smiling back as fetchingly as she could. "Though, I reckon myself the fortunate one."

"And this is my wife's brother, Midshipman Charles Chenery, sir," Lewrie added. "My aide, and temporarily our clerk."

After the introductions were done, Middleton groped under his boat-cloak and coat to draw out his pocket watch.

"Yes, I suppose so," Lewrie said. "Time to depart, my love."

"Give us a hug, Charley," Jessica said. "Be a good lad, follow your Captain's orders, and stay out of trouble. And write, often as you can, to me and Father."

"I will, I promise, Jess," her brother said, sounding as if he was embarrassed by the attention.

"And, farewell, darling," Jessica said, giving Lewrie a last, long embrace, and a more formal kiss, now they were in company.

"Farewell, and *adieu*, love," Lewrie replied. "Take care of the beasts."

All three dogs were there, drawn by the novelty of guests at such an early hour. Bisquit got up on his hind legs to put his paws on Lewrie's chest for some last "wubbies", but he got back down just as quickly, as if he knew that he would be staying.

Out the door and into the coach the men went, waving at the door and at Jessica, who stood in the rectangle of warm light, before the coachman whipped up and rattled them away.

Lewrie shut his eyes and took several sorrowful breaths.

"A hard thing, parting from the wives," Middleton said.

"Damned hard," Lewrie fiercely agreed.

"I was fortunate enough that my dear wife could sail overseas with me when I had the yards at Gibraltar," Middlton went on, "and my new posting is here in London. Well, only a month's separation, before I'm back. Just in time for warmer weather, hah!"

Oh, do stop yer gob! Lewrie thought; *For ha'pence I'd leap from this coach and tell the Navy t'kiss mine arse! This is the hardest parting ever I can remember. Even leavin' Caroline and the children never hurt this bad.*

"Your good lady had a nice basket packed for the trip, sir," Deavers spoke up, opening the straw basket and poking round. "Cold ham, slices of last night's roast, bread, mustard, pickles, berry tarts, and . . . hmph. What's this in there for?" he asked himself as he drew forth a long-dried sprig of rosemary. He held it up in the faint glow of a single candle lant-horn.

"That'd be for me," Lewrie said with a fond smile. "I wore it on my lapel at our wedding."

Damme, does she suspect I'd stray overseas? Lewrie asked himself; *She insists on fidelity, then I'll do my best.*

"Some wee sausages and dry meat strips, too, sirs," Deavers said. And Chalky, in his wicker cage, let out a loud meow to claim those.

CHAPTER TWENTY-FOUR

*B*oat, ahoy!" came a shout from HMS *Boston* as Lewrie's hired boat neared its starboard side, steering for the main channels under her entry-port.

"Aye aye!" a boatman shouted back, showing four fingers aloft to warn *Boston* that a Post-Captain was arriving, and creating a dash to form a side-party, and hunt up the Bosun and Bosun's Mate to pipe him aboard.

The newcomer went up the battens and man-ropes, gaining the deck inboard of the entry-port with a last tug on the cap-rails, and a skip-step as the silver calls tweeted the greeting.

"Captain Sir Alan Lewrie, Baronet," the newcomer announced himself, doffing his new-styled bicorne hat to the flag and the waiting officers.

"Ehm, Lieutenant Fletcher, sir, First Officer," the senior-most officer replied, doffing his own. "I say . . . we've met before, sir . . . I was Agent Afloat for the cavalry transports you escorted to Cape Town five years ago."

"Ah, Mister Fletcher, aye," Lewrie said, smiling and offering his hand. "You were partially lamed, then, as I recall. It is good to see that you've recovered, and gained a proper sea berth."

"Thank you, sir," Fletcher said, grateful to be remembered. "I must ask, sir . . . you are come aboard to command? We all thought the ship is to be stricken." His junior officers looked anxious that the frigate would get a last-second reprieve, too.

"I fear she will be, Mister Fletcher," Lewrie told him, "But I am come to ah, commandeer, as it were. I have need of your services, and those of your officers and Mids, as well as *Boston*'s people. Has your Captain departed yet?"

"He has, sir," Fletcher said, "and left the duty of dis-arming her and landing all stores ashore to me. Us, rather."

"So, his great-cabins are vacant? Good," Lewrie said. "Please summon your officers, Mids, Sailing Master, and Mates there and join me, so I can explain things to them."

"Aye aye, sir," Fletcher said, utterly mystified.

Boston's age was not noticeable on deck, but once aft in the empty great-cabins, the years of hand usage were evident from the wear of the painted canvas deck chequer, and dents in the hull timbers where the guns had been served. It was chilly, too, and depressing.

Fletcher did the introductions to Lieutenants Hoar and Creswell, and Midshipmen Kirby, Thornton, Peagram, Jolliffe, Cotter, and Mabry, Sailing Master Trotter, and his Master's Mates.

"Gentlemen, you have a chance to keep your crew *somewhat* together, continue in active commission, and take part in an experiment that, if successful, will make you pioneers," Lewrie began, "and if successful, will prove to be a grand adventure."

He explained that three troop transports of the proper size were to be bought in and manned by Royal Navy crews, not merchant seamen, each rated as His Majesty's Ship, equipped with six eight-oared twenty-nine-foot barges to carry soldiers ashore, altogether at the same time, then retrieve them when their shore raids were done, and gave them a thumb-nail sketch of how that would be accomplished.

"Each of you gentlemen will command a King's Ship, no matter how humble," Lewrie said to the Lieutenants, "and you older Midshipmen are to be re-rated as Sub-Lieutenants. Mister Trotter, you will be the Sailing Master of one transport, and your Mates will be elevated to Sailing Masters of the other two. Bosun's Mates will be promoted, and new men chosen to be *their* Mates."

That pleased most of them right down to their toes, and Lewrie could discern which Mids would be promoted; there were at least three fellows in their mid to late twenties who had not yet passed the exams before a Post-Captain's Board, and this un-looked-for stroke of luck might give them a leg up to their Lieutenancies.

Rough details were laid out; continue dis-arming *Boston* and sending her shot and powder ashore, but retain enough small arms, cutlasses, and swivel-guns to give the future landing-boat crews the means to defend the beaches; keep at least a month's rations aboard 'til they could go aboard their new ships; choose or find men who could cook rations for the crews and from one hundred to one hundred and fifty soldiers, and *Boston*'s Purser to appoint his Jack-in-the Breadroom, and another man, to serve in that office.

"Your Marine complement has already departed?" Lewrie asked.

"Went ashore yesterday, sir," Lieutenant Fletcher replied.

"Pity," Lewrie said with a scowl. "We could have used them to keep order, and re-enforce the landings. As to who among your present crew would best serve each ship, I leave that decision to you, Mister Fletcher, you and your officers. Just so long as you present me with a going concern aboard each transport, and equal in skills and experince. Anybody from the dockyards gives you any guff, tell them to see me, and I'll wave my orders under their nose, right?"

"Right, sir!" Fletcher said enthusiastically.

"I'm to take command of a sixty-four, the *Vigilance,* as soon as she comes in from the blockade," Lewrie said, "and we can hold the change-in-command ceremony. 'Til then, I'm lodging at the George Inn, so if something comes up, send for me. You will, from time to time, be dealing with a Captain Robert Middleton, who is an Admiralty Commissioner, and I may send my aide, Midshipman Chenery, to you. He speaks with my voice, young'un though he is, so . . . tolerate him, if ye will, hey?" Lewrie cajoled. "Lastly, there are a lot of nay-sayers who don't think this experiment will work, but if you throw yourselves fully into the plan, you can prove a lot of them wrong. If we can pull it off, we could end up with five transports in the squadron, with an entire army battalion to work with, and staging even bigger raids against the French, hurting them where they don't expect. In, rampage, then out and away before they can react, what? In the future I am counting on you all to get us ready to sail, and once at Malta and Sicily, and we get our troops aboard and trained, I trust that we will work ourselves to perfection . . . and have a lot of wicked fun in the doing."

Hmm, that seemed to go well, Lewrie told himself as he landed ashore and turned to look seaward at the *Boston* frigate one more time. With hopes that Captain Middleton had turned up at least one suitable transport ship, he returned to the George Inn for a late-morning pot of coffee and a scone, drenched in jam. He spotted Middleton in the dining room, hailed him, and went to join him.

"How's the hunt going, sir?" Lewrie asked as he sat down, waving for a waiter.

"I have discovered just one ship, Captain Lewrie," Middleton glumly told him. "She's about three hundred tons burthen, full-rigged, and just returned from carrying troops to Lisbon. She's named the *Bristol Lass*, and there's the problem."

"Hmm?" Lewrie commented over the rim of his coffee cup.

"Her owners and ship's husbands are at Bristol, and any offer on her purchase must be done by mail, *if* her owners decide that to sell at the price I may offer is preferable to her continuing being leased at the top rate per ton from the Transport Board. And if they *do* wish to sell, they'll surely haggle, which may take weeks of negotiating back and forth, by mail, before we could get her."

"Oh," Lewrie grunted, wondering why he had imagined that things were going well. "Damn. Nothing else available?"

"Oh, there are nigh sixty merchantmen in port, of which the men at the local Transport Board offices tell me there are at least seven which might suit," Middleton gravelled, looking morose. "Unfortunately, they are all spoken for, and loading to sail in an escorted convoy to Spain and Portugal, so they would not come free 'til they *return* from overseas, d'ye see. Weeks? An entire month?"

"Oh, shit," Lewrie groaned, setting down his cup before the urge to fling it cross the dining room struck him. "Christ, what'll I do with *Boston*'s crew, then? They're available *now*, and if they have to sit idle that long . . . Oh, God! Her scrapping's scheduled, and their pay and rations might be stopped before we could get 'em off her!"

"Lodging them ashore would be impossible," Middleton said. "If we even *found* an empty barracks or warehouse, half of them would take 'leg bail' and desert before we could get them aboard the new ships."

"Or a Captain recruitin' for a new ship doesn't steal 'em," Lewrie griped. "Needs of the Service . . . mine arse on a band-box! And here I thought we had orders, writs t'wave under people's noses to smooth the way! Surely, you can find *something* available in port!"

"Well, I've only been at it one morning," Middleton said, with a touch of "don't blame me!" snarl.

Lewrie's scone arrived, along with a jam pot and a butter dish, and he split it and slathered it, though he had suddenly lost his appetite. "Not every ship in port is hired on by the Transport Board," he suggested. "There must be some available."

"I would imagine there are, Captain Lewrie," Middleton gloomed, as if an inspection of every hull in Portsmouth might be necessary. "How many, though, are fitted for troop berthing, large enough, able to be converted?"

"Blackbirders?" Lewrie tossed out.

"Slave ships?" Middleton scoffed. "Only if you plan to chain the soldiers belowdecks. Most of them are smaller than what we need, can't accommodate your large Navy crews, or berthing space for soldiers who expect to be able to stand upright and walk about. And, most of the slavers work out of Bristol and Liverpool, anyway. Not exactly ready to hand."

"Hmphf!" Lewrie commented. "I suppose it'd take half a year to get the stink out of them, too," and Middleton nodded an amen. Both men had encountered "blackbirders" at sea, and the reek of their West-bound wretched cargo could never be forgotten, and could even put rats and roaches off their feed.

"Insult the Army, too," Middleton agreed.

"Well, what'd they expect, passage in an East Indiaman?" Lewrie scoffed. "Here now, you went aboard this *Bristol Lass*, spoke to her master?"

"Spent a couple of hours at it, aye," Middleton informed him. "She's already fitted out for troops, though her four-man cabins will have to be rebuilt. You know how soldiers are, Lewrie. Give them a cabin, and built-in cots, and they'll knock down the in-board partitions and sleep on the decks, and you show them hammocks, and they'll riot. She's leased at twenty-five shillings per ton per month, and currently under a six-month contract."

"What if we offered thirty shillings per ton?" Lewrie wondered. "Surely that'd be cheaper than buyin' her for nine or ten thousand pounds. That'd be uhm . . ." He had to scribble with a finger on the tablecloth. "That'd be five hundred and twenty-five pounds per month and . . . three thousand one hundred and fifty pounds for a six-month contract. A whole year'd be double that. Christ, why sell for nine or ten thousand, when her owners are makin' 'chink' hand over fist, already!"

"It would save the Navy *some* money," Middleton said, stroking his chin. "What would we do with her Master, Mates, and skimpy crew, though? And if she's only hired, not bought in, she can't exactly be called a King's Ship."

"Don't we have armed transports in service?" Lewrie pressed.

"Aye, we do, with Navy crews, Lieutenants' commands, but they are meant to carry troops independently, or carry troops but act as escorts to the convoy they're in," Middleton pointed out. "The merchant crews are left ashore, able to run the owners' other ships."

"We could *hire* them as armed transports," Lewrie enthused, "but leave the guns off, and that way, they *would* be King's Ships, in name only. Offer the owners a year's contract up front, a note-of-hand by mail or courier, and we just might have ourselves a ship!"

"Good morning, sirs," Midshipman Chenery cheerily said as he entered the dining room, after running some early morning errands for Middleton. "My, the scones look good! Here, waiter?"

"Take half of mine," Lewrie offered, peering at Middleton who was mulling the idea over with several Harumphs and Hmms.

"Thank you kindly, sir!" Chenery said, quickly snatching half a scone and gobbling it down before he could ask for a coffee cup.

"You know, Lewrie, it just might work, at that," Captain Middleton slowly said, at last. "We should go speak with her Master, again, and let you have a look over her."

"No time like the present," Lewrie declared, slapping a hand on the table top.

"Aye, let's go, this instant," Middleton agreed.

"Ye wish t'look over a trooper, Mister Chenery?" Lewrie asked as he rose and dug out his coin-purse to settle the bill.

"Ehm, aye sir," Chenery replied, getting up, too, and casting a longing look at the other half of the scone, and his lack of coffee to wash down what he'd devoured. He was still chewing and probing with his tongue for crumbs as they stepped out into the street.

"*Thirty* shillings a ton?" *Bristol Lass*'s flint-faced Master said after they made the offer. "Bless my soul, thirty? This very minute, sirs? Well, now, that'd be up to the owner and his partners. She is already under hire, only two months into a six-month contract, ye know. And an *armed* transport, ye say? With a *Navy* crew? Ye trying to put me and my Mates out of work?"

"The owner has other ships in which you could serve, sir?" Lewrie asked him.

"Nigh a dozen, all hired by the Transport Board, even cavalry ships," the Master boasted, "and more building all the time. Aye, we could . . .

but we'd have to coach to Bristol or Liverpool to go aboard one of the new ones. Lost wages 'til we do."

"We could offer to pay your fares, with *per diem* to cover meals and lodging atop that, sir," Captain Middleton said to sweeten the pot. "Your sailors . . ."

"Bugger them!" the Master scoffed, looking about to see if any of his crew could hear. "A sorry pack of sulky 'sea lawyers' and lack-wits I'd as soon see the back of. A touch of the lash would keep them on the hop, but I can't, not like you in the Navy, more's the pity. We tell them they're pay-ing off, they'll drink and fuck their money away, and find new ships the next morning, as easy as 'kiss my hand'."

"So, if we continue their pay 'til your owners agree to the new terms, you could remain in port?" Middleton asked him.

"Makes no matter to me," the transport's Master spat. "Even if you of-fer them their pay, half of them would jump ship before the ink's dry on a new contract. We were *supposed* to take a fresh draught of soldiers aboard, but, if you tell the Transport Board Captain that there's a better offer, I'll sit here at anchor 'til the next Epiphany!"

"I will do that this very afternoon, sir," Middleton vowed. "And write your owners with the new offer by the evening post."

"I'd like to take a look below," Lewrie said.

"Why, then, let me give you the ten-pence tour, sir!" her Master almost whooped in glee, leading them below while boasting that *Bristol Lass* was built to be a trooper, that she was only three years old, and her copper-clad hull had been scoured of weed and barnacles only two months ear-lier, and how she could turn a fair ten knots on a quartering wind, made little leeway, and didn't "gripe".

Down either beam of the lower deck there were dog-box-styled cab-ins, rather tiny in all, with room for only four private soldiers each, and as Captain Middleton had described, the deal-and-canvas partitions had been torn down to leave the cabins open to the midships, for air circula-tion most-likely, so the soldiers who would idle and sleep in them would not feel cut off from the world and crammed into a wee, dark box. The foremost and aftermost cabins either side were usually for Corporals and Sergeants, while gentleman officers, subalterns, and Captains would be berthed right aft where the wardroom for Master and Mates lay. As in any ship, the overhead was low, and here where cargo would usually be stowed, there were no gun-ports that could be opened when at anchor to allow cir-culation; only grated hatch covers for air.

Stores, water, salt-meat rations, and other victuals were stored on the orlop, along with whatever the troops needed ashore, but not at sea, like their tentage and camp cook pots.

"Be a tight fit for your sailors," Captain Middleton pointed out as they went up one deck. "And, I'd suppose the galley is big enough to feed sixty or so crewmen, plus soldiers."

"About an hundred and fifty troops, all told," the Master told them, "with officers and servants included. Thick as cockroaches!"

Lewrie puzzled over how many seamen he could assign to the ship, considering that the six rowing barges would require at least fifty-four oarsmen and tillermen, the bulk of the sixty-five or seventy available for each transport from *Boston*'s crew. Once anchored, the nets lowered, and the boats manned, there wouldn't be a complete Harbour Watch still aboard, should anything go smash, the anchor dragged, or the weather suddenly piped up foul!

Christ, can we take the risk? he asked himself; *Now I see the reality of it, can it really work? Looked fine on paper, but . . . I'd be better off back home with Jessica!*

"Will she do, sirs?" the ship's Master asked once they were all back on the weather deck.

"Looks suitable to me, sir," Lewrie grudgingly allowed, loath to sound too eager.

"Splendidly," Captain Middleton declared, though, "and I shall communicate with her owners this very day!"

In for the penny, in for thirty shillings a ton, Lewrie thought as Middleton shook hands on the prospective bargain.

"And if your owners have other ships like her available, I shall contract for them, as well," Middleton said, in happy takings. "Whilst we wait to hear what the owners think of the arrangement, you just may speak with other Masters in port, sir, who have similar ships under contract. Never can tell," he said with a wink to one and all. "The higher fee might tempt them, too!"

CHAPTER TWENTY-FIVE

*T*he situation looked a little brighter two days later, when HMS *Vigilance* entered port, and Lewrie could go aboard her just as soon as she was anchored by bow and stern, and her Bosun and Mates could be rowed round to see that her yards were squared away. Things would have been sunnier had his new ship not looked dowdy and worn down by several months on the blockade of the French Biscay coast. Paint had been scoured nigh to bare wood by the clash of heavy seas and winds, and what little gilt her present Captain had trimmed her with was about gone. As his hired boat came alongside her main channels, Lewrie saw that the man-ropes along her boarding battens had faded dull grey and were slimed with green on the lowermost steps.

It was with some misgivings that Lewrie took hold of the man-ropes, tucked his everyday hanger behind his left leg, and began a careful ascent to the entry-port, and a hurriedly-gathered side-party.

"Captain Alan Lewrie, to see your Captain," he announced after the last notes of the the Bosun's silver call had died away.

"Oh!" *Vigilance*'s First Officer cried in surprise. "Captain Lewrie! Welcome aboard, sir!"

"Mister Farley?" Lewrie exclaimed in like surprise. "I haven't seen you since *Thermopylae* paid off. Good to see you, again."

"And you, sir, ehm . . . ," Farley replied, returning to a proper Sea Officer's sternness. "Captain Nunnelly is aft, sir. We were not told who his relief would be. This way, sir. I am sure he will be delighted to greet you."

"Ill is he, Mister Farley?" Lewrie asked as they crossed the quarterdeck to the door to the great-cabins.

"Barely able to walk, or anything else, sir," Lieutenant Farley told him with a sad shake of his head. "Our Surgeon, Mister Woodbury, says it's the worst rheumatism he's ever seen, but then, Captain Nunnelly has been almost continuously at sea nigh on fourty years, by now."

Damme, just thinkin' of it makes me *feel creaky!* Lewrie told himself, happy that his own thirty years in the Navy hadn't crippled him, too.

"Enter," a voice from within bade after the Marine sentry had bellowed to announce their presence; a weak, weary voice that was followed by a bout of coughing and throat-clearing. Once inside the great-cabins, Lewrie beheld a shambling, bent-over stick-figure of a man who was taking a long time to ease himself to his feet behind his day-cabin desk, a haggard, lined face of a wizened ancient, wincing in pain with every movement. Captain Nunnelly's hair was completely grey, long, and unkempt, fluffed out from the sides of his head as if combing was too much of a bother any longer.

"Lewrie, is it?" Captain Nunnelly rasped. "You're to be my replacement?"

"I am, sir," Lewrie told him, "but this is more of a courtesy call today. I'll not read myself in 'til you've completed your arrangements. No real tearing rush."

"Harumph," Nunnelly replied to that, more of a gargle of phlegm, followed by several more throat-clearing coughs. Nunnelly wiped his mouth with a handkerchief before speaking again. "No matter to me, sir. I cannot get off this ship fast enough. Already halfway packed up and . . . harumph. I'm old, I'm tired, and so crippled that I'll leave her by Bosun's chair, and might need another to leave the boat for the top of the landing stairs. I *tried* to hold out, but . . . ," but he had to break off to cough into his handkerchief for a moment.

"We'll see you safe ashore, sir," Lieutenant Farley promised.

"Coffee, Captain Lewrie?" Nunnelly asked once he was in control of his voice, again, and came round his desk to shake hands, resting his other hand on the desk-top to support himself.

"That would be welcome, sir," Lewrie agreed, though wondering if Nunnelly would make it to the settees and chairs without falling down.

Captain Nunnelly called out to his cabin steward, a man about as ancient as himself, to fetch coffee and the makings, then finally eased himself down into a shabby wing-back chair, wincing and sucking his teeth in pain, even grunting before he got settled.

"Damned fool, me, Captain Lewrie," Nunnelly said with a first glimmer of mirth, which was as quickly gone. "So many years as a Mid, *ages* as a Lieutenant in peace and war, and at least I can boast that I never spent more than a Dog Watch on half-pay 'tween ships. I made Commander and got a sweet Sixth Rate in 1805, and I was feeling the first twinges then, and I *should* have faced the truth, but they offered me promotion to Post-Captain, and *Vigilance*, a year and a half ago, and I couldn't refuse. Too much thick-headed pride, d'ye see. Make the Captain's List, at last, after a whole life spent trying for it?"

"One hopes that time ashore will ease you, sir," Lewrie said as the coffee came.

"Hah!" Captain Nunnelly spat. "*Death* will ease me. Laudanum, brandy, mustard poultices, hot flannels . . . nothing else has worked, harumph." He took a moment to wipe his mouth. "Maybe a summer spent in front of a roaring fire *might* help, but I doubt it. I don't envy you having *Vigilance*, Captain Lewrie, not at all, and God help you."

"Sir?" Lewrie tentatively asked, with a brow up in wonder.

"They say that officers with any sense pray, or curse, to get out of serving on sixty-fours," Nunnelly sourly growled. "They're all old, half worn-out, too slow to act like a frigate, and too weak to stand in the line of battle. The blockade is all they're good for, unless you're in the Far East, and that's a death sentence in itself. Foreign fevers will carry you off before you can get your cabin furnishings settled."

"Oh, I don't know, sir," Lewrie said. "My last ship was a fifty-gunner Fourth Rate, and we accomplished rather a lot with her."

Nunnelly scowled at him as if he'd just spouted moonshine, and Lewrie's lack of sash and star, or his medals made him appear as just one more Post-Captain who would accept *any* active commission at sea as a God-given favour.

"If you say so, Captain Lewrie," Nunnelly said, waving an idle hand in response. "At any rate, I'm halfway packed up, as I said, and intend to leave the ship Wednesday at Eight Bells of the Morning Watch. We can hold the change-in-command then, if you're eager, or you could read yourself in Thursday."

"Whichever *you* prefer, sir," Lewrie offered.

"Hmm, since it is the end of my naval service, I suppose that I might as well go out in style," Nunnelly gruffly allowed, "so, let's make it Wednesday."

"Happy to oblige you, Captain Nunnelly," Lewrie said. He sipped his coffee in silence for a bit, and Nunnelly seemed to feel no need to speak further. "Ehm . . . how does she sail, sir? How fast has she been?"

"On the way to her station, or on the way back to port, she'll turn a fair ten or eleven knots on a beam or quartering wind, and she'll go to windward as well as one can expect. A heavy, steady sea-boat in a gale, too. Fourteen hundred tons. They took her lines off a French sixty-four, though I still think her entry's not as fine as it could be, like the French design them. But, she's stouter and stiffer than any of theirs. The French build too light, with too few frame timbers. I think you can find her , , , tolerable, for as long as you're saddled with her."

Her officers, her petty officers? The experience, or lack of it in her crew? How many pressed men, County Quota Men, or petty criminals dredged up from gaol? Any to be cautious of? Nunnelly was just too soured on her use on blockade work, but he had no real complaints except for the general low morale that that dull duty engendered.

Nunnelly thought that her First Officer, Lieutenant Farley, was able, but too much of a wag. Her Second, Rutland, was fool enough to marry, and moped to be apart so long from his young wife, but a good officer for all that. The Third, Lieutenant Greenleaf, was a bluff and hearty "bulldog", too loud and profane for Nunnelly's taste, and prone to be stricter with the hands when on duty, and her Fourth Officer, Mister Grace, was only twenty-five or so, able, but shy, according to the wardroom, and perhaps a bit too popular among the hands.

"Mister Farley served under me in the *Thermopylae* frigate, sir, and Mister Grace was a volunteer when I was fitting out my first 'Post' ship, the *Proteus* frigate, at the Nore during the Mutiny. I made him a Midshipman and gave him his first 'leg up'," Lewrie related with a happy grin on his face.

"Came up through the hawse-hole, did he?" Nunnelly queried with a grunt. "No wonder his lack of polish, or social poise. Not that *this* ship will ever have call for showing off to her betters, hah!"

"Came from the Nore fisheries, he did, sir," Lewrie told him, "his father and grandfather, too, after their boat foundered. Good men, all."

Nunnelly coughed into his handkerchief again, after nigh strangling on a sip of his coffee. Lewrie wondered where Nunnelly had come from, and what his family's social status was, for it was rare to find people in the Navy who made light of "tarpaulin men" who had risen from the lowest rates; perhaps he was just sour on the whole world after a thankless climb from Midshipman to Post-Captain himself, only to see it snatched away.

"Well, I thank you for the coffee, Captain Nunnelly," Lewrie said as he set his cup and saucer aside at last, and prepared to rise and depart. "I'll be alongside at Six or Seven Bells of the Morning Watch this Wednesday for the change-in-command."

"I'm looking forward to the relief, do believe it, Captain Lewrie," Nunnelly replied. "You'll pardon me if I do not rise or see you to the quarter-deck, sir, but I ache hellish-bad this morning."

"Of course not, sir."

"Need any cabin furniture, Captain Lewrie?" Nunnelly suddenly offered. "Should I leave anything other than the bed-cot behind?"

"Well," Lewrie said, taking a long look round the cabin, and spotting the table in the dining coach. "I did leave my old eight-place dining table and side-board at my house, else I'd deprive my wife, so . . . may I look at yours, sir?"

Captain Nunnelly waved him leave to go inspect it, too busy at hocking up a lung full of phlegm, and Lewrie walked over to find that Nunnelly possessed a twelve-place table and set of chairs, sturdy and non-collapsible, made of highly polished oak, and much too fine to take to sea. The side-board was fine, too, elaborately carved and inlaid with contrasting woods on the doors and top.

"I would admire your dining coach furnishings, sir," Lewrie told him as he returned to the day-cabin. "Name your price."

"Hell's Bells, Captain Lewrie," Nunnelly gargled and wheezed. "I doubt I'll have any need of it six *months* from now. Say, twenty pounds, enough to buy me a good coffin, and pay the parish sexton his fee to plant me, and that'll do."

"Surely you jest, sir," Lewrie gently protested. "Some time to rest, thaw out away from the sea? Twenty pounds is more than fair."

"Done and done, sir. See you Wednesday . . . if I live that long, that is," Nunnelly grumbled.

"Grace," Lieutenant Farley said with a sly grin as he entered the ward-room a deck below. "You'll never guess who's to be Captain Nunnelly's relief."

"Who?" Lieutenant Grace asked, looking up from his hand of cards. "Admiral Hosier come back from ghosting?"

"Who do you recall who likes cats?" Farley gaily hinted.

"No! It can't be!" Grace perked up. "The 'Ram-cat'?"

"Can't abide cats," Lieutenant Greenleaf hooted. "Too damned sneaky for my taste. Gimme hounds, anytime."

"Well, you'd better get used to them, Charles," Farley said in glee, "the last time I served with him, he had two."

"Captain Lewrie, really?" Grace marvelled. "Good Lord!"

"Who?" Greenleaf demanded.

"Captain Sir Alan Lewrie, Baronet," Farley announced, "knighted for bravery, and they call him the 'Ram-cat' for the way he goes after the enemy, too."

"One of the fightingest, most successful scrapers in the whole Royal Navy," Grace told him. "Oh, he's a wonder!"

"An honest-to-God fighting Captain *here*, in *Vigilance*?" Charles Greenleaf scoffed. "What a waste!"

"Just about to say, Tom," Farley said to second Grace's opinion. "I could tell you stories, Charles. Whatever brought Captain Lewrie to *this* old barge, I doubt it's his skill at blockade work that sent him to us. We might just have a shot at seeing some action, for a change."

"Oh, God, please let him take us *anywhere* but back to the coast of France!" Greenleaf exclaimed, looking aloft to the overhead, so piously that even gloomy Lieutenant Rutland laughed.

"Just you wait," Grace assured them, "I'd wager a month's pay we'll be choking on powder smoke before the winter's out. Captain Lewrie will find a way. He always does."

A change-in-command ceremony was something new to Lewrie, all of his previous ships had been newly commissioned or re-commissioned from a spell in-ordinary. Even when he'd replaced *Thermopylae*'s Captain at Great Yarmouth, that man had already left the ship. He showed up at the appointed time in his best dress uniform, wearing the sash and star of the Order of the Bath, both his medals, and his fifty-guinea presentation sword. Captain Nunnelly, though, emerged from his great-cabins in much the same state as when Lewrie had first met him, though someone in his retinue had combed his hair, and his steward and senior servant took him by the elbows to support him, in addition to his walking-stick, making

Lewrie wonder how long the poor fellow had stubbornly endured his af-
fliction.

Afflictions, Lewrie thought as they briefly shook hands, for Nunnelly's
hands were swollen and gnarled, his fingers permanently cupped like tree
roots. When Nunnelly got to the cross-deck hammock stanchions at
the forward edge of the quarterdeck, his voice was still capable of a volume that could reach the bowsprit. He then stood aside while Lewrie
drew out his commission documents and read himself in. A turn, a doff of
his hat, and a formal "Captain Nunnelly, sir, I relieve you," a last shake of
hands, and a call for three cheers to see the old fellow off followed, and
the crew's cheers sounded heartfelt, lasting 'til Nunnelly had suffered the
indignity of being hoisted aloft in the Bosun's chair to be lowered overside, and was deposited like an empty water cask into a waiting boat.
Lewrie stood by the open entry-port, hat raised in salute 'til Nunnelly's
boat was at least two hundred yards off, then turned to his waiting officers and Midshipmen.

"Mister Farley," Lewrie said, "how is the ship laden with stores? Enough
for the next few days, at least?"

"Well, aye sir," Lieutenant Farley replied. "We've salt-meat, bisquit, and
victuals enough for another month and a half, and fresh bread and beef is
coming from the dockyard daily."

"Very good," Lewrie decided. "Once all my dunnage is aboard, do you
pipe 'All Hands' and announce 'Make and Mend' 'til the end of the Second Dog this evening. Tomorrow, we'll start taking on fresh stores. I'll
also want the Master Gunner and his Mates to sort through the powder to
see if any of it's damp. I'll want that replaced."

"Aye, sir," Farley agreed.

"Once we've fully replenished, we'll put the ship Out of Discipline for
a day or two," Lewrie added, turning to a lean fellow in a plain blue coat
he assumed was the Purser, who spoke up before being asked.

"Ship's Purser, sir, Leonard Blundell," he said, doffing a civilian hat.

"I'd admire did you see that the ship's people get their back-pay before
we let 'em dance and rut, sir?" Lewrie asked. "So long as you're ashore . . .
which I assume will be often, Mister Blundell?"

"Aye, sir," the man replied, more formally, wondering if he was being
put on notice. Lewrie rewarded him with a quick little smile, as if to do
that very thing, which was always a good place to start with a civilian
merchant appointed aboard a warship as an independent contractor.

"If you would be so kind as to introduce me to the rest of the officers and Mids, Mister Farley," Lewrie said, and he went down the rows, making his own rough appraisals of Lieutenant Rutland and Lieutenant Greenleaf, then greeting young Lieutenant Grace warmly, and asking of his family, though old HMS *Proteus* had cost the Graces the father and grandfather before her commission had ended.

Lewrie met the Marine officers, a Captain Whitehead and a Lieutenant Webster, asking if they might be eager to do something out of the ordinary off the ship in future, and getting a warm response.

God, but there were a lot of Midshipmen, sixteen of them in all, and over half under the age of twenty, with very little time at sea, in addition to the sprinkling of older young men, and it might take Lewrie weeks to sort their names out properly. He also met the Sailing Master, Francis Wickersham, the Surgeon, Mr. William Woodbury, the Master Gunner, Mr. Carlisle, and found them suitable.

"Gentlemen, I will make no promises yet about what new duties we will be performing, or where *Vigilance* will be going," Lewrie summed up their first encounter, "but I will say, and you may pass this on to the ship's people, but we will definitely *not* be plodding off-and-on in the Bay of Biscay any longer, so everyone should be ready to sharpen his gunnery, musketry, cutlass work, and boat-handling.

"Now, Mister Farley, you may dismiss all hands," Lewrie said to his First Officer, "and I'll fill them in later. My goods are coming alongside, I see, and must be carried to my great-cabins. Upon that head, I need to speak with the Carpenter."

"Mister Gregory, sir, aye," Farley said, "I'll send for him."

"I'll be aft, seein' what I have t'work with," Lewrie told them all, and went to the doors to the great-cabins, being saluted for the first time by his Marine sentry as he entered the yawningly empty cabins, peering round and pacing about, looking for a place to hang his hat from the overhead deck beams.

The sentry announced the presence of the Ship's Carpenter, and a round, red-haired fellow of middle years entered, a shapeless felt hat clasped to his chest.

"Ye sent for me, Cap'm sir?"

"Ah, Mister Gregory!" Lewrie warmly replied. "There's a few things I need done, if you'd be so kind. First, a wider bed-cot, say, thirty inches across? I'm prone to toss and turn. Next, I need a box made, about eight inches deep and two feet on a side, open-topped, for my cat's 'head', with very snug-fitted bottom boards so his sand don't dribble out."

"Bed-cot and a box, aye, sir," Gregory said, nodding sagely.

"Lastly, the door to the stern gallery," Lewrie said, crossing to the rear of the day-cabin and the lazarettes either side of the glazed door. "On warm days, I like to leave it open, and the cat will try to get out and chase sea birds, so . . . I need a door *frame* hung in addition to the real one, with twine strung like a fishing net across it, good and taut, so fresh air can get in, but he can't get out and drown his silly self."

"Bed-cot, a jakes for a cat, and a twine door," Gregory said, screwing up his brows and forehead. "Got it, sir. Be at it directly, sir," he said, bowing himself out with a knuckle to his forehead, in a tangle for a moment with seamen bearing in the first of Lewrie's sea chests, and his folded-up collapsible wood and canvas deck chair.

It would be far too cold and rainy, or snowy, to set it up on the poop deck above, not 'til *Vigilance* had made a goodly Southing nigh to the latitude of Cádiz; for now, the sailor who carried it in raised his brows in puzzlement as if he bore a set of golf clubs.

Familiar faces entered next; his new steward, Michael Deavers, his servant, Tom Dasher, and his cook, Yeovill, fetching Chalky in his wicker cage, and more chests.

"Ah, good," Lewrie said, glad to see them. "You all know where things go, so I'll be out on deck, and out from underfoot, for now. If you've any questions, Deavers, give me a shout."

"Aye aye, sir," Deavers said with an easy grin, "but, between the three of us, I think we can sort it out. Wash-hand stand in the sleeping cabin, plates and glasses in the side-board, and your wine-cabinet to larboard, right, sir?"

"Got it in one, Deavers," Lewrie said, clapping his hat back on and going out to ascend to the poop deck. He took in the view, looking round the vast anchorage, the many warships present, and the flotillas of rowing or sailing boats working between them and the shore. Birds swirled in the hundreds, a fairly insistent wind out of the Sou'east snapped flags and pendants, and made his boat cloak flail about his legs. At least, though, it was a sunny and clear day, a perfect one for reading himself in to take command of a new ship, and for a Winter day, it was not too chilly, and the sun felt good.

An auspicious sign? he wondered. That hopeful idea lasted just as long as he peered outward. When he turned his gaze inboard and saw the length of his new ship, nigh one hundred seventy feet on the range of the deck, and the sight of hundreds of men in her crew, some idling, some scurrying on duties, on her sail-tending gangways and in the ship's waist, Lewrie felt a qualm of trepidation. Most of those sailors, boys, and Marines peeked aft at him, as if wondering what sort of a Captain they'd gotten this time round. He spotted the Carpenter, Mister Gregory, and his crew making their way aft with tools, lumber, and with fresh, white storm canvas with which to line his bed-cot, sharing quick comments with crewmen as they passed, who looked up again in response to those comments, most with quizzical looks on their faces.

A bed-cot almost wide enough for two, a twine door, and a box for a cat's relief? Who *was* this new'un, anyway? he was sure they were asking themselves. Most sailors were mortal-certain that Captains were a quirky lot, but . . . how much quirkiness and eccentricity could they abide? And would it be good for them, in the long run?

Me to know, Lewrie told himself; *and you to find out.*

He paced the poop deck, from the hammock stanchions at the edge overlooking the quarterdeck all the way aft to the flag lockers and the taff-rail lanthorns, back and forth, impatient to at least have his desk set up in the day-cabin. He had only written Jessica twice since they had gotten to Portsmouth, whilst she had written him a brief, one-page letter almost every day, and he felt guilty for being remiss.

CHAPTER TWENTY-SIX

*S*ettled in aboard, are you, Lewrie?" Captain Middleton asked over coffee at the George Inn where he and Midshipman Chenery still resided.

"Quite well, sir, thankee," Lewrie told him.

"I note you haven't hoisted a broad pendant," Middleton added.

"I wasn't authorized one," Lewrie said with a *moue*. "Perhaps if the plan is successful, and we get all five transports allowed us, and a couple of brig-sloops for additional escorts, they *may* make me a Commodore, again, who knows."

"Speaking of transports," Middleton said, all but rubbing his hands in glee, "I've heard from *Bristol Lass*'s owners. Not only will they accept a new contract for her for a full year at thirty shillings a ton per month, they've offered us a second, the *Spaniel*, of the same tonnage and age as the first one, for the same price."

"Why, that's grand, sir!" Lewrie hooted. "*Spaniel*, hey? That will please my wife. She has a cocker. How soon will she get here?"

"They write that she can be in Portsmouth within ten days to a fortnight," Middleton told him. "I've let London know of the arrangement by yesterday morning's post, Admiralty seems delighted that we could hire on *Bristol Lass* at the rate for armed transports, which is cheaper than purchasing them outright, and, they have allowed us to deem them King's

Ships, so that's out of the way. The local Captain of the Transport Board, though, had to be brow-beaten. He had plans for *Bristol Lass*, to take part of a regiment to Lisbon, and I put his nose out of joint, looking for a replacement. God, what a hide-bound lot. I don't envy them their posts, being Commission Sea Officers but desk-bound ashore 'til God knows when, shuffling papers and wrangling contracts for ships they'll never set foot on."

"But, *Bristol Lass* is ours, outright?" Lewrie pressed. "I can shift part of *Boston*'s crew aboard her today, or . . ."

"As soon as the signed contract is in hand, and the lease fee is in their bank account, aye," Middleton told him. "A few days hence, I'd imagine."

"Days!" Lewrie groaned. "The Dockyard Commissioner is on my arse t'get *Boston* to the breakers. He's a schedule to keep, and I'm holdin' him up. I'd imagine that's why he hasn't said when he can even start to build the eight-oared barges we need."

"Well, perhaps if I wave my orders under his nose as an Admiralty Commissioner, I could light a fire under him for you," Middleton offered with a look of sly glee. "What's the use of being one, if you can't use that *august* power, now and then, hey?" he joshed.

"I'd be grateful if you did, sir," Lewrie assured him. "For that matter, I'd like to swap *Vigilance*'s cutters, pinnace, and jolly-boat for three more new barges, too. Well, I'll leave the gig aboard. The Boson, Mister Gore, has t'have *something* to row about in. He'd feel slighted if he couldn't, if only to see to squaring the yards.

"Ehm . . . boarding nets for *Vigilance*, too," Lewrie added, "and an ocean of paint and tar. Fresher gunpowder than what I have, as well. At least a quarter of it shows signs of damp, and . . ."

"We'd best make a list," Middleton said with a dramatic sigh as he opened a folio-sized leather ledger which served as a portable desk, replete with several pencils in some slots in the inside. "Best that we let the dockyard know what's lacking all at once than coming back hat-in-hand day after day. Paint . . . tar . . . boarding nets, heavy duty, and three more twenty-nine-foot eight-oared barges. And?"

"And nigh an hundred other wants, sir," Lewrie admitted as he fumbled in a side pocket for a list of his own. "My Purser, Bosun, and First Officer have already submitted most of the usual items, and this is a rough copy."

"Oh, rough indeed," Middleton said as he squinted at the list, turning it about to decypher the scribbles. "Your clerk writes like a scratching chicken."

"My hand, in haste, sir," Lewrie confessed. "I've been too busy to hire on a new clerk. There's a Midshipman Severance aboard whom I've called upon to help with the usual submissions, he has a good copper-plate hand. Late twenties, a Passed Midshipman, but hasn't had any luck at gaining his Lieutenancy, yet. I'd love to promote him to Sub-Lieutenant and make him my aide, even if I have to pay him extra out of my own pocket."

"Hmm, well . . . why not?" Middleton said after a long moment to mull that over. "Whether Admiralty allowed you to hoist a broad pendant or not, you do need an aide, and a clerk, someone with more authority than young Mister Chenery when dealing with the transports, and the Army contingent, when you get them. Write me a formal request, which I will authorise and forward to Secretary Croker, making it all legal, soon as you're back aboard, and your man will be a Sub-Lieutenant by nightfall."

"Excellent!" Lewrie said, breathing out in relief. "Then, I can enter Chenery on ship's books . . . but still at your disposal 'til we sail, of course."

"Capital," Middleton agreed. "I've found him extremely helpful. Ah, speak of the Devil!" for Midshipman Chenery entered the dining room with some letters in his hand.

"Fresh from the morning post, sirs," Chenery announced, handing over some he'd already sorted out. "Yours, Captain Middleton, and yours, Captain Lewrie. One from my sister," he said with a wink.

"And one from your sister to you, peeking from your pocket, is it, Mister Chenery?" Lewrie teased.

"And one from Father, too, sir," Chenery said, blushing.

"When you write them back, tell them that I've a sudden opening in the Midshipmen's mess, and you will be filling it, sir," Lewrie told him. "Of course, 'til we sail, you'll still help Captain Middleton."

"Glad to hear it, sir!" Chenery all but crowed.

"Now, if we could only find our third transport," Lewrie said wishfully.

"Is there *no* pleasing you, man?" Middleton pretended to object.

"Not 'til I hoist sail and leave the Lizard astern, sir!" Lewrie rejoined with a laugh. "Nor, 'til I'm at Malta, and picking up a battalion of soldiers."

"Very well, Lewrie, I'll see what we can do to please you," Middleton mock-grudgingly said. "Mister Chenery, go fetch your pen and ink. You've a good, legible hand . . . unlike your Captain . . . and I've a fresh list to be copied down."

"And, whilst you're doing that, I'll hire a boat and go aboard *Boston* to speak with Lieutenant Fletcher, and let him know that we'll have the first transport to be manned within a couple of days, and the second to arrive within a fortnight. *That* should get the dockyard off his arse, and mine."

"Very good, sirs," Chenery said, ready to dash up to their lodgings to fetch the writing materials, and a sheaf of good bond paper, though he looked as if he would dally long enough to at least scan his letters from home.

As soon as Midshipman Chenery returned, Lewrie penned his request for Midshipman Severance to be promoted, which he handed over to Captain Middleton, who wrote a letter of approval that instant, then added news of that to his latest letter to be sent to First Secretary Croker.

"There, see how simple that is?" Middleton japed.

That was the easiest thing that Lewrie accomplished that day, for when he went aboard the aged *Boston* frigate, Lieutenant Fletcher told him that the Victualling Board ashore had deemed the ship de-commissioned and had listed her as In-Ordinary, vastly reducing the rations issued to her, barely enough to sustain the tiny crew of Standing Officers carried on idle hulks to maintain them.

Back to *Vigilance* Lewrie went to rouse out his Cox'n and boat crew, dig into his desk for the precious documents authorising all of his requests and needs to further the experiment, then back ashore to the Victualling Board offices to set things right.

"Who's the new stroke-oar?" Lewrie whispered to Desmond as the boat got under way.

"Kitch, sor," Desmond told him in a like mutter.

"'At's me, sir," Kitch spoke up as he plied his oar smoothly and strongly. "Johnny Kitch. I woz Cap'm Nunnelly's stroke-oar, an' Cox 'ere tells me ye'd be needin' a new'un."

"He ain't Pat Furfy, sor, nor Irish neither, but he'll do," Desmond grudgingly allowed. "They all will, I reckon, sor."

Kitch was about as tall as Furfy had been, but was much leaner with wide shoulders and corded muscles. He had long light brown hair clubbed back into an impressive queue, and the face of a professional boxer, battered and rough, right down to a broken nose, but he had a set of merry but sly eyes.

"Right, then," Lewrie said, giving Kitch a approving nod. "I'm sure Desmond told you that you're steppin' into the shoes of a hellish-good man."

"'At 'e did, sir," Kitch replied. "Won't let ya down."

⚓

Mr. Pettijohn of the Victualling Board, once Lewrie was let in to see him after a half-hour's delay, struck Lewrie as a proper "Captain Sharp", the sort of minor tyrant who, if appointed aboard a ship as a Purser, would have to be watched exceedingly carefully lest he not only make the Discharged, Dead, and the deserters "chew tobacco" but list them as needing new issue slops, buckled shoes, and try to make it look as if they'd signed their pay over to him to safeguard.

I wager he got his start by stealin' the coins from his dead mother's eyes, Lewrie thought.

"But, Captain Lewrie," the oily little git lazily drawled with a half-hidden smirk, "*Boston* has been dis-armed and de-commissioned. She is to go to the breakers, and, most importantly, she has no Captain at present, so I do not quite understand why you involve yourself in her victualling."

"I am, as Captain of the *Vigilance* sixty-four, to take under my command the officers and crew of the *Boston*," Lewrie told him, "to man three armed transports, two of which will be under contract with the Transport Board, and will both be in port within a fortnight. The third is being looked for, but it may take another fortnight to find her and issue a contract on her. *Boston*'s people must be supplied in all respects 'til they can leave her and take charge of them."

"I know nothing of that, sir," Pettijohn said with a dismissive laugh, leaning back in his desk chair, toying with a letter opener between both forefingers. "Perhaps you should take it up with the Transport Board."

"*They* do not victual," Lewrie almost hissed. "*You* do, and you must. Not only salt-meat and bisquit but fresh bread and meat, along with water, small beer, and their rum issue, 'til the transports are here."

"Ah, to my knowledge, sir, *Boston* is laid up In-Ordinary 'til she's turned over to the breakers," Pettijohn smirked, "and her crew has been reduced to only the Standing Officer party and their wives and children. I am not authorised to issue more, sir."

"Want me t'row you out to her, sir?" Lewrie spat. "Let you see the nigh two hundred and fifty people still aboard?"

"Are you sure they are not deserters, sir?" Pettijohn replied, "lurking aboard a hulk, looking for handouts?"

"What does your position pay, Mister Pettijohn?" Lewrie asked. "Two hundred pounds a year, at best?"

"Well now, sir . . . ," the uppity clerk began to dispute.

"What's the goin' rate, two thousand pounds for a job where you can reap thousands in jobbery and graft? Declare fit rations as rotten and sell 'em to merchant masters under the table?"

"I think this conversation will prove to be un-fruitful, sir, so I suggest . . . ," Pettijohn snapped, getting heated by Lewrie's true-to-the-mark accusations.

"Think you have patrons who'll save your arse, sir?" Lewrie said with a savage grin as he pulled his orders from a pocket of his coat. "Read that . . . sir."

Grudgingly, frowning, Pettijohn took the document and read it. His eyes blared and his brows shot up as he noted the names associated with the orders: Sir Alan Lewrie, Bt.; First Secretary of the Admiralty John Croker; First Lord of the Admiralty Henry, Lord Mulgrave; and even Secretary of State for War, Lord Castlereagh.

"I, uh . . . ahem," Pettijohn stammered, his ruddy, well-fed visage paling, "I did not know, I wasn't told, Captain Lewrie . . . Sir Alan, my pardons. A fortnight, did you say? Perhaps a whole month? Victuals for two hundred fifty men to be continued 'til *Boston* is officially turned over to the breakers? I will see to it, Sir Alan, I assure you."

"So I, and Admiralty Commissioner Captain Middleton, won't have to write London to lay a complaint, aye," Lewrie said with a sense of satisfaction, snapping his documents back from nerveless fingers.

"No need for that *at all*, Sir Alan," Pettijohn quickly said, sure that his patrons would never lift a finger to help him should he be sacked, and their share of his illicit profits be revealed.

"Then I bid you good day, Mister Pettijohn," Lewrie told him, furling up his documents and putting them back in his pocket, sure that they would have to be shoved into the faces of a great many more petty drudges before he was through.

Patrons, Lewrie mused on his way back to his boat; *can the men who tried t'keep me on half-pay the rest o' my life have clout down to ink-slingin' clerks? They give orders t'block me so the experiment's a failure 'fore it even starts? Oh, horse manure! I'll be lookin' under my mattress for monsters, next!*

After a short row to the shipyard, though, and a confrontation with yet another smugly self-satisfied official, Lewrie began to wonder.

"Bless my soul, Captain Lewrie!" the fellow said with a start. "Twenty-one barges, all at once? Good, seasoned oak, too? See here, sir," he said, sweeping an arm round the long stretch of shoreline where the keels, stems, and stern posts of ships under construction stood like skeletal fingers spearing to heaven, where laborers shaped piles of hull timbers, and saws and hammers and adzes rang. "We've enough on our plate as it is, sir, and seasoned oak is all spoken for. Even new frigates and brig-sloops are being built out of fir, these days, Stockholm pine, New England fir when we can get it. And ship's boats would be the last thing we'd be slapping together."

"So, you've no idea where they could be obtained on short notice?" Lewrie asked, already hot under the collar from his last encounter at the Victualling Board warehouses.

"Not from a Navy dockyard proper, sir," the official said, "the best bet would be to speak to the people who build on speculation 'back of the beach'. That's where most ship's boats get built, anyways, and they'll be fir-built. I expect any of the minor yards would turn hand springs to get such a large contract."

"And you have no twenty-nine-foot barges to hand at present?" Lewrie asked him.

"No more than three or four, that I can recall, sir, and those are waiting for a pair of Second Rates finishing their refit or construction, sorry," the fellow said with a hapless shrug.

"Back of the beach, then," Lewrie said with a heavy sigh.

Another contract for Middleton to wrangle, Lewrie thought as he went back to his waiting cutter, sure that Middleton would feel even more put-upon. At least after his spell in command of HM Dockyards at Gibraltar, he'd know to a penny what each barge should cost, and negotiate a fair price that wouldn't make the Admiralty officials kick furniture.

When he got back to his boat, he noted that there was a carter with kegs of ale aboard, with a row of wood piggins hanging on pegs down one side, lingering quite near, and the itinerant merchant having a slanging match with his men, who, upon his arrival, suddenly found great interest in the shore birds, the clouds, and the boats stirring near the piers.

"Penny a pint, sir," the carter announced as Lewrie drew near. "Right refreshin', even on a cold day, it is!"

Kitch and Desmond looked up at him, both faces innocent as new-born babes, but Desmond gave the game away, licking his lips.

"Penny a pint, is it?" Lewrie asked the carter. "Well, give us eight pints, then," he said, pulling out his wash-leather coin-purse and extracting a shilling. "It's a dry row, back to the ship."

"Thankee and arrah, sor!" Desmond was quick to say, scrambling up to the quay ahead of the rest. "An' a foin gentleman ye are!"

Long ago in his Midshipman days, barely a week aboard his first ship, the old *Ariadne,* Lewrie had sprung for ale for the crew of the cutter he'd taken to the piers, and been bent over a gun to "kiss the gunner's daughter" by the First Officer upon his return.

Think my bottom's safe now, Lewrie told himself, savouring an ale, too; *So long as I don't make a habit of it.*

Once back aboard *Vigilance* and in his great-cabins, Lewrie sent Dasher to pass the word for Midshipman Severance. As he waited, he peered slowly round his cabins to see if there was anything lacking that he must buy in Portsmouth before sailing.

The hull bulkheads and deal-and-canvas partitions which separated the dining coach, day cabin, and bed space had been re-painted in a pale sky blue, with louvres and false wainscots white. The cushions of the settee and chairs, and the cushions atop the lazarette lockers were now upholstered in ruby red storm canvas. His Turkey and Axminster carpets were faded and a tad ratty after years of use, but were still serviceable. The overhead deck beams had been freshly linseeded, and the overhead was now a brighter white, whilst the black-and-white canvas deck chequer had been touched up. Coin silver or bright brass lanthorns hung from the beams, slowly swaying with the faint movement of the ship at anchor. Satisfied, he sat behind his desk, and his eyes were naturally drawn to his wife's portrait, prominently displayed on the forward bulkhead. Despite Jessica's protestations that Madame Berenice Pellatan had rendered her too wispily and romantically, Lewrie thought it a perfect representation of her; bareheaded, with her lustrous nigh-black hair done up, with hints of flattering candlelight to warm her with touches of amber; her dark blue eyes so alive that he could swear they followed him as he paced his cabins; a hint of a wee smile on her lips, and her graceful neck bare to mid-shoulders before the embrace of a white-trimmed blue satin gown.

God, why'd I accept this commission? he chid himself, thinking himself a fool to part from her, all for his wounded pride!

"Midshipman Severance, SAH!" his Marine sentry bawled.

"Enter," Lewrie responded.

"You wished to see me, sir?" Severance said, his hat under his arm as he came to the day-cabin desk.

"Aye, Mister Severance," Lewrie began, finding at least one good thing to come of his frustrating day. "I have spoken with Commissioner Middleton, and he has seen fit to appoint you a Sub-Lieutenant and aide to me."

"Oh! Ah, thank you, sir!" Severance gawped in surprise, "Thanks to Commissioner Middleton, too, sir!"

Severance was an impressive young fellow on his mid-twenties, tall and fit with broad shoulders and lean waist, handsome in a rough-hewn way, with chestnut hair worn short, and green eyes.

"What rumours have circulated are mostly true, sir," Lewrie told him. "We are forming an ad hoc squadron, with three troop transports to sail with us, manned by Navy crews. You will be instrumental to me to liaise with the officers commanding them as they fit out for overseas service, and, as they train themselves and the troops they take aboard for the task we've been assigned."

"I see, sir, I think," Severance said with a cock of his head.

"Clear as mud, now," Lewrie said with a smile, "but all will be made clear once we sail. Midshipman Chenery, the young'un? He's been helping me, but he's barely a year in the Navy, and I need an experienced fellow who can deal with our transports and Army officers, when we obtain them. Think of yourself as a Flag-Lieutenant to a man who's not an Admiral. Of course, I'll still need you to stand in as a clerk when you can, at least 'til that office proves too demanding on your time."

"I'm sure I can handle both, sir," Severance assured him.

"Good. I suppose you should see the First Officer, Mister Farley, and tell him of your promotion," Lewrie said. "The wardroom has a spare Flag-Captain's cabin, which I'm sure Mister Farley will be more than happy to take for his own, leaving a dog-box free. You can shift your berth to the wardroom. And, once at sea, I'm certain that the Sailing Master will be spending more time in his sea cabin than in his space in the wardroom."

"Ehm . . . perhaps you should tell Mister Farley, first, sir," Severance suggested after a quirky look. "He's a grand fellow, but I've found he's not one who likes being blind-sided."

"Ah, perhaps you're right, Mister Severance," Lewrie agreed. "As you depart, pass word for him to come see me."

"And the ship's office off the quarterdeck, sir?" Severance asked.

"That'll be the chart room," Lewrie said. "I found that arrangement worked well on my last ship, handy to officers of the watch."

"Very good, sir," Severance said, "and thank you again for the promotion, and the trust you put in me, sir."

"Good, then," Lewrie said, rising from behind his desk to see him out. "Take joy of it, *and* the stir it'll cause in the cockpit with your *former* fellow Mids. Mister Chenery will take your place, there. I'd admire did you take him aside and let him know all the cautions a newcome needs to know of doings in your old mess."

"That I will, sir!"

A brief meeting with Lieutenant Farley five minutes later, and Lewrie was free of demands for the rest of the afternoon. As Eight Bells of the Day Watch chimed and the First Dog Watch began, he opened a desk drawer to get some of his new bond paper and his steel-nib pen; he'd not yet written Jessica today, but he'd barely gotten past *My dearest darling Wife* when Deavers interrupted.

"Slipped my mind, it did, sir, to brew any more of your cold tea, but would you be wanting anything instead, sir?" Deavers asked.

"Hmm, a mug of ginger beer from that anket I bought'd suit," he told him.

"Aye, sir. I'll fetch it directly," Deavers replied. He was back in a trice with a bright pewter mug. "Ehm, sir."

"Aye, Deavers?" Lewrie asked, just after *How I long to see you.*

"I've been speaking to Yeovill, sir," Deavers hesitantly began, "about the dining arrangements?" and Lewrie laid his pen aside to hear him out. "Well sir, with more officers aboard to dine in, and if we're going to be dealing with Army people come aboard for meetings and such, Yeovill thinks Dasher and I might need some help at-table, and keeping your cabins tidy, sir."

"Another cabin servant?" Lewrie asked, frowning a tad.

"Aye, sir," Deavers replied, a little more at ease since Lewrie had broached the topic. "There's a young fellow we've spoken with that might suit, name of George Turnbow. He's a seventeen-year-old lad, as neat as anything, a waiter from a good chop-house here in Portsmouth who got swept up in the Press, and he knows his way about a fine table. He even showed me how to lay out the forks and such proper, sir. Not that Pettus didn't before."

"Full time, or just when we dine in more company?" Lewrie asked.

"We were thinking full time, sir," Deavers said. "He's no good at 'pulley-hauley', or knows the first thing about what even a Landsman lubber should when it comes to seamanship. We think he needs to be either fish or fowl, sir."

"Well, I suppose," Lewrie said with a sigh, recalling how many servants some Captains had in their retinues. "We'll give him a try and see how he works out."

"Thank you, sir," Deavers said, grinning.

I s'pose I can afford a second servant, Lewrie told himself; *but I still miss Pettus, and Jessop. And Furfy, and a lot of people. And Jessica most of all. Ah, well. Times change.*

He took a deep sip of ginger beer, but in setting the mug down on his desk, he slopped some of its contents on the letter he'd begun.

"Oh, damn," he growled, balling the sheet of paper up and tossing it cross the cabins, which was just fine with Chalky, who sprang from a sprawl on the settee, where he had been "decorating" the red cushions with white fur, and happily began to football it round the day-cabin.

> *My dearest darling Bride,*
> *One of the many Joys of being your adoring Husband, which I miss*
> *terribly, is sitting close with you in pleasant Intimacy as our day*
> *ends, snugly embraced and sharing either our mutual Cares, our*
> *Successes, or our Frustrations. Imagine me holding your hand, at*
> *long Distance, and relate to you what a perfect Hell this day has*
> *been. First off . . .*

CHAPTER TWENTY-SEVEN

*N*o barges available?" Captain Middleton asked, looking as if he would tug at his hair as he faced yet another hurdle, and it was too early in the day, and his breakfast from the kitchens at the George Inn had been, 'til that news, too good to be ruined. "You will put me off my feed, sir," he grumbled.

"And no help in that direction from the Portsmouth Dockyards, either," Lewrie had to tell him, feeling a tad guilty to impart such news, and equally bad news almost every morning.

Lewrie had already had a fine breakfast of his own aboard HMS *Vigilance,* but Middleton's fried eggs, pork chop, and mound of spiced hashed potatoes looked too tempting; he snatched a slice of toast off the bread barge and began to butter it.

"The yard suggested that we'd do best issuing a contract for 'em with one of the independent builders 'back of the beach' somewhere along the hard," Lewrie added hopefully. "What does a fir-built barge cost, d'ye imagine?"

Middleton's response was a heavy sigh, and a hard frown at his plate, with both hands nigh-balled into fists either side of it. "It may be about an hundred pounds for each, labour included."

"We did save on leases versus purchases on the transports, so . . .

wouldn't we be under budget?" Lewrie pointed out. "Assuming that we even *have* a budget, that is."

"It's rather nice, being a Commissioner Without Special Functions, you know, Lewrie," Middleton said. "Well, it *was*. Breeze in at a decent hour, read some paperwork, ring for a pot of tea and the newspapers, go out for a good dinner, then pack up and be home with my feet up before supper. Now, though. Ah, me. Getting you to sea is become akin to the Labours of Hercules."

"Sorry, sir," Lewrie pretended to apologise. "But, this is all new, and nothing we need is in the cupboard, ready to go."

"Oh, I know, dammit," Middleton griped, then took a sip of his coffee and resumed with his knife and fork. Between bites he said, "I was going to inspect a promising ship this morning, and speak with her owners, who keep offices at Southampton, but . . . if you don't mind, we could do that together, *then* prowl about the minor shipbuilders'."

"I am at your *complete* disposal, sir!" Lewrie vowed.

"Just as I seem to be at yours, sir," Middleton said rather frostily. "I think all that can wait 'til I've had my breakfast . . . don't *you*, Captain Lewrie?"

"But of course, sir! *Bon appétit!*"

They took Lewrie's cutter out into the harbour to inspect the ship in question, just come in from the American Chesapeake. Once in the holds, she was still redolent of kegged tobacco, West Indies rum and molasses, and the dry, musty smell of baled cotton which she had just landed. The *Lady Murray* was not fitted out with many small cabins like a trooper, but she was more than big enough belowdecks to carry at least one hundred and fifty soldiers, and constructing the partitions and berths would be an easy task. She was bigger than *Bristol Lass*, too, longer and beamier, and of four hundred and fifty tons. In all respects she would more than suit their purposes, and she was in very good material shape.

"If her owners are amenable, we might contract with the people who'll build our barges to do the conversion, sir," Lewrie suggested, once they were back on deck

"Hmm, we'll see," Middleton said with a shrug as he thumped on her larboard main stays. "If they're amenable, depending on how many other ships the owners have, and how lucrative their trade has been. Cotton, is it?" he asked, looking at a wad of cotton lint that had come loose from a bale.

"I'm told it's the coming thing, sir," Lewrie told him. "Finer feel for bed linens and undergarments. Not as scratchy as flax."

"If you say so," Middleton said, rubbing the boll about in his hand. "Looks more like the dirty lint one finds under furniture, in its natural state. Well, let's go keep our appointment with *Lady Murray*'s owners, and see if thirty shillings a ton will tempt them."

Thirty shillings a ton per month for an entire year *was* tempting to the ship's owners, a dour pack of money-grubbers who struck them as impoverished counting house clerks. The West Indies trade with British colonies was alright, both for exports and returning import cargoes, but the American trade was getting harder and harder to deal with, and Lewrie got an earful about the Royal Navy's enforcement of the embargo of American ships bound for Europe and the predations of man-starved warships stopping and inspecting, then pressing, sailors suspected of being British deserters, even the ones with legitimate declarations of US citizenship, which practices had enraged the Americans and engendered bad feelings and hard dealings in American ports. The motto "Free Trade and Sailor's Rights" was becoming widespread. And even British ships were not immune to being stopped and robbed of crewmen once in Soundings of Great Britain, either!

If the Navy wished to take *Lady Murray* over that instant, it was fine with them, and they would shift her present crew into other ships of their burgeoning line!

Just as soon as they had the money deposited, of course!

"Bless my soul, sirs," the owner of a small yard down-river from Southampton exclaimed after they had put in to begin their search for a boat builder. "You've come to the right place if it's boats you want, and in pudding time, to boot. We've just finished launching a brace of fishing yawls, and I've been at sixes and sevens wondering where and when our next work was coming from. Fancy Admiralty barges, would it be?"

"No sir, standard twenty-nine-foot ship's-boat-type barges," Captain Middleton told the fellow. "Nothing fancy, but sturdy."

"I've a twenty-five-foot cutter here, sirs," the man said as he led them to a six-oared boat on skids, hauled out for a bottom clean. "You look at our workmanship, sirs, you won't find better in any yard on the coast. Tight and snug, and will keep as dry as a stone crock. Sound as the pound should she be run ashore, on sand, shingle, or rock. You said barges, plural, sirs. How many did you have in mind?"

"Twenty-one," Lewrie told him as he and Middleton inspected the cutter, with Middleton making approving "Hmms!"

"All at once, sirs? Well, bless my soul!" the shipbuilder said in wonder, removing his knit cap to scratch his head. "With every man working sunup to sundown, I doubt we could turn out eight a month! Kills my soul to say it, but . . . what do you need so many for?"

"For troop transports," Middleton said, not wishing to give any more clues. "To land soldiers, if docks aren't available."

"Hmm, there's another yard just down-river of mine, sirs," the man said, "decent sort of fellow runs it, and hard as it is to throw him some business, between the two of us we might be able to build at least sixteen or seventeen a month. You're in a tearing rush, sirs?"

"Unfortunately yes," Lewrie said, which earned him a glare from Middleton.

"Well, now," the fellow said, shrewdly rubbing his raspy chin, "I doubt between the two of us that we could turn them out for less than, oh . . . an hundred and fifty pounds apiece, with oars and all."

That made Middleton cough into his fist, and throw another glare in Lewrie's direction. "That, ah . . . seems fair, sir," Middleton said. "Your competitor down-river would be free to begin them at once, do you imagine? With the same fine quality as your yard, sir?"

"If you can row me down there, we could see," the fellow said with a sly smile.

"One hundred and eighty-five pounds per boat, Captain Lewrie," Middleton complained as he and Middleton left the cutter for a moment at the King's Stairs in the naval base hours later. "Three thousand, eight hundred and eighty-five pounds all told. You really don't know *how* to negotiate, do you, sir? Paid full price for everything, haven't you."

"They saw us coming, sir," Lewrie attempted to apologise. "It's a seller's market? Soon as we admitted how soon we need 'em, it was out of our control. Could I dine you aboard to make amends, sir?"

"No no, not tonight," Middleton wearily griped. "I have to write London to tell them how much we're costing them, write up the contract for the boats, look for the contract for *Bristol Lass* and *Spaniel* . . . *and* the contract for *Lady Murray* has to be laid out. I'll be at it 'til Midnight, if I'm lucky."

"Well, I'll take my leave, sir," Lewrie said, "and call upon you in the morning."

"Oh, joy," was Middleton's parting comment.

And, after doffing his hat to Middleton's departing back, and a hapless shrug, Lewrie got back into his cutter and allowed himself to be stroked back to his ship in a rueful silence.

CHAPTER TWENTY-EIGHT

*I*t took an approach to a third minor shipyard for enough of the barges to be constructed as soon as possible. The contracts for the *Bristol Lass* and *Lady Murray* were signed, monies dispersed; the *Spaniel* came in and she was leased, at last. Finally, the crew of the *Boston* could leave her, be split up into lots of ninety men, and go aboard the transports, and *Lady Murray* rang and hummed as cabins for soldiers were built. Indeed, all three transports had their troop accommodations altered, with four-foot-high half-walls between for better ventilation, and lower berths boxed in inches above the deck and uppers three feet over the lowers. Provisions were made for weapons racks down the midships centrelines. It took some further wrangling with the Victualling Board, and that Mr. Pettijohn to provision all three ships with rations for three months, but, finally, all that was wanting were the barges. In the enforced delay, Lewrie had all long guns aboard *Vigilance* notched with rudimentary sights, but no amount of explanation could convince the ship's Master Gunner, his Mates, the Quarter Gunners, or the gun-captains that aiming would ever make a lick of difference. But then, Captains were supposed to be eccentric, and a Captain who had a fish-net door was quirkier than most!

⚓

"Swung by the boat yards yesterday," Captain Middleton said at breakfast at the George Inn as he sawed away at a slab of ham. "They'll be in the
water, soaked, and ready for your sailors to pick up by the end of the week.
They didn't know what colour to paint them, so I went ahead and told them
to make them all dark blue, with white gunn'ls."

"That's *grand* news, sir," Lewrie enthused between slurps of hot coffee
and a large bite of jammed and buttered toast. "And dark blue's a good
choice, do we go in before dawn or a little later. Harder for the foe to see,
and target if they have guns ashore."

"Lewrie," Middleton said after a long moment of chewing. "I've come
to notice a certain, ehm . . . reluctance on the part of the yard, the Victualling Board warehouses, everyone we've dealt with. In the beginning,
I put it down to interrupting the usual bureaucratic laziness, but lately
I have begun to suspect that it's organised. Have you any reason to believe so?"

"I've riled several people in my career, sir," Lewrie freely admitted with
a rueful grin, "and was pretty-much told why I didn't get a ship right away
after *Sapphire* paid off that *their* patrons were a lot more powerful than *my*
patrons. But no, I thought that any lack of co-operation was just sloth, or
the lack of bribes to speed the work."

"Hmm, I must tell you of some correspondence I've had with Mister
Croker in London," Middleton said with a frown, setting aside his utensils. "Early on, some influential people in Parliament, and the Navy, wrote
Admiralty to disparage the project as wasteful of monies and effort . . . to
be expected, of course, if something is too novel.

"Lately, though," Middleton went on, "the critics have grown more specific in the details. They've complained that *Boston*'s crew could be better
employed by turning over entire into a newly-commissioned frigate. That
Vigilance has spent too long idle in port when she could have returned to
the blockade once *another* Captain was appointed into her, and they seem
to know *too* damned much of the costs we've run in hiring the transports
and re-fitting them, the barges, the boarding nets, small arms, I don't know
what-all. As if people here in Portsmouth are in league with these carp-
ers, in their pay, or beholden to them for their positions."

"Anybody write to say that I'm a damned fool who doesn't know what
he's doing?" Lewrie growled in frustration, wondering how far and how
powerful this seeming cabal might be.

"They're much too subtle for an outright denunciation, no," Middleton said with a mirthless grin. "But, if you're ready for sea in all other

respects, I'd suggest that you hoist anchor just as soon as your barges are aboard your ships, before they find a way to scotch the entire project."

"Christ, do they *run* the Navy, or do they imagine that they do?" Lewrie gravelled in growing anger. "How did we get this far along, if some spiteful people who don't really know me from Adam can throw so much delay at me? Can they influence the Army at Malta or Sicily? Deny me decent soldiers, none at all, or a pack of cripples?"

"I envy you, in a way, Lewrie," Middleton said with a touch of worldly-wise amusement, "For a man your age, you've not had many brushes with 'interest', faction, or the politics of grasping men who would've displaced Nelson with their favourites if they could have. It's all a game of power over others, gaining the power to enrich oneself at the expense of others. Good God, that's the essence of Parliament and the Navy, the Army, of trade and government. All this time and you're as innocent as a babe in the woods. Don't you know that there are people who would strip General Wellesley of his command in Spain despite the victories he's won, if they could put their pet *protégé* in his place?"

"I'm clueless, is what you're sayin'," Lewrie said, groaning.

"Wouldn't go that far, no," Middleton said with a shake of his head, as if what he'd said was kindly meant. "Get to sea as soon as you can, Devil take the hindmost, and prove that large-scale raids work. If only to spite your foes."

"Before their spite sinks me?" Lewrie asked with a puckish grin.

"Exactly so, sir," Middleton said. "Exactly so."

It was a fretful time, the few days waiting for the barges to be picked up. At last, rowing boats from *Vigilance* and the transports were despatched up-river towards Southampton, and a flotilla of boats returned to the main anchorage, their old boats and some of the new barges being towed. It took several trips to gather them all in and hoist them onto the cross-deck boat-tier beams, with the main course yards employed as cranes. More rowing took older, smaller, boats to the dockyards to be disposed of, or re-fitted and issued to other ships in need.

Lewrie wanted to hoist the Out of Discipline pendants to give his crews a last-minute rut and some welcome ease, but he began to fear that the in-visible but powerful cabal would discover a ploy to steal it all right out from under him, cancel it at the last minute, or give it to another officer, so, that next Monday, when a favourable slant of wind came from the

Nor'west, he hoisted the signal flags for hoisting anchors and to make sail, and breathed a vast sigh of relief when the signals were struck to order the Execute.

Lewrie had had his last shore supper, a last fresh-water bath, and had mailed his last letters. He had spent the last day in harbour explaining their coming duties to his officers and Midshipmen. Now, as yards inched upwards from their rests, as topmen laid aloft to free canvas, and jibs and stays'ls billowed out to the squeals of blocks, he stood at the forward edge of the poop deck, belly pressed against the iron stanchions and the rolled hammocks, watching his new ship come to life. Sailors tramped round the capstan, and the best bower anchor was barely out of the water, not yet rung up or fished, as *Vigilance* began to shuffle, to stir, and to make a feeble way as the winds filled freed square sails not yet properly braced about or drawn down. But she was moving, making a slow and ponderous knot or two. A glance down showed the helmsmen on the large double wheel on the quarterdeck spinning to and fro, searching for the first of the rudder's bite.

We're really doin' this, he told himself; *we're finally on our way. Do forgive me, Jessica, but I want to do this, even if it means bein' apart from you. It'd be so sweet to stay ashore with you, but, this is what I do, what I'm good at, and so long as there's a war, it's what I have to do!*

"Cast of the log, there!" Lieutenant Farley barked, and a Midshipman at the taffrails tossed the line over, let the line run through his fingers 'til the sand-glass ran out. "Three knots, sir! Three knots!"

"Helm bites, sir!" the senior Quartermaster reported.

"Make for mid-channel down to Saint Helen's Patch," Lewrie said in a louder voice than any he'd used the last few weeks.

"Mid-channel aye, sir!" came the welcome response.

Lewrie looked aft at his transports, all under sail but not yet in line-ahead formation, sails pressed full, though, with frothy mustashios under their forefeet and cutwaters.

Further casts of the log showed five knots, then six and a half, and *Vigilance* began to stride over the sheltered harbour waters, sure and steady, with a reassuring solidity, and Lewrie cocked an ear to hear the first glad seething, chuckling, and burbling of seawaters parting.

A look astern showed Lewrie the beginnings of a churning bridal train of wake. Courses, tops'ls, jibs, and stays'ls were now properly braced round, drawn down to full deployment, and bellied out full of power and drive. Sea birds wheeled between them, trying to perch for a moment before fluttering off in dis-appointment, and astern more of them skimmed over, or dove, into *Vigilance*'s wake for unwary fish, or strands of green slime-weed scrubbed off the hull after weeks of idle growth. The ship moved well, somewhat like *Sapphire* had, but heavier and surer, and Lewrie could feel her beginning a thrum that felt so pleasing to him, right up from her keel to his boot soles.

On a quartering wind, *Vigilance* and her consorts threaded their way through the anchorage at St. Helen's Patch, where many warships, transports, and merchantmen had anchored awaiting a favourable slant of wind to carry them out into the Channel, now rapidly emptying as squadrons, convoys, and escorts hoisted anchors and spread sail, and for a time it was a dicey situation 'til the many other ships gained control of their courses and sorted themselves out.

The Isle of Wight loomed up to starboard, and Bembridge and Foreland came abeam; with fishing smacks and dredgers working close to shore, well alee of the many out-bound ships. As the log showed nine knots, *Vigilance* met the first chops of the Channel, her bluff bows and forefoot smashing into them, parting them, and riding over them with an implacable forward drive, flinging the first sprays of seawater up to the beakhead rails and wetting the feet of the inner, outer, and the flying jibs, and pattering salt rain on the forecastle that made idle ship's boys screech and caper about, forcing them further aft.

Lewrie looked aft at his small convoy, and found them lined up like beads on a string, in line-ahead, with about two wary cables of separation between them, just clearing Ventnor.

"Mister Farley?" Lewrie called out as he descended the windward ladderway to the quarterdeck. "Nine knots is all very fine, and I am delighted that our ship is faster than my old one, but, we're leavin' our transports behind. Once we're a good five miles clear of the Isle of Wight, I'd admire did you take in a bit of sail, come about to West, Sou'west, and let 'em catch up."

"Aye, sir!" Lieutenant Farley cheerfully replied. " 'Tis a pity we're saddled with them, though, sir. On our own we could let her have her head, and really fly."

"I haven't 'flown' since my last frigate," Lewrie reminisced. "That would be fun, indeed, but . . . they're the reason we're here and I'd hate t'lose 'em, after all the trouble it took t'get 'em. A good day to be back at sea, anyway."

"Oh, aye sir, it is!" Lieutenant Farley quickly agreed, eager to shake off the weeks spent lying idle in port.

"Carry on, sir," Lewrie said, taking his rightful place at the windward corner of the quarterdeck, just by the ladderway that led to the waist, and hooked an arm round a mainmast stay. From there, he could look forward down the weather deck and waist to the forecastle belfry and manger, well shaded from fitful, passing sunlight by the four big twenty-nine-foot barges stowed on the cross-deck boat-tier beams. His crew, hundreds and hundreds of strange new faces, sailors, both Able and Ordinary, pressed or volunteered Landsmen, Marines minus their red tunics and hats, and ship's boys dressed any-old-how milled about, some idle, some engaged on last-minute tidying of sheets, halliards, braces, and clew lines into neat coils on the decks, or tidy loops over the pin-rails and fife rails. Many idle men stood on the starboard sail-tending gangway for a last, longing look at England, and Lewrie was forced to take a long look, too, knowing what was in many hearts.

Loss of loved ones, real wives and children, or sweethearts left astern. There would be relief for some who'd fled girls with "belly pleas", debts they couldn't pay, or gaol sentences. Older, more experienced tars had done it all many times, but the Johnny Newcomes, the volunteer Landsmen and the pressed men and Quota Men rounded up by the counties to fulfill their obligations, or the gaol sweepings who took the Joining Bounty, would be "all asea", unsure of anything beyond the next rum issue or call to stand watch, dreading the separation and the chance that battle, disease, or dumb accidents would deny them a sight of their homeland once it fell below the horizon for the last time.

All of them, at one time or another, would turn and look aft to the quarterdeck, and at their strange new Captain, wondering if this new fellow would be a tyrant, quick with the lash, reckless, or a poor seaman who'd find a way to get them maimed, crippled, or killed.

"Bosun Gore!" Farley bawled of a sudden. "Pipe hands to stations to alter course and take in some sail!"

"Hands to the braces and foresheets! Topmen, trice up and lay aloft," Bosun Gore yelled in a deep *basso* after his pipe had shrilled.

"One reef in the fore course might just do, Mister Farley," Lewrie suggested, turning his attention in-board. "If not, we'll take a second."

"Aye, sir," Farley replied. "Mister Upchurch, hoist signal to the transports. Make, Alter . . . West, Sou'west. In line astern."

"Aye, sir," that Midshipman said, dashing for the poop deck and the flag lockers right aft, and Lewrie tried to fix a name and a face in his memory. There were seven of the sixteen Midshipmen aboard who were older, nineteen to twenty-five, and Lewrie *thought* he'd memorised them by now; the other nine lads were fourteen to eighteen, but except for Charles Chenery and a wee'un of only fourteen named Page, the rest were so many blanks, yet.

Think, *ye shitten fool!* Lewrie chid himself; *Surely, I ain't so old that I can't remember. Be losin' my hat, next! Or use it for the shavin' bowl.*

He put it down to the many hours of each day he'd spent ashore, away from the ship, depending on his officers to see to the provisioning, discipline, the painting and maintenance whilst he was fighting tooth and nail for scraps from the dockyard authorities. Once at sea, with daily familiarity, he was sure he'd do better.

Vigilance came about, her jib-boom and bowsprit sweeping cross a stretch of sea, putting the Undercliff and the light at St. Catherine's Point on her starboard quarter. With one reef taken in the fore course, she seemed to sag a bit, to slug through the Channel chops with a little less exuberance, and Midshipman Monkton, a lad of twenty, was sent for a fresh cast of the log.

Monkton! Straw hair and pimples the size of pistol shot! Lewrie prompted his memory; *He ought t'wash more often.*

"Steady on West,Sou'west, sir," Farley reported, "and we make only eight knots."

"Good enough, Mister Farley," Lewrie said with a grunt of satisfaction. "And if our transports can't keep up with that, I'll put 'em all on bread and water."

"Ehm, time to set the Forenoon Watch, sir," Farley reminded him.

"Very well, sir, do so," Lewrie agreed. "I'll be puttering about for a while. You and Mister Rutland have the deck."

"Aye aye, sir," the First Officer said with a nod, and a glance at his replacement who was waiting at the top of the larboard ladderway from the waist.

Rutland, Lewrie thought; *strange man. Dark as a "Black Irish".*

The Second Officer was tall, lean, with dark hair and eyes, and a well-tanned sailor's complexion. He must not have shaved in the last two days, for his stubble was so dark it appeared that he'd shoved his face into ashes, coal dust, or black gunpowder. Rutland was the gloomy one in the wardroom, as opposed to the cheerful First Officer, Mr. Farley, the loud and irreverent Third Officer, Lieutenant Greenleaf, or the sweet-natured and earnest Lieutenant Grace. He looked to be in his early thirties, was married with one child, and neither he nor his wife could afford to travel to see each other whilst *Vigilance* was in port, so he probably had a reason to be glum.

Lewrie exchanged a nod with him, then went down the ladderway to the waist, approaching the Bosun, Mr. Gore, so they could stroll forward to make an informal inspection of the neatness the crew had attempted to put right after altering course.

Lewrie and Gore made their way up to the forecastle, past the galley stove chimney, the thick base of the foremast, the forward fife rails to where they could stand and look down on the bowsprit and the knightheads, the beakhead rails, and the seats of ease.

"How's our lion, Mister Gore?" Lewrie asked of the figurehead.

"Peerin' fit to bust, Cap'm sir," Gore said with a grin.

First, Second, and some Third Rate ships of the line, with famous classical names, had ornate carved and painted figureheads tailored to those names, but 64s and Fourth Rate 50s usually got a variation of a crowned lion, some so distinctive, though, that sailors could name an espied ship by the sight of them. HMS *Vigilance* wore a crowned lion, crouched on its haunches, tufted tail wrapped round its left front paw, with the right paw held just above its yellow-and-white-painted eyes, as if to shade them for greater sight, and the buff-painted lion with its dark brown mane had been shaped as if the beast was leaning forwards, ready to spring, with its mouth and lips curled into a snarl of warning, with long white fangs and red tongue rendered in a permanent roar of defiance. The only gilt was on the long-spiked crown, all newly touched up and ready to prowl the world's oceans for prey.

"He's scary-enough lookin' for me," Lewrie said with a laugh, "and certain to make the French wet their trousers."

"Lookin' forward t'that, sir," the Bosun said. "Spent too damn long on the blockade, I almost forgot what a good ship's for."

"Tomorrow morning we'll exercise with the great-guns," Lewrie promised. "And remind our people what a good ship's for. I'll be aft. Carry on, Mister Gore."

"Aye aye, sir!"

Lewrie went down a ladderway to the waist and took a peek into the manger, just to see how his rabbits and quail were doing. He'd been advised long ago to carry them aboard for they bred fast and made a good small supper for the evenings when he'd dine alone. It appeared that they were thriving, but . . . his cabin servant, Tom Dasher, was squatting on the deck with a bunny in his lap, stroking it and cooing to it.

"Oh, sorry, sir," Dasher said, holding the rabbit to his chest. "Just checkin' on 'em. Fond, wee things, they is, sir. Never seen 'em where I grew up."

Oh, God, he's got a pet! Lewrie thought.

"Buck or doe, Dasher?" he asked.

"Ehm, I dunno, sir. 'Ow d'ye tell?" Dasher said with a puzzled look, holding the bunny up to inspect its hindquarters.

"Either way, we'll need at least one of each so they can keep on makin' bunnies," Lewrie told him. "Edible bunnies, for my table?"

Dasher clutched his bunny even closer,

"Whichever it is, Dasher, put a hank o' riband round its neck," Lewrie instructed, "so we'll know to not skin it and cook it."

"Oh, aye sir, thank ya, sir!" Dasher said, all but crying out in sudden relief. "I'll do that directly, sir!"

Christ, the cares of a Post-Captain! Lewrie told himself with a silent laugh as he made his way aft; *He'll be havin' it in my cabins, next, for Chalky t'play with!*

BOOK FOUR

Ne defice coeptis.
Falter not in what thou hast begun.
— VALERIUS FLACCUS, *ARGONAUTICA,*
BOOK II, LINE 596

CHAPTER TWENTY-NINE

A damned eerie-looking place," Lieutenant Greenleaf commented as he took a long moment to gaze about Malta's Valletta Harbour. "Nothing but rock and stone fortresses as far as the eye can see."

"Hemmed in," Lieutenant Grace pointed out. "Dry as a bone and not one green thing in sight."

"Just going to say," the First Officer, Lieutenant Farley, chimed in. "Arabic-looking. Like Morocco, or Egypt."

"A little bit of everything, Mister Farley," the Sailing Master, Mr. Wickersham, contributed. "Arabs, Greeks, Romans, Sicilians, the Normans, the Spanish, now us? Who *hasn't* owned the place over the years? Crusader fortresses all round the harbour were likely build on top of Roman forts, to keep the Carthaginians out."

"Well, let's hope that everyone's left their mark on the local cuisine, hey, Rutland?" Farley joshed.

"Rather have a beef steak, but God knows how they keep cattle on such a dry and rocky island," Lieutenant Rutland laconically carped. "It'll mostlike be goat, or salt beef."

"Nothing wrong with goat," Lieutenant Greenleaf said with a laugh. "A tasty kid? Beats cold, boiled mutton, any day."

"Shore liberty," Lieutenant Grace suggested of a sudden, and all turned to look up to the poop deck, where the Captain stood with a telescope to one eye for his own survey of Valletta.

"Since I deprived everyone of liberty at Gibraltar, we most certainly will allow the people liberty here," Lewrie assured them as he lowered his glass and compacted the tubes, satisfied with his viewing. "We worked 'em hard enough on the way here, and they deserve it. You can pass word of it . . . after we've re-provisioned."

As soon as *Vigilance* and her consorts had stood out of the Channel into the open Atlantic and turned South down the Bay of Biscay, the days on-passage had been filled with drills; striking then erecting topmasts, reefing then making sail, so Lewrie could judge the efficiency and skill of his new crew. Cutlass or boarding pike drills were held each afternoon, and exercise on the great guns was piped almost every morning for at least one hour.

From his first raw days as a Midshipman, Lewrie had found that gunnery was almost his sole joy of shipboard life, the most exciting part of a drab existence, and his former superiors had drummed exacting standards into him. Months on dull blockade duties, with more effort required to merely keep the sea in winter gales, had blunted *Vigilance*'s gun crews' skills, and, when looking over the Lieutenants' journals, Lewrie had found that Captain Nunnelly had used very little shot and powder, even less than the parsimonious amounts that Admiralty allowed. Before the Battle of Trafalgar, before the Spanish withdrew from their allegiance with France, nobody had minded much if Captains shot off the top tier of powder in their magazines to keep their gun crews at their peak. Now, though, those journals cited concerns that Admiralty might frown on anyone *too* wasteful.

It took the first four days on-passage before Lewrie felt his crew was ready for anything other than dumb-show practice, running-in then pretending to load, ramming powder and wads, playing at loading shot and second wad, ramming, then running-out. On the fifth day, he began live-firing; by broadside, as they bore (which went more like a timed salute since there was nothing to aim at), then ordered one of the transports to hoist sail on one of their new barges and tow a keg well astern off either beam, at varying distances from the ship.

Three rounds per gun every two minutes was Lewrie's standard, and after much practice, *Vigilance* could do it, even with the heavy 24-pounders on the lower gun-deck, and broadsides could be concentrated within an imaginary ship's length, with most shot striking the sea in a dense flurry of shot-splashes like a blast from a fowling piece.

Then, with the barge sailing much closer in, Lewrie got his gun crews familiar with those newfangled sights, one gun at a time 'til the towed keg was swamped by a close hit, or shattered and replaced, with tobacco or full measures at the twice-daily rum issues, with no deduction for "sippers" and "gulpers", paid for out of Lewrie's pocket, and once his Vigilances caught on, they became most proficient, and competitive with each other. They didn't even mind when their ship sailed right past Gibraltar without putting in for liberty in such a fabled port for wine, women, and song.

It is *a damned odd-lookin' place,* Lewrie thought as he had one last look about, then ambled down to the quarterdeck to join his officers. "Boats in the water, then, and we'll see what Mister Blundell can scare up by way of fresh victuals from shore for supper tonight, right? Firewood and water today, then replacement shot and powder tomorrow," he told his Lieutenants. "Mister Blundell? I'll go ashore with you, if you don't mind. Whoever commands round here doesn't seem to be in port at the moment, so I'll have to ask about to discover when we get our troops, and what sort they are. Carry on with the boats, and I'll be aft 'til they're in the water."

And find if there's a chief spy on Malta who might know what's goin' on round here, he told himself.

Malta seemed even more exotic and alien to his senses a few hours later when Lewrie stepped ashore, at last. Swarthy, Arabic-looking men and women in the cobbled streets babbled away in an unknown language that sounded like a mix of Italian, Spanish, and Arabic, with rare familiar words popping up. Most were garbed in long, flowing costumes that appeared practically Biblical, in sandals, shapeless hats, or head scarves. Street vendors' stalls and carts gave off a variety of odd but tempting aromas, and, for a dry-appearing island, their vegetable and fruit bins overflowed with bounty.

Hardly anyone could understand him, of course, or direct him where to go, so it was a relief to enter the massive gates of one of the imposing fortresses to discover British Army sentries who *could.* He was directed to the headquarters offices of a Brigadier-General by the name of Geratty, who was pleasantry itself, giving Lewrie a warm welcome.

"Sit you down, sir, sit you down!" Geratty insisted, "Care for tea?" he asked, ringing a wee china bell to summon his orderly. "Now, I've orders from London round here somewhere concerning you, sir, if you'll give me a moment . . . ah!" he said after digging through a pile of correspondence and finding the pertinent letter. "We're to supply you with a battalion of troops, and . . . ten companies?"

"I'm only authorized three troopers, at present, sir," Lewrie corrected him. "An experiment, really. I can only accommodate about six companies for now, no more than four hundred and fifty soldiers. I thought I would have to report to the General commanding on Sicily for . . ."

"Sicily, Lord no, sir," Geratty said with a laugh. "The French have already staged one attempt to cross the Straits of Messina and gain a lodgement, a few years back. Nothing much came of it, a complete flub, but since then, the commanding General is loath to give up even a Corporal's Guard detail, lest Murat over in Naples try it on again. It was thought that the French, and their Neapolitan allies, cannot stage an attempt on Malta. Admiral Cotton's fleet at sea, the impregnability of Malta's forts, the lack of good landing beaches, what? If they did try, they'd have to come in fishing smacks and little coasting boats, and it's a long sea passage from fishing villages in Calabria or Basilicata in the Bay of Taranto to here, haw haw! A lot further than three miles from Scylla to Messina."

"So, I came to the right place," Lewrie agreed, relieved that the Army sounded prepared for his arrival.

"Indeed you did, sir," Geratty said with a beamish grin. "Room for only four hundred fifty or so, is it? Hmm, I *was* ready to offer you the Second Battalion of the 65th, but . . . ah, Dindwiddy, please do fetch us a pot of tea. No fresh milk or cream, sir, sorry, but I find that lemon and honey go down well."

"Sounds good," Lewrie said, explaining how he kept a pitcher of cool tea with lots of lemon and sugar aboard ship.

"Cool tea, ah," Garatty mused, "sure to be most refreshing here, when Summer rolls round. Sell my soul for a cellar full of ice to make it even better! Stop at Gibraltar on the way, did you, Captain Lewrie?"

"Ah, no sir," Lewrie replied, wondering when Geratty would get down to business.

"Then you haven't heard about the Spanish Lines!" Geratty hooted in mirth. "Saw it myself, when my ship put in there on the way here. When the French marched South into Andalusia and laid siege to Cádiz, the Spanish, and our Army engineers, blew them up so the French couldn't use them. Terrific, *titanic* explosions, loud enough to be heard as far away as Madrid, and not one block of stone left standing atop another, haw haw! Simply *magnificent* show! The Spanish armies just melted away, of course, and our General Blayney got himself caught by the French by mistake, so all we hold in Andalusia at present is Cádiz, but . . . ," he concluded with a large shrug.

That don't sound too promising, Lewrie thought; *but at least The Rock still holds, and will, and all the Spanish gunboats at Algeciras are guardin' the bay, and Gibraltar's harbour.*

They got their pot of tea and went through the social motions for a bit before Geratty finally set his empty cup and saucer aside and picked up his orders once more.

"Ah, troops, Captain Lewrie," Geratty said. "There *is* one battalion available which does not require splitting it in half, one raised by a patriotic committee of gentry and wealthy merchants round Peterborough about five years ago when Napoleon looked likely to invade us cross the Channel. I believe they only had about six hundred men back then. A *one-battalion* regiment, do you see, is the 94th, and, once the danger of invasion passed, the enthusiasm of its founders dwindled, as did recruiting, or plans to become a proper two-battalion regiment with a home barracks. Horse Guards didn't know quite what to do with them after that, but I believe they took part in the Walcheren Expedition a few years back, some guard duties round Dover Castle, then they shipped them out here two years ago. Diseases, desertions, well . . . they only muster about, ah . . . three hundred and thirty, rank and file, as of the last month. In six companies, since a fair number of their officers lost *their* enthusiasm, too, and quit the service, and damned lucky they were to get the cost of their commissions back and use it to purchase a commission in a proper regiment, or simply call it quits."

"That sounds, ah . . . ," Lewrie tried to say, dumbfounded and with his mouth hanging open, wondering if his enemies extended into the Army, too. "Christ, General Geratty! Christ!"

"Quite," the Brigadier agreed with a grim look. "Sorry about it, but . . . there it is. It's the 94th or nothing, I'm afraid, about all I can spare from the Malta garrison."

"Hate t'look a gift horse in the mouth, sir, but . . . mine arse on a bandbox!" Lewrie gloomed. "An *experienced* battalion, are they? Decent morale? Well-trained? Full o' piss and vinegar?"

"As much as one might expect after two years of doing 'sentry-go' on the ramparts, Captain Lewrie," Geratty said. "They do well on musketry, and 'square-bash' smartly. And, I would expect that did one offer them a shot at active duties, they'd be eager enough."

"Right, then," Lewrie said, surrendering all hopes that his experiment had a ghost of a chance to succeed. "Where do I find 'em?"

"The 94th, quite by chance, is garrisoned right here in this fortress, Captain Lewrie," Geratty told him, "and I do believe that it is about time for their officers to take their mid-day dinner in their mess. Shall I introduce you to them?"

"If you have to, sir," Lewrie wryly replied, setting aside his tea cup and getting to his feet. "Beggars can't be choosers, what?"

Across the vast quadrangle, past drilling soldiers and snarling Sergeants, then up innumerable flights of stone stairways, and arched stone galleries that led off to artillery batteries, barracks, kitchens, and armories, and the immensity of the place, the yards' thick construction, and the gloom, put Lewrie in mind of vast caverns deep under the earth, like the natural caves and tunneled-out gun galleries that he'd toured in the mountain that brooded over Gibraltar.

At last they reached an upper level near the ramparts with real windows and sunlight overlooking the expanse of the quadrangle, though the windows were rather small, and at the end of deep, arched recesses large enough for a decent front parlour, there was a vestibule with a wood sideboard, Turkey carpets, and some hanging flags, and an incongruous oil painting of the Lake Country that Lewrie could have sworn was a copy of a Turner. On the side-board sat rows of stiff felt infantry officer shakoes, and two fore-and-aft bicornes, one featuring an egret feather plume.

A Colonel, a Major, Captains, and subalterns, he told himself, noting that there were no stiff, upright white plumes that would have denoted officers from a Grenadier Company, and that two shakoes had the silver hunting horn emblems denoting a Light Company.

There was a pleasant hubbub coming from a room beyond and Brigadier Geratty led him into it, where Army officers of the 94th Regiment of Foot stood about with pre-prandial drinks in their hands, waiting for dinner to be announced. They all perked up and looked to the door as Geratty cleared his throat.

"Ah, Brigadier," a tall, lean man with salt-and-pepper hair said in surprise. "Welcome to you, sir, though . . ."

Maybe senior officers showin' up in a regimental mess just ain't done without an invitation, Lewrie thought; *like me turnin' up in the wardroom and askin' for a plate and a drink*.

"Colonel Tarrant, Major Gittings, gentlemen," Geratty replied.

"Will you be *dining* with us, sir?" Colonel Tarrant asked with a brow up in question, as if it *was* an imposition.

"Sorry, no, sir," Geratty brushed off with a smile, "but I have a fellow with me whom you might make welcome. Allow me to name to you naval Captain Sir Alan Lewrie, Baronet," and he went on to introduce the regimental officers to Lewrie. "Captain Lewrie is in need of soldiers to conduct an experiment that London has approved."

"And you thought of us, Brigadier?" Colonel Tarrant asked with a weary, and leery tone, as if Geratty could not rid himself of the 94th faster.

"Only if you wish to get out in the fresh air, spend a week or so at a time at sea," Lewrie interrupted, "and make landings and raids against the French below Naples, Colonel Tarrant,"

"Oh, I say!" that worthy replied, looking startled, nigh gasping.

"Would we be coming back here, Captain ah . . . Louis?" the Major, Gittings, asked, sounding too cynical to be hopeful.

"To rest up between raids, I'd imagine," Lewrie told him, "while we plan the next, enjoy your bragging rights, and make the rest of the garrison envious. And it's Lewrie," he added, spelling his name.

"Out of here, sir?" a Captain with the wings of the Light Company on his shoulders, queried, looking ready to whoop in glee. "Get to do some *real* soldiering? Hallelujah!"

"Well, I'll leave you to it," Brigadier Geratty said, dismissing himself. "Captain Lewrie, gentlemen."

"Do please dine with us, Captain Lewrie," Colonel Tarrant grandly offered, "and allow me to name to you my officers."

A glass of Rhenish was shoved into Lewrie's hands and a flurry of names were shared before dinner was announced, and they all went into a dining hall beyond to take seats. Lewrie's guess was right, the 94th didn't have a Grenadier Company any longer, only five Battalion Companies, and one Light Company, though Colonel Tarrant declared that he had been playing with the idea of forming a second Light Company from the most agile of his unit, and post them on the right of the line, if there *ever* would be a call for the 94th to take the field.

The dinner was un-remarkable; a rice-and-barley soup that barely tasted like beef stock, a stringy and tough roast beef, but the salads and vegetables were a welcome marvel, for their like back home would not be seen 'til much later in the Spring. No one really took time to savour it, though, for, against the tradition of never talking business in the mess, Lewrie was eagerly pumped for explanations. Towards the end of the meal, before the port, nuts, and sweets, he ended up standing over his end of the table, with a glass butter dish for a transport ship and a half-dozen walnuts for rowing barges.

"My sailors protect the boats and the beach," he said, "you go in, with my seventy Marines as re-enforcements, raise merry Hell, then come back to be picked up and returned to the ships. No packs, cooking pots, or camp gear. Rucksacks with sausage, cheese, and bisquit, your spare flints, gun tools, and another fourty rounds of ammunition, All else remains on the ships. Oh, two canteens of water per man."

"We get to *practice* this, don't we, Captain Lewrie?" a Captain Sydenham from one of the Battalion Companies asked.

"Oh, indeed we do, sir!" Lewrie assured him. "In the dark, in the light of day, 'til you and your soldiers are sick of it. We won't launch the first raid 'til it's second nature."

"Well, I daresay we won't be emulating the Battle of Maida, but it sounds the very thing to get us out of this garrison drudgery," Major Gittings said with a laugh. "Sounds delightful!"

Lewrie vaguely recalled accounts of Maida that he'd read once back in England to heal up after *Reliant* had paid off. In 1806, the French over-ran the Kingdom of Naples and the Two Sicilies, isolating the last remnants of the Neapolitan army in the fortress town of Gaeta. To relieve the siege and extricate them, Admiral Sir Sydney Smith and General Sir John Stuart put about fifty-two hundred British troops ashore in Calabria, with some Corsican Rangers, Sicilian Volunteers, and man-hauled foot artillery. He met a much larger force under the French General Reynier, caught them at a clumsy dis-advantage, shot them to pieces with overwhelming musketry volleys, left their wounded and dead strewn in windrows, and drove them from the field, resulting in the first victory of British soldiers against the nearly invincible French.

"Do we prove the concept, there are plans for more transports, and full regimental landings," Lewrie hinted to encourage them more.

"Ah, but then they'll whistle up a *proper* regiment and turn the game over to *them*, and the poor old 94th ends back on the ramparts of this stone cess-pit," a Captain Bromhead griped.

"Unless the fame you gain results in fresh companies recruited back home, sir," Lewrie pointed out, "Nothing draws more friends than a winner. With ten full companies, again, you'd be the pioneers."

"Haw, it might even make the value of our commissions go up," a Captain Meacham said with a cynical laugh.

Lewrie could see the sense in that comment. A Lieutenancy in a famous regiment might go for upwards of £1,500, a Captaincy £2,500. What had they paid to join the 94th, £500 or so?

"Brigadier Geratty said you'd been in the Walcheren Expedition?" Lewrie asked, referring to the disastrous landings in Holland in 1807.

"Nothing but rain, mud, snow, and Walcheren Fever," Colonel Tarrant gravelled. "Wet boots, foot rot, and disease that took a quarter of the regiment. We ended as camp guards, and hospital tenders, with never a real shot fired. I was Captain of the Light Company, then, and Major Gittings was a Lieutenant of a Line Company."

"Bags of promotion available after that, yes," Gittings spat. "If one could afford to buy a dead man's post."

This is gettin' too damned gloomy, Lewrie thought; *Best I leave 'em on a happy note.*

"I'll speak with the Brigadier to take your battalion out of the rotation on the ramparts," Lewrie said, finishing his last half-glass of port and wadding up his napkin preparing to depart. "Let's say that we begin boarding practice in the harbour on Monday. We'll row you out to the ships from the main quays, let you get used to boarding nets, and settle into your cabins. Tuesday, we'll begin practicing the embarkation into the boats and back, row to the quays, land you, then do it all over 'til we're ready for landing on a real beach."

"Oh, good luck with that, Captain Lewrie," Captain Meacham said with a snicker, "for I doubt there's a real beach wider than a sidewalk on the whole damned island."

"Ehm, the outer islands, then?" Lewrie asked,

"Gozo?" a Captain Fewkes scoffed. "Comino, Cominotto, or Filfa? Saint Paul? Most of them are un-inhabited, with no harbours, no landing places, and certainly no beaches."

Shit! So much for a happy note! Lewrie fumed.

"We'll find a place to practice," Lewrie assured them, "even if we have to sail over to Sicily. *And* get you your sea legs on the way, hey?"

⚓

No bloody beaches? he furiously thought as he tried to find his way back to ground level through the maze of passages, galleries, and stairways; *Mine arse on a band-box! Should'o' thought of that beforehand, ye damned idiot!*

He considered going back to Brigadier Geratty's offices, if he could find them, that is, and ask if he knew where they could practice landings. *And* find out if Foreign Office's Secret Branch had an office on Malta, where he could trade thoughts with the local senior agent, and learn all he could from him about conditions in Calabria and other provinces round the toe, arch, and boot of the Italian peninsula. It would speed his operations to no end if the Neapolitans had anything like the irregular partisan bands in Portugal and Spain that gave the French so much gory grief.

At last, he found a stairway that led down to a promising patch of sunlight on a stone slab floor, and a massive doorway out to the quadrangle which was already shimmering in Springtime Mediterranean light and warmth. On his way to what he took for an exit to the quays, he found himself crossing paths with a Colonel in stainless white stockings, breeches, under a plumed bicorne that bent down to his nose and the nape of his head. The fellow was puffing lazily on a *cigaro* as he ambled about. Lewrie doffed his hat in salute, and the Colonel put his hand to his hat, palm out, in a return salute.

"I say, sir," Lewrie hopefully began, "but are you familiar with a certain, ah . . . trading company here on Malta that might be able to provide information on what's acting over in Naples and Calabria? The Falmouth Import and Export Company, Limited?"

"*Trade,* sir?" the Colonel said with a dis-believing sniff, and flicked some ash off his smoke. "And what would an English gentleman wish of a *trading* firm, what?"

"They're more than a trading firm, sir," Lewrie blundered on in fading hopes, "more like an ah, information gathering . . . ?"

"Oh, you mean the *spying* lot!" the officer barked, understanding. "Bless me, sir, but I don't know which is worse, spies, or mere money-grubbin' tradesmen. Yayss, I know *of* them, though I have no dealings with them, no no, none at *all*, sir! They just ain't . . . criquet, are they? If one *must*, I do believe that one would have to go to Messina, where the General commanding on Sicily *has* been known to listen to the rumours they gather. Good luck to you if you must sully yourself with *their* sort, sir!"

"Thank you for the information, sir, and a good day to you," Lewrie said, doffing his hat once more, then turning to watch the fellow stroll away with a scissoring-legged gait, blowing aromatic clouds of smoke at the sky.

Messina, my God! Lewrie thought; *Sufferin' Christ on a crutch! I* told *'em, I made it clear as* day *in my proposal that without information, any landing we try could set us in a* hornets' nest! *No spies? No good targets t'hit! Mine arse on a . . .* !

Lewrie found himself a patch of shade and watched soldiers hard at their square-bashing. He recognised some from the 94th in their single-breasted coats trimmed with gilt button holes either side of the joinings, the odd dark green stiff stand-up collars and dark green cuffs with the gilt-laced white button holes and shiny brass buttons. They *did* drill smartly, for all he knew of soldiering, their shakoes were stiff stovepipes, with flat leather brims over their eyes, with large regimental plates on the front that were well-polished. Blue-grey trousers and decently blacked ankle boots stamped below them.

A shoddy, half-strength cast-off unit or not, they looked as if they'd do. And it seemed a damned pity that the whole experiment was scotched from the outset!

CHAPTER THIRTY

*W*ot in 'Ell're we gettin' into, den?" a soldier shouted.

"Int'r bloody *boats*, ya idjit!" came the reply which was quickly becoming a semi-humourous refrain as harbor training went on for days on end. Down to the quays they marched each morning, got into waiting boats, and were rowed out to the transports, where they scrambled up the boarding nets and mustered by companies on deck. A brief quarter-hour belowdecks to stow their equipment for the day, then they formed above the channels of the fore, main, and mizen masts to practice disembarking down the nets and back into the barges to be rowed ashore and formed up atop the stone quays. After a while, the 94th could perform in mostly good order, and with creditable speed. They would share the Navy's rum issue at Seven Bells of the Forenoon, dine aboard, then return to practice 'til the second rum issue in the First Dog Watch, which they much admired, compared to the Army's over-zealous caution of their "scum of the earth" soldiers even getting a whiff of more alcohol than the one-a-day dole.

Lewrie could hear the gripes, though, over the abuse that they suffered each morning and evening when they marched out of the fortress, and when they returned to it. Other garrison soldiers and artillerymen hooted and called them "duckfeet", the "mer-men", jeering questions of how wet they got, and deriding a battalion that had low morale already as "Tarrant's Tadpoles".

Lewrie sent his clerk, Sub-Lieutenant Severance, riding about the island on a lowly donkey to see if there was *any* sort of beach that could serve for more useful practice, and Severance returned with news that a beach in Mellieha Bay on the Nor'west corner of the island *might* be sandy enough, and deep enough, to allow all the boats to land at once, and that there was a rocky slope behind it that the soldiers could scale without too much difficulty. At that welcome news Lewrie hoisted Captain(s) Repair on Board and made plans to sail there just as soon as the wind and weather allowed. Once the Captains of the transports, and his own First Officer, had been briefed, he rushed to share the news with Colonel Tarrant and his officers at the fortress.

"Will you be coming ashore with me, Captain Lewrie?" Tarrant asked as he re-adjusted his rucksack to a more comfortable position after all ships had come to anchor about a mile offshore of the beach in Mellieha Bay.

"Oh, I fear not, Colonel," Lewrie breezily said, all the while taking note of the strength of the wind, the commissioning pendant and how it streamed, the readiness of *Vigilance*'s barges alongside the fore- and main-mast chain platforms, and the ship's Marines, who would go in alongside the 94th. "I'll observe from here, so I can shout, stamp on my hat, and curse in private. All ready, Mister Farley?" he asked over his shoulder.

"The Man Boats signal is ready to be made, sir," Farley replied.

"Very well, sir, hoist it," Lewrie snapped, frowning deeper as he glanced over the side at the wave height of the waters in the bay.

"Make the signal, Mister Acford!" Farley shouted aft to a Midshipman by the signals halliards. "You may man your boats, Mister Whitehead!" he called to the Marine Captain.

"And God help the wicked," Lewrie muttered under his breath. *Vigilance* rumbled to the footfalls and shuffles of her Marines going over the bulwarks, and boarding nets groaned as they scrambled down to the waiting barges, but he was pretty sure that they would perform the evolution as well as, if not better than, the soldiers of the 94th, who were clambering down into their boats for the first time from a slowly rolling, bobbing ship, into barges that rose and fell and swayed to the scend of the bay's waters. Lewrie's attention was focussed upon his telescope, and *their* doings.

"How long, Mister Severance?" he asked as he pulled out his own pocket watch.

"Seven and a half minutes, so far, sir," Severance replied. "I do believe they might be all aboard in ten, as they managed in port."

"Good, good," Lewrie said with a quick nod or two, impatient, but concerned that someone might slip and hurt himself with a fall into a barge, or fall in the water and drown, even under the reduced weight of their equipment.

Was it his imagination, or were the soldiers of the 94th managing better than his first tentative training exercises with those two borrowed companies off Gibraltar in 1807? They were in their boats and sitting upright, muskets erect between their knees, almost all . . .

"Ten minutes, sir!" Severance piped up, sounding triumphant.

"Mister Farley, hoist Form Line Abreast, and Land the Landing Force!" Lewrie said, breathing somewhat easier, sharing Severance's enthusiasm. A few minutes later, though, and he was slamming his fists on the bulwark's cap-rails. "Shit, shit, shit! Do half of 'em know what Line Abreast is *supposed* t'look like? Oh, Christ! You lack-wit, cunny-thumbed . . . !" as three boats swanned so close together that their oars had to be hoisted aloft before they snapped. They fell behind the loose row of barges stroking for shore, a line abreast that looked more like a snake swimming sideways, first one part far ahead, then the other end, or the middle, advancing further.

"Hmm, early days, sir," Lieutenant Farley dared comment.

Lewrie's reply to that was an inarticulate "Aarr!" He snatched off his hat to swipe back his hair, muttering.

"Mine arse on a band-box," Lieutenant Grace mouthed behind his back, to which Lieutenant Farley grinned widely, and mouthed a silent "Just going to say" back at him.

"If not at the same minute, ye'd think they could all land on the same bloody *day*!" Lewrie fumed as one small packet of barges drove their bows onto the sand and shingle of the beach, followed by others in twos and threes. "Now, get outta the bloody boats and *do* something, you . . . ! Gawd!"

He couldn't hear the officers' shouts, but he could make out a flash of sword blades through his telescope, and soldiers tumbled over the bows onto the sand, into ankle-deep surf, and began to bunch up by companies. Lines were formed in two ranks, with the first ranks kneeling, and there were more flashes of sunlight as bayonets were fixed on their muskets.

Boats were landing, driving their way between the ones already ashore, and, at last, the 94th colour party unsheathed their flags and shook them out to bare the King's Colours and the Regimental Colours. Someone in a fore-and-aft bicorne hat waved his sword, and the front rankers rose to their feet, the Colours went forwards, and in two ranks, the six companies of the 94th began to scramble their way up the slope behind the beach, the orderly lines becoming ragged, but they were headed for the top.

"I wonder what the locals make of this, sir," Lieutenant Grace said to Lieutenant Farley. "Did anybody warn them?"

"No, they didn't," Lewrie answered for Farley, disgusted with himself for not thinking of it. "I hope they don't take them for the French." He raised his telescope once more and espied some sheep and goats grazing along the scrub atop the slope, and some Maltese talking with their hands in quick, alarmed gesticulations. A moment later and Maltese, goats, and sheep scattered as Colonel Tarrant had his soldiers load and fire by platoons at an imagined enemy, one volley, followed by a second, then they dashed out of sight down the back of the slope in a bayonet charge, leaving a low thunderhead of spent powder smoke to mark their passing, and the faint sounds finally reached *Vigilance* as a crackling like burning twigs, followed by something that might have been taken for a massed shout of "Huzzah!"

"Well, sir, they pulled it off," Lieutenant Farley hopefully pointed out, "no one drowned or broke their neck, and they did . . . well, whatever soldiers do once they all got ashore. Wasn't neat, but . . . ," he summed up with a shrug.

"Hmmf," was Lewrie's comment. "Let's hope, then, that *someone's* watching, and hoist the Recall signal. We'll get 'em back aboard and have 'em do it, again."

"Aye aye, sir," Farley said, going up to the poop deck to speak with the signals Midshipman. A moment later, and he was back at the hammock stanchions to call down to the quarterdeck, though. "A signal from our shore party, sir."

"From shore? What do they say?" Lewrie asked.

"It's spelled out, sir," Lieutenant Farley reported with an embarrassed cough into his fist. "It's Tea, sir. They're brewing tea."

Lewrie looked up at Farley with a wearily tired expression, and slowly shook his head. "Tea. Mine arse on a band-box."

⚓

All troops were back aboard their transports, eventually, after some ma-
noeuvring ashore, just in time for the rum ration and the mid-day dinner,
The embarking, forming up, and landing was practiced twice more that
day, conveniently ending just at the start of the First Dog Watch, the second rum issue, and an hour or so of idling about on deck in the fresh air
without tunics, crossbelts, shakoes, or their stiff collars, before the evening mess was doled out. Lewrie's boat crew was busy, rowing him from
one transport to the next during the First Dog to speak with the Army
officers and the transports' officers, holding quick conferences as to what
went right, what went wrong, and how they planned to correct their faults
on the morrow.

To get the soldiers used to future duties, just after supper was served
out, he hoisted the signal to up-anchor and make sail, taking *Vigilance* and
the transports far offshore to stand off-and-on for the night. At last, he
and his supper guests could sit down to take their own meals, with Lieutenant Farley, Colonel Tarrant, Major Gittings, and Captain Whitehead
of his Marines attending, along with the Sailing Master, Mr. Wickersham.
Between them, Tarrant and Whitehead had "liberated" a lamb from shore,
had brought it bleating to the deck, and had generously offered to share it
with the Captain's table and the wardroom, and Yeovill and the wardroom
cook had done it to a fine, tasty turn, along with succulent shore vegetables and fresh bread.

"I trust your soldiers will sleep well tonight, sir," Lewrie offered to
Colonel Tarrant, lifting a wine glass in his direction to encourage a toast
between them. "Something to get used to, rocking to sleep aboard ship
instead of a thin cot in one of those fortress galleries that won't move."

"Oh, I wager they will, Captain Lewrie," Tarrant allowed with a smile
of satisfaction. "We put them to it rather vigourously, today, so I'm certain they are ready for a good rest. Do it all again tomorrow, Hey?"

"Thought we'd close the coast in the dark, if the wind remains moderate," Lewrie told him, "and start just after breakfast. We could get in three
or four landings, then stand out to sea for another night before we return
to Valletta Harbour."

"And the Colonel and I might round up a stray kid goat for our table,
what, sir?" Captain Whitehead said with a laugh.

"Amazing how they stroll up to be adopted, yes!" Tarrant agreed with
a hooting sound. "Don't know if it's done in the Navy, Captain Lewrie,
but . . . how do you assess our performances today?"

"Well, the first'un I'd not write home about, Colonel," Lewrie replied, "but, we seemed to sort things out main-well on the others. Another day at it, so long as the waves and surf in the bay stay moderate, I'd say your people did well."

"Pleased to hear you say so, sir," Tarrant said, puffing up with a touch of pride. "It's been a long time since the 94th could imagine that they've done anything right, or anything to enthuse about. Time in garrison was wearing their spirits down to nothing. So! How soon do you imagine we might be doing it for real, sir?"

"I wish I could tell you, sir," Lewrie replied with a sigh, and laying his knife and fork aside for a moment. "But it's intelligence, or so far, the utter lack of it, that keeps us leashed."

He gave Tarrant and the others a rough sketch on how he had had access to an active network of spies, informers, and Spanish patriots when he'd raided along the Andalusian coast in 1807, but so far no one on Malta would even admit that the British government had thought that Naples and Italy were worthy of a resident agent, none that he could discover at any rate.

"Most reports come from ambassadors and consuls, *diplomats*," Lewrie said with a sneer, "too gentlemanly to dirty their hands with spying. They might lay out money to scoundrels and shifty sorts who'd do the actual risky work, skulkin' about in enemy country, but *they'd* never. Foreign Office *does* have a Secret Branch, but if they're operatin' in the Mediterranean area, the closest agents may be as far away as Messina, on Sicily. At least, that's what one Colonel I met in the fortress told me,"

"Don't we have a consul on Malta?" Captain Whitehead asked. "I would have thought we had one."

"I spoke to him," Lewrie said, grimacing in memory of that meeting with a complete nullity. "We're too far away from Italy to learn anything actionable, he said, and thought Secret Branch *might* be found on Sicily, which is much closer, and more subject to French invasion. Who to write to, he couldn't say, and to wait for a real reply . . . my word!"

"Well, why don't we sail for Sicily, then?" Tarrant suggested.

"Aye sir, why not?" Captain Whitehead seconded eagerly. "Even if there is no network such as you described, surely the Army there would be much better informed, and might run some smugglers back and forth."

Lewrie took a tasty forkful of lamb dabbed with mustard to chew on while he considered that, washing it down with a swig of Rhenish.

"Hmm," he said at last, "I'd have to leave a letter for Admiral Charlton, maybe send one off to the commander of the Mediterranean Fleet, Sir

Charles Cotton, too, to let them know that we're almost in business, and have swanned off looking for work. For the nonce, once we get back to Valletta, we'll provision all ships to the deckheads, and prevail upon Brigadier Geratty to give you license to steal from the arsenals and store houses, Colonel. With luck, *someone* on Sicily will know where to send us."

"Gentlemen," Major Gittings cried, raising his glass. "I give you Sicily, and an host of spies!"

"Sicily and spies!" the others chorused, then tossed their wine back to "heel taps", and banged their fists on the table in exuberance.

"Hear that, George?" Dasher whispered wide-eyed. "Real, honest t'God spies, secret codes an' ev'rything!"

"Fresh bottles, Dasher," the older, more experienced lad said in a return whisper, nudging Dasher towards the wine-cabinet. "Aye, though. I'd care t'see that," he admitted, losing his air of superiority over the younker.

CHAPTER THIRTY-ONE

A final interview with Malta's sole British consul assured Lewrie that he'd not have to make a port call at Palermo on Sicily's Northern coast; that was civil government's seat, whilst British military command, and a Foreign Office representative, could be found at Messina.

Not wishing to sail his three un-armed transports into reach of French warships and gunboats, and the remnants of the Neapolitan navy in the narrows of the Straits of Messina, with only *Vigilance* as their escort, Lewrie decided to shape a course along Sicily's Southern coast, round the Western end, then passing Palermo and the Tyrrhenian shores, where many promising practice beaches lay, then to stand out to sea by Capo d'Orlando and get a glimpse of the fabled Aeolian Islands of Greek myth, finally coming to anchor East of Milazzo, near the West side of the peninsula on which Messina sat.

A last practice landing of troops was staged, and the 94th was allowed off the ships for a period of rest, setting up a tent camp and cooking facilities above a wide beach, in the shade of olive groves, and immediately swarmed by urchins, farmers with produce and livestock to sell, hand-carts loaded with barricoes and ankers of rough wine, and the inevitable whores.

Lewrie found horses for him and Deavers, and rode into Messina to find someone in charge who might direct him to potential targets for raids, and

someone from Foreign Office Secret Branch who could supply information. It did not go well.

Lewrie's familiarity with Italy was limited to brief stays in Genoa, Naples, and Leghorn, where there had always been *someone* who understood
perfectly good English, or made sense of his stab at signing what he
wanted, and no one would ever declare Lewrie as a man skilled in foreign languages; French and Greek at his various schools, Hindee in the
Far East, Portuguese or Spanish the last few years, they were all beyond
him. And it did not help that Messina was, for all of its mythic fame,
rather squalid, and simply teeming with suspicious-looking . . . *foreigners*
packed elbow-to-arsehole, stirring about as busy as a whole herd of
shipboard rats, slanging away in a loud, angry babble, with their hands
flying about in accompaniment. It was only when he finally came across
some off-duty British soldiers, as drunk as Davy's Sow, that he could
barely gather from their drink-slurred Cockney accents where to find
Army headquarters.

That did not go well, either.

"What? Mean t'say you've only four hundred or so effectives?" a Brigadier finally sent down to deal with him scoffed. "Pinpricks, a flea bite,
by God! An experiment, is it? It is the principal intent of the Army on Sicily
to hold the island, for the first part, sir, and in future, any planned thrusts
cross the Straits will require a re-enforcement of massive proportions by
at least two or three times the current size of the garrison. I doubt, sir, if
your paltry four hundred or so could make the *slightest* contribution to
that in the face of the fifty thousand or so French soldiers, and allied
troops, that Marshal Murat has over there," the Brigadier simpered.

"Aye, I see that, sir," Lewrie replied, getting hot under the collar to be
lectured and dismissed, "but surely you have made up a list of places to
be probed, attacked in quick in-and-out raids that keep the French on
their toes. Small fishing ports, gatherings of coastal trading ships that could
support another French landing here? Watch towers, semaphore chains,
small strongholds?"

"To what end, Captain Lewrie?" the Brigadier scoffed, amused. "Were
plans in hand to stage such raids, they would envisage *brigade*-sized forays, perhaps division-level incursions, much like Stuart's at Maida. But
then . . . that would require the full co-operation of the Navy, with a fleet

of transports, a protective squadron, and the ability to land substantial cavalry and artillery to support and screen the infantry, artillery especially, since the French seem so fond of it and must be countered in matching strength. You have the ability to land cavalry, do you, sir? Your troops have *any* artillery?"

"We have the guns of my ship, Brigadier," Lewrie sullenly shot back. "And we don't plan to go much beyond their range."

"Pinpricks and flea bites, as I said, Captain," that officer waved away with a languid hand like shooing flies. "A nip from a wee terrier, at best, I'm afraid, which contributes nothing to the effort to expel the French from Naples and Italy, and might only serve to alert them to strengthen their coast defences."

"Leaving the partisans inland to have a freer hand, perhaps, sir?" Lewrie said hopefully.

"Partisans?" the Army officer gawped with a laugh. "If there *are* Italians who emulate the Spanish and Portuguese, it's the first that I have heard of it, sir! I fear that if you truly wish to conduct your, ah . . . experiment, the Army here on Sicily has no suggestions, or encouragement, to give you. You must operate on your own."

"In that case, sir," Lewrie said, ready to strangle the simpering buffoon, "is there anyone from the Foreign Office in Messina who deals with intelligence-gathering cross the Straits? Might you steer me to him?"

"What, sir?" the Brigadier exclaimed, shocked. "You would base your operations on rumour-mongerers and smugglers, haw haw? Well, on your head be it, and God help you."

"If ya don't mind, sir, I'm thinking we should make an open show of our pistols. This looks more like a lawless London stew."

"Aye, it does," Lewrie agreed as they reined their horses to a stop in the middle of a teeming harbourside street reeking of pitch, tar, and fish where that fool Brigadier had directed them to the lodgings and offices of a Foreign Office representative. He looked at the storefronts and signs above the warehouses and chandleries for a familiar Falmouth Import & Export Company sign, but evidently that cover identity had become too well-known, or was only used at Gibraltar, Lisbon, and Cádiz. There was a solid block of stone houses or office buildings in the middle of the street on the shore side. The middle edifice had a Sicilian version of an open-air tavern, either side of which were elevated doorways above grimy stone stoops. Beside each, wooden signs had been screwed to the walls, listing the offices within, and Lewrie kneed his horse closer to try and read them.

No, nothing in English at all, he thought, taking off his hat to swipe a sleeve over his brow; *all Sicilian businesses.* He reined his horse past the tavern to the next, very aware of the fierce and threatening glares of its patrons, who looked like a parcel of off-duty pirates who'd drunk up or whored away the last of their booty who contemplated how much the horses, saddles, clothing, and shoes of these interlopers might go for.

The new sign he discovered listed peoples' names, with numbers of their spaces, and, wonder of wonders, there was one English name, a Mr. Nicholas Quill, Esq.

Can't be a British *lawyer,* Lewrie thought; *he'd starve to death on a practice here! He* has *t'be our local spy!*

Lewrie swung down, looking for a place to lash his horse's reins but there was nothing. Deavers alit and took both reins. As they both dithered as to what to do, a boy came out of the doorway.

"I say there, lad," Lewrie began with a grin, "Does *Signore* Quill live here? The British fellow?"

"*Scusa, signore?*" the lad asked, "*Signore* Quill, *si si*" followed by a flood of utterly incomprehensible Italian, though it sounded helpful. "*Numero quattro,*" he said, pointing inwards and upwards. "Something something *stalla* something *cavallos?*" he asked, pointing to a narrow alley at the end of the building that might lead to stables, or a slash cross the throat.

"Think he means stables, sir," Deavers intuited.

"You show?" Lewrie asked, pointing in that direction, then at their horses, which elicited a broad grin, a vociferous "*Si si, signore!*" and a reach for the reins. "Go with him, Deavers," Lewrie ordered.

"Can I write my will first, sir?" Deavers said, sounding as if he wasn't joshing, but followed the boy down the alley. Both were back in five minutes. "Proper stables for the lodgers, sir," Deavers informed Lewrie, "and there's a great brute with a fowling piece who'll stand guard over them. I slipped him six pence, so they might be there when we leave."

"Right, then," Lewrie said, promising to re-imburse Deavers once inside, "he's in number four. Let's see if he's in."

"Ehm, what if he's not, sir?" Deavers asked.

"Then we'll look like bloody fools," Lewrie told him. "Lad, is *Signore* Quill at home, uh . . . in his . . . *casa?*" he said, hoping that the Spanish word would translate to Italian.

"Ah, *si, signore*," the lad said, bobbing his head, "*a casa, adopera la casa come unufficio.*"

Whatever the Devil that *means!* Lewrie thought.

The boy led them up a dark, grimy stairwell and knocked on a door which was slowly opened in a cautious manner. A muttered conversation took place, at the end of which the occupant opened the door wider and peered out, putting Lewrie in mind of a mole who'd accidentally broken through a lawn into sunlight.

"Mister Quill, I take it?" Lewrie said. "I am Captain Sir Alan Lewrie, and I dearly wish to speak with you, concerning doings over on the mainland."

"Ah, Captain Lewrie, Sir Alan, rather," Quill said, acting as if he had expected French grenadiers had come to bayonet him, and much relieved to find that his visitors were British. "Come in, sir, you and your man, come in!"

He thanked the lad for his assistance, gave him a pat on his head, then securely locked and bolted the door before he steered his visitors to seats, or offered tea or wine.

Mr. Nicholas Quill was a tall, slim, and slightly built fellow who more resembled a university drone who spent his life in libraries, with a long, sorrowful face and a Cornish hook of a nose, and a first appearance that did not fill Lewrie with confidence.

"I've no tea brewed, Sir Alan, but there is a rather nice wine," Quill offered, "a very fruity white, with a big finish."

"That'd be grand, Mister Quill," Lewrie said, and Deavers all but licked his lips to be included in the offer, not dismissed as some officer's catch-fart. "Ah, that is tasty!" Lewrie said after a first sip.

"May I ask what brings you to my offices and lodgings, sir?" Quill asked after a long sip of his own, and an appreciative Aahh!

"You're Foreign Office, I trust, sir," Lewrie began. "I have a small squadron of ships with which I'm charged to conduct boat raids against the French on the mainland, and I'm in need of guidance as to targets, where I can hurt the French the most at the least risk to my small force. I need information, Mister Quill."

"I *am* with the Foreign Office, sir," Quill replied after a long moment of staring. "And, if you are familiar with Secret Branch . . . but of course you are, sir. My mentor, Mister Zachariah Twigg, recruited me from Trinity College, Cambridge, and he mentioned your name in recounting some of his past exploits. How remiss of me to even *ask* if you knew anything of Secret Branch, ha ha!"

Quill had a laugh that sounded like hiccups and the inhalations of a half-drowned man, rocking back and forth with a prominent Adam's apple bobbing in his skinny neck; it was quite off-putting, and Lewrie began to doubt that he'd come to the right source. Even the bland Thomas Mountjoy at Gibraltar looked more like a spy than this'un!

"I, unfortunately, do not take such an active, or exciting, part in intelligence gathering, Sir Alan," Quill told him with a gloomy look.

Oh, Christ, have I come to the wrong place, again? Lewrie thought.

"I fear that I am not the skulking sort, sir," Quill said, "no midnight meetings, or letters in invisible ink, ha ha. But my superiors have endowed me with an operating budget with which I have engaged, ah . . . dare I call them agents, who are willing to share information or gather it, and bring it to me. A most colourful lot they are, too, sir. Smugglers, petty thieves, out-of-work fishermen . . . Sicilians for the most part, and, when it comes to guile, one cannot do better than a Sicilian. They cost me an horrendous sum in hard currency, but their reports of French troop movements and such I've found to be spot-on and truthful for the most part. Though, some *will* embellish, if you get my meaning, hah?"

"Is that the reason you live down here?" Lewrie asked him. "I'd expect that you'd lodge and keep offices up in the *castello*."

"Poor as these rooms are, sir, they are quite handy for meeting with all sorts of suspicious sorts, at all hours of the day or night. And besides," he added with a rueful look, "in the *castello* I would be dining with the general staff mess, at greater cost, amid Army officers who have no time for my sort, or the information I could provide them, if they would ever give me the time of day. Rumour-monger, ungentlemanly tradesman, 'the gullible ghost' . . . I've been called all those, and more, sir."

"So, you could introduce me to your ah, agents, so they can begin scouting for me?" Lewrie asked.

"The principal men who call the shots, as it were, are in port even as we speak, sir," Quill assured him. "I can get a message to them and you could meet them this evening. Here would be best, I think. We can't have you gallivanting round the quays in full uniform, now can we, sir? That would attract too much attention, and put my people at risk were they seen meeting with you publicly."

Gawd, that means we'll have t'sleep over here, Lewrie thought, giving Quill's squalid lodgings a hard looking-over, a mix of poverty-stricken genteel student's quarters, and the roughest sort of peasant hut, dreading the possibility of fleas, lice, bed bugs, mice, and, given the closeness of the seafront, wharf rats in the middle of the night. It smelled like a garbage midden, too, and Lewrie wondered what sort of toilet facilities might be available if caught short; a communal bucket in the odd corner, or an empty stall out back in the stables.

"Aye, tonight would be best," Lewrie grudgingly said, "and we can get back to my ship tomorrow morning."

"Oh, good, then!" Quill exclaimed. "I'll whistle up Fiorello . . . the lad you met? And send him to fetch Caesar. In the meantime, we can send down to the tavern for dinner."

"Caesar?" Lewrie asked.

"Full pseudonym is Julio Caesare," Quill said with a cryptic smile. "God knows his real name, I don't. A thorough scoundrel, but damned good at whatever it is that he does, and does for me."

"Looking forward to it," Lewrie lied, plastering a co-operative grin on his phyz.

CHAPTER THIRTY-TWO

$\mathcal{J}$ulio Caesare, or just plain Caesar, and his crew came skulking in after dark, swaggering rather, though still making sure that they were not followed or watched, and a dangerous-looking lot they were. All sported daggers in their waist sashes, the bulges of small pocket pistols in their baggy, loose slop trousers, and additional sailors' work knives. They looked a blend of Sicily's history of Greek, Roman, Saracen, and Norman blood, all dark, brooding eyes, sun-bronzed skin, and shaggy, clubbed-back hair under shapeless hats or knit caps.

Lewrie had met pirates in the West Indies and Bahamas, Asiatic pirates in the Far East and South China Seas, and had unwillingly dealt with Serbian pirates in the Adriatic, and was convinced that this lot could give all of them a run for their money. Quill did the introductions, explaining that Lewrie had no Italian, which admission made the leader break into a crafty smile as if he was contemplating just how badly this *Inglese* could be fleeced.

"My *capitani, Signore* Luigi," Caesar said in surprising English.

"Lewrie," Lewrie corrected.

"*Non importa*," Caesar shrugged off, "This is 'Tonio . . . Paulo . . . 'Tonio . . . Alfonso . . .'Tonio . . . Pietro . . .'Tonio . . . and, Antonio. His *madre* insists."

"Gentlemen," Lewrie said in greeting, nodding to each one. He took a quick glance over at Deavers, who was frozen in a rictus somewhere 'twixt awe, and an urge to reach for his pistol. "Delighted to make your acquaintance."

"Captain Lewrie thinks he has need of your services, Caesar," Quill said, translating to Italian right after, phrase by phrase. "He has one large warship and three transports with many boats, and about four hundred troops, all told. He wishes to land them over on the mainland to kill Frenchmen."

"*I Francesi!*" Caesar spat, making a slit motion over his throat, and his captains growled their dislike, with "*bastardi!*", "*diavoli!*", "*donnaccias*", and other vulgar expressions of disgust. They spat, too; on the floor and the one ragged carpet, which would do it no good.

"The whores, they are brutes," Caesar growled, "and bad for business. They swarm like the *locusta,* eat up and steal everything in Campania Naples, Basilicata, Calabria, even to Puglia! The poor people they starve, suffer in fear, and no woman is safe! I wish to kill all of them!" He then lapsed into Italian in his rage.

"The French are bad," Quill translated in snatches. "The Poles, Germans, Dutch even worse . . . he hates the Genoese, Piedmontese, Lombards, and Neapolitans worst of all. Whores, slavish . . . traitors to Italy . . . bootlicking turncoats . . . act like Huns and barbarians out of their own provinces . . . Vesuvius should wake and burn them all to Hell. How can he help you kill some?"

"I need information, most of all," Lewrie began to explain as Caesar and his men calmed down from their rant. "Places where a small force can land, make a raid, then get out quickly. Places where there are good, sandy beaches. Watch towers and semaphore towers with weak garrisons, small ports where the French gather boats to use to invade Sicily."

Slowly, in both English and Italian, Lewrie and Quill laid out the need for the presence of French and allied soldiers, how many at a certain location, whether there were forts or artillery batteries, and soundings near those forts and beaches, so *Vigilance* could close the coast to use her guns on the forts, and the transports could anchor close enough to make for a quick row ashore. He'd need to know if a particular beach had easy access to the targets, an easily-ascended slope behind it, a coast road, or a steep cliff.

"You know which place you want to go?" Caesar asked, scratching his stubbly chin with a shrewd expression.

"Not immediately, no," Lewrie had to confess. "That's why I need the information you would supply me. Think of a weakly held place that would hurt the French, a place with good beaches, easy access, so that my troops could get in, raise the Devil, then get out quickly."

Quill translated that for all, making them share looks with each other, before Caesar began to grin. "I know a place, *signore*," he said, "a small fishing port, where coastal traders put in, too. There is a small fortification to one side of the harbour, but it is old, very old. Maybe the Vandals or the Normans put it there, so I do not see openings for cannon, except on the top, and that is small. The place is held by Piedmontese lap-dogs, no French, but killing Piedmontese is almost as good." He turned to one of the 'Tonios to palaver for a bit, then resumed his description. "'Tonio says the last time he was there, he did not think there were more than five hundred soldiers, but their *Colonnello* sends many of them to loot inland, and collect the taxes, so not all would be there all the time. There is a good beach North of town, close to town, and there is a road just above it that leads to the town and the piers and store houses. At the piers there are many boats and small ships that can be burned or taken away. How you say, the prize-money; *si*?"

"It sounds perfect," Lewrie said, curbing any enthusiasm that he felt. "Far enough away from other French garrisons?"

"Two hours or more, by foot," Caesar informed him with a shrug. "Alfonso knows the place, too, and does not remember cavalry."

"Where is it?" Lewrie asked. "What's it called?"

"Tropea," Caesar said with a grin. "*Signore* Quill, have map?"

A much-folded map was produced, and Caesar traced a grimy finger over it, then stabbed at the map, "There, *signore*. Tropea."

Lewrie leaned over and laid a finger on it, himself. Tropea was about thirty miles North of the narrowest point of the Straits of Messina, just North of a West-trending bulge of land, and seeming isolated from other towns by at least ten miles.

Damme, do we hoist anchors from our current location round Four am, we could be off Tropea by Eight or Nine in the morning, Lewrie speculated; *Leave by Two in the morning, and we could be there by dawn! If the bloody weather lets us, of course.*

"I and my ships are anchored East of Milazzo, about halfway between there and Messina," Lewrie told Caesar. "Once one of your boats has a chance to scout the town, the beach, and the depth of water off the fort, can you report to me there, sir?"

"Hmm, give me three, four days to go there, do what you ask, and come to your ship, *Signore* Luigi," Caesar promised. "I get all you need to know."

"It's Lewrie, actually," Lewrie corrected again.

"*Signore* Quill," Caesar said, turning to the weedy Foreign Office man. "For this, I think we need one hundred pounds, in gold guineas. For the expenses."

"You shall have it, *signore*," Quill vowed, "though guineas are rare these days. Would one hundred and five pounds in silver do?"

"Same value? *Si, non importa.*" Caesar agreed, explaining the sum to his swarthy compatriots, who bared stained teeth in cheerful grins. Well, one of the 'Tonios had few left, and they were green.

To seal the bargain, one of Caesar's men produced a stone crock of what he said was *grappa,* and Quill managed to turn up some suspect and grimy glasses so they could all toast.

Ain't brandy, or grape-based, Lewrie thought, taking a cautious sniff of the spirit; *looks like gin, or water. Might be harmless.*

A second later and he changed his opinion. He'd drunk a raw, clear back-country whisky when he'd played spy in Spanish New Orleans— once!—but that harsh brew had nothing on *grappa.* Lewrie's lips, tongue, and gums were on fire, his throat was searing, and what *grappa* would do when it reached an indifferent supper was best not contemplated!

"Whew, my . . . mine arse on a band-box!" he wheezed, which gave Caesar and his compatriots a good, back-slapping laugh.

It took all Lewrie had to very slowly finish that first glass, and he almost groaned aloud when one of the 'Tonios splashed a convivial finger or two more of *grappa* atop the remaining swallow. Liquid fire or not, Caesar and his smugglers sloshed down a fair amount of it before they decided at last to take their departure, by which time even Mr. Quill, more familiar with *grappa,* surely, was looking pained but too proud to show it. Hands were shaken all round before they left, slipping out into the hallway and stairwell as furtive as house-breakers to slink back to their lodgings, boats, or another tavern.

"Well, that was . . . different," Lewrie said as he got his wind back. "Thank you, Mister Quill, for the introduction . . ."

"I've found that a white wine helps," Quill suggested, going to one of his storage chests for a bottle, and poured them all liberally.

"What the Devil *was* that stuff?" Deavers muttered after tossing back the wine and swizzling it round his mouth to cool it. "Satan piss? Ah, thank you, sir. The wine does help."

"Just doing my part for King and Country, Captain Lewrie," the fellow replied, letting out a long "Aah!" of relief, then yawned. "It is late.

We should turn in, do you not think? I have but the one bed-stead, but your man Deavers can doss down on the settee. If you do not mind sharing a bed for the night, sir."

I'll keep my boots and breeches on, Lewrie swore to himself; *and I hope this fellow don't snore as queer as he laughs.*

CHAPTER THIRTY-THREE

*T*hey woke to cocks-crows, and the lad Fiorello rapping on the door, dressed and packed by the light of one candle, and had a quick breakfast at the nearby tavern, cinnamon-and-raisin rolls washed down with incredibly strong black coffee. Their horses were led out by the giant with the fowling piece, who got another silver six pence in reward, and Lewrie and Deavers were ready to set off and return to the ships' anchorage, and the shore camp of the 94th.

They rode in silenee for some time, savouring the coolness and and relative quiet of pre-dawn. Away from the quays and harbour, and the town of Messina, the air was a lot fresher, too, and the odd reeks they encountered were from farms, and livestock manure, which was down-right homey.

"Why'd a gentleman live so poor, sir?" Deavers asked, breaking the silence at last. "That Mister Quill?"

"The gentlemen at Army headquarters don't think anyone in his line o' work *is* a gentleman, Deavers," Lewrie replied. "And, he can't have his sources and his spies like Caesar and his men droppin' in to tell their tales, either. They probably don't want their connexions to us known, Might be bad for business, in their circles, too."

"Lord, sir," Deavers said with a little laugh, "but we do meet the odd-est sorts in the Navy. Might be mermaids and Amazon women, next."

"As Mister Quill said, the things we do for King and Country!" Lewrie hooted.

They reached the Army camp a little after Noon to find the 94th at their mid-day meals. Not too much cooking was being done by the men of the regiment, though, for the camp had been invaded by local Sicilian women and children who had set up pots and skillets over fires to cook ration salt-meats with local victuals on the side. Lewrie noted that several soldiers, a fair number, stood guard under arms to protect the olive and fruit groves, and patrolled the tent lines.

"Ah, Sir Alan," Colonel Tarrant called out, alerted to their arrival as he came from his pavillion in his shirt sleeves. "Welcome back. It's good news, is it, sir?"

"We have our first place to strike, Colonel," Lewrie told him as he dis-mounted and turned the reins over to an orderly. "Full details are coming within three or four days, then we'll be ready to go."

"Thank the Heavens for that, sir!" Tarrant exclaimed, sounding re-lieved. "This camping ashore may just be the ruin of my troops!"

"Ruin, sir?" Lewrie asked, taking off his hat to fan himself, and mop his brow with a handkerchief.

"It's the bloody locals," Tarrant carped. "Soon as the tents were aligned, they swarmed us, with lashings of fresh bread, pasta and wines, vegeta-bles, fruit, rice, all welcome, mind, but they're like the flies . . . they're everywhere! It's not that their prices are high, but my men only have so much money in small coin, and they'll run out soon. Then, there's the whores, the old hags who've damned near taken over the cooking, in place of the regiment's own wives and camp followers, the children . . . my God, sir! Sicily must train their thieves well, from the cradle. I swear they could steal the band instruments, which they've tried several times, and leave the *music* playing! Then, there is the *grappa*. A plague worse than gin in Hogarth prints!"

"Heard of it," Lewrie cryptically said. "Rough stuff."

"Now, I have to place guards over the men's possessions to keep them safe," Tarrant continued to gripe, "pat down every trader to keep *grappa* out of camp, and on top of all that, keep my own men out of the groves so they don't chop down olive trees and fruit trees for firewood, and the regimental chest has had to pay out for the ones they *did* chop down. I do believe we'd have been better off staying aboard those awful bloody ships!"

"I assure you we'll be shot of this place by the end of the week, Colonel," Lewrie promised him. "Though, we may have to return here to await information, and plan future raids."

"A day or two of respite, sir?" Tarrant demanded, "then right back here? Good God. I'd have thought we'd sail back to Malta and replenish, first. I've sent Major Gittings to Army headquarters in Messina, to find out if we could draw from the local garrison stores 'til then, but they've been *most* un-cooperative. Do we want pay for the troops, rations, or ammunition, they said we're still officially part of the brigade on Malta, detached to the Navy temporarily or not, d'ye see. Does the 94th wish to transfer to the Army on Sicily, they *would* supply us, but the paperwork back and forth to London, Malta, and Messina would take weeks. We're told that even barracks accommodations would be un-available."

"Well, damme," Lewrie spat, seeing what fragile plans he'd made tumble like a house of cards. "We *can't*! My . . . our sources of information are here on Sicily, the man from the Foreign Office they work for is in Messina. Without his money, we'd get nothing, and it would take *weeks* to go back to Malta, wait to hear from him, then sail back here, camp, get the final details, stage the raid, and . . . ! Back and forth from Malta? Good Christ!"

"At least my soldiers could be sure to see their wives and children," Colonel Tarrant said with a gloomy expression.

"Hey? What?" Lewrie gawped. "Who?"

"The regiment's wives and children," Tarrant explained as if it was self-evident. "When we sailed for Malta, when we were close to our full ration strength, we held the lot-drawing for the sixty wives allowed, and they sailed with us. They're still on Malta, the most of them, about fifty or so by now. My men are growing anxious to see them."

"Oh, my sweet Christ!" Lewrie groaned aloud. "Dependents didn't even cross my mind, I just assumed . . . ! Didn't see 'em at the fortress, so . . . !"

He'd seen it during the American Revolution, at the failed incursion at Toulon, at Gibraltar's garrison, and the landings of British troops in Spain, and it had completely slipped his mind, didn't even factor in his plans as far back as the paper study he'd written in London!

The British Army allowed wives, children, and camp followers at their home stations to live in barracks with their men. When deployed overseas, only sixty lucky wives won the drawing of lots to go with them, and the rest were left to their own devices, perhaps never to see their husbands alive, again. As disease and desertion depleted the ranks of the 94th, surviving widows had no choice but to take new husbands to support them and their children. They did the sewing, the tending to the sick and wounded, the cooking, the carrying of packs (and tots) on the march, and helped pitch camp each evening, then break it down each morning.

Wives aboard ship were so rare that Lewrie hadn't even thought to account for their accommodations, and when calling upon Tarrant and his officers, he had *seen* women and children round the fortress drill grounds, but hadn't thought that some of them might be from the 94th!

I'm a God-damned, witless, blind fool! Lewrie chid himself; *No one should trust me with organising a drinking party! I could foul up a two-horse race! Christ, what'll I tell Charlton, if we ever cross his hawse, and he asks what my plans are?*

"It's possible that some of the younger lads might take up with the Sicilian girls," Tarrant speculated, looking round his encampment with his hands on his hips. "Beyond the whores, there are *some* pretty. I'll still have to hold them to the allotted sixty, but . . ."

"They've no English, your men have no Italian," Lewrie pointed out, hoping in vain that that would keep the numbers low.

"Oh, love will find a way, Captain Lewrie," Tarrant mirthlessly replied. "That, or plain lust, haw haw."

How well I know! Lewrie bleakly thought; *Dammit! More mouths to feed, at Admiralty expense! We stay here on Sicily, I have t'shuttle their womenfolk and brats here for a rut? Or carry 'em all back to Malta for it? Can things get more hopeless?*

"Care to join our mess for dinner, sir?" Tarrant offered.

"Ehm, what? No, thankee for the offer, but I really should go aboard my ship," Lewrie decided. "It's a Banyan Day, and I can manage on cheese, oatmeal, and bisquit from the general issue."

With my luck, the crew's found grappa, *too, and they're ready for a drunken mutiny!* Lewrie gloomily thought as he ambled down to the beach and waved his hat to summon a boat to come fetch him.

He doffed his hat at the top lip of the starboard entry-port as he got back aboard, lost in a worried stew, and only somewhat re-assured by the ceremony of bosuns' calls and the side-party's salutes.

"Nothing's gone smash in my brief absence, Mister Farley?" he asked the First Officer once the salute was done.

"Nothing to report, sir," Farley replied, "and the purser has established dealings with the locals, so we've ample firewood, fresh water, bread, and vegetables coming aboard daily."

"My compliments to Mister Blundell for it," Lewrie said.

"Ehm . . . there is one problem, sir," Farley admitted. "There are four hands due Captain's Mast. A fist fight, sir."

"Who are the miscreants, then?" Lewrie asked, frowning.

"Ehm, sir," Lieutenant Farley confessed, "Able Seaman Kitch, Ordinary Seaman Beckford, Landsman Stubble, and . . . your cabin servant, Dasher."

"Dasher!" Lewrie exclaimed in shock. "And my stroke oar? What the Devil was it about?"

"Dasher's bunny, sir," Farley reported. "Beckford and Stubble cruelly teased Dasher, I gather, saying they'd skin it and cook it, taking it away from him and passing it back and forth, out of Dasher's reach. Treated it rather roughly. Kitch stepped in to make them stop and things went bad from there. Kitch laid into them, Dasher got his bunny back into the manger, then *he* tried to fight them as best that he could, before the Master at Arms, Mister Stabler, and his Corporals broke it up, frog-marched them to me, and I ordered them put in irons 'til you returned aboard, sir."

"What? All of 'em in irons? Dasher, too?" Lewrie gawped.

"Aye, sir," Farley said. "Seemed fair at the moment, sir."

"Well, just damn my eyes," Lewrie allowed. "Aye, your action was fair. Poor tyke, though. How long have they been in irons?"

"Since half past Noon yesterday, sir," Farley told him.

"Very well," Lewrie said with a sigh. He pulled out his pocket watch to note the time, which was near one in the afternoon. "I'll eat first, then we'll summon all hands to hold Mast at Six Bells. Let 'em stew 'til then. I'll be aft."

"Aye aye, sir," Farley said, doffing his hat.

Deavers was already back at his duties in the great-cabins, and the new lad, George Turnbow, was there to take his hat and sword belt.

"You've heard, Deavers?" Lewrie asked.

"Aye, sir," Deavers replied. "He dotes on that bunny, but I didn't know he had that much spirit in him."

"A game'un, is Dasher, sir," Turnbow said. "What those bastards did was just evil-cruel. I'd've laid into 'em myself, were it me they were teasin'. Hope you don't go too hard on him, sir."

"I'll hear them out, but I think I know who I'll go hard on," Lewrie promised. "Anything for dinner, Deavers?"

"Yeovill brought round some cheese, bread, and something the Sicilians call a *salami*, sir," Deavers announced, "and there's fresh grapes just come off shore, too."

"No *grappa*?" Lewrie teased as he headed for his dining coach.

"Thank the good Lord *no*, sir!" Deavers declared.

"What's *grappa*, then?" Turnbow asked, puzzled.

"Pray God ye never know, lad," Lewrie said with a laugh.

Six Bells of the Day Watch, three in the afternoon, and bosuns' calls and shouts for All Hands roared through the ship as Lewrie appeared at the forward edge of the quarterdeck, his punishment book resting atop the hammocks in the racks, as the prisoners were led up from the orlop deck far below, their wrist chains and irons clanking. Crewmen lined the boat-tier beams, the sail-tending gangways, and crowded in the waist, eager to see justice done, or merely curious to see what their new Captain deemed as justice.

"Mister Farley," Lewrie snapped at his First Officer sternly, "pray do name the defaulters, and enumerate the charges against them."

Lieutenant Farley stated the defaulters' names, accusing them all of violating the 23rd Article of War. "If any person in the Fleet shall quarrel or fight with any other person in the Fleet," Farley recited, "or use reproachful or provoking speeches or gestures tending to make quarrel or disturbance, he shall upon being convicted thereof, suffer such punishment as the offence shall deserve, and a Court-Martial shall impose."

"The particulars, sir?" Lewrie growled, and both Farley and the Master at Arms described the offence. Some of the crew grinned, or laughed behind their hands about the bunny which had been the source of the disagreement.

"Landsman Dasher," Lewrie said, turning to his cabin servant. "What do you have to say for yourself in your defence?"

"You were away ashore, sir, and I didn't have no duties, so I thought to visit the manger an' feed my bunny, Harriet, some lettuce an' such what come aboard," Dasher began with many gulps. "Beckford an' Stubble come up an' snatched her away from me, wavin' her around, like they were goin' t'wring her neck, skin her, and get the cook to fry her on th' sly. I pleaded with 'em t'give her back an' not hurt her, sir, but they thought that was funny, an' took t'tossin' her about like a shoe, swingin' her by her ears or her legs, an' I yelled for anyone t'come help me get her back. That's when Kitch come up and told 'em to leave the bunny be, and give her back t'me, They thought that was funny, too, an' dared him t'try takin' her. So Kitch says, if ya two cowards an' bullies don't, he'll box their ears an' make their bungs spout claret, they said come ahead an' try, and Kitch lit into 'em, knockin' Stubble clean off his feet, That's when I got my bunny from him, then Beckford an' Stubble both started swingin' at him. I got my bunny back in the manger, an' it looked like Kitch needed some help, so I started kickin' an' hittin' them, too. An' that's when Mister Stabler, Geary, and Kirby came an' stopped us fightin', Cap'm sir."

"And for you, Able Seaman Kitch?" Lewrie asked. "What have you to say for yourself?"

"I've never cared much for cruel, motherless bastards abusing younger lads, Cap'm sir," Kitch declared, "I was coming back from the beakhead rails, sir, saw what Beckford and Stubble were doing from the foc's'le, and went down to the waist to make them stop. Dasher was beginning to weep, pleading most dreadful in fear of what they would do to hurt or kill his wee pet. I never much cared for what people do by way of evil to wee beasts, either, sir, so I tried to get the rabbit away from them and for them to leave off. One thing led to the next, sir, and aye, it turned into a fight. The only way to keep *some* evil, godless people from doing bad, Cap'm sir. And aye, harsh words and curses got said on both sides, I admit."

"And you, Ordinary Seaman Beckford, and Landsman Stubble. What do you have to say for yourselves?" Lewrie demanded.

With much shuffling of their feet, shrugs of their shoulders in dumb show, and gazes directed mostly at the toes of their shoes, they wheedled out a tale that it had all been done in idle fun, that they had meant no harm, that the rabbit wasn't really hurt, and that Dasher couldn't take a joke. If they pulled at their forelocks and called Lewrie "Yer honour, sir" as they would to their magistrates back home, they could not have appeared more contrite, or innocent.

"Th' lad's too much of a babby, Cap'm sir," the burly and dim-witted-looking Stubble concluded, with an attempt at a sly smile, "an' Kitch, 'e cursed us an' hit us f'r no good reason. We 'umbly beg your pardon, Cap'm sir, an' we won't be doin' such, again."

"Idle fun, was it?" Lewrie barked. "Malicious and cruel evil is what I call it. If I could prove that you *planned* to bully a young lad just 'cause you could, for *sport*, I'd have your backs laid open!

"I will not tolerate anyone quarrelling, or fighting, on my ship, a *King's* Ship, nor will I tolerate bullying or taking unfair advantage of anyone aboard *Vigilance*," Lewrie went on, pausing to pencil entries in the punishment book, then looked them in the eyes once more. "Not only are you guilty of violating the Twenty-Third Article of War, you forgot that Dasher was tending *my* part of the manger, and the rabbit you tossed about is *my* rabbit.

"The punishment is one-dozen lashes for each of you, to be administered at Six Bells of the Forenoon tomorrow," Lewrie decreed, "and following that, ten days' bread and water, ten days with no rum issue, and ten days of no tobacco, whether you're a member of a successful gun crew or not. Mister Stabler, see the miscreants to the orlop!"

"Aye aye, sir!" the Bosun replied with a note of delight in his voice, and there was a general stir and murmur from the watching crew, though it did not sound dis-approving, making Lewrie think that Stubble and Beckford were not the most popular tars belowdecks, or in their eight-man mess.

"Silence on deck!" Lieutenant Farley snapped to still them.

"Able Seaman Kitch," Lewrie said, turning to the stroke oar of his personal boat crew, and Kitch raised his chin to look him straight in the eyes. "What you did to stop their cruel bullying in any other situation would be commendable. Were you ashore and *not* in the Navy, I expect you'd be due a round of drinks from your mates, but . . . you *did* quarrel, responded with speech that further provoked the situation, and you did exchange blows in a fight, and the Articles of War leave me with little room. Good order *must* be maintained.

"*Six* lashes," Lewrie ordered, and Kitch nodded silent agreement, which surprised him, "at Six Bells of tomorrow's Forenoon, but . . . you will be un-shackled and allowed to resume your duties 'til then."

That prompted many nods of agreement from the ship's people, but in silence this time. Some even broke out relieved grins.

"Landsman Dasher," Lewrie said, and the lad looked up in terror, whey-faced. "The evidence given shows that you did nothing to start it, and that you . . . and *my* rabbit . . . were the victims. You both were innocent, though . . . you *did* admit to delivering some kicks and blows to aid Seaman Kitch once the fight became general, so . . . you will be bent over a gun and given a half-dozen strokes on your bottom with the Bosun's starter. Will you wish to wait 'til Six Bells tomorrow, or would you prefer to receive your punishment now?"

"Ehm, ah . . . I'll take it now, Cap'm sir," Dasher said, betwixt relief that he was too young to be lashed to a hatch grating and flogged, dread that "kissing the gunner's daughter" would hurt, and trying to pluck up his courage and accept his punishment as gamely as Kitch had.

Bosun's Mate Loftis took Dasher by the arm and led him to the nearest 18-pounder, tipping the lad a sly wink that Lewrie took as a sign that those half-dozen strokes from a stiffened rope starter would not be as hurtful as the ones he'd received when he was a Midshipman.

"And Dasher," Lewrie called out before he was bent over the gun, "I do believe that in future you might keep your bunny in a safer place, like my great-cabins. Caged, of course. You'll be responsible for its care. And, if it chews the legs off my furniture, or leaves pellets on the deck, there might be another half-dozen in your future."

Gawd, though, what'll Chalky make o' that? Lewrie wondered.

Whack . . . whack . . . whack! came the first slow-timed strokes.

No, Loftis ain't puttin' half *himself in 'em,* Lewrie told himself, glad that he wasn't; *How'd my first Captain in old* Ariadne *say it? "I didn't say* dust *him, Bosun! Make Midshipman Lewrie* sting!"

The last stroke was delivered, and Lewrie nodded to Lieutenant Farley, who shouted for the hands to be dismissed from watching punishment, and Lewrie went aft into his cabins, stowed away the rarely used punishment book in his desk, and sat down to pretend to read a novel. After a while, Dasher came in, still wincing a little even if Loftis had been lenient, carrying the plain grey rabbit in a wood-slat cage.

"Over by the starboard quarter-gallery, for now," Lewrie said.

"Aye, sir," Dasher replied. "An' she won't be no trouble."

"Tell that to my cat," Lewrie japed, for as soon as the cage was on the deck, Chalky came prowling, whiskers stiffly forward, his tail cautiously lashing, in a stalk. Some sniffs, a tentative paw at the slats or two, and a curious *Mrr?* and he leaped atop the cage to try and paw down from above, claws out.

"Now where'll we be gettin' fresh greens for it?" Turnbow asked.

"Oh, Harriet gets by just fine on ship's bisquit," Dasher said, kneeling by his doe-rabbit's cage, "the staler the better. Keeps her teeth from gettin' overgrown!"

I always wanted to go to sea with a menagerie, Lewrie thought; *Wait'll I write Jessica about this!*

⚓

"Ya did good, Kitch," Lewrie's Cox'n, Liam Desmond, told him as off-watch sailors gathered round to commiserate.

"Still gonna hurt, though," another sailor in Kitch's mess said.

"Ain't the first time I've been licked by the 'cat'," Kitch told them with a mirthless grin. "Ah, well. Only six? Won't be all that bad. And I still get full rations, rum, and tobacco."

"Cap'm shouldna given ye any at all," another sailor groused. "'Em two bashtits 'ad it comin', long afore ye lit into 'em. Like 'e said, ye should be 'avin' a round o' drinks."

"Didn't have no choice," Kitch objected. "I fought, I called 'em bullies and cowards, and I earned my punishment."

"The worst went where it was most deservin'," Desmond added.

"I still say . . . ," the upset sailor tried to continue.

"Oh, hesh yourself," Kitch shot back. "Liam's right. The true villains are payin' for what they did, and Cap'm Lewrie'll have his eye on them from now on, and I'll lay ya a guinea to a pinch of pig shit it won't be the last time they're seized up and flogged. He let that lad off, didn't he? That was more than fair."

"'What you two forgot is,'" Desmond said, loosely quoting the Captain, "'you feckin' idiots were feckin' with *my* rabbit,' hee hee!"

"I'll tell you true, lads," Kitch sternly announced. "And it's not because I'm in his boat crew trying to crawl up his bung hole . . . this ship's got herself a *good* Captain for a change, a firm but fair man."

"And when we finally get into a battle," Desmond assured them, "we'll have a blood-and-thunder *fighting* Captain!"

CHAPTER THIRTY-FOUR

"*F*ive fathom!" a leadsman in the foremast chains shouted. "Five fathom o' water!"

"Just as those smugglers said, sir," the Sailing Master, Wickersham, said with a sniff of satisfaction. "And I make it only half of a mile to the fort."

"Mister Farley, you may open, as the guns bear," Lewrie ordered.

"As you *bear*!" the First Officer yelled, "Fire!"

And the bucolic view of a peaceful seaside fishing port vanished as a rising cloud of spent gunpowder smoke blotted it out for a while, before slowly rolling shoreward on a light breeze.

Just like their sketches, and their maps! Lewrie exulted to himself. There was the town to the right on a higher spur of a headland, there was the sandy beach to the left, the slight slope above it that led to a road, and rows of houses, barns, and storefronts, just as described, with the little harbour notched deep between, a harbour full of boats, from wee rowing boats to larger sail-rigged fishing boats to a gaggle of coastal trading vessels, some of them rigged in ancient Arabic lateen style, tied up along the low stone quays as if unloading cargo into the stone warehouses that took up a goodly stretch of the town along the water.

"Troops are going in now, sir!" Lieutenant Farley pointed out as soon as the gunsmoke cleared enough for him to see.

Sure enough, the barges filled with soldiers were well clear of the quickly-anchored transport ships and rowing quickly towards the beach, in a fairly good line-abreast formation, a far cry from their initial practice landings. Within five minutes, those eighteen barges would be grounding their bows on the sand and shingle, and the soldiers of the 94th would go leaping ashore.

"Return fire, sir!" Lieutenant Farley said.

The ancient castle-like fort that brooded over Tropea did not, as Caesar had said, have any openings for guns, having been built long before artillery came into general use. There were some wee windows and arrow slits, and the only places to site cannon were atop the old round tower, and along the seaward ramparts of a long, barracks-like adjoining building.

Lewrie raised his telescope to watch tiny ant figures in French blue uniforms and shakoes scurrying round some artillery pieces, and a blossom of smoke here and there as a gun was fired. Shot whistled and moaned overhead, a couple of balls skip-splashed between *Vigilance* and the shore, and the ship drummed to at least one hit.

"Aim closer, aim closer, you buggers!" some gunner was crying.

"Not too many of them, it appears," Lewrie said to the quarterdeck with his glass still pressed to one eye. "Twelve pounders? They should have twenty-fours, or thirty-twos to defend proper."

"Might not have had guns at all, sir, 'til the French came," the Sailing Master commented. "Oh, well shot, I say!"

Vigilance's sketchy efforts at close aiming were beginning to pay off, for, still firing individually instead of broadside, her guns were hammering the notched stone ramparts at the top of the tower, and stone blocks, raised and mortared into place perhaps six hundred years before, were coming loose, falling down in cascades with each roundshot's impact, leaving the few cannon atop the tower nakedly exposed, and the fort's guns without ring-bolts for run-out or train tackle. One cannon got dragged off the tower roof as the stones in front of it gave way!

"That was a field piece, by God!" Wickersham laughed. "A high-wheeled twelve-pounder, by God!"

"And some very surprised Piedmontese gunners," Lewrie agreed.

He swung his telescope over to see how the soldiers were doing, wishing yet again for some way that he could devise that could provide the element of surprise. The small squadron had sailed from Sicily in the wee hours, after taking apart the shore camp and bringing all that and the troops aboard the transports the afternoon before. They had come to an-chor off Tropea round Ten in the morning, and no matter how fast they had gotten the soldiers into the boats, the enemy in the fort and the town had had bags of time to prepare to receive them. Lewrie could only see the road above the beach and the low buildings behind it, the lower part of town and the old fort, and what lurked beyond, up in the maze of nar-row lanes leading up to a rather fine church and a hint of a public square or two, a *palazzo* or two, was completely unknown.

Lewrie glanced up at the ship's fighting tops and cross-trees, where he had posted three Midshipmen with telescopes. Perhaps, they could see fur-ther, or deeper into the town. He opened his mouth to shout a demand of what they saw, but stopped after taking a deep breath. He'd given strict orders for them to sing out if they saw troop movement, or a threat to Col-onel Tarrant's soldiers, stressing that the 94th's safety was in their hands. He had to trust that those Mids would take their duties seriously.

Over to the left, Lewrie caught a flicker from the corner of his eyes; the troops of the 94th were all on top of the road, now, and had stripped the leather covers off their furled colours, freeing the King's Colours and the dark green Regimental Colours to flutter in the soft morning wind. He could see that Colonel Tarrant was cautiously deploying skirmishers to guard the road approaches from the next town up the peninsula, Vibo Valentia, and others were set to breaking in doors of every building along-side the road before marching into Tropea's warren of streets and dock-side district.

"Load grape atop roundshot!" Lieutenant Rutland's deep voice could be heard shouting to the gun crews of the upper gun-deck. "Let's make it hot for their damned gunners!"

"Oh, crash-bang and down it goes, hah!" Mr. Wickersham roared in joy to see a substantial part of the old tower crumble from continual heavy blows from the ship's lower-deck 24-pounders, The few remaining can-non crammed into its top, and the gunners manning them, fell in a jumble of stone blocks. Some of it collapsed onto the skree slope and steep cliffs at the fort's base, and some crashed down onto the roof of the long barracks-like building, smashing even more guns into ruin, and silence. *Vigilance*'s sailors gave a great cheer at the sight.

"Shift fire to the left, to the long building!" Lieutenant Farley was shout-ing through a brass speaking trumpet. "D'ye *hear*, there? Shift to the remaining guns!"

"Wouldn't work on a properly built stone fortress, you know," the Sailing

Master was idly informing the two Midshipmen who stood waiting to run messages from the quarterdeck. "A modern fortress is stronger than that old ruin. But, we could do one of those harm, young sirs. Oh, my, yes! Our eighteens and twenty-fours from just one side of the ship is the equivalent of an entire army's siege train."

"How many guns remain ashore, Mister Farley?" Lewrie asked the First Lieutenant.

"No more than two, or three perhaps, sir," Farley replied.

"And, they're busy dealing with us," Lewrie said, making up his mind. "Time to send our boats in and raise Hell in the harbour and the quays. Mister Whitehead? Mister Greenleaf? Off you go!"

"Marines, stand to!" Captain Whitehead roared. "Man the boats!"

Seventy Marines, barge crews, and a party of armed sailors under the Third Officer swarmed over the bulwarks, onto the boarding nets, and clambered down into the boats arrayed along the ship's larboard, disengaged side. Their departure took longer than usual since the starboard side could not be used, but in short order, all four barges and the gig were stroking over the relatively calm offshore waters close to shore, and into the much calmer waters in the harbour.

Vigilance's upper gun deck 18-pounders and the lower gun deck 24-pounders were still banging away at the longer building, turning its upper ramparts jagged where blocks had been shot away, and some of the roof platform stone had fallen inwards, exposing the floor below. The upper parts of the building seemed to shine with flinty sparks where Lieutenant Rutland's grapeshot struck and whined away in ricochet. One minute, then two minutes passed, and there was no more return fire from the fort. It, and its guns and gunners, had been shot to silence.

"Mister Farley," Lewrie said, stepping close to be heard over the din of the ship's guns. "Lay a spring on the cable, and direct our fire at the vessels in harbour, and the Quays, to cover our boats as they approach them."

"Over their heads, sir," Farley said, trying not to make it a question, for it would be a risky proposition.

"Slow, aimed fire, sir," Lewrie repeated. "Over their heads."

"Aye aye, sir! Bosun Gore! Spring on the cable!" Farley called.

Before that could be obeyed, though, all three Midshipmen in the tops and cross-trees shouted together in a babble of excitement. "Deck, there! Enemy troops ashore! Moving from behind the fort for the town centre, and the quays!"

"Numbers!" Lewrie shouted aloft even as he stepped on the slide carriage of a starboard carronade, the stubby barrel, then to the bulwarks so he could take hold of the mizen stays to get a higher, closer look.

"Hundreds, sir!" was one guess, "Two hundred!" was a second.

Settling in with one arm laced round a stay, Lewrie raised his telescope to make a guess of his own. He beheld wee ants crawling into view, black shakoes with flashing brass face plates, blue tunics with white crossbelts, dingy white waist-coats and trousers, bunched into three distinct groups of soldiers marching at the double-quick, muskets erect and close to their shoulders.

He had seen French soldiers at the Battle of Vimeiro as they'd marched in dense columns into the fire from General Arthur Wellesley's army, and learned how they'd form round a gilded eagle like ancient Roman legions. These soldiers didn't display one of those, but did have pole-mounted flags hung vertically from cross-pieces.

Company flags? he wondered; *three full companies, that'd be round three hundred men? Well, damn!*

Whether they had been sheltering in the fort or behind it, whether they had been spurred to deploy at last by the sight of his barges rowing ashore, or by reports of Colonel Tarrant's soldiers entering the town, he did not know, but, either way they presented a danger. And he had no shared signals to display to warn Tarrant of their presence!

He looked to the left of the town, hoping to spot the 94th, or their colour party, but they must have advanced beyond the point where the road from the beach entered Tropea, and his view was now masked by two- or three-storey houses and buildings close to the shore, and the steeper cliffs above the way to the warehouses and quays.

Dammit! He could do nothing, but could only hope that Tarrant was a wily and cautious soldier, and had put out his Light Company as skirmishers in advance of his march, and would be warned! Lewrie felt a rare helplessness, a frustration that he was not ashore himself with sword in hand! As satisfying as it had been to reduce that old fort, and glorying in the roar and power of his ship's guns, there was nothing more that he could do but watch events unfold. A sea fight, hull-to-hull, was one thing, but this?

"The starboard battery will now bear, sir," Lieutenant Farley yelled up to him.

"Very well, sir!" Lewrie snapped, slamming the tubes of his telescope shut and turning round to jump back down. "Engage the quays and those damned soldiers. Slow aimed fire, and warn Mister Rutland that grapeshot is *not* required, at present."

He made his way to the quarterdeck, then went up to the higher view on the poop, where he extended his telescope once more. The enemy soldiers had reached the quays and had deployed in company blocks, four ranks deep, to oppose Captain Whitehead's and Lieutenant Greenleaf's approaching barges, which had already threaded their way through the fishing boats anchored outer-most of the harbour.

He had to grin, even so, as he saw men on those boats abandoning them like so many rats leaving a sinking ship as they suddenly realised that their boats, and their livelihoods, would be taken. Italian fishermen were pouring into their rowboats in a rush, some diving into the harbour waters, to row or swim for the nearest shore.

"Mister Rutland, the upper-deck battery may engage!" Lieutenant Farley shouted down. "Aimed fire, by gun! Six-pounders will also open fire!"

Once more, *Vigilance* awoke fresh thunder and clouds of powder smoke, and the roar of her 18-pounders and lighter 6-pounders echoed off the shore, loud enough to shake the bell towers in town, creating faint *Bongs!* from the nearest churches.

"That's the way!" Lewrie shouted as the smoke cleared, and he could see what that careful demi-broadside had wrought. "Oh, spot-on! Skin the bastards, lads!"

Large, barn-like wooden doors of the warehouses were blown open or down, shot holes in the wooden buildings stood out starkly, and on the stone or brick warehouses there were deep indentations. The Piedmontese soldiers' ranks had been ripped apart as heavy roundshot tore through the front ranks then the ones standing behind them, tearing off limbs, driving right through chests, and mangling bellies and taking off heads!

Soldiers! Lewrie sneered; *They* never *understand what a ship's broadside can do! They just stand and suffer for their ignorance!*

The 6-pounders were quicker to load than the 18-pounders, and they got off second rounds whilst the heavier guns were still running out, again, and the enemy soldiers were slinking away from the gory remains of their comrades.

"What the Devil?" Lewrie blurted as he saw something a little to the left of the quays. "Hold fire, Mister Farley! Cease fire!"

It was smoke, gunsmoke, a sudden cloud of it rising above the houses as Colonel Tarrant's 94th Foot deployed into two-deep ranks and engaged the enemy soldiers, taking the nearest-company block, what was left of it, under sudden, concentrated fire. A moment later and there was a rush of red-coated figures dashing forwards with bayonets glittering under the muzzles of their muskets, mouths open in a battle yell that could not carry out to *Vigilance*.

"Huzzah for the army! Huzzah!" a Midshipman on the quarterdeck cried. "Go it! Get them all!"

The Piedmontese had not affixed bayonets of their own, expecting to engage the Marines and sailors with musketry, so they were not ready for a spirited bayonet charge, and stood stunned and flat-footed too long. Some quicker off the mark simply dropped their muskets and ran for their lives, a few smarter soldiers quickly held their weapons aloft, muzzle down in sign of surrender, though that did not spare them all from a Redcoat with his blood up.

That first company disappeared, swarmed over by Tarrant's men, and the middle company could not wheel about to present a firm front with loaded muskets. Some shots were fired before the 94th slammed into them, too, and that company, still with gaping holes in their ranks, suffered the fate of the first.

The last company block of Piedmontese did try to wheel about, but by then, realising that they were now out-numbered by at least three-to-one, simply broke and ran, shedding shakoes, muskets, cartridge boxes, and back packs, heading up the lanes into the upper town.

"I think you can unload, swab out, and secure the guns, Mister Farley," Lewrie said, leaning over the cross-deck hammock stanchions to call down to the quarterdeck. "It appears that Tropea is now ours."

"Aye aye, sir!" Farley replied, beaming fit to bust.

It was hours later, though, that the troops could march back to the beach, re-board their boats, and return to their transports, laden with booty. It took hours before *Vigilance*'s Marines and armed sailors could finish up their duties ashore, as well.

The ruins of the old fort and tower had to be gone through for papers, the search for information limited by the fact that very few of the ship's people had any Italian, spoken or written. The warehouses had to be searched, as did the coastal trading vessels alongside the quays or anchored out, their ownership papers seized along with their manifests, and the vessels set alight to deprive the French of the means to stage another invasion attempt upon Sicily. Those fires made quite a show, and a welcome to the Piedmontese soldiers who had been out in the countryside to forage,

loot, and collect taxes, As the last of *Vigilance*'s boats came alongside, en-
enmy soldiers could be seen in the upper part of Tropea, drawn back by
the sounds of cannon fire and the great pillars of smoke.

The work of searching the warehouses had been made difficult by the
citizens of Tropea. Once the gunfire had ended, they had swarmed out of
their houses' basements and places of hiding and had rushed to loot the
warehouses like so many starving wolves. With hand-carts and donkeys,
even wheelbarrows, goods of all sorts had been carried away as if the occupying troops had kept every morsel of food, every bottle of wine in the
town and its environs for themselves, starving Tropea's people.

"What was that bee swarm about, sir?" Lewrie asked Marine Captain
Whitehead once he was back aboard, and had slaked his thirst at one of
the scuttle-butts. "Was all the food in town in there?"

"Lord, sir," Captain Whitehead said, his eyebrows pumping as he
chuckled. "What *wasn't* in those warehouses! Food, of course, aye, dry
pasta, flour, and grains by the sacks, piled to the roof beams, along with
oceans of wine in barricoes, ankers, kegs, and pipes. The locals carried
off a lot of that, but they seemed more interested in bolts of cloth, furniture, paintings, and sculpture. Linen, cotton, drapery material, silk, satin,
as if the French are stripping every museum, fine house, and palace of their
wealth."

"They do that everywhere they go," Lewrie growled, "the greedy bastards. I heard they have special Commissioners who travel with the army
whose job it is to steal the best and ship it back to Paris, so the art can be
shown in the Louvre, or Napoleon's palace."

"Wouldn't have thought that this part of Italy would yield that much,
sir," Whitehead replied, "the best pickings would surely be in the larger
cities, Naples, Rome, and the cities in the North. Why all that's here in
Tropea is beyond me. Oh, we fetched off cured hams and flour, coffee and
cocoa beans, about ten pounds of tea, sacks of sugar, and lots of dried
fruit for puddings and duffs. The crew can thank my Marines for that,
later, hah!"

"Most welcome, Captain Whitehead," Lewrie said, "though, that is
against the Articles of War, if one wanted t'get strict about it, looting a
prize before it goes to the Prize Court."

"Well, sir," Whitehead said with a sly look, "I doubt we could fetch
warehouses and burned ships away to a Court. Our . . . *foraging* took place
on land, and could be termed the spoils of war."

"Do I get a ham out of it?" Lewrie said, smiling back.

"You do, indeed, sir!" Whitehead assured him.

"Spoils of war it is, then," Lewrie amiably agreed.

"Hoy, the boat!" a Midshipman shouted, drawing Lewrie to the bulwarks. It was one of the twenty-nine-foot barges from *Spaniel,* the largest of the transports, bearing Colonel Tarrant, Major Gittings, and their orderlies, and what looked to be another small hoard of loot. Those two officers had sailed to Tropea on *Spaniel* so they could go ashore with their men, but, now that the raid was done, they were returning to their better quarters aboard *Vigilance.*

Tarrant and Gittings made it up the ship's side to the entry-port easily, though their loot had to come up in a cargo net, and the sacks gave off some metallic clinks and jangles when they landed on the deck.

"Gifts of the Magi, Colonel Tarrant?" Lewrie japed as their orderlies and some off-watch hands carried the sacks below to the wardroom.

"War relics, Captain Lewrie!" Tarrant jovially boasted. "Things to adorn the officers' mess, and items to put in a place of honour in my home. The gentlemen who funded the creation of the regiment didn't go so far as to bless us with a lavish silver service, just some few items. Well, we have a lavish set now!"

"The enemy regiment's service, is it?" Lewrie asked, curious to see it.

"Not at all, sir," Tarrant told him. "We found it in the warehouses, crated up. Pitchers, creamers, sugar bowls, tea and coffee services, candlesticks and candelabras, decorative vases and figurines, and tableware enough for thirty or more, we haven't counted it yet."

"I didn't see any of that," Whitehead said.

"Ah, but the Army got to it first, sir," Tarrant drolly said. "A king's ransom in coin-silver. Finders keepers, what?"

"The question is, where did the enemy *get* such a trove?" Lewrie posed. "Were the crates marked for shipment to Paris or somewhere in France?"

"No markings at all, Captain Lewrie," Tarrant said, "and we did look. It was all we could do to lay hands on what we got, what with all the locals ripping boxes, crates, and barrels open and running out with what they took. They were everywhere, underfoot, fighting over what they wanted with each other, with my troops. It was like a mob back home when the first Spring vegetables show up at the greengrocers'."

"That makes as little sense as the artwork and the furniture," Lewrie said, puzzled. "This part of Italy can't have *that* many rich houses to loot."

"Curiouser and curiouser, sir," Captain Whitehead agreed.

"Oh well, I expect our hired spies can sort it out, eventually," Lewrie decided. "Mister Farley?"

"Aye, sir?" the First Officer, who had been listening to the conversation nearby, responded.

"Pipe stations to raise anchor and make sail," Lewrie ordered. "And have a signal hoisted to the transports to that effect."

"Aye aye, sir!" Farley said.

"Where to, might I ask, Captain Lewrie?" Colonel Tarrant said.

"Right back to your old camp on Sicily, sir," Lewrie told him. "But, I assure you that I'll send one of the transports to Malta to pick up fresh supplies, and your regiment's dependents, as soon as you are established ashore. Let's go up to the poop deck, out of the way."

"Oh, Gittings and I brought away several pounds of sausages," Tarrant said, once they were on the poop deck. "Salamis, and those spicy, peppery ones. I understand you've quite a store of sausages laid by for your cat. You're welcome to some."

"Thank you, sir," Lewrie said, "Chalky adores 'em, though the pepperoni is too spicy for his old tummy. *I'll* relish those. Did you have any casualties, Colonel?"

"We lost two men to musketry, and one to a bayonet," Tarrant said, turning sobre, "and I've six down with light injuries. Our Surgeon is established in *Spaniel*, where there is more room for a surgery and for them to convalesce. They'll be laid up for a time, but . . . ," he ended with a hopeful shrug. "It all went rather well, for a first try, and my soldiers are happy with their loot."

Enemy shakoes, hangers, coins, watches, pipes, and tobacco taken from the dead and wounded had gone aboard the transports, along with sausages, and the calfskin backpacks the French issued, whose straps didn't half-strangle those wearing them like British-designed packs did, Tarrant explained, along with the difficulty of keeping his men *sobre* enough to re-enter the boats and scramble up the boarding nets, after prowling the warehouses for wine barrels to be broken open, or searching their rucksacks and new back packs for smuggled bottles and flasks.

"It appears that the fires from those ships you set alight are spreading to the warehouses, sir," Colonel Tarrant said, taking a pocket telescope from the rucksack on his hip for a better look. "The stone ones may survive, but the wooden ones will surely burn down, more's the pity. They're still rather full of goods that the locals might have used."

"Hmm, someone's set fires in the fort, too, sir," Lewrie noted after extending the tubes of his own telescope. "Some locals, I see civilians milling about over there. With muskets."

"Those won't do the townsfolk much good," Tarrant said with a frown. "Soon as those surviving soldiers, and the ones that were out in the country, come down to the lower town, I expect they'll shoot anyone armed out-of-hand."

"You did not gather up the enemy arms, sir?" Lewrie asked.

"We did, but we left them in a pile," Tarrant told him. "Hah! We stripped the prisoners of their boots, trousers, and coats, and set *that* lot afire. Should have done the same with the muskets and cartridge pouches. That would have saved the people of Tropea a lot of grief . . . though I'm sure that what's left of the garrison will be vindictive enough."

"Or thrown them off the quays into the harbour," Lewrie added.

"Ah, well, we'll do that, next time, what?" Tarrant promised.

"You're right, though, Colonel," Lewrie said, taking a longer look at the ruin they'd made. "For a first try, things did go well. About a dozen coasting vessels burned, about the same number of fishing boats? That'll take pressure off Sicily, and force the French to move everything by road, which'll be much slower than by sea. You and your troops should feel proud of a job well done."

"Ehm, what about those three fishing boats sailing out, sir?" Tarrant pointed out.

"In case we can't trust our Sicilian spies, I'd like to have a way to skulk along the coasts, for myself," Lewrie told him with a grin.

"Hands are at stations, sir," Lieutenant Farley reported, "all ships have the signal hoisted and are ready to do the same."

"Very well, Mister Farley," Lewrie said, "strike the signal to show Execute, and get us under way."

CHAPTER THIRTY-FIVE

I think he's scared o' Harriet," Dasher said to Turnbow as they polished Lewrie's shiny pewter service, drawing Lewrie's attention from sealing yet another letter home. He leaned back in his desk chair to peer round into the dining coach where they were working, to see Chalky nose-to-nose with the rabbit, sniffing, crouched down with one paw up as if to slap. The rabbit made a short hop to one side, and Chalky went skyward, stiff-legged and backwards, two feet high, and a yard away with a startled *Rrowr!*

He'll get over that, soon, and then the fur will fly, Lewrie thought, sure that his cat would see the rabbit as large prey once the strangeness wore off.

"Third Officer, Mister Greenleaf, SAH!" the Marine sentry bawled.

'Oh, good," Lewrie muttered, then shouted for him to enter. He rose from his desk to greet him as Greenleaf came into the cabins.

"We think we've found a better place, sir," Greenleaf said at once, unfolding a quickly done map of the coast and the bay. "Major Gittings and I went ashore, and it looks good."

He and Lewrie leaned over it as Greenleaf speared a finger at a spot a few miles West of the current anchorage and army camp, closer to the shelter of the peninsula, and the tiny fishing port of Milazzo.

"Just below the fork in the roads that leads to Milazzo and Barcellona Pozzo di Gotto . . . however ya say *that* sobre, sir . . . there is a wide, sandy beach for the boats to land," Lieutenant Greenleaf told him, "and behind the beach there's a great, level area, some pasture, and some forest, none too thick. *And*, along the East side, there's a low gully with a fresh-water stream that runs into the sea, sir."

"Closer to *two* villages," Lewrie frowned. "That means even *more* pick-pockets, petty thieves, and smuggled spirits. What did Gittings say about that?"

"He and Colonel Tarrant thought they could cope, and keep their troops in check, sir," Greenleaf said with a shrug. "That it would be no worse than what they're dealing with already. The fresh water is welcome, and the fruits and vegetables will still be available from the locals. The Major said that at least there'd be no need for guards over the olive and fruit groves there, and that we might be able to cut some timber from the woods, for a fee, to make the camp a little more substantial, now that their dependents are coming."

"Well, if he wishes to move the camp, that's fine with me. But, what sort of anchorage would we have, Mister Greenleaf?" Lewrie asked. "Sufficient depth? Decent holding ground?"

"Four to five fathoms within a cable of the beach, sir, and the bottom is eight to ten fathoms deep two cables off," Greenleaf said, running a finger along his line of soundings. "The 'dipsy' lead on a shorter line brought up coarse sand and thick grey mud everywhere we let it run, sir, so the anchors should hold well enough except in a stiff blow from the North."

"And we'd stand out to sea and stand off-and-on if that should happen, aye," Lewrie agreed. The waxed bottom of the "dipsy" lead had brought up samples that were not all that different from the bottom of Portsmouth harbour, so he thought that the ships would be safe, in most instances.

"Those two villages, sir," Greenleaf suggested, "we could let the men have a poor sort of shore liberty. And, there's room ashore for football and criquet, and sea bathing, or just beach idling."

"I could consider it, once we've . . . ," Lewrie began to say but there came a shout from the deck of "Sail Ho!", followed by a yell from the Marine sentry that a Midshipman Langdon wished to see the Captain.

"Enter!" Lewrie called out.

"Beg pardon, sir," Langdon, a gawky twenty-five-year-old Mid said, "but there is a boat entering the anchorage, sir. It appears to be a fishing boat."

"Headed into Milazzo, or here, sir?" Lewrie asked.

"She looks to be bows-on to us, sir," Langdon reported.

"Good ho! Fresh fish for supper, sir!" Lieutenant Greenleaf said with eagerness, rubbing his stomach. "A nice snapper, I hope."

"We'll see," Lewrie said, picking up his telescope to go on deck to spy out the strange boat in his shirtsleeves. "Thankee, Mister Langdon. Well done, Mister Greenleaf. Let's go 'smoak' our visitor."

"I say, sir," Greenleaf said as they bustled to the door. "Is that rabbit *chasing* your cat, sir?"

The strange fishing boat, about forty feet long, was scabrous and filthy at first glance, its once colourful paint fading and peeling, and her sails much patched, but her rigging, and her crew's handling of her coming to anchor and handing her sails were first rate. An equally shabby rowboat was led out from towing astern and several men went down into her. Lewrie recognised the largest fellow as their spy-chief he'd met at Mr. Quill's lodgings in Messina, Julio Caesare.

Lewrie thought the man would come aboard *Vigilance*, but his boat only came alongside so Caesare could shout up, inviting Lewrie to come ashore, where Caesare could speak with both him and Colonel Tarrant. Reluctantly, Lewrie called for his boat crew, donned coat and waist-coat, and followed in Caesare's wake, to land on the beach and wade ashore.

"Ah, *Capitano Inglese, buon giorno*!" Caesare cried, arms out as he came to embrace Lewrie, slapping him on the back and bestowing a hairy kiss or two on his cheeks, "*Buon giorno! Miracoloso! Una vittoria*, ha! You cut the Piedmontese *balls* off! *Bello, bello!* Everything smashed, and many enemy dead. So many ships and boats burned, but I see you take some away, *si*? Everything I tell you is true, *si*? Julio Caesare is man of his word, knowing everything on the coasts."

"Indeed you are, sir," Lewrie replied, freed from the garlicky kisses and the bear-hug, at last, and stepping back a half-step so the man couldn't grab him a second time. "Your information guaranteed our success. You did damned well."

Damned excitable . . . foreigners! he thought: *Try* that *in London and they'd lock you in the stocks!*

"And now you wish to strike again, not so?" Caesare asked with a shrewd look, and a rub at his unshaven chin. "I come to have the *progetto*, the . . . plan? Oh, these are your *soldati*? Head of *soldati* is here? A *colonnello*, is he? Good! We put the heads together, ha ha!"

Colonel Tarrant, Major Gittings, and many of the company officers had come down near the beach to see what the commotion was, and Lewrie did the introductions. Either Caesare could not pronounce Tarrant and Gittings, or he did not care; they became *Colonnello Inglese* and *Maggiore Inglese*. Tarrant invited them all into his pavillion, the largest tent in the U-shaped encampment with the open end facing the sea and the beach. Even in late morning, the interior was stifling, though two sides had been rolled up and the fly was open. Glasses were produced, and some white wine chilled in a bucket of seawater was poured.

"Might I ask, *Signore* Caesare," Colonel Tarrant began, "just how much damage did we do? We took to our boats before the fires really took hold."

"Oh, *Colonnello*!" Caesare hooted. "Fort and tower is gone, when gunpowder blows up. Cannon buried in ruins, carriages burned. All of wood warehouses burned up, and Tropea people set fire to goods inside the others, so all is lost, and the damned *Francesi* left with nothing! Piedmontese *Colonnello* and half his *ufficiali*, great brutes and thieves, dead. I tell you half his *soldati* will be out in country? Was true, *si*? Three hundred in town, I learn after. Maybe a hundred run off to cathedral, beg the *santuario*, eh, sanctuary? Rest dead or wounded and some who throw guns away get killed by townspeople. *They* set the many fires, in revenge.

"But," Caesare sobred, looking pained, "Piedmontese who come to town from looting in country take great revenge. Many firing squads, half-dozen at a time shot, bayonetted for having guns or swords. Much pity, uhm . . . *great* pity."

"Damme, I *knew* we should have thrown those muskets into a fire!" Colonel Tarrant exclaimed, angered by the enemy response. "Put them in the boats you burned, Lewrie, or tossed them into the harbour. But, the locals were snatching them up as quickly as we piled them up."

"Take away, next time, *Colonnello*," Caesare suggested. "Corsican Rangers, Sicilian Volunteer *reggimento* need guns, even made by *Francesi* . . . and ammunition to fit them. My men and I need guns. To spy along coast is dangerous business without guns. You bring me guns, next time, I pay well. *Signore* Quill, *he* wishes guns to give to . . . partisans?"

"And is there a partisan movement over on the mainland?" Lewrie asked.

"Ah, not so much, yet, *signores*," Caesare had to confess. "One time, *Signore* Quill get four dozen muskets, *molti* cartridge, pouches, say he gets letter from man in Maratea, up coast, who say he have hundred fighters eager, but no guns. I go meet him on beach with muskets, but there is only one old man in Neapolitan army coat, a priest, ten men, and one donkey. They take away two dozen, could not carry more, then we never hear from him again. I think the *Francesi* and their *Maresciallo* Murat, a great Devil, scare the people too much. Not like my Siciliani! *Francesi* try to come here, every man, woman, child cut their throats in their sleep! Never make a Sicilian angry, no no! The Corsican *vendetta* is nothing to ours!"

"One thing that struck me as odd, *Signore* Caesare," Colonel Tarrant said as he made free with the semi-chilled bottle of wine, "was so much wealth, so many remarkable things stored in those warehouses, silver, silks, fine art, grains, and foodstuffs. What was it doing there in an out-of-the-way place like Tropea?"

"Ah, *Colonnello*," Caesare said with a wordly-wise smile, "I tell you Piedmontese *Colonnello* and his *ufficiali* are great thieves? Send loot to their homes, their banks. Take away food and wine and pasta, then sell it back to locals at great profit, and people pay or starve. Their *soldati* feast like old Roman emperors, the pigs.

"You will see the same everywhere you strike," Caesare went on, "I hope you keep some for yourselves, *si*? Heh heh heh. Now, there is a place I will scout where *molti* boats can be burned, no fort or guns, but warehouses, rich warehouses, *si*? Garrison is *Tedesci*. Germans."

"Might put up a stouter defence than Piedmontese," Gittings said.

"Is it urgent?" Lewrie asked. "As you see, *Signore* Caesare, one of our transports is off to Malta for fresh provisions, mail, and the regiment's dependents."

"Dependents?" Caesare repeated, one syllable at a time, with a quizzical look on his face.

"Their families," Lewrie said. "Wives, sweethearts, and children."

"Ah, the *famiglia*!" Caesare brightened. "You *Inglesie*," he said, shaking his head in wonder. "Go to war with wives and babies? *Straordinario!*"

"Well, not so many," Tarrant said, describing the lot drawing, and army limitations on the numbers allowed. "In the meantime, we mean to shift our encampment closer to Milazzo, where there is a stream for fresh water, timber for sale, and slightly better shelter for Lewrie's ships. Show him, Gittings."

"Ah, *si*," Caesare said after poring over a copy of the Major's hand-drawn map. "*Bello!* Is very good anchoring there, and I can help. I am knowing *molti* people in Milazzo and Barcellona, ones who sell the fresh fish, goats, and sheep, milk for *bambini*, fruit and vegetables. Timber? Wood to build with?"

"We thought that with our dependents arriving, we'd lay floors and risers to get the tents a bit off the ground," Tarrant told him, "raise some walls for semi-permanent huts, roof trusses, and use our tents for the roof coverings."

"I get you all the wood you want, *signores*!" Caesare boasted. "Nails and tools, and workers, too, if you wish! I know *everybody*!"

"Well, that would be wonderful if you could, *Signore* Caesare," Tarrant cautiously allowed, not willing to leap into an agreement at once. "We could break camp and march down there tomorrow morning, and allow you time to speak with your friends and associates to make the arrangements for supplying us. Ehm, how much might they ask for their goods, though?" he asked, worried about his regimental chest funds.

There goes his new mess silver, Lewrie cynically thought; *Arm and a leg sound about right?*

"Milazzo and Barcellona are poor towns, *signores*," Caesare explained with his hands out as if pleading. "A little amount of coin is going a long way, *comprendere*? New customers, *soldati*, the *famiglia*, and *Capitano Inglese*'s sailors make a big market they not have before. You be very welcome, great friends! Allies!"

"Just so long as they don't rob us blind," Major Gittings complained. "We're already surrounded by thieves."

"The ignorant, greedy *paisani*?" Caesare spat, then laughed. "You have no trouble in new place, *signores*, I guarantee it. Caesare say no stealing, then there is none. Mention my name *anywhere* in the East of Sicily, say you are friend of *Don* Julio Caesare, and all the doors open to you! Your camp will be safe, and your *famiglia* will be safe when you go to make the great raid! I cut the balls off anyone who steals, or bothers you, and make them *eat* them! Hah hah hah! We drink to bargain, *si*? Drink to promise!"

And drink they did, though they had to open a second bottle of white wine, one not cooled in the tub of salt water.

Who is *this bugger? Is he* that *powerful?* Lewrie wondered.

"Ah, is good," Caesare said after tossing every drop down his throat and holding out his glass for more. "*Capitano*, I wonder, though. As I say, Milazzo is poor, and they have no way to build big boats," he said to Lewrie. "Little rowing boats, only, *si*? And, I have very few boats that

I can use to seek places to strike for you, and go ashore to get the information you need."

"Yayss?" Lewrie drawled in wariness, sure that his goat would be got.

"If you give Milazzo two of the big fishing boats so they can go far out to sea and catch more fish, they, and all your people eat better," Caesare wheedled with a wide smile, and some humble shrugs. "And I could use just one more boat that comes from Basilicata region to spy for you all. You give me all three, and I can assure you that the timber, the nails, and all you and *Colonnello Inglese* need or want will cost you nothing, and the food and wine, the fruits and the vegetables will be very inexpensive. A bargain?" he said, holding out a hand to be shaken.

"Oh, well I say, Lewrie!" Colonel Tarrant marvelled with delight at the offer. "What d'ye say to that, sir? It's not as if they would be worth much at the Prize Court on Malta. What use would you have made of them, anyway?"

I think I'm bein' fucked, Lewrie thought; *but I don't see how, yet. There's something about this bugger that's . . . shifty.*

"Oh, why not," Lewrie said, surrendering to the greedy looks of the others. "Aye, all three fishing boats are yours, *Don* Julio."

"*Bello, bello!*" Caesare cried in joy, shaking Lewrie's hand.

Their meeting broke up soon after that, Caesare vowing that he would sail instanter to Milazzo and lay the groundwork, whilst some of his spare hands aboard his own boat would make sail and take away the former prizes. Lewrie sourly took note of the fact that Caesare's crew suddenly tripled in size, as if many of them had been down below, out of sight 'til he'd struck his lop-sided bargain.

Colonel Tarrant offered to dine Lewrie in, and he accepted, telling his boat crew to return to *Vigilance* 'til he wig-wagged a signal for them to return for him, so they would not miss out on their own mid-day meal, and the first rum issue of the day.

Just before a dessert of berries and sweet bisquits, a rider approached the camp, was challenged, and asked to see the *Inglese Capitano* "Luey". With a sigh, and a quick explanation to his fellow diners that foreigners *never* got his name right, Lewrie rose and went out to see Quill's lad, Fiorello, on a saddled mule.

"From *Signore Quill, signore,*" Fiorello said, pulling a sealed letter from a bag on his hip, where he also kept a long sausage which he also produced, and bit into.

"Thankee, lad, ehm . . . *grazie*, Fiorello," Lewrie said, delighting the lad that his name was remembered.

Under the pole-stretched fly of Tarrant's pavillion, he opened the letter to read it.

Sir Alan,

I am in receipt of the results of your initial raid, and I must say it appears to have been a smashing success, which I shall praise to the skies far and wide, though not drawing too much attention to the choice of Tropea as your first landing, should anyone in London look too closely into the town's use as an entrepot for smuggled goods in addition to the loot amassed by the Piedmontese commandant and his officers.

Tropea, you see, the choice of which I was unaware, is, or rather was, controlled by one of Julio Caesare's principal competitors in bed with the Piedmontese commandant, and given protection for a share of the profits on both sides of the bargain in smuggling to Sicily and the province of Basilicata, and the luxury items stolen from the wealthiest families of said province.

Do watch Caesare like a hawk, for he is one of the greatest scoundrels, but alas, a most useful one! Now that he has ascendancy over the trade in smuggled goods, he may be satisfied, but I fear that, given the situation as it exists, he will use us as much as we will make use of him!

I knew it, I bloody knew *it! I felt* he wasn't straight! Lewrie fumed in silence. This revelation was nothing to share with Tarrant, his officers, or Admiral Charlton in his written report of the action.

He's made me . . . us! . . . his partners in crime! Lewrie goggled.

CHAPTER THIRTY-SIX

*L*ieutenant Fletcher had returned from Malta with fresh provisions, more war *matériel* that Tarrant had added to his "absolutely essential" list, the 94th's dependents, and mail. Lewrie could look shoreward from his stern gallery or the poop deck at almost any hour of the day and see smoke from laundry cauldrons, feminine clothing drying on lines between trees, and children shrieking round the tent lines at play, or running along the beach, and splashing into the surf.

"And how was Mister Fletcher's voyage, Mister Upchurch?" Lewrie asked the Midshipman who had gone over to *Bristol Lass* to collect their mail.

"I gathered that he'd rather have carried cattle, or soldiers, sir," Upchurch said with a sniff of humour, "both are less noisy, or disorderly than the regiment's wives and children. Less messy, too."

Mail, now! News from home; at last!

After leaving Portsmouth for Malta, weeks before, *Vigilance* had sailed into a figurative black cavern, and the ship, and her consorts, had departed Valletta Harbour before a mail packet could arrive with anything for them. Whilst still at Portsmouth, Lewrie had received at least two letters a week from Jessica, his father, family, or long-time friends, but, after departing there had been nothing. Likewise, Lewrie was sure that Jessica must have thought that he had sailed off the edge of the world, for the long "sea letters" he'd written her had been delayed 'til arrival at Malta, and might take weeks more to reach her. He'd sent off another flurry of letters when *Bristol Lass* went to Malta, in hopes that those made amends, hoping Jessica could inure herself to a naval wife's lot, so unlike the same-day deliverance of letters sent cross town by footmen, maids, or neighbourhood lads.

Now, he had such a high-piled feast of letters that he didn't know where to begin, looking for the dates on which they had been dispatched. Was Jessica that orderly? Unfortunately, no, so he just dove in, tearing open the first that came to hand.

"Bisquit *sings?*" he muttered aloud. "He *likes* music?"

> . . . *the drollest thing, dearest Alan! Do recall that I learned to play a harpsichord which we used at St. Anselm's, and, quite by chance I was able to obtain one, used of course, but in fine condition for only £60 from your friend Clotworthy Chute's emporium. Harpsichords are rapidly going out of Fashion, piano fortes are all the rage, but I cannot abide how loud and clangy they strike my ears. It looks grand in the drawing room, and, when I and my lady friends had a tea, we gathered round it to play some songs. Wonder of wonders, Bisquit, Rembrandt, and the kitchen terrier, Bully, came running to sit and marvel. Bisquit, though, began to croon whilst the other dogs shewed less interest. When I stopped, he whimpered and yipped for me to continue! Perhaps it is only your penny whistle that irritates his ears, but he seems quite enamoured of Music, especially the slower Ballads.*

"Well, just damn my eyes!" Lewrie said in wonder. "Wish I'd been home t'see that! Wait. Sixty pounds?"

Reading further, Lewrie discovered that Sir Hugo had ponied up more than half the sum, and Jessica had used some of her earnings for the purchase, which prompted him to gawp once more over the idea that his father would be *that* generous!

In another letter, Jessica described how grand their back garden was progressing, and how she had chosen the flowers to be bedded, the saplings she had had planted, and how lovely the aspect would be when the imported crape myrtles, dogwoods, and cherry trees would be in a year or two when they put out blossoms. She had hopes for some dwarf Chinese magnolias, but London weather, and the pall of coalsmoke, might disappoint her.

. . . Catherine writes that she was safely delivered of her third Child,
weeks before the predicted date round Midsummer Day, a healthy
Boy, and that she is now most marvellously Fat!

Who the Devil's Catherine? Lewrie asked himself, dredging his memory but coming up with nothing.

She was attended by a Surgeon-trained mid-wife, a Male one. I
have never heard the like, but he was most Insistent on Cleanliness,
and everything went well. With a Baby, and two other Children,
their Household is quite Chaotic, so it may be some months before
they take leave of the Church at Windsor and coach to London to
show him off.

Windsor. Oh, her sister-in-law, *and her husband's in the family church*
trade, Lewrie thought with an "Aha."

I am most Envious, dearest Husband. I know that Babies are not
placed by fairies under cabbages, but, I had most dearly Hoped that
there would have been a Heavenly Result of our Divine Intimacies.
And now you are far away Overseas, and that Hope must be put in
Abeyance 'til your most-desired Return. I comfort myself with the
thought that the Marriage I hoped for since girlhood came at last, and
was all the Sweeter for the Delay. So, too, I Trust, that once your grim
Duty is done, we shall be Blessed with at least one Child of our very
Own, a Boy who shall grow up to be as dashing, handsome, kind,
generous, and loving as you, my Dearest, or a Girl who shall be as
Impish as me! Dare I wish that she is a better Horsewoman?

Lewrie opened a third letter from Jessica and found that she had dated them, at the top of the first page. That prompted him to open all of them at once and sort them out in chronological order.

You once alluded that your Father was not the most Hospitable man,
having grown used to his Solitary Pursuits, and a quiet, ordered Life.

Pray God ye never learn what he solitarily pursues! Lewrie told himself with an audible snigger.

*I must own that Sir Hugo initially inspired in me a Dread, being so
fierce in visage in his old Age, and so sharp of Tongue even in idle
Conversation. Imagine my Surprise, dearest Alan, that Sir Hugo has
invited me to dine at his house, escorted me safely when I am required
to go to the rougher parts of town, and, in short, has become a doting
Father-in-Law, and the Delight of my lady friends when invited to
Tea!*

Aye, he likes t'sniff round the ladies, Lewrie thought; *though he did stand
as Sophie's 'grand-père' when she lived with me and Caroline as our ward. Sophie adored him!* He *can be pleasing, damn him.*

*Poor old thing, he is now most Vexed by the London Season, for not
only is he hosting your Daughter Charlotte, and Governour and
Millicent Chiswick, for the Summer, his neighbours have let out their
house next door to his, as they did before, and have gone down to the
Country, resulting in a constant Din and Bustle of comings and
goings. Your Father is of a mind to go down to Anglesgreen, and has
suggested that I might accompany him, but, alas, I have much too
much to do by way of illustrations commissioned, due by September.
Perhaps after?*

" 'Poor old thing'?" Lewrie growled aloud. "Mine arse!"

*Alan, as hard as I try to form true Fondness for your former brother-
in-law, Governour, I find it is a Trial. Millicent, I pity, and do like
her, though she has no Conversation and is Awkward in social
settings. Governour, though, I find the most Opinonated and Acerbic
man, used to trampling over anyone who would hold an opposing
Idea!*

Got him *pegged right*, Lewrie thought; *He is a trial!*

Jessica complained about Charlotte, and how cloying her façade of
sweetness was, as if sugar would not melt in her mouth, but there was a
snippish, dismissive air about her, and an idle arrogance that sometimes
arose, as if she believed that she had been born on equal station with the
Quality, and had little patience with people that did not impress her, right
off, or be of immediate or future avail.

*As her Step-mother I have hosted Charlotte and the Chiswicks to
Supper and Teas, my Dearest, and I got the distinct impression that
she was dismissive of our Tasteful and Delightful House, and that it
did not rise to her Tastes. Despite the press of my Commissions, I did
offer to do her Portrait, gratis of course, and shewed her some of my
best Work, including your Portrait, and she did sit for half an hour
whilst I did a most lifelike coloured pencil sketch (if I do say so
myself), but she demurred. And Governour had the gall to suggest
that should she desire a Portrait in the future, he'd seek out a
Professional! Hah, I say! Hah!*

*Charlotte and Governour both seem to imagine that I must gad
about the mantua makers, milliners, shoemakers as her guide to the
latest London Fashion, and then spend my nights chaperoning her to
subscription balls and other social Occasions where she may shew
herself to likely Beaus, and it is becoming a bit too Much! I would
like to like her, be Supportive, win at least a grudging Relationship
with your Daughter, but my Lord! I will not, and cannot serve as her
"buttock-broker", as your Father so amusingly termed the Role!*

Aye, that's Governour, and Charlotte, to a Tee, Lewrie angrily thought,
disgusted that his former brother-in-law had turned into such a bullying
tyrant, and that his daughter, who had once been so sweet and loving, had
been raised under Governour's roof after Caroline had died, the utter ruin
of her.

If Charlotte needed a "buttock-broker", there were plenty of match-
makers in London who made their living prancing hopeful young men
and women round the town, dressing them, shoeing them, instructing in
how to be pleasing, and introducing them to other likely prospects.

Once more, the long time it took to send a letter irked Lewrie painfully,
for he had a sudden idea to write Jessica to tell her that such services were
available, even if Governour would scream bloody murder to shell out
money to some grande beldame, who like as not was a sham, a former
brothel keeper, or recruiter for one if fallen on hard times.

He'd write Clotworthy Chute, too, who'd made his own living playing "Captain Sharp" to unwary newcome heirs who came up to London
to gain some class. Clotworthy had had platoons of clothiers, hatters, shoemakers, saddlers, horse brokers, carriage sellers, and owners of somewhat fashionable lodgings to which he steered the gullible, and had gotten
a share of everything the naive fools had spent. All but the better brothels

he'd shown them to; the flinty-eyed Mother Abbesses did *not* share. Well, a free whore for an hour or so every now and then, but money? Never!

Clotworthy could steer Charlotte, and it would quite droll to the old scamp, and Lewrie, to lighten Governour's purse, to boot!

He *would* write those letters, instanter, but, the temptation to read the rest of his wife's wondrous letters was just too strong, and there were dozens of them still to go. Six Bells of the Forenoon rang and he had nothing else to do 'til his solitary dinner, and no demands from an anchored ship with one watch away on a brief shore liberty, so he picked up the next in the pile and read on.

> *My Dearest, most Loving Husband,*
>
> *What an unimaginable Surprise greeted me last morning when I called at your Father's house! I met your elder Son, Sewallis, who is come up to London to outfit himself for his Promotion to Lieutenant, mere days after receiving the glad news of it, and his posting to a Frigate that he describes as a Fifth Rate 38, the Daedalus, in which he is to be Third Officer! She is to be launched at Deptford within a fortnight, and I, Charlotte, your Father, and the Chiswicks plan to coach down for the day to witness it.*

"Well, good for him!" Lewrie said aloud, then explained his son's promotion to his cabin servants as the reason for his outburst.

> *One sees merchant ships in the Pool of London every day, but I have never seen a Warship and am looking forward to doing so, so that I can better imagine the life you lead, dearest. Oh, what Joy Sewallis's arrival caused, and even Governour Chiswick seemed elated, for once.*
>
> *Soon after Charlotte's and Sewallis's initial Elation to be reunited, though, she commented rather sourly that your Sons had both been sent to Sea to rid yourself of Children, and that to do so with the Eldest, and Heir, was especially Cruel; an opinion Sewallis was quick to scotch, explaining that he had joined the Navy by choice, to avenge his late Mother's Murder by the French, against your Will. He boasted that he had beaten his Brother to it, by Subterfuge. He hinted of saved Money, Letters altered written on Hugh's behalf. Forgeries? Sewallis's introduction to the Navy sounds nothing like my Brother's. You must write and explain it all to me, Dearest.*

Be sure your sins will find you out, Lewrie thought, wincing; *Forgery seems to run in the family!*

> *He seems a responsible young man, serious, sobre, and of obvious*
> *fine intelligence, though rather grave of mien, much like a young*
> *Curate who has just taken Holy Orders, though my long Experience*
> *with Churchmen may influence my Observation.*

He always was, Lewrie remembered; *Quiet, bookish, serious, and . . . rather dull, really. The only things that made him laugh were his setters, and his pony. And for some reason, he was always in competition with Hugh, when it should've been the other way round.*

For variety's sake, Lewrie opened a letter from his father next, to get his view of Charlotte's London Season, and Sewallis's surprise appearance. Sir Hugo was his usual acerbic self, so much so that his letter was actually amusing. At least until he got to the part where Sewallis's new uniforms, and replenishment of shirts, neck-stocks, and such, cost much more than the lad had, and Lewrie now owed his father £24/9/8 to repay him for the outlay. Jessica had given him those two scenic paintings she'd done of Sir Hugo's house at Anglesgreen, and the view of the countryside from its deep front gallery, and he was most pleased with them, and had hung them in a prominent place. Once Sewallis's ship was launched, he *would* go down to the country, if only to get away from the bustling, and from the former in-laws' continual company. Sir Hugo had little patience with the dull vacuity of Millicent Chiswick, sweet and kind though she was, and Governour and his host of loudly voiced opinions on anything and everything. He wished Charlotte the best of good fortune in husband-hunting, though she was a tad young for marriage, expressing a wish that she would become someone else's problem! Soon!

> *I fear, though, for my House and Property should I leave for the*
> *Country before the Chiswicks depart, for God only knows what ill*
> *Use they might make of it in my Absence, and how many of my*
> *Servants quit me for a quieter Place due to their many Demands.*
> *May this Season end tomorrow one way or another!*

There was a letter from his son Hugh, still aboard *Undaunted* on the North coast of Spain. Hugh related how active that station had become of late, after the arrival of many more warships under the command of Rear-Admiral Sir Home Popham. Not only were French merchantmen still fair game, Popham had instigated a series of landings, going after the chain of semaphore towers, coastal artillery batteries, and small fortifications, and staged cutting-out raids into enemy harbours to take, sink, or burn cargo ships, and setting fire to supplies in the warehouses, and the means of transportation inland. Dray waggons, carts, and even humble hand-carts were put to the torch, and, sad as it was, draught horses, mules, and oxen were shot dead, if there were no partisan bands close by to steal them away.

Naturally, Hugh hadn't seen Lisbon half as often as he had in the past, for *Undaunted* stayed at sea months on end, most enjoyable months. Popham was even training some borrowed Army troops to land from transports if a large-scale raid was envisaged, and had boasted that he had come up with a new and novel form of warfare!

God damn his blood! Lewrie fumed; *That vain coxcomb read my work, and now he's claimin' credit for it? He'll get away with it, too, he's gotten more ships than* I'll *ever have, the official backing that no one will allow* me! *God, will he claim he* wrote *it, too? And every last son of a bitch who's tryin' t'blight* my career will *praise* him *for it!*

"Life's unfair," Lewrie growled aloud, "and I need a drink!"

"More cool tea, sir?" Deavers asked from cross the cabins.

"Whisky!" Lewrie demanded. "A full bumper!"

"Ehm . . . aye, sir," Deavers replied, going to the wine-cabinet.

Chalky took that unfortunate moment to hop atop the desk with a play-ful trill, tail whisking in delight to nose, then paw, at the un-tidy pile of opened letters.

"Get out of it!" Lewrie roared in a tone so harsh and out of character that Chalky scrambled in fright off the desk, taking Jessica's letters down in an avalanche of good bond paper, scattering them over the deck. "Oh, just damn your blood, you clumsy . . . !"

"I'll pick 'em up, sir," Dasher quickly offered, sounding as if he was as cowed as the cat. "Bad boy, Chalky, bad cat. Oh, don't you be diggin' at 'em!" For Chalky, over his shock, was pouncing on one, then another, skit-tering them ever further afield.

"I'll take 'im," Turnbow said, scooping Chalky up and holding him against his chest with both hands. Surprisingly, he did not get clawed in a frantic escape attempt; the cat seemed to tolerate being held. His tail did not lash, his ears were not laid back, and he was looking up at Turnbow's face most calmly. "Think I've a way with 'im, I do, sir," Turnbow cooed.

"*Think* I got 'em back in order, sir," Dasher said as he brought the tidied stack to the desk. "By date it was written. Must be wondrous things, letters. Never got one, or wrote one, though I know how. Never had call to."

"I send me Mum a letter now an' again," Turnbow chimed in with a sad shake of his head as he paced round the cabins with the cat in his arms. "Never hear back."

"Aye, lads," Lewrie told them, "News from afar can please you, or make you want t'pull your hair out."

"Whisky, sir," Deavers said, placing a glass on the desk-top.

"Speck o' bad news, was it, sir?" Deavers asked in a whisper.

"Not from home, no," Lewrie confessed. "Though there are people suddenly more successful than we've been, doin' the same things."

"The raids, sir?" Dasher piped up.

"Aye, the raids," Lewrie told him, giving them all a brief explanation of what was happening on the coast of Spain.

"Well, beggin' yer pardon for sayin' so, sir, but we've barely got goin' yet," Dasher said with an irrepressible grin. "Soon as we hit our stride, we'll run neck-and-neck with anybody!"

"I'm glad you're so confident, Dasher," Lewrie said, grateful for his naive trust.

If only our next'un hurts the French, and doesn't make that Don *Julio richer,* he thought as he took a brooding sip of his whisky.

CHAPTER THIRTY-SEVEN

*W*hat the Devil's he waving his shirt for?" Lieutenant Rutland groused as he peered shoreward at the Army encampment with his day-glass. An Army officer stood at the edge of the light surf line. "Damned fool. He can't shout loud enough for us to hear him. Mister Page, go aft and alert the Captain."

"Aye, sir," a fourteen-year-old Midshipman replied. Going aft was a matter of a few steps to the Marine sentry who stood guard by the door to the great-cabins. "Mister Rutland's duty, and I'm to—"

The stamp of boots and the slam of his musket's brass-bound butt interrupted the ritual as the sentry bawled, "Midshipman Page t'see the Captain . . . SAH!"

"Enter!" came a shout from within.

"Captain, sir," Page began again, "Mister Rutland's duty, and I am to inform you that there is an Army officer on the beach, waving a shirt and trying to get our attention."

"Very well, Mister Page," Lewrie replied, wiping his chin and plucking his napkin from his waist-coat. "My compliments to Mister Rutland, and I will be on deck, straightaway."

"Aye aye, sir," Page replied with a curt nod, turned about, and plunked his hat back on his head as he exited.

Damned good breakfast, too, Lewrie thought, rising from his table and abandoning a very cheesy omelet, toast, and local salami. A last sip of Arabic coffee, laced with sugar and fresh goat's milk, and he was out on the quarterdeck.

"Now what's he doing?" Rutland gravelled as the Army officer produced a pistol, cocked it, and fired a shot into the air.

"Pass word for my boat crew, Mister Rutland," Lewrie ordered. "I believe there may be a need to speak with Colonel Tarrant."

"Aye aye, sir," Rutland said, cupping his hands round his mouth to bawl a "Do ye hear, there?" and a summons.

"Sword, sir?" Deavers asked as he brought Lewrie his hat.

"No, I think I'm safe from the 94th," Lewrie quipped, "though I haven't met their wives and children yet."

Liam Desmond, Kitch, and the bow man and oarsmen came boiling up from belowdecks, went down the starboard boarding-battens to a waiting barge, and prepared to row the short half mile to shore.

Minutes later, Lewrie waded up the beach in ankle-deep water to see what the matter was. "A letter came by mounted courier for you, sir, from Messina. Colonel Tarrant has it in his pavillion," a Leftenant whom Lewrie did not know told him. "If you will follow me this way, sir?"

Colonel Tarrant's breakfast had not been interrupted, and his orderly was just clearing the campaign table when Lewrie was shown in.

"Ah, Sir Alan, a good morning to you," Tarrant jovially said in greeting as he rose, "or *buon giorno,* rather, hey?

"*Buon prima colazione,* too, sir," Lewrie said in reply, stumping Tarrant for a moment. "Good breakfast, I mean."

"Ah! Take your word for it," Tarrant laughed off, "Italian is nothing like my school Latin. There's a letter come for you. Coffee, whilst you read it, sir?"

"Aye, that'd be fine," Lewrie told him as a very young officer, a cavalry Cornet half-covered in dust from his joyously exuberant ride, handed Lewrie the letter, produced from his sabretache with a flourish.

"It's from my Admiral, Charlton," Lewrie announced as a cup of coffee was poured for him. He broke the seal and quickly read it. "He expresses his approval of our raid on Tropea, Colonel, he got my action report. Didn't know which regiment I'd get at Malta . . . congratulations to the 94th . . . he's left his flagship at Catania and boarded one of his brig-sloops to come to Messina for discussions with the commanding General on Sicily as to an operation he's had in mind for some time, and I'm to report to him at the Castello 'with all despatch' . . . which is Navy for 'as soon as dammit'. Have you any horses, Colonel?"

"Well, no, actually," Colonel Tarrant had to confess. "Garrison at Valletta, travelling by ship here, there is no way to feed or stable them, and no way to land them ashore. My dignity suffers, but . . . ," he said with a shrug.

"Hmm, it'd be quicker by boat, then," Lewrie decided. "Jib and lugs'l on a barge. I think you should come with me, sir."

"Sailing?" Tarrant balked. "In a *small* boat?"

"Call it a yachting jaunt," Lewrie said with a smile. "Might I borrow pen and paper? I'll send Charlton a quick note to confirm my receipt of his orders . . . make a suggestion. That Foreign Office fellow, Quill, should be there, too. It's his informants who'd have the freshest assessments of what we'd face . . . wherever we're going."

"And *Don* Julio and his cut-throats?" Tarrant asked with a sham shiver.

"I very much doubt the commanding General would want *them* there!" Lewrie japed as he sat down to scribble. "They'd most-like make off with his silver services, ha ha. Or, get his staff drunk on *grappa*."

He wrote his note, read it over twice, then signed it and stood to hand it to the cavalry Cornet, who had been patiently standing by, intrigued by the hint of a landing on the mainland, a battle, informants, and *grappa*.

"Off ye go with it, young sir," Lewrie urged, "and I'd wager you will take great, galloping joy of the doing. Your horse blown?"

"No sir, she's a goer," the Cornet said, beaming. "All day long!"

"I must go back aboard for a while," Lewrie explained, "make my arrangements, pack a kit for an overnight stay, if we must, and put on my best dress. I'll be back to pick you up shortly, Colonel Tarrant."

"Small boats," Tarrant said, blowing out a breath of exasperation. "Small, *tippy* boats, not like a steady ship. My Lord!"

It had been a beautiful day for a short sail up the coast, with blue skies, high-piled white clouds, and a fresh breeze that bellied out the barge's quickly rigged loose-footed lugs'l and jib, a breeze that cooled the beginning warmth of the day. The barge *had* taken on an angle of heel that had made Tarrant grip the thwart on which he sat, white knuckled and a tad pale in the face, but Lewrie had fiddled with the sheets, and Desmond had tweaked the tiller 'til the ungainly barge had gained a fair turn of speed, in relative safety. Within two hours, they handed the sails and rowed to the main piers, where Lewrie found temporary quarters, victual issues, and even a rum issue for his men with the Navy shore parties. A shabby open coach was whistled up to carry Lewrie and Tarrant to the imposing Castello, and off they went through the confusing maze of Messina's grubby streets.

Stone walls, brick galleries, and stone floors made the Castello much cooler and dimmer than the glare and warmth of a Spring Sicilian day. An orderly Sergeant led them to a vast and imposing office of the commanding General, and Lewrie was pleased to see Charlton there.

"That was quick, I must say," Rear-Admiral Charlton said as he came forward to shake hands, "Hallo, Lewrie, good to clap 'top lights' on you, again. Keeping well?"

"Very well, sir," Lewrie replied with a broad smile, then made the introductions. "Where is it you wish to strike, sir?"

"Not so much me as it is the Army," Charlton countered. "They've taken notice of my reports about what my lesser ships have seen along the coast from Cape Spartivento to Catanzaro, and Crotone, the other side of Calabria on the Ionian Sea and the Gulf of Squillace. There's even more worthwhile places to raid round Taranto, French *corvettes* and smaller warships. But, that would take a rather *large* army. Ah, here are our hosts!"

A dashing Army officer in an immaculate uniform came bustling in, bearing the marks of a full Colonel, followed by three Leftenant-Colonels, and a Major. There were Ensigns or Leftenants to carry the map stands and maps, too. Lewrie was pleased to see Mr. Quill slink in behind them, dressed all in Beau Brummell black suitings, looking more like a whipped cur, though, as if he knew just how thin his welcome was in such an august gathering.

"Gentlemen, good day to you," the Colonel energetically said. "I am Brigadier Charles Caruthers. The commanding General has left it to me to brief you, since it will be my brigade that will be landing on the far Calabrian coast. The Colonels of my regiments?" he said, introducing them. As he did so, his junior officers set up the map stands, backing boards, and unfolded maps to pin to them.

"Admiral Charlton, and Captain Sir Alan Lewrie, aha! Delighted to make your acquaintance, sirs. And you are, sir?" he said, turning to Tarrant. "The 94th Regiment of Foot? Highlanders, are you?"

"Line, sir," Tarrant told him. "The number was used for the Royal

Highland Emigrants regiment during the American Revolution, but it was retired when they disbanded."

"I see," Caruthers said with a nod. Higher numbers usually were assigned to Highlanders; he looked dis-appointed that the 94th was not. "Admiral Charlton, perhaps you may enlighten the officers of my brigade as to what your ships have discovered along the coast."

With a borrowed pointer, Charlton stood and approached the main map, tapping small seaport towns from Brancaleone Marina to Bovalino Marina, Locri, Siderno, Marina di Gioiosa, Roccella, Monasterace Marina, Soverato, and Lido Catanzaro, explaining that a suspiciously large number of coastal trading ships had been noted in those small harbours, where there was little prospect for trade. Each time one of his ships had peeked in, they had noted a few more at each port, anchored, and not moving from one week to the next.

"Our best estimates total over sixty-five or seventy of them, gentlemen," Charlton told them. "Each capable of carrying a company of French troops, and, from examining those few we've been able to intercept at sea, the French seem intent upon selecting, then storing, only those with shallow draughts, able to be run ashore on some beach to allow the soldiers aboard to scramble down over their bows.

"Your commanding General wrote me after receiving my reports, and suspected, as did I, that the French have hidden them from plain sight cross the Straits of Messina in out-of-the-way harbours where we would not think to look 'til they marched an invasion force cross the Aspromonte mountain chain from their main enclaves round Reggio Calabria, board them, then make a surprise landing near Catania or Syracuse, out-flanking the defences closer to Messina.

"The Navy's part of the plan is to bring my entire squadron, with re-enforcements from the Mediterranean Fleet, to sail right up to these small harbours and take, sink, or burn their transports, staving off a threat of invasion here on Sicily. All at once, every port hit at the same time," Charlton said with a faint smile. "That's my part in it. Now you, Brigadier."

Brigadier Caruthers jumped to his feet like a coiled spring and took the pointer, posing before the map with his booted feet spread, and tapping the pointer into the palm of one hand for a moment, with a confident smile on his face.

"Right, then!" he barked.

I don't think I like this bastard, Lewrie thought, casting a look over his shoulder to Mr. Quill, who was slumped against a side-board at the rear of the gathering, arms folded over his chest. Quill gave him a shrug, and a well-concealed roll of his eyes.

"The bulk of these transports are mostly concentrated from Locri here, to Roccella, here," Caruthers began, whacking the map with his pointer, "There is a rather poor coastal road all along from Reggio Calabria, but rather a long march for the French when they put their plan in motion. There are two roads, however, that cross the peninsula and the mountains. One comes to Locri, the other to Marina di Gioiosa, and *that* is where it makes the most sense for the French to have put stores of arms, ammunition, rations, and artillery, ready to hand when the troops of the invasion force arrive. Whilst our compatriots in the Navy are blazing away at all the ports, it is my intention to land the three regiments of my brigade here . . . at Siderno, halfway 'twixt Locri and Marina di . . . however you say it. We believe that the French have only small, guard garrisons in the ports so far, mostly to protect the stores from local pilferers, and the Navy's doings should pin them down in place, too unsure of what's happening to think of concentrating to oppose us for at least two days, and allow us to eliminate the stores, further hobbling any invasion of Sicily in the near future, what?"

"Three full-strength regiments should be more than enough to fight off the two or three companies scattered up and down the coast," one of the Leftenant-Colonels agreed with a rumble of amusement.

Lewrie shrugged; it sounded as if it might work.

"We have been able to scrounge up twelve ships to carry us over, so far," Caruthers told them, "some transports, though some of them are cargo ships, not suited or fitted out for troops, unfortunately, but they could suffice. Captain Lewrie, I'm told you have three transports. I'll need you to lend them to me for the operation."

Hello? Lend *them*, mine arse! he thought; *Buss my blind cheeks!*

"I'm afraid, sir, that my transports are allocated to the 94th Regiment, and our operations," Lewrie stated. "I was given to believe that the 94th would be a part of your operation, since they're trained in amphibious landings, and have already carried out one, quite successfully, mind. That's why I was invited here, is it not?"

"Well, perhaps we *could* employ the 94th," Caruthers allowed with a polite smile frozen on his face. He coughed into his free fist. "What is your troop strength, Colonel, ah . . . ?"

"Tarrant, sir," that worthy reminded him. "I've six companies, less ten killed and wounded at Tropea, there are three hundred twenty men, though when we sail, I'll probably have to leave at least a Corporal's guard at our encampment to prevent theft by the Sicilians."

"A rather paltry force, sir," Caruthers drawled, amused. "Why, I intend to land ten times that."

"Ah, but the 94th can be ashore in half an hour from the time we come to anchor, sir," Lewrie pointed out. "And my own ship can contribute another seventy Marines, and an equal number of armed sailors."

"Half an hour?" one of Caruthers's Colonels scoffed. "Surely you boast, sir! Why, it may take half a day to get all of ours ashore."

"I've eighteen large oared barges that can bear the whole force ashore in one wave, sirs," Lewrie explained. "Colonel Tarrant can set his troops and my Marines out as advance guards whilst you're coming ashore, and send scouting parties inland or up the coast road in either direction."

"You've artillery?" Caruthers asked.

"Not a stitch, sir, not even swivel-guns," Lewrie told him.

"Then I don't see . . . ," Caruthers said, shaking his head.

"You expect no more than two companies of French troops at each harbour, sir," Lewrie pressed, "perhaps with half of those out in the country to forage, loot, and patrol. *They* would have no artillery. And if they did, they'd be busy firing at Admiral Charlton's ships."

"As long as they last, that is," Charlton bragged.

"Well, we'll certainly need artillery," Brigadier Caruthers insisted. "My plans envisage at least two batteries of twelve-pounders."

"Horse-drawn, or man-hauled, sir?" Lewrie asked.

"Horse-drawn," Caruthers told him, " 'flying batteries' able to roam about wherever they're most needed."

"So you've a horse transport, and a ship to carry the guns and carriages, limbers, and caissons?" Lewrie pressed further. "No? Then how do you intend to get guns ashore?"

"I'm told that horses can be forced over the side of the ships and led ashore, swimming behind a rowing boat by their reins," Caruthers answered. "As for the guns, I note that there are many barges in harbour at Messina, probably more like them at Catania and Syracuse."

Christ, he hasn't the first clue! Lewrie thought, appalled by the blithe assumptions on which Caruthers's plan was based.

"Those are crude, flat-bottomed scows, sir," Lewrie said, with his face blandly set, "low-sided, too, good for taking cargo out to an anchored ship, or carrying goods from ship to shore, and propelled by sweeps. They're not seaworthy. Outside a flat-calm harbour, they'd be swamped by any sort of moderate sea. Use them for horse teams and your artillery, and you'd lose them halfway there.

"If you really wish to land guns and horses, it would be better if the 94th landed as close to the outskirts of Siderno and cleared the town," Lewrie went on, "then you can bring the ships carrying guns and horses right to the quays . . . assuming you have ramps built for the unloading. Wide, strong . . . with side-rails so the horses don't panic?" he added. "Though, how you get them all over the bulwarks . . ."

"Two sets of ramps, I'd think," Admiral Charlton chimed in. "To get everything over the bulwarks, *then* down to the quays. By the by, *does* Siderno have stone quays? How high are they, and what is the water depth right alongside them, if they do?"

Charlton gave Lewrie a hooded look, as if to say that this was all a load of manure, and sounded more improbable by the minute.

"If the ship, or ships, carrying the guns and horse teams draw too much depth to get alongside the quays, then you'd need really *long* ramps," Lewrie added. "More like bridges. They would take up a lot of deck space, unless one could tow them behind the ship, then hoist them into place, but . . . your ships, sir. How many sailors are aboard? Ramps that size would be extremely heavy, and I don't see the fifteen or twenty sailors, cook and ship's boys included, paid for by the Transport Board . . . a *most* parsimonious lot, believe you me . . . able to 'pully-hauley' anything that heavy. They might not even be strong enough to hoist your guns and horses from the holds."

"If the ships could get right by the quays, sir," Charlton said, "it would require your gunners, teamsters, and several dozens of your infantry to hoist everything up and over. Do you really need two full batteries? My ships, do they get within three-quarters to a half mile to the shore, can provide all the artillery support you'd need, sir."

"In one broadside battery, sir, *Vigilance* mounts six nine-pounders, thirteen eighteen-pounders, and thirteen twenty-four-pounder guns," Lewrie told the gathering. "If there is sufficient depth for me to get within that half a mile, I can reach out, line-of-sight, to almost two miles. Which brings up the question . . . how hilly is the coast, what's the lay of the land? The harbour depth, the height of those quays as Admiral Charlton posed, and how many troops are ashore, and in town at any given time? Just where *are* the arms and rations kept, and in what amount? It seems to me that we'd need topographical maps and current navigational charts, and some scouting, before we launch any action. Mister Quill?" Lewrie called, making everyone turn and look over their shoulders at the lone civilian. "Do you have any informants familiar with the vicinity?"

"Not as many as I would like, Captain Lewrie," Mr. Quill said, stepping forward from his slump on the side-board, though he did keep his arms folded cross his chest. "Not that side of the Calabrian peninsula. My concerns have been focussed on the West coast, from Naples to Cape Spartivento. I've gathered *rumours* of the French marshalling ships and war *matériel*, but nothing solid.

"I *could*, however, send some ah . . . people in my employ there to 'smoak' out the situation," Quill went on more confidently. "Along that poor stretch of coast, the appearance of smugglers with desired goods to sell would be most welcome to the locals, *and* the French garrisons."

"Just so long as your spies show up in dowdy fishing boats," Lewrie japed, "nothing the French might confiscate as troop transports."

"Goes without saying, sir, hah!" Quill said, finding that amusing, and, unfortunately, treating them all to his wheezy, gasping laugh.

Lewrie looked at Brigadier Caruthers, whose breezy confidence had evaporated. The fellow's face was flushed, his brow deeply furrowed, and his eyes were slitted almost shut in anger.

If looks could kill, Lewrie thought: *Now, maybe you'll take more time t'plan your little escapade. This ain't like puntin' from one bank o' the Thames to the other, up round Henley where it's calm and narrow.*

"It would take me and my, ah, associates, about ten days to a fortnight to make their scouts, and report back, sir," Quill estimated.

"That would give you more time to hunt up the last transports that you need, sir," Lewrie stuck in, "and figure out a way to land at least *one* battery of guns . . . man-hauled, perhaps?"

"Without artillery, the whole operation could take no more than twelve hours ashore," Colonel Tarrant spoke up. "Anchor, board boats, get rowed ashore, clear the towns of Locri, Siderno, and Marina di Gioiosi, find the stored goods and burn them, then re-embark."

"We had hoped to do more than *that*, sir!" Caruthers spat in some heat. "Do we draw the attention of French forces in the area, we plan to meet them and give them a bloody nose into the bargain!"

That drew a hearty series of growls, roars, and "hear, hear" from Caruthers's officers.

"*Our* raids, sir," Lewrie said, "go ashore with two canteens per man, eighty rounds of cartridge, a rucksack for sausage, cheese, and bisquit, get the job done then skip clear before the enemy *can* concentrate. We give the French bloody noses, but then dance back, like a skilled boxer, to avoid giving them a hope of hurting us. I'm told it is very bad for their morale."

"That's the way of it," Colonel Tarrant seconded. "Unless one is desirous of emulating the Battle of Maida."

Christ, I'll bet that's what he had in mind! Lewrie realised.

"Sir Alan, and Colonel Tarrant, are correct, sir," Admiral Charlton spoke up. "The principal aims of the expedition are to eliminate those coasting ships, and secondly, to burn and eliminate the arms and supply depots. The Fleet can support a limited operation, but anything more ambitious than that would keep my ships on the coast too long, and to no good end, should the French response be too swift or too powerful. Warships can only sit and watch a hurried evacuation, and if the lay of the land does not lend itself to line-of-sight gunnery support, we would be little aid to you, sir."

"Aye, let us allow Mister Quill time to gather as much information as he can," Tarrant summed up as if it was his meeting, not that of the Brigadier, "and you can hunt up additional merchant ships for your troops, Brigadier."

Meanin', get your head outta your arse and come up with a plan that'll work, Lewrie thought, unable to hide a smug expression.

"The need for updated information does require us to delay, for a time," Brigadier Caruthers hissed, his jaw working and his teeth grinding in frustration and embarrassment. "Very well. Once Mister, ah . . . Quill is it? . . . reports back, we will meet again, to finalise the plans for the operation."

As maps were un-pinned and folded, as hats, gloves, and swords were gathered up, Lewrie could not help sticking another pin into Caruthers's backside. "Your transports, sir . . . how many boats do they possess, and how many merchant sailors do you have to do the rowing? My transports have Navy crews, and nine or ten men per barge. A matter to look into, what?"

"Uhmhmm," Caruthers answered, more a feral growl of a cornered beast.

"Well, that was rather fun," Colonel Tarrant remarked as they left the imposing Castello into bright sunlight.

"Nothing against *you*, Colonel, but *soldiers* understand nothing of ships and the sea," Lewrie told him, feeling glee to have deflated such a puffed-up coxcomb, "and that fellow's plan had more holes in it than a colander. He's bound and determined to do *something* grand and glorious but one hopes that reality hits him 'twixt the eyes."

"Amen to that, Captain Lewrie," Tarrant enthusiastically agreed. "Especially if my poor old battalion seems a part of it."

"Lewrie!" Admiral Charlton called out as he and Quill caught up to them, after a long palaver between them. "Good fellow. You made some good points in there, as did you, Colonel Tarrant. Now, perhaps the Brigadier will trim his sails to a reasonable wind, and not emulate Wellesley's large battles in Spain. For a minute there, I imagined that he'd camp out, guns, tent lines, and cooking cauldrons, waiting for a battle to make his name in the papers."

"Garrison duty can be boring in the extreme, sir," Tarrant said with a *moue* of distaste. "Believe me, I know."

"We've bought you time, Lewrie," Charlton said. "Let us hope, most earnestly, that Caruthers makes the best use of it."

"Back to your flagship, sir?" Lewrie asked.

"For the nonce, aye," Charlton allowed. "Once at sea, I'll lurk close to Messina and Catania, waiting to hear what the final plan is to be. Close enough for a despatch boat to reach me easily. I will plan the naval part of the operation and pass them to all of my Captains, so they'll be ready to sail for the coast at the same time as you and Caruthers's transports sail from Sicily. Before I do so, hmm. Mister Quill, do you know of a particularly fine place to dine in the town?"

"Not down in your neighbourhood, pray God, sir," Lewrie japed.

"Not today, no, Sir Alan," Quill said, pointing towards the town centre and the grand public square. "There's a lovely *trattoria* quite near the church, the Duomo. Norman and Romanesque, you know, built ages ago by King Roger the Second. Most impressive."

"My treat, gentlemen?" Charlton offered, to which they all were most eager to accept. "Let us go there, then. I wish I had the time to take a look at the Duomo, but, time and tide."

"After dinner, we must collect my boat crew and sail back to Milazzo," Lewrie said, none too eager for a tour of a cathedral, either.

"Boats, again?" Tarrant groaned. "You're right, Lewrie, soldiers know nothing of the sea. By preference, hah!"

CHAPTER THIRTY-EIGHT

*L*et's see what we have, then, Lewrie thought, opening a hefty packet that had come from Mr. Quill, a fortnight after the first meeting in Messina; *Aha! Those scoundrels've done us proud!*

Don Julio and his compatriots had sailed over to Locri, Siderno, and Marina di Gioiosi with cargoes of wines, pastas, fruit from citrus groves on Sicily, olive oil, bolts of cloth, and various and sundry goods chosen to tempt the poverty-stricken locals, already limited to short commons by the presence of French occupiers, to come and haggle fair prices. Quill's notes that accompanied the packet amusedly told of how off-duty enemy soldiers, Genoese this time, had also come down to the quays in search of bargains, and had been engaged in conversations which had unthinkingly yielded a wealth of information. Officers had taken a couple of *Don* Julio's leaders aside and grilled them on British doings on Sicily, on troop strengths, and what they might have heard about future plans! Those smugglers had lied like blazes, or claimed that they knew little, or could care less what the *Inglese* were up to, as long as they did not interfere with business!

The local townspeople, in their *tavernae* over wine, cheese, and sardines, had revealed a lot, too. The depots *were* there, under canvas at all four corners of the roads cross the mountains where they met the coast road. The garrisons of the towns from Bovalino Marina to Monasterace Marina were

from the same Genoese regiment, no more than eighty to one hundred in
each town, and half of those would stand guard over the depots, whilst
the other half, less a small cadre to police the towns, would be out in the
country, inland, foraging, stealing, and looting whatever took their fancy
at any given time.

Quill's spies learned that the Genoese were utterly despised; they talked
too fast, they were arrogant and dismissive of how poor Southern Italy
was compared to their own lush province of Liguria.

There were rough maps of the coast and beaches, the hinterland behind,
and rough layouts of the towns. The heights of the quays had been estimated at high and low tide as the smugglers' boats had lain alongside, and
the depth of the water in the harbours had been sounded, on the sly. Idle
strolls along the shore had revealed the softness of the sands and had been
noted. *Don* Julio's men had even managed to sound the coastal waters, up-
dating old charts to show how close ashore the transports could anchor,
no more than half a mile off. There were rough drawings from seaward
indicating how open the farmland round the towns was before encoun-
tering a series of rising ridges further inland, giving Lewrie the impression that if *Vigilance* came to anchor half a mile offshore, her guns could
cover the first ridge easily and protect the soldiers ashore, if they stayed
below the crests, among the olive groves and wood lots.

All in all, it was a Godsend, a cornucopia of information that laid the
coast as bare as a baby's bottom. Of course, there would have to be another meeting with Brigadier Caruthers in Messina, whilst the information went off in another packet to Admiral Charlton, whether he actually
could attend or not. All he would need to know would be the day upon
which Caruthers planned to strike, so he could have his ships in place to
support him.

Lewrie leaned back from his desk after an hour or more poring over
every scrap of paper in the packet, called for Deavers to bring him some
of his cool, lemoned and sugared tea. Should he summon his officers in,
officers from the transports, right away, and call for Tarrant and Gittings
to join them? Or, should he put that off 'til he'd met with Caruthers?

Time enough for that, later, he decided. One matter *did* need immediate attention, though.

"Turnbow, go on deck and pass word for Mister Severance and the
Bosun, Mister Gore," Lewrie said. "I need to speak with them."

Those worthies showed up at his door minutes later and he bade them
enter.

"Mister Severance, you're aware that there's going t'be a landing soon, over on the mainland?" Lewrie began.

"Aye, sir," Severance said with a faint grin. "The ship's been laying wagers on what day it will be."

"Of course they did," Lewrie said with a shake of his head in wry amusement. "Nothing stays secret for long aboard any ship. When we do, I'll need some way to know what's happening ashore, and can't wait for word of it to come by boat from the beaches. Do you know of how semaphore stations work?"

"Ehm, I've *read* about them, sir, and I *vaguely* recall what the positions of the arms mean, letter by letter. But I would not swear to a working knowledge, no sir."

"Flag signals?" Lewrie asked.

"Of course, sir!" Severance brightened. "Not to brag, sir, but I can roughly make out a signal hoist without referring to the code book, most of them time."

"Better and better," Lewrie perked up. "Mister Gore, we need to rig a spare royal yard with a cross-piece, two blocks, and halliards on which to hang signal flags, so our people ashore can speak to me, and can reply to any signals we make to them."

"Matter of an hour, no more, Cap'm," Gore assured him.

"Excellent!" Lewrie praised. "Glad to hear it! Now, as to how many signal flags you should take ashore, Mister Severance."

"I will be going ashore, sir?" Severance eagerly replied.

"You will, indeed, sir," Lewrie assured him. "I can't waste a good man on my ledgers and letter copying *all* the time. I'm thinking that some Midshipmen should accompany you, as well. One to read the signals to Brigadier Caruthers, one to assist you making up hoists, and one to Colonel Tarrant and his staff. I fear there will be some ink smudges and finger cramp 'twixt now and then, making up several code books pared to the necessities. Can't risk the *real* code books or the private signals falling into enemy hands, should things turn ugly. I'll leave it up to you who you think best from among our Mids to accompany you."

"Ehm, I'll get started on the spar, sir?" Gore asked.

"Aye, Mister Gore, have at it," Lewrie said, standing to see him out. "Care for some cool tea, Mister Severance? We'll be at it for some time. Now, which flags from our spare set do you imagine might prove useful?"

"A suggestion, sir?" Severance posed. "If there is no wind on shore, the flags may just hang there, un-readable. I think that we'd need to find some thin slats to hold them out horizontally, top and bottom."

"Hmm, good idea," Lewrie agreed. "There must be something like that available in Milazzo . . . though I don't know what, right now."

Severance opened a copy of the Popham Code book. "Obviously, sir, we'll need Number Ten . . . Enemy in Sight."

The second meeting in Messina's Castello was much more muted than the first, and Brigadier Caruthers did not enter the offices with a bounce of over-confidence. His highly polished boots still creaked, though, as he paced before his map, which was now marked over with coloured pencil of various hues, the result of Mr. Quill's flood of information from his paid agents. Quill was not present, this time, evidently still thought too *outré*, too un-gentlemanly and tainted by his association with the lower sorts, and spies, and . . . as Lewrie suspected . . . Quill had filled in too many blank spaces in Caruthers's preconceptions, making him appear an ill-prepared fool.

"Right, then!" Caruthers began as he had at the first meeting, slapping his wood pointer in a palm, "After conferring with our commanding General, this operation has been scaled back a bit. We shall emulate the 94th Foot, in that all troops will go ashore with muskets, bayonets, hangers, two canteens of water, and eighty rounds of cartridge. Rucksacks with one day's dry rations will replace the heavier field packs. And, given the absence of any artillery, as noted by ah, local informants, we will dispense with the two batteries of 'flying artillery' twelve-pounders. It will be land, rampage, burn anything of value to the French, then retire to the boats to be extracted, an operation that may take no more than twelve hours on the outside."

"Still wish the enemy was there in strength," one of the brigade's regimental commanders gruffly said. "We'd've shown them a thing or two."

"Later landings upon Catanzaro and Crotone, where there surely are larger French garrisons, may fulfill our wishes," Caruthers said. "Sir Alan, Colonel Tarrant, if you would be so good as to land there," he went on, tapping at a long, wide beach just East of Locri, almost within the town's outskirts. "One of my regiments will land just West of Siderno, the second just East of the town."

He envisioned a rapid pincer movement to swarm over the defenders of Siderno, clear it, then meet at the depots just inland beyond the road junction. The third regiment of the brigade would sail right up to the quays and dis-embark over gangways. All troops, at Locri and Siderno, would gather flammables and advance on the depots to set them alight.

Caruthers wished that the 94th and *Vigilance*'s Marines and armed sailors would throw out piquets to the North and West to watch for any French troops drawn to the noises and conflagrations, as would the troops of the third regiment once they'd marched off the quays.

Lewrie explained the signals staff his men would bring ashore, which would have to be attached to Caruthers's staff, but had to ask of messages from his men to Caruthers, and from Caruthers to his third regiment, and what the Recall signal would be.

"Once ashore, be prepared to send runners, Sir Alan," Caruthers told him. "Perhaps we could commandeer some donkeys for gallopers, hey?"

"You might have to wait for the third regiment to land, sir," Lewrie told him. "The Navy's going to be very busy towing out or burning ships in Siderno's harbour, so it's goin' t'get smoky and chaotic."

"I think we'll cope," Caruthers replied, back to being confident. "Speed will be of the essence, gentlemen."

Our army? Lewrie scoffed to himself: *'Quick' ain't in their vocabulary. Like as not, they'll brew up once the fires are set!*

Caruthers set a date five days hence, with time enough for word to reach Admiral Charlton, and for him to alert his frigates and sloops and be off the towns by dawn of that day.

"Perhaps, sir," Lewrie said as a last caution, "it would be best did the Navy have its go at the shipping, first, and clear the harbour at Siderno before you send your transports to the quays."

"Sit back and watch the bombardment for an hour or so, hey?" Caruthers said, frowning at yet another objection to his thinking. "I *suppose* that would so frighten the French present that our landings would go in mostly un-opposed. And, as we discussed previously, the Navy's attacks at many towns all along the coast will confuse and discomfit them. Very well, Sir Alan, we shall do as you suggest."

"I still don't trust the gleam in his eye," Colonel Tarrant said as they dossed down in borrowed lodgings that night in the Castello. "An assault all up and down the coast just might draw enemy forces down to respond, and save their depots. Then, Caruthers could get his battle that he's wanted from the outset."

"*Don* Julio's cut-throats placed the bulk of their forces up at Catanzaro, or cross the peninsula at Reggio di Calabria," Lewrie said, "Several hours' march away. If we're back aboard the ships by Six in the afternoon, we should be hull-down by the time they arrive."

"Hope you're right, Lewrie," Tarrant said, frowning over the thinness of his mattress as he sat to pull his boots off.

"Someone senior sat on him," Lewrie said, yawning as he pulled a thin linen sheet up to his chest, and plumped the lumps that passed for pillows, "and told him to aim smaller. He's a Brevet Brigadier, only in charge 'cause he's senior to the regimental Colonels, probably for the first time they've let him off the Army's leash. Most-like, it's been stressed that his future prospects'd be rosier if he did a good job, with few casualties, not over-reach and get his, and the Army's nose, bloodied. Don't be a Sir John Moore, don't re-enact a Walcheren campaign, and *don't* suffer a defeat."

"Where's the damned chamber pot?" Tarrant groused, peering round their room as he undid his breech's flap.

"Under the wash-hand stand, I think," Lewrie said, yawning once more. "Ehm, you don't snore, do you, Colonel?"

"Most horribly, sir," Tarrant exclaimed as he found the chamber pot and began to piss. "Most horribly, I assure you!"

"Oh, Christ," Lewrie groaned.

"That's my revenge for having to gad about with you in that bloody barge," Tarrant laughed.

CHAPTER THIRTY-NINE

S*o damned nice t'be back with the Fleet,* Lewrie thought as he raised his telescope to admire the sight of Charlton's squadron as it loomed up from the Sou'east at the appointed "rondy". Column after column of frigates and brig-sloops, already sorted out into smaller groups which would break off and proceed to the seaports they were assigned to bombard and raid. There were at least three Third Rate 64s, and a 74-gun ship of the line, Charlton's, flying the Blue Ensign, and a command pendant. He lowered his telescope to look round at his own clutch of transports strung out astern of *Vigilance* in line-ahead, and a proper one-cable's separation. Further off, and seaward, stood the fifteen vessels that Brigadier Caruthers had managed to round up, also separated into packets of five which carried the ten full companies of each regiment of the brigade. They were not manned by naval crews or officers, only merchant masters and seamen hired on by the Transport Board, or dragooned into the expedition locally. They made a distinctly un-tidy showing, especially the smaller cargo ships not fitted as troop transports, continually making or taking in sail to maintain a safe separation from the one ahead.

Stifling his longing to be an actual part of that squadron, Lewrie went down from the poop to the quarterdeck, just in time to hear the Sailing Master, Mr. Wickersham, express his own feelings.

"Here we are, poor relations," Wickersham said with a cackle, "only had in at Christmas for scraps, like a cack-handed, red-headed bastard step-child, haw haw!"

"Most apt, sir," the First Officer, Lieutenant Farley, seconded. "Just going to say. Dear as I wish to be part of that, it could be worse. We could end up on blockade duty. Plod, plod, plod!"

"We'll be the only ship close ashore of Locri, or Siderno, and we might be called upon to fire at shore targets, Mister Farley," Lewrie told him, with his face stern in "proper Captain's gloom" and a bit of ice in his tone. "Should the time call for it, I trust you'll see that we shoot accurately, and take joy of it."

"Of course, sir," a chastened Farley replied.

"Duty well and gladly done," Lewrie said as he went to his place at the windward bulwarks, "*any* duty, is satisfaction enough."

Even if I don't believe a word of it, either, he told himself.

Seven Bells of the Forenoon was struck, and a cheer went up as the gilt-trimmed red rum keg came up from below, accompanied by the Marine drummer and fifer.

"Your chronometer and sextant, sir," Deavers announced as he came from the great-cabins with a mahoghany box in each hand.

"Ah, thankee, Deavers," Lewrie said, opening the felt-lined chronometer box to test once more that the timepiece was ticking away, and tautly wound. Eight Bells would mark the beginning of any ship's official day, and time to take Noon Sights. He compared the time on the chronometer to what his pocket watch said, and uttered a faint grunt as he reset his pocket watch. He'd spent several more pounds than he'd wished on it, but it still ran almost five minutes fast in a full day.

The ship's clerk's office on the larboard side of the quarterdeck had become the chart space, and Lewrie went in there to pore over the chart of the Ionian Sea, following the trace of X's along their course done by Dead Reckoning and the casts of the log since the last sun sight the day before. Near 38 degrees North and 17 degrees East already, out of sight of land or any coast watchers, he noted, within easy striking distance for when Admiral Charlton hoisted the Execute, which would order the packets of warships and transports off to their assigned targets, though that might not come 'til dusk, and all ships would have to stand off-and-on their assignments 'til dawn of the next day.

Tapping an estimated position when all officers had taken their sights, Lewrie put the pencil away and went back to the quarterdeck to scan the skies, looking for bad omens in the weather. The chosen day could turn foul, another thing that soldiers never seemed to take into consideration. So far, so good, he decided. He rocked on the soles of his boots, impatiently, reviewing night signals in his mind, and the few he could expect the merchantmen to read, despite the notes he'd sent round to them. And would they obey his order to douse all taffrail lanthorns during the night as they closed the coast? Could they, without colliding, or straying too far afield as they stood off-and-on off Locri and Siderno?

He determined that he would take a good, long nap after Noon Sights, before the order to disperse was hoisted, and before sundown, for he doubted if he'd get an un-troubled wink of sleep after.

"Ready, gentlemen? Ready, you Mids?" the Sailing Master called out, and Lewrie got out his sextant.

Eight Bells chimed. "Time, sirs! Time!"

Pre-dawn, and all was grey gloom, three-quarters of an hour to the first paler hints of sunup. Dark specters ghosted all round HMS *Vigilance,* what looked to be a frigate and two brig-sloops ghosting past to starboard, and three brig-sloops only guessed at to larboard, imagined by the white foam-froth of their bows' mustachios, and wakes creaming down their flanks.

"Can anyone make out the brigade's transports?" Lieutenant Rutland demanded in frustration. "Are they still with us? Lord, trusting slack-wit civilians to do the Navy's job is impossible!"

"I *think* I can make out bow waves, sir," Midshipman Randolph hesitantly said. "Well clear aft of us?"

"Hard to tell," the Sailing Master commented. "The sea's got up since the end of the Middle Watch. Could be white-caps and white horses breaking."

"Take a good sniff, Mister Wickersham," Lewrie suggested. "Does it smell fishier?" He inhaled deeply, himself, fearful that there was bad weather offshore, rolling down on them, which would abort the landings, if not the attacks on the enemy transport gatherings. Fish-rack smell came with a heavy storm, strong enough to stir the bottom, and a smell of fresh water meant rain and winds.

"No, nought fishy, sir," Wickersham slowly decided, "though I do get a whiff of rain in the offing."

"Christ!" Lewrie spat, under his breath.

If the surf was up too high, sending boats ashore with soldiers in them could cost lives, and cancel the landings altogether. The frigates and sloops could do their jobs, and send armed parties into calmer harbour waters to cut out ships, or set fire to others, but there was no way that the troop transports could stand offshore waiting for better weather. Surprise would be lost, and God only knew how many French troops would swarm to the area during the delay, leaving them nothing to do but sail back to Messina and Milazzo.

"Proper sunrise is when, Mister Wickersham?" Lewrie asked.

"Half an hour from now, sir," the Sailing Master said, checking his pocket watch in the light of the compass binnacle, then looking up to see if the skies were any lighter. Lewrie caught his eye and led him into the chart space for another peek at the Dead Reckoning marks since Midnight. A single stub candle burned, its weak glow barely illuminating the trail of X's pencilled in after each cast of the log.

"Twelve miles off the coast, perhaps a bit less," Lewrie said after stepping it off with a brass divider. "A bit quicker than I like, even if we've been under reduced sail all night. If we didn't have to wait and let the warships clear the harbours first, we could almost put the troops ashore round Seven in the morning, a proper dawn raid."

"No real chance of surprise, even so, sir," Wickersham said as he scratched at his unshaven chin. "We'd have to go in after Midnight for that, the ships totally darkened, so no one ashore sees a thing 'til the barges are in the surf line, and with an ungainly mob like ours, I doubt it could ever be done."

"We did it in Spain, a time or two," Lewrie told him as they left the chart space, "but that was with only one transport. I wish we *could* manage that, someday."

"If wishes were horses, sir, we'd all be riding thoroughbreds," Wickersham replied with a brief chuckle. "It is getting lighter."

"Aye," Lewrie agreed, heading up to the poop deck for a better view, scanning about fretfully at the sky, the sea state, the faint hint of the long commissioning pendant high aloft that would show the strength and direction of the wind as it streamed, and the long paler streak on the Eastern horizon that presaged the dawn.

In the few minutes spent in the chart space, the skies had become lighter, indeed. Lewrie could make out the frigates and sloops ahead of his ship as they made more sail and began to stride away for their bombardments, and once again he felt a pang of envy that those ships and their crews would be having a lot more destructive fun than he would. He looked aft and could espy his transports hobby-horsing over long-set waves, bows high for a long moment, then bows dipping into grey-white foam. It still smelled like fresh water on the wind, but the wind was still steady, not gusting, and the long, rolling waves did not clash in confusion. There were white-caps and white horses, but the sea didn't look threatening, yet.

Yet! He crossed fingers against the worst.

Even further astern and off the starboard quarter, he could make out the lead ships in that gaggle of transports carrying the brigade. Looking closer with his telescope, they even appeared in somewhat good order.

Perhaps this'll work, after all, he thought, looking forwards down *Vigilance*'s length, able to make out details that could only be guessed at a half-hour before. And to the East, the long pale streak low to the horizon had taken on an odd, pale lemony colour, revealing a greyish overcast above it. There was no hint of the ominous red that the old adage warned against.

A grey, gloomy, cloudy day, he surmised: *it may rain, but there isn't a real storm in the offing. Please God, no storm!*

Four Bells of the Morning Watch were struck, and the Bosun and his Mates piped hands to their breakfast, a Banyan Day meal of oatmeal, cheese, bisquit, and small beer, and people who had been idling on deck in the fresh air trooped below to join their eight-man messes, some of them appointed as messman for the day, the ones who would go to the galley to fetch everything back to their mates.

Was he hungry? Not at the moment, but Lewrie doubted if he'd eat; by the time he usually took his breakfast, the transports would be coming to anchor, and the troops would be going over the side into their barges, and there would be no time for it, later. Perhaps he'd stow some of those spicy Sicilian sausages in his coat pockets, and munch on them on the sly.

"Dawn, sir!" the Sailing Master shouted up at him.

And anyone awake, or on guard, ashore can see us plain, Lewrie grimly thought.

"Did you ever *see* the like, ha ha!" Lieutenant Farley cried, in awe of the sight. "It's like the entire coast is burning!"

Indeed it seemed so, and not just at Locri and Siderno. Their intended targets were being pounded with roundshot, broadside after broadside. Frail fishing boats in the harbours were being shot right through, and the coastal trading ships anchored in the ports were being boarded, sailed out as prizes, or set afire by armed cutting-out parties from the frigates and brig-sloops. Stray shot was slamming into houses, taverns, and shops along the waterfronts, and the stone quays. Great, greyish-white cloudbanks of gunsmoke rose into the sky, joined by the swirling, rising darker grey and black smoke from the burning boats, towering high above Locri and Siderno.

Further up the coast to the East, as far as Monasterace Marina, and down the coast almost to Cape Spartivento, huge palls of fire and smoke rose from every small, sleepy seaport town where the French had gathered boats and small ships. Admiral Charlton's warships ranged as close as they dared risk their bottoms, methodically eliminating the threat of a future invasion of Sicly, coming to anchor and concentrating their broadsides on anything afloat, then loosing their sailors and Marines to row into the harbours and cut out or torch them. And if there had been any artillery ashore that had traded fire with them, it had not lasted long, or had not been there in the first place, for no one aboard *Vigilance* could spot a single gun in or near Locri.

Hell on Earth was what it looked like, and the stink of burning ships and flaming wood mingled with the rotten-egg reek of gunpowder even half a mile offshore where *Vigilance* and the transports were anchored.

"Damned near Biblical," Lieutenant Greenleaf commented. "Like a forest fire I saw once on Nova Scotia. Hellish-satisfying, and confusion to the French, hah! Good show, hey, Rutland?"

"Mmm," was the dour, taciturn Second Officer's reply.

"A hard man to please," Greenleaf said to the rest who stood on the quarterdeck.

"Springs rigged on the cables, Mister Farley?" Lewrie asked.

"Aye, sir," Lieutenant Farley answered, drawn from his own enjoyment of the scene. "Though I see nothing to shoot at, so far. If something turns up, we'll be ready. We can range the top of the nearest ridge quite easily, which Mister Wickersham says is about one mile off."

"Very good, then," Lewrie said, looking at his watch, and then at the beach ashore. What was going on in Locri proper lay well to the East, and would not hinder the landings, except for the haze of smoke that would limit visibility. The orders had been to give the warships an hour to do their work, and that hour was almost up.

He raised his telescope for a better view ashore, wondering how people scrabbled out a living in such an arid-looking environ. Large rocks, dry and dusty soil, and very little green to be seen but for olive groves, low wind-stunted and wind-sculpted bushes, and small trees that put Lewrie in mind of the *maqui* woods he'd seen on Corsica.

There were people above the beach! Two-wheeled carts, hand-carts, donkeys and mules, and a rare horse or two, sprinkled like raisins in a duff of people streaming out of Locri. He looked closer but could not spot any of those small figures in French blue uniforms.

"The Devil with it!" he growled. "Mister Farley? Signal to the transports to man their boats, we've waited long enough. Bosun, pipe our shore parties to stand to and man their boats."

"Aye aye, sir!" Lieutenant Farley said, yelling for the Midshipman in charge of signals to hoist the prepared signal away.

"Away you go, Whitehead," Lewrie cried down to the waist where *Vigilance*'s Marines stood under arms. "Good luck, and good hunting."

"Aye, sir!" Captain Whitehead roared back.

Lieutenant Rutland and the Fourth Officer, Lieutenant Grace, shook hands with their compatriots, then trotted down the ladderway to the waist to take command of the boats and the armed sailors who would augment the landing, one with a grave expression, and one with a boyish glee, accompanied by the Midshipmen they had selected to assist them. The ones who would remain aboard jeered them enviously.

"The transports acknowledge the hoist, sir," Lieutenant Farley said.

"Very well, strike it," Lewrie snapped.

Down it came briskly, the signal to Execute, and all three transports burst into a flurry of action, bow men, armed oarsmen, Mids, and Cox'ns scrambling down the boarding nets first, followed by a flood of red-coated men of the 94th. As soon as the barges had been filled, they were rowed clear in loose gaggles, shuffling themselves into a ragged line-abreast, rocking and tossing on the scend of the sea and the rushing of the waves beneath them. An officer from the largest transport, *Spaniel,* stood and waved a red pendant, and all eighteen barges began to stroke for the beach half a mile away.

As soon as the fleeing townspeople saw that, they goaded their livestock and draught animals into a panicked rush, and people broke into full-out runs or fast trots.

"Go, granny, go!" a Midshipman hooted at the sight of the older women in their monotonous black gowns and head scarves trying to run with sacks of their most precious belongings on their backs, or balanced on their heads, surrounded by sheep and goats flooding past them with bleats and the tinkle of bellwethers' bells.

Lewrie was peering shoreward, as well, though his gaze was on the surf that was breaking on the beach, trying to discern if it was too high for the boats to breast, and make safe landings. On the way to their anchorages, in shallower waters, there had been more white-caps and white horses as off-shore waves had met the sea bottom, and a slight increase in the wind that had sprung up, driving those waves to break in white-crested rollers. As the barges merged with the shore he held his breath, expecting the worst, transfixed by the sight of the troop-laden boats stroking hard over a disturbed strip of white foam, riding the breakers, soaring atop them, and . . . !

"Aha!" he cried as the barges drove ashore at last, oars held aloft like spears at the last moment as they grounded, bow men leaping into foam that surged shin-high or knee-high to steady the boats, and oarsmen going overside to steady them at right angles to the beach. A moment later and it was soldiers who stood and tottered to the bows to jump over and slosh through the surf to the hard-packed sand, scattering shoals of sea birds who took wing and complained of it in mews and squawks. Up the beach the soldiers went, onto the looser deep dry sand, to the overwash barrows and low sea grasses, congealing from a loose pack into two-deep ranks by companies. The King's Colour and the Regimental Colour were freed from their leather cundums and fluttered to the breeze. There was a young drummer and two fifers dressed in the green facing colours of the others' uniforms, and Lewrie could not hear them, but the drummer raised his sticks and began to beat as the battalion began to march up to the coast road, with the Light Company out as skirmishers ahead of the colours, which sight made the villagers begin to gallop even further and faster away.

"There's our part of it done, sir," Lieutenant Greenleaf announced with a whoosh of relief, "and it seems good, so far. Now all we can do is twiddle our thumbs 'til they return."

The road into Locri was now empty of villagers and townspeople, who were well on their way to Bovalino in search of haven, though the pall of smoke rising down there offered scant promise. The 94th was making their way towards the town, and the arms and supply depot behind it, and in Lewrie's ocular, it appeared that Colonel Tarrant was setting his men into two columns abreast of each other, three companies in one further into the scrub and cactus, two closer to the road, but all angling out inland, with the Light Company far out in front in pairs, at least an hundred yards in advance of the columns. He scanned to the right and found his Marines and sailors right on the road, Marines in loose order, and the armed sailors shuffling along behind them like so many farmers headed to the fields for a day of reaping, muskets held on the backs of their necks like scythes or rakes.

The fires in Locri's harbour were still raging, though the warships had mostly ceased fire. A few more of the most seaworthy enemy transports, worth more at the Prize Court, were sailing out of port in British possession, short-tacking in gross confusion and barely avoiding collisions, and Lewrie smiled as he imagined the curses being shouted by the officers or Mids in charge of them.

He lowered his telescope and let out a long breath, satisfied in a way that things seemed to be going well, so far, but frustrated that he had no hand in it, and must stand by, pace, grumble, and watch the hours go by with no word of what was happening ashore.

He turned his gaze back up the coast to Siderno, searching for Caruthers's brigade. He could make out the anchored ships, some thinly manned boats rowing back and forth, and Lewrie thought that he *might* have seen one regiment's set of colours on the beach West of the town, but the smoke made that speculative.

Bloody man, Lewrie thought, reaching into a side pocket of his uniform to pull out a sausage and take a bite; *He doesn't have enough boats to get all his troops ashore in one go, and the transports that hold his third regiment don't look as if they've even entered harbour yet!*

He chewed, swallowed, then roared aloft. "Mastheads! What can you see at Siderno?"

"Deck, there!" a lookout in the mainmast cross-trees shouted back. "Soldiers ashore . . . *two* sets o' colours! Boats workin' in-an'-out!"

"Can you make out our signal party?" Lewrie demanded.

To make Sub-Lieutenant Severance's improvised signal yard more visible, he had taken a red broad pendant ashore and affixed it to the tip of the yard to mark its position prior to hoisting any messages.

"No, sir, can't make it out, yet!" the lookout bawled back. "Too much smoke!"

"They're not brewing tea, are they, sir?" Lieutenant Greenleaf japed.

"They're what, no more than three miles away?" Lieutenant Farley fretted. "We should be able to see *something*!"

"Different operation than ours," Greenleaf opined, "perhaps they have nothing to say to us."

Lewrie had been about to snap at Greenleaf, to tell him to stop his gob, but his second observation gave Lewrie pause to consider it.

He and Caruthers were *supposed* to co-operate, act in tandem as part of a single attack, but, minor though the separation was, they were on different pages. *Vigilance* and the 94th Foot were junior partners to Caruthers's larger assaults, a street show to the drama playing in a proper theatre! Caruthers would only send a message if his force had to be bailed out of trouble. The man was on a different errand, and doing it slowly, too slowly, no matter how aggresively he had talked at the meetings about quickly clearing Siderno and marching on those depots. Perhaps the troops already ashore, not yet ready to march off, really *were* using their idleness to brew tea!

To Hell with 'em, Lewrie sourly thought; *we'll take care of our objective, and bugger what he's doing with his!*

"Deck, there!" a lookout called down. "Gunfire! There's enemy in Locri, and lots o' shootin'!"

Lewrie raised his telescope and saw yellow-white spurts of powder smoke in the town, and behind it, followed a second or two later by the crackle of musketry. His Marines and armed sailors were firing at the outskirts of Locri, and there was powder smoke forming in the windows of some houses either side of the road.

Seventy, eighty men in town? Lewrie scoffed; *What in the Devil have we walked into?*

CHAPTER FORTY

*M*arines and sailors rushed forward, first the sailors in one large mob, then Whitehead and his Marines, bayonets quickly fixed, by tens, pressing their attack on the houses 'til they were right up to the walls, jabbing muskets in the windows where the enemy troops were firing, jabbing with their bayonets. Lieutenants Rutland and Grace were sending their sailors down the fronts and backs of the houses they were attacking, finding other windows, then doors which were kicked in, so men with cutlasses and musket butts could rush in. In a furious minute, it was over, and men in French uniforms were being herded out of the houses, hands raised in surrender, being prodded by bayonet points. Lewrie let out a breath in relief after he scanned the ground, and could not see any of his men down. As if to reassure the ship that all was well, Captain Whitehead stuck a white tablecloth on his sword and waved it high in the air, wigwagging back and forth, and Lewrie could almost make out the sound of a "Huzzah!"

There had been several larger volleys beyond the houses, back of the town, the crackly crash of at least one hundred muskets going off in the same second, then silence as a pale pall of spent powder rose and drifted away on the breeze. A party from the 94th came into sight, shoving and prodding about a dozen French soldiers out to the road to join the other prisoners, and the officer in charge of them also performed a great, victorious wave to the ship, On the tip of his sword, he lifted up an enemy shako.

"Think Locri's ours," Lewrie said with a smile as he saw his Marines and sailors going into the town, warily, with muskets held low and aimed at every doorway and window, to search every building for more enemy soldiers, on their way to the quays to complete the destruction that the warships had wrought. A small party stayed behind on the road to guard the prisoners, no more than twenty in all, who were forced to sit in the dust with their hands behind their heads.

"There will be a grand trade in souvenirs tonight," Greenleaf prophecied with a laugh, "once our lads've picked the prisoners clean. I'm hoping for an officer's sword to send home, myself, though it'll cost me a pretty penny."

"It'll cost your family a pretty penny, too, Charles, when the postage comes due," Lieutenant Farley reminded him.

Lewrie pulled out his sausage again, picked some pocket lint off it, and took several satisfying bites to make up for the breakfast he'd missed. He could hear no more firing, not even a single gunshot from the town, so he felt safe in assuming that all the French . . . Genoese, really . . . were eliminated, and almost empty of panicked citizens.

"Deck, there!" a lookout called out. "They's big fires breakin' out back o' th' town! Acres an' acres o' tents are burnin'! An' our sodjers is a'comin' back!"

Lewrie pulled out his pocket watch, and had to smile once more, for the 94th had torched the arms and supply depot they'd been assigned to destroy, and it had all been done in a little over an hour since the barges had grounded on the beach. In another hour, they would all be back aboard their transports, and his little squadron would be ready to hoist anchors and put back to sea; and if God was just he could boast in his report of the action that not a man had been wounded or lost!

Feeling smug, he went up to the poop deck for a better view down towards Siderno, to see how Caruthers was faring, and he could not help feeling superior. The gunsmoke from the warships' broadsides had long ago dispersed, and the smoke from the many burning ships had subsided to thin wisps, so he could finally make out details.

The rowing boats were *still* shuttling back and forth from the transports to the beaches and back. The ships carrying the third regiment were *still* pacing up and down the coast, unable to enter the harbour for one reason or another, and he could see the colours of Caruthers's other two regiments further inland, but the arms and supply depot they were assigned to destroy had yet to be set ablaze; he could almost see faded rows of tents stretched out in long lines, almost a square form, protecting crates, kegs, and loaded waggons from the elements, with tiny red-coated figures among them as if they were taking an inventory before they did their duty, so the totals would impress when their report was submitted to Army superiors!

"Oh, come *on*, you cunny-thumbed bastards!" Lewrie groused. "Do get on with it! Are ye *shoppin'*?"

"It would appear that Army work is much like church work, sir," Lieutenant Greenleaf sniggered. "It does go slow!"

"Damn my eyes, are the brigade's troops *inland* of the depot?" Lewrie fumed. "What *is* he playin' at? And where'd they get horses?"

Wee, dark brown forms could be seen, mounted men in uniforms of senior officers Lewrie guessed from the hints of gold lace and bright gimp. Other wee mounted figures were dashing about between the depot and the nearest ridge, putting Lewrie in mind of an impromptu steeplechase on captured mounts, though *Don* Julio's spies had not reported any cavalry anywhere along the coast.

"Aha, sir!" Lieutenant Farley exclaimed after a long squint with his telescope. "I think I've discovered our signalmen, at last."

"Where away?" Lewrie snapped.

"Atop a tall house, sir," Farley said, "just to the left of the town church. See it?"

After a moment, Lewrie spotted it, too. "Aye, I do."

"Damn my eyes, is he showing Number Ten?" Lieutenant Farley cried in surprise. "Mister Ingham, your signals code book, if you please. Is that Number Ten?"

"Ehm, *aye*, sir," the Midshipman said after fumbling through his book. "Enemy in Sight, sir."

"Enemy in Sight?" Lewrie gawped aloud. "*What* enemy? There was no reports of more than a company in Siderno, and they've surely done for them, by now—"

"Another signal, sir!" Midshipman Ingham interrupted. "Need G . . . N . . . R . . . S. That's down, and . . . Gunners? Numeral Two . . . B . . . A . . . T . . . Repeater. Batt, batteries? H . . . O . . . W. God knows what that means, sir."

"Howitzers," Lewrie spat. "Show them Understand, then haul it down, and make Unable, and Evacuate. D'ye have t'spell that out?"

"Ehm, how about Unable, then Recall, sir," Ingham suggested.

"Add Immediate to Recall," Lewrie ordered, then shouted as if Caruthers could hear him several miles away, "Set the God-damned depot afire and get the Hell out, you shit for brains!"

Ingham hoisted the signal, reported that the shore signal yard had struck theirs, then, a minute later, read out their new hoist as "Enemy in Sight . . . Need G . . . N . . . gunners, sir!"

"What in the world?" Lieutenant Greenleaf puzzled as he directed his telescope back to the beaches and transports for a second. "They are *still* fetching troops from the ships, sir, as if they have no intention to withdraw. Spoiling for a battle, if you ask me."

"What do we do, sir?" Lieutenant Farley asked, perturbed. "We can't just *watch* them get knackered."

"No, we can't, dammit," Lewrie seethed through gritted teeth. "Repeat our signal, Mister Ingham, and add Advise to it. Do we have a strongly advise?"

"Don't think so, sir, unless we spell it out," Ingham replied.

"Advise, Burn, Immediate Recall," Lewrie fumed.

"Aye, sir," the Mid said, hustling aft to the flag lockers and halliards. Long minutes later, the shore signal yard replied, and Lewrie could read it from the deck. Unable . . . Need . . . G . . . N . . . R . . . S.

"Just God-damn it," he raged, "and God-damn *him*!"

He took a deep breath, held it, then let it out in a whoosh, thinking hard. He looked shoreward, and was relieved to see the troops of the 94th formed up on the beach by companies once again, marching by twos down to the barges, ready to re-embark. He could see Colonel Tarrant with the Colours, which were being furled round their poles and re-inserted into their leather cundums. Round the houses where the enemy soldiers had engaged his men, a shambling mob of sailors and a smarter column of Marines were just leaving Locri, and there were new fires in the town. One Marine by the drummer and fifers paraded with a broom held aloft, an old sign of a victorious clean sweep.

"Mister Farley," Lewrie said, striving for a calmer voice, "I'd admire did you signal the transports to hurry loading their troops, so they can get out to sea at once. Send Recall to our people. But, as soon as the Marines are back aboard, you will take command of the ship, while I will take charge of the armed sailors and our boats."

"Sir?" Farley asked, puzzled.

"We've gunners among our landing party, enough to manage those howitzers Caruthers reported," Lewrie went on, "a few of the guns, any-way, and . . . *unfortunately,* I'm the only person here who knows the first bloody thing about howitzers, and fused explosive shells, so . . . if I can't order, or bludgeon that miserable, cack-handed moron to get his people off the beaches, and set fire to that bloody depot, I'll have to support him . . . damn his blood!"

At that moment, Locri's depot, which by then was burning furiously, began to explode when the fires reached the tons of stored powder. Pre-made artillery cartridges lit off, thousands of them together, and cartridges with roundshot attached, those which would propel canister or grapeshot, went flying into the air like a royal fireworks trailing smoke like errant Congreve rockets. Hundreds of thousands of paper musket cartridges flared up yellow-white, crackling like millions of burning twigs or whole cauldrons full of bursting maize kernels, and the ground shook as if God was stomping his feet!

Flaming powder kegs that did not blow up in sympathetic blasts whirled skyward, staves crushed inwards, and tumbling over and over to whirl trails of fire before they exploded high in the air or fell all about, coming down on the seaport of Locri like a bombardment to crash through roof tiles and set the entire town alight.

The crews of the ship and the transports, the sailors on the beach, and the soldiers filing into the boats, stopped to give great cheers, mixed with "Oohs and Ahhs," though some yelped when kegs and flaming debris fell near the filled boats on their way out.

"Deavers!" Lewrie shouted through the open door to his cabins. "Round up my Ferguson musket, the pair of Mantons, and see if you can find that wood canteen, and fill it with cool tea!"

"Tea, sir?" Deavers called back from within.

"I have to go ashore!" Lewrie took time to explain, "Hurry!"

Vigilance's boats were coming alongside, and the ship's Marines were tentatively standing in half-crouches amidships of them, ready and eager to get back aboard. Lewrie went to the bulwarks to shout down.

"Mister Rutland, Mister Grace, keep the sailors and boat crews aboard," he ordered. "We will be rowing up the coast to the nearest beach where the brigade landed. We've more work to do!"

"Aye aye, sir," Lieutenant Rutland replied, calmly, as if surprises did not faze him; Lieutenant Grace just looked slack-jawed.

Deavers, Dasher, and Turnbow all came boiling out of the cabins with his weapons and accoutrements, and Lewrie hurriedly hung cartridge pouches, priming flasks, and the full canteen over his shoulders.

"The Ferguson and the pistols are loaded, but not primed, sir," Deavers said, standing back after helping him. "Fourty rounds for the musket are in the black pouch, fourty paper cartridges for your pistols are in the brown one, and both priming powder flasks are full. I put the tea in the canteen, but there wasn't all that much left, so I topped it up with some ginger beer, sir."

"Capital, Deavers," Lewrie said with a forced smile, "I thank you. You lads always do your best for me. Keep Chalky and the bunny happy whilst I'm away. I should be back aboard in a few hours."

"Thought our job was done, sir," Dasher said, pointing to the massive cloud of smoke rising above Locri, and the tongues of flame that licked upwards almost as high as the ship's main top.

"Down the coast, to help the Army," Lewrie said, going to the nearest boarding nets, waiting for the Marines to finish their scrambles up. "Mister Farley?" he shouted to the quarterdeck. "Once the transports are ready to up-anchor, take *Vigilance* to sea with them, but fetch-to or re-anchor off the closest beach this side of Siderno, and await our return."

"Aye aye, sir!" Lieutenant Farley replied, "Ehm . . . side party?" he called out, unsure if there was a Navy ceremony for a Captain's departure in such an odd way.

The Bosun, Mister Gore, stepped to the bulwarks on the larboard sail-tending gangway and raised his silver call to his mouth as Lewrie swung a leg over.

"Oh, for God's sake, Mister Gore," Lewrie admonished him. "Do save it for when I come back aboard the proper way."

"Er . . . aye aye, Cap'm sir," Gore said, with a nervous cough.

Now, how do I get down this bloody thing? Lewrie wondered as he straddled the bulwark, looking down into the waiting barge below that contained Lieutenant Grace and Midshipman Chenery, armed sailors from the landing party, and oarsmen, all of them looking up expectantly. The starboard rowers held the bottom of the net to tension and steady it, and to keep the barge alongside.

Lewrie's booted foot sought a square in the net, for a starter, put his weight on the horizontal cross-rope, and he swung the other leg over, fingers groping for hand-holds. The net lay so close to the bulwark that he had to fumble lower before getting firm grips. Then, he found that boot soles would slip right off if he didn't cock his feet toes-down and catch his boot heels on the supporting rope.

This is harder than it looks, he told himself as he lowered himself a foot or so: *It looked good, on* paper. *Oh, God,* please *don't let me fall in the boat and break my damned neck, fall in the water and drown . . . or look as stupid and clumsy as I* think *I do!*

He couldn't swim a stroke, he'd never learned, but then most of his crew couldn't swim, either, and he suspected that his Marines and the men of the 94th were in the same situation.

We haven't drowned any of them, yet, so . . . maybe I won't, he tried to cheer himself; *Oh, shit!*

It *was* harder than it looked, for every time he lowered himself his sword hilt or the drag of his scabbard caught on something. So did the butts of the pistols shoved into his coat's side pockets. So did the cartridge pouches strapped cross his chest, and every time he let go with his left hand to find another rope to grasp, the sling of his musket threatened to slide off his shoulder, and the faint rolling of the ship, the scend of the sea that lifted and dropped the boat, and the tension of the net, that canteen full of tea and ginger beer swung wildly about, spanking him on his buttocks.

He looked down, once, and gave that up as a bad go, for the boat didn't seem any closer for all his efforts, but the sea did, and if he fell, his weapons and accoutrements would drag him right down.

How long, Oh, Lord! he thought, scrabbling for new hand-holds as he found new places to put his feet, cursing the naval architects who designed ships with so much tumblehome above the gunwales, for the net lay almost flat against the ship's sides, and the sides of his boot soles were of more avail.

I must *be there by now!* he assured himself as he passed the last of the pale tan-painted lower gun deck wale. Left foot down, and scrabble, right hand lower, right foot down, and left hand . . .

The Ferguson rifled musket almost slipped off his shoulder once more, and when he shrugged it back into place, the barrel knocked his hat off. But, a grope with his left foot found something solid under the rough, tarred boarding net, and he dared a peek, discovering that his boot was on the barge's starboard gunn'l.

" 'At's it, sir, 'at's th' way," a sailor encouraged, reaching up to steady him as Lewrie stood with both feet on the gunn'l, with the boarding net's squares sure hand-holds at last. A long stretch of one leg and he was standing on a thwart, his leg muscles trembling. He stumbled to a seat on the after-most thwart by the tiller.

The bow man reached overside and retrieved Lewrie's hat, shaking water off it, then passed it aft. Midshipman Chenery took it, poured the last water out of it, and handed it to him.

"Your hat, sir," Chenery said, trying not to laugh.

"Ah, thankee, Mister Chenery," Lewrie replied, clapping in on his head despite how damp it felt, "Been having fun ashore, have you?"

"Immense fun, sir," Chenery said with an impish grin. "Wait 'til I write my sister of it," drawing a warning glare.

"Right, show of hands," Lewrie said, "How many of you are in a gun crew? Good. We're going ashore up by Siderno to save the Army from themselves. They've found some guns in their depot, and none of 'em know a bloody thing about 'em. Let's shove off, and row along the coast."

"Why would the Army need artillery, sir?" Lieutenant Grace asked him as the bottom of the boarding net was let go, the bow man pushed his gaff against the ship to make room for the starboard oarsmen to work, and the barge's Cox'n ordered larboard oars rigged.

"They sent some scouts out over the nearest ridge and found an enemy force, no idea how big, coming this way," Lewrie told him, "and they want t'give 'em a bloody nose before they fire the depot. That will take guns, and they didn't land any."

The barge was clear of the ship by then, stroking for Siderno, so Lewrie could shout over to Lieutenant Rutland to repeat his explanation.

"Twelve-pounders, sir?" Lieutenant Grace asked. "I believe that's what the French prefer."

"Don't know their calibre," Lewrie told him, "but they're not guns, exactly. They're howitzers. Short, stubby barrels like a wee carronade. They throw fused explosive shot at higher angles than a proper cannon. Where there's howitzers there must be fused shot, so . . . that's what we're t'play with. There have t'be fuses."

"How far off are the French, and how much time do we have to figure the guns out, sir?" Lieutenant Grace asked with a furrowed brow.

"That I don't know," Lewrie confessed, "but once I see the Brigadier, I'll know more. And why he hasn't set the depot alight, and why he wants a battle in the first damned place," he grimly added.

Vigilance's barges slithered onto the sands to the far right of the beach, as close as they could get to Siderno, and the inland road junction where the arms depot sat. Amazingly, boats from the brigade's transports were still

landing soldiers to re-enforce whatever it was that was in Brigadier Caruthers's head.

Once ashore in the softer sand at the top of the beach, Lewrie took a
look round. He could see why the third regiment had not been able to land
their soldiers on the quays, for the harbour was choked with sunken,
burned-out wrecks, and the waters littered with floating debris. Many had
been sunk right along the quays, which were chipped and scarred by
roundshot, too.

He looked seaward, and was gratified to see the 94th's ships standing
out to sea, and *Vigilance* slowly approaching Siderno under reefed tops'ls
and jibs, over a mile offshore and feeling her way back to a fresh anchorage closer to the beaches, with leadsmen in the fore chains sounding the
depth. No matter what happened, *his* part of the expedition would get away
un-marked.

"No horses for us, it seems," Lewrie said, pointing inland as an Infantry Ensign cantered by on a rather fine horse. "Let's go see what the Army
wants. Forward!" he called to his men.

It was only half a mile from the coast road and the shattered town of
Siderno to the depot. There were some working parties of soldiers there,
but the Lieutenant in charge of them informed Lewrie that the regiment
proper was out beyond the vast depot, and that was where Brigadier
Caruthers could be found.

"When do you set it on fire?" Lewrie asked, waving an arm to take it
all in.

"I was told that it would be set afire as we evacuate, sir," the Army officer said, "but I have no idea when that would be. We are ah, helping
ourselves to whatever might be of use to us, at the moment," he said with
a wink.

"Hmph!" was Lewrie's comment to that.

Once out beyond the last rows of tent-sheltered *matériel*, it was a brisk
five-minute walk to where Lewrie could see the signalling yard standing
erect, with the red broad pendant atop it fluttering. A clutch of officers
stood round a man on horseback nearby; Caruthers was mounted, and
looking rather grand and commanding, sitting stiffly upright in the saddle,
and pointing at various things much like commanding generals had been
portrayed in paintings of famous battles. Someone in the group spotted
Lewrie's party, said something, and Caruthers reined his horse about to
face his approach, a broad grin on his face.

"Ah, you're here at last, with your gunners!" Caruthers cried out. "Topping!"

"And you're still *here*, no matter how daft that is," Lewrie re-joined, tapping fingers on the brim of his soggy hat instead of doffing it in salute. "*Why?*"

"There's a French column coming, and I intend to give them a battle, sir," Caruthers archly stated.

"How many, how far off are they, and if they're too strong for you, how do you intend t'get your troops off, *and* fire the depot? I believe its destruction *was* the main idea for this expedition in the first place?" Lewrie said, equally arch. "*Not* offer battle?"

"The enemy, sir," Caruthers shot back, "consists of at least one regiment of infantry, a troop of cavalry, and a battery of cannon. As you can see, I've two of my regiments ready to receive," he said with a wave of his arm to indicate the troops out half a mile inland below the nearest ridge, sitting or napping on their backs in long lines. "We estimate that they will be coming through that draw atop the ridge in two or three hours . . . sufficient time for you to emplace the guns we found. I would have all my brigade, but for your Navy clogging the port," he accused.

"That's because *their* orders were to sink, take, or burn every hull in sight, sir, as their part of the operation," Lewrie replied. "Two or three *hours*? You expect to waste the rest of the day, fight them round dusk, *then* get your troops off in the *dark*? Perhaps if you can do that by the light of the burning depot, you *might* pull it off, but I doubt it. If you march your men back to the beaches, you might get them all off before the French arrive, but you'd have to start *now!*"

"I fully expect *your* ships and their boats would aid in that endeavour, *after* we've bloodied the enemy's noses . . . sir," Caruthers snapped, abandoning genteel conduct, seething, hissing through his teeth.

"*My* transports, and *my* boats, are back at sea, sir," Lewrie told him. "The 94th achieved all their objectives without loss, and their part of the operation is also over. I came here imagining that the French were at your throats this instant. I am not of a mind to hang about for hours so you can re-stage the Battle of Maida, sir."

"You would sail away and abandon us, sir?" another officer spat.

"You've *almost* fulfilled your orders, sir," Lewrie turned to say to him. "Fire the depot, get your troops back aboard their ships, and you've achieved everything asked of you."

"There is always something more to be done," Caruthers snapped, "a golden opportunity discovered that must be exploited."

"Fine, *get* yourselves knackered," Lewrie growled. "Mister Severance?" he called to the signal party. "Head back to the beach and set up to speak to our ship. Nothing more for you to do here."

"Aye, sir," Severance said, looking relieved to be freed from the Army.

"And would you abandon us, sir?" Caruthers demanded.

"If you won't take my advice, Brigadier, there's not a lot the Navy can do for you," Lewrie told him. "I could provide fire support to cover your evacuation. My ship's gunners are hellish-good, but we have only round-shot. Broadsides of eighteen- and twenty-four-pound shot might pin the French on the back side of the ridge whilst you withdraw, but the last thing I wish is to encourage your folly."

"Let me make this plain, Captain Lewrie," Caruthers said as he shifted in his saddle, placing both hands on it to lean forwards. "I am senior officer ashore. *Your* command ends in the shallows along the beach. I *order* you to remain ashore, and man the guns my men have discovered. If you do not do your utmost to aid me, I shall prefer court-martial charges, no matter how this turns out, and if I do fail, your refusal will be to blame for it! You, alone, sir!"

"That's grossly unfair, sir!" Lieutenant Grace exclaimed.

"I did not speak to *you*, puppy!" Caruthers snapped.

He's got me, Lewrie miserably thought; *I should've stayed aboard and let him get beaten. No, he'd say I didn't send him gunners, and he'd see me court-martialled for that! Fuck it. We're here, so . . .*

"A court-martial could find you reckless, too, sir," Lewrie told him. "Remember Buenos Aires, and General Whitelocke?"

That stung the man! Whitelocke had been so inept, so foolish, and had lost an entire British army to *gauchos* and un-trained volunteers, and had been ruled out of any further military service in any capacity as a total incompetent.

"Very well, I will stay, and I'll man your bloody guns," Lewrie said in surrender, seething though he was. "I'll say for the record, though, that you're a damned, glory-huntin' fool. Now, where's the fuckin' howitzers?"

There were twelve of them, lined up at the back end of the vast depot, stubby bronze barrels, wooden wheeled carriages, limbers and caissons that held propellant cartridges and explosive shells together as if readied for inspection. On the wide trails behind the barrels sat more boxes for ready-use ammunition. As Caruthers and his staff sat and watched Lewrie and his men inspect them, Lewrie opened one of the boxes to peer inside.

"There's a plate on the carriage, sir, "Lieutenant Rutland grumbled. "It says, ah . . . Systeme AN XI . . . eleven. Fourteen cent-i-metre, whatever the Devil that means," he said, stumbling over the strange word.

"Dumb-arsed French measurements," Lewrie scoffed. "I think it's close to five inches, maybe five and a half? Anyone else know Frog mathematics? No?"

"Maybe higher numbers to measure length make the French think their members are longer," Lieutenant Grace sniggered.

Lewrie hefted one of the heavy shot from the ready-use box with difficulty, for it felt as if it weighed more than twelve pounds. He turned it over a little to look at the plug in its side.

"Where's the fuses?" he asked.

"Right there, sir!" Caruthers snapped, jabbing a finger at the plug.

"No, that's a wood plug t'keep the gunpowder from spilling, and to protect the charge from anything that might set it afire," Lewrie contradicted. He sat the shell on the trail ahead of the box, pulled the plug, and held it up. "Wood. Solid wood. I'll ask again. Where's the bloody fuses?"

"Uh," was Caruthers's response.

CHAPTER FORTY-ONE

*F*or a hopeful moment, Lewrie wished that there were no fuses in the depot; Caruthers couldn't prevail against the French without artillery, and he'd see sense, and Lewrie could go back to his ship with not a shot fired. But, no, tons of explosive shot were found marked AN XI 14 Cm, and boxes of fuses, at last.

Nothing for it, then, he told himself.

With no draught horses, eight of the howitzers were wheeled out by hand, all that Lewrie thought his sailors could manage. He placed them in a line well behind Caruthers's infantrymen, and well apart from each other to avoid return fire from that rumoured French battery hitting something vital that might take out two or three guns at once, and killing or wounding too many men.

Soldiers were ordered to dig pits for the flannel cartridge bags, and canvas was fetched from the depot to cover them 'til needed. The explosive shot had to be piled into French army waggons and hauled to the howitzers to be piled up with a supply of at least fifty rounds per gun. Empty shot boxes were placed well behind it all, where the fuses would be cut before being inserted into the shot, just before it was rammed home down the barrels.

Lewrie gathered reliable men with some education to handle the fuses, patiently explaining and demonstrating the markings on the fuses. Ignore the Froggish *millimetres* painted down one side, measure the seconds on the other side, and cut off the fuses straight across with their clasp knives. He would call how many seconds of flight were required when fired. The exploding powder in the bores of the howitzers would light them . . . hopefully.

They *had* to try them out. Lewrie decided on three seconds, and had the fuses cut, inserted, and the shells carried to the guns.

"Charge your guns!" Lieutenant Rutland roared in a voice that would carry in a full gale, and flannel cartridges were fetched, inserted, and rammed down. "Shot your guns!" and the shells were rolled down the barrels and rammed snug.

"Light your linstocks!" and the slow-match was ignited with some flint fire starters, with more long lengths of it coiled round the top of the swab-water tubs, as it would be aboard ship, though the lack of flintlock strikers was troubling to the experienced naval gunners' routine.

"Prime your touch-holes!" and fine-milled gunpowder from copper flasks was poured over the vents.

"Let's give it a try, Mister Rutland," Lewrie said, wishing for some cotton or candle wax to stuff in his ears.

"Aye, sir. By broadside . . . fire!" Rutland yelled.

Some howitzers were slower to take fire, so the guns stuttered out a salvo, rolling back from the recoil, but seeming to squat upon their carriages, as well.

"One one thousand, two one thousand, three . . . ," Lewrie counted aloud, waiting for the results. "Whoo! They work!"

High above the ridge, too high really, and almost behind it, a row of shells cracked in ugly black smoke flowers, shattering the iron shot into jagged shards of death.

"Let's try lowering the barrels a bit, Mister Rutland," Lewrie ordered, "and let's cut fuses for two and one-half seconds."

"Swab out your guns, stop your vents, and crank the elevation screws to lower the aim," Rutland yelled.

The second salvo all exploded, too, the bursting shot this side of the ridge, and the draw through which Caruthers expected the French to come, lower in the air, where shards would cover a troop-killing area.

"I think that will do quite well, Mister Rutland," Lewrie said.

"Wheel position, sir," Rutland said, frowning, and pointing to the nearest howitzer carriage. "They roll back each time we fire, and we need to mark where they must be pushed back before firing again. On ship, we run out to the port sills, but here, we could end back by the depot after ten or twelve rounds."

"Hmm, empty boxes in front of the wheels, and we'll roll 'em back against 'em. Send men t'find some," Lewrie decided.

"Speakin' o' lookin' for things in the depot, Cap'm sir," Kitch intruded, snatching off his tarred straw hat. "We were wond'rin' if th' Frogs have food stored yonder. We've eat up what little we came away with, and it's well past mid-day mess."

"Aye, sor," his Cox'n, Liam Desmond, chimed in. "There must be some o' those waxed cheeses, hard bisquit, and such like we found off Spain when we took their supply ships."

"Water's runnin' low, too, sir," Kitch added with a hopeful look. "The wells back in Siderno . . ."

"The *ratafia*, the brandy, the wines," Lewrie skeptically said, with a wry grin. "Mister Grace? Form a working party to fetch water from town. Take all the canteens. And root round the depot for food, in the town shops. There must be hundreds of sausages there. But . . . any man who gets drunk will pay a stiff price when we get back aboard ship. Hear me, Desmond? Kitch?"

"Aye, sor," Desmond answered, sagging in defeat, "though it's a hard thing to ask of sailors, Irish or no."

"Handling gunpowder and fuses drunk is a good way t'blow your fool heads off," Lewrie said. "Didn't ye hear the Brigadier? There's to be a grand battle in a few hours! Get ye gone with Mister Grace, and no spirits!"

Once the working parties had trudged off, Lieutenant Rutland returned with some broken wood crates, which he placed snug against the front of all eight howitzers' wheels, explaining to the gun crews why they had to "run-out" to them as they did aboard ship, then came over to join Lewrie, who was scanning the ground out beyond the idle infantry lines, and up the slopes to the ridge, and the draw.

"They're said t'have artillery, six guns at least," Lewrie said with his telescope to his eye. "But, I don't see where they could put them 'til they're down on the flat . . . that shelf to the right of the road would suit. Cavalry? Once they get down to the foot of the ridge, there's little our howitzers can do to 'em."

"Rain, sir," Rutland said in his usual pessimistic way. "It's almost a full overcast, and smells like water. If rain sets in, there is no way to fire the guns if the priming powder turns to slush. How dearly I miss flintlock strikers!"

Lewrie looked at the sky, and pulled out his pocket watch; Lieutenant Rutland was right, it was gloomy, overcast, and dimmer than the skies had been when they went ashore earlier in the day. There was nothing to say, nothing to do, but wait it out, and pray for the best.

There had been cheeses, sausages, and fresh-baked loaves in the town shops, though a cursory search of the depot had turned up little. It was just too vast to search row after row of tentage piled with all an invasion force would need, but blankets, shirts, stockings, boots, and eight-man tents held little appeal to hungry sailors, or those seeking wine or brandy. Some jugs of wine from Siderno had been brought back to the guns, in spite of orders, but the wine was doled out between the men, one swallow at a time, passing the jugs about, and once their meals were done, Lewrie ordered them smashed or spilled out.

Another hour or more passed, and the men napped round the guns, or nodded sleepily on watch, 'til . . .

"Riders, sir!" Midshipman Chenery gave a warning shout.

"Where?" Lewrie snapped, springing to his feet.

"Top of the draw, sir!" Chenery answered. "Five or six, so far."

Lewrie raised his telescope and made out several mounted men, officers by the look of them. He could see gilt sashes, gilt-trimmed hats with egret feathers, blue uniforms, white trousers, and well-polished boots. He couldn't tell a French Lieutenant from a General, or an artillerist from infantry or cavalry, but . . . there was one cove up there in a red coat, tall shako, with a gilt-trimmed *pelisse* half-draped over his shoulder. He must be cavalry!

"Quarters! Stand to your guns, there!" Lieutenant Rutland was yelling. "Prick cartridge, and prime your guns!"

Ahead of them, closer to the ridge, Caruthers's two regiments were getting to their feet and arraying themselves in two-deep ranks, and officers and Sergeants were barking orders to load, prime, fix bayonets, and stand ready to receive.

"Shift aim to the draw, where the road comes through!" Lewrie ordered, trying to remember whether his pistols and Ferguson musket were loaded, or primed.

Men lifted the trails of the howitzers by leather straps with loops, as if made for humans as draught animals, then set them down as gun-captains signalled their satisfaction with their aim.

"Ready linstocks, blow them hot and bright!" Rutland warned.

There! The French officers in the draw at the top of the ridge wheeled their mounts about and rode out of view. A long minute went by, during which every man's hands gripped his gun tools tighter, and all breathed a little harder.

"Aha!" Lewrie shouted. "It's a gun battery! You may open on them, Mister Rutland!"

The senior French officer would want his guns deployed, first, to support the infantry's march through the draw, down the road, and form. One, two, three horse-drawn cannon hove into view, carriages, caissons, and limbers, with their crews sitting on the waggons and on the draught horses.

"By broadside . . . fire!" Rutland yelled.

Eight howitzers bellowed, lurching back, in an irregular stutter, and two and a half seconds later, the pre-cut fuses exploded the shells, big, ugly black bursts barely fifty feet above the first three enemy guns, and it was chaos! Wounded horses screamed, gunners were scythed off the horses and waggons, and the third crashed into the second. Neat order was lost as caissons and limbers went one way, panicked gun teams and guns on their carriages went another, running off the road, and overturning as they met ditches and rocks jutting from the hillside.

"Stop vents!" Rutland bawled. "Swab your guns!"

There was a breeze off the sea running to the Nor'west, but it could not disperse the pall of powder smoke fast enough for Lewrie. He beckoned Midshipman Chenery to him.

"Run out to the right about a long musket shot, lad, and spot the fall of shot for me," Lewrie told him with a hand on his shoulder. "Whether we're over, short, or spot-on. Go! And shout loud! Cut the same two and a half seconds on the fuses!" he called to the men behind the battery as they prepared the next rounds.

"Charge your guns!" Rutland roared. "Get the bloody shot up here, damn your eyes!"

"Lord, sir!" a sailor puffed as he waddle-ran forward with a shell cradled in his hands, low by his waist. "'Ese things must be as 'eavy as twenty-four-pounder roundshot!"

Twenty-four-pounder explosive shell? Lewrie thought; *I love 'em! I want them aboard ship someday!*

"Shot your guns, and ram them snug! Prick cartridge! Prime!" Rutland yelled, then took time to look outwards at the ridge, hunting for fresh targets to slaughter. The smoke had mostly blown away, and everyone could see the draw, by then. What would the French send next?

"Infantry, sir!" Chenery yelled. "In column of fours!"

Just like at Vimeiro, Lewrie marvelled.

He'd been ashore to witness General Sir Arthur Wellesley's first victory in Portugal, and the French soldiers looked just the same; the flash of bayonets and shako badges, the white crossbelts over blue coats and white trousers, swaying side-to-side like a glittering worm. This lot broke column as they dodged round the ruin of the enemy battery, where wounded horses still screamed and kicked, wounded men shredded by hot, jagged iron shards whimpered, cried out for aid, or cursed for a chance of survival. They came on fast, at double time, re-forming a column of fours once downhill from the carnage, company after company of them, marked by their burgee-shaped flags on poles.

"By broadside . . . fire!"

The howitzers roared and bucked, again, and the view was gone in a fresh cloud of spent powder smoke. There were eight distinct cracks of bursting shells, though, and then the sound of "Huzzah!" from nigh two thousand British throats as the regiments in front cheered.

"Spot-on, sir!" Midshipman Chenery yelled. "There's a whole lot of them down!"

"Re-position your guns! Swab out!" Rutland shouted.

"They are scrambling over the ridge, either side of the draw, sir!" Chenery warned. "Hundreds of them! They are coming over the top in *mobs,* slipping and sliding downhill!"

Lewrie trotted out near him for a better view clear of smoke, devoutly wishing for his gunners to be more proficient with their unfamiliar howitzers. Aboard ship, they could manage three rounds every two minutes; here, they were lucky to get off one round a minute, and it wasn't enough to stop the French soldiers swarming over the ridge like a horde of ants. He looked left down the line of guns, watching his men charge, ram, shot, prick, and prime the howitzers.

"Damn my eyes!" he exclaimed after he looked back at the French. He saw two emblems in the centre of those mobs; gilt eagles on tall poles. The Emperor Napoleon Bonaparte had issued them to each regiment after he'd crowned himself in 1805, emulating the Roman Empire's legions and their eagles which had been signs of sacred honour.

"There's *two* regiments up there!" he gawped. "Mister Rutland, what's the fuse setting?"

"Two and a half seconds, sir!" the fellow replied,

"Spread out the aim, and I'll want *two* seconds for the next salvo!" Lewrie ordered.

"Aye, sir! Ready? By broadside . . . fire!"

Lewrie trotted back to the fuse-cutters and told them the same, then spotted an infantry Ensign trotting his horse near the battery to see what he could see.

"Hoy, you sir!" Lewrie shouted at him, and the young man seemed to cringe, as if he was not wanted there. "Can you carry a message to the beach for me?"

"Well, yes sir!" the subaltern, no older than sixteen, replied.

"There's a flag signal yard on the road above the beach," Lewrie rushed out. "Tell Sub-Lieutenant Severance that he is to signal to my ship. The signal is, Engage Ridge, and I hope he has the flags that he needs if he has to spell it out!"

"Engage Ridge, right, sir!" the Ensign repeated, puzzled, but he jerked the reins of his captured horse about and thumped his heels to urge it to a rapid canter.

"The enemy is forming either side of the road, sir!" Midshipman Chenery reported once Lewrie was back, sounding a tad more anxious as he beheld the two regiments congealing into four-deep ranks, looking in good order, at last. Drums began to rattle, bugles sounded, and the regiments began to shift in complex manouevres to form columns, twenty men across and about fourty deep, with the eagles glittering in the wan daylight in the centres alongside the drummers.

Buh-buh-boom-boom-boom, buh-buh-boom-boom the drummers beat out as the two columns began their slow advance, followed by the shout that Lewrie had heard at Vimeiro, "*Vive l'Empereur!*"

"Mister Rutland, the damn fools are *obliging* you!" Lewrie cried, almost laughing. "Do you aim for the regimental column to the right of the road!"

"Aye, sir! Shift aim right! Lower your barrels, screw the elevating screws up! Ready? By broadside . . . fire!"

Buh-buh-boom-boom-boom, "*Vive l'Empereur!*"

Sharp cracks went off above their heads, quick red blossoms of fire, black flowers quickly replacing them, with trails of smoke flying outwards to mark the flight of the largest hot shards.

"Oh, right atop them, sir!" Midshipman Chenery enthused to see such carnage. "Dozens and dozens of them down! Uh . . . they've cleared the wreckage in the draw, sir. There are three pieces of artillery on the road, moving to the right, off the road! And there is cavalry in the draw, now!"

As their gunsmoke cleared, Lewrie could see the bad news for himself; sixty, an hundred cavalrymen trotting over the draw and down into the road by twos. Generals, Colonels, and Majors on horses preceded them. The horsemen rapidly formed a two-deep line across the centre of the French troop dispositions, with the officers just behind them.

"Mister Rutland, those guns are setting up on the shelf of land I pointed out to you before!" Lewrie urgently yelled. "Cut fuses for one and a half seconds, and take them out before they can open upon us!"

He had a cruel choice, destroy the artillery quickly, shoot at the cavalry before they charged, or continue to pummel the columns of infantry. He remembered his former brother-in-law, Burgess Chiswick, speaking of how infantry dealt with cavalry; they would have to form square, bristling with kneeling men with bayonets and standing ranks firing their muskets, to deter cavalry. If they had to, the squares would fall victim to artillery, then the cavalry would eat them alive!

Caruthers, your regiments are on your own, now, he thought.

The drums still beat, and the French infantry shouted out their *"Vive l'Empereur!"* He'd seen that at Vimeiro, too; British guns with shrapnel shell had winnowed the tightly packed columns, but, no matter the casualties, they had still come on, hoping to get within musket range where they would fan out into line, deliver a massed volley, and then charge with the bayonet.

"Ready? By broadside, fire!" Rutland roared, sounding hoarse.

The French gun teams had wheeled into position on the level land of the shelf to the right of the road, trails dropping and the ammunition caissons were positioned yards in the rear, swarmed by artillery-men, and the horse teams and limbers led off smartly. It was like he watched a clockwork wind-up toy, so practiced were the French at their grim trade, Napoleon's favourite branch of his *Grande Armée*.

The howitzers roared, lurched back, seemed to wish to dig themselves into the ground as their cleverly designed carriages absorbed the downwards thrust of recoil, and the view of the French battery was blotted out. Lewrie heard the welcome series of cracks, and all but crossed the fingers of his right hand that they had hurt them, stymied them for a minute or so.

"Huzzah, huzzah!" Midshipman Chenery shouted, capering and waving his hat in the air. "Eat that, you snail-eating bastards!"

Where'd the boy learn that? Lewrie had to ask himself, hoping it was good news; *Am I a bad influence? Aye, I probably am.*

Now his gunners were cheering, as were the British regiments, jeering and hooting, daring the French to come on. The smoke drifted clear, and Lewrie could see that those three French guns still stood in place, but most of the men serving them were on the ground, men and horses killed and wounded, the horses thrashing in their traces and harness, a few galloping away trailing entrails.

"Good God, yes!" Lewrie shouted. A look to the road, though, damped his enthusiasm, for the French cavalry were drawing sabres and holding them aloft. Which British regiment would they attack?

Before anything could happen, though, the sky was filled with unearthly moans, and the roar of distant guns. Drones in the air, a harpy's shriek, rising in tone as something passed overhead, dropping in tone and volume, then . . . it was roundshot from *Vigilance*, slamming into the slopes down which the French regiments still marched with the drums and the now-and-then shout in praise of Bonaparte. They could not explode or even shatter as they struck the dry, rocky gound, but they could rock the ground when 18-pounder shot hit, and raised great gouts of dirt, sand, and dust almost as frightening as explosive shot.

Hardly had that broadside landed when a deeper, heavier moaning soared overhead, and 24-pound shot from the lower gun-deck battery hit, making the ground shudder as if there had been a sudden, distant earthquake, and cloaking the French positions in a cloud of dirt.

Cavalry horses and their riders were just splattered when a direct hit was made, and the French regiment on the left of the road was parted into several smaller columns as soldiers were ripped apart. As the dirt settled round them, the French columns both staggered to a halt, and the drums fell silent.

Oooh! a broadside from the upper-deck 18-pounders moaned over-head again, better-aimed this time, now that the guns were warming up, and the left-hand French regiment was shredded. A roundshot even hit near the clutch of senior officers, making horses rear and buck, and tearing one of the officers from his saddle in a bloody bloom.

"The brigade will advance!" Lewrie heard Caruthers shout to his men, and trotted out in front of them on his stolen horse, sword pointing towards the enemy. British drums beat, fifers tootled out "The Bowld Soldier Boy," and the colours went forward. Stunned French soldiers shuffled about, turning their stalled columns into line, waiting for the British to approach musket range.

"Think we should discourage them, sir?" Lieutenant Rutland shouted, his face and uniform gone smutty with powder smoke.

"Aye, let's finish off the cavalry," Lewrie agreed as more shot moaned in from the sea. "One-and-a-half-second fuses, there!"

"Prime your guns! The target is cavalry! Ready? By broadside . . . fire!"

This time, the explosive shells burst right over the horsemen, and the clutch of staff officers. The surviving red-coated troops at last turned their mounts and trotted back to the draw atop the ridge. Some staff officers dismounted to kneel by one of their own who had fallen, even as more gunfire rolled in from *Vigilance*, as regularly as a metronome.

There came a higher-pitched rattle of musketry, massive volleys from the French, overtaken by the platoon fire that rolled continually down the ranks of the British regiments, delivered by men who actually trained in live fire to get off three, perhaps four, rounds a minute. By the time the last Light Company on the left of a regiment's line had fired, the Grenadier Company on the right had reloaded and were leveling their muskets to start the ripple again, and the French could not stand it. They began to give ground, pacing back from their dead and wounded, *over* their dead and wounded.

"Charge!" came the cry, and the British regiments lowered their muskets and raced forwards to fight with the bayonet, and the French, pummeled and decimated, broke, the ones in the rear ranks abandoning their comrades to run back up the slope, heading for the draw.

"Gut the bastards, make 'em bleed!" a sailor-gunner was yelling.

Lewrie went forwards of his now-silent guns for a better view, thought to climb up on the carriage and stand astride a barrel, but a touch on the bronze tube made him jerk his hand back. It was hot!

He caught sight of the Ensign out of the corner of his eye as he trotted back from the beach. The silly sod had his sword drawn, and a look of joy on his face.

"Hoy, Ensign!" Lewrie shouted, jogging out to intercept him and his horse, but the lad seemed too intent on entering the battle. "Hoy!"

The Ensign hauled reins. "Yes, sir?"

"I need you t'ride back to the signals party and tell 'em t'cease fire," Lewrie told him.

"Oh, but *sir*!" the young fellow all but wailed, pointing at the fighting with the tip of his sword like a tot that had been denied the last morsel of a figgy-dowdy.

"Our troops are going up-slope, and they'll run into the shot from my ship's guns," Lewrie explained. "We can't have any of our soldiers splattered right at the moment we're winning, hey? Gallop back, and tell Mister Severance to show Cease Fire."

"Yes, sir," the Ensign replied, sulkily, then sawed his reins and heeled his horse into a gallop, sword still drawn.

Lewrie let out a sigh of relief and walked back to the gun line, where Rutland, Grace, and Chenery were standing, watching the battle as it petered out. French troops who'd been abandoned by their mates had their muskets held out, muzzles down in sign of surrender, and some who had dis-armed were tending to the wounded. The quicker of them looked as if they were apes scrambling on their hands and feet to get up the slope and over the crest of the ridge, through the draw on the road, to escape the roundshot that still moaned and keened in from *Vigilance*.

At least someone's *got a lick o' sense,* Lewrie thought as he saw that the British regiments had halted their charge short of the foot of the ridge, jeering and cheering as the French escaped, still pursued by spurts of earth dug up by 18- and 24-pound shot.

After two more broadsides, the ship's guns fell silent, musket fire fell silent, and the battle was truly over.

"Oh, damn," Lieutenant Rutland gravelled in a laconic tone.

"A good show, while it lasted," Lewrie said.

"It's raining," Rutland pointed out as the first large drops hit the dry ground like miniature roundshot that raised mud spurts. Rain hit the hot howitzer barrels, and made sizzling noises. "All that we bloody need."

There was a gust front rolling in from the sea, turning the humid warmth of the day much cooler for a minute, but it faded, leaving only a pleasant zephyr. With the gust front, large rain drops came in wave that rattled hats, but the rain subsided to a gentle shower.

"Better now than half an hour ago," Lewrie told him. "Nobody could prime a musket, much less these guns. We'll have to destroy them, spike them, of course. I'll be damned if we roll them back into the depot."

"Can't be spiked, sir," Rutland informed him. "The vents and touch holes are tubes that screw in. The depot's probably full of the things. Damn all French cleverness. We'll have to burn them."

"We've lots of flannel cartridge bags left, sir," Lieutenant Grace said, "Pile them up under the guns, with the leftover fuses, set that afire, and the wood carriages will burn up."

"Pull the wood plugs from some shells, ram them down, and when they explode in the barrels, they'll burst, too, sir," Rutland added.

"Right, let's get to it, then," Lewrie decided. "And perhaps the Brigadier will make the connexion. Fire, depot, burn?"

"Ehm, we wouldn't have to wait around 'til then, would we, sir?" Midshipman Chenery asked.

"No, once we've got good fires going under these guns, we can stroll back to the beach and get rowed out to the ship," Lewrie told him. "Unless you'd like to see a second depot blow up?"

"No, one's enough for one day, sir," Chenery said, laughing.

"Here comes the Brigadier now," Rutland warned.

Oh, God's Balls, Lewrie thought; *Now I'll have t'hear him crow!*

"Lewrie!" Caruthers shouted as he rode up on a fresh horse, but where he obtained it was anyone's guess. "I've had a horse shot from under me! Isn't that grand?"

"Well, not for the horse, sir," Lewrie drawled.

"But it will go down well in my despatches," Caruthers replied, sounding positively chipper. "This 'un, now, belonged to one of their Hussars who has no future need of it. Be a shame to put a bullet in its skull when we leave, but it'll probably end up back in French service when I let it loose. See the white flags? My Brigade Major's having a parley with their senior surviving officer. They officially yield the field to us, take no more martial action, and all prisoners we've taken, whole or wounded, will swear on their parole not to serve in the field against British forces 'til they're exchanged."

"They'll lie like blazes," Lewrie told him, "they'll only honour that 'til your last soldier is off the beach."

"Well, of course they will," Caruthers hooted. "Gad, who'd trust the word of a Frenchman, haw! Magnificent, sir! What you did with the guns, and your ship's guns, was truly magnificent, and I shall say so, fulsomely, in my report of the battle. Had you not come ashore, had you not brought gunners, it might have neen a close-run thing, and I would have lost a lot more than the hundred or so we have in killed and wounded. I daresay you saved my bacon, and I will be forever in your debt, sir!"

Wouldn't have lost any *if you'd done what you were supposed to do in the* first *place*, Lewrie thought; *Still, give a dog a good name.*

"You do me a great honour, sir," Lewrie replied, doffing his hat in salute, and putting a "sweet" face on. "Thank you for the compliment, which I shall pass on to my crew."

"Well, sir," Caruthers said, doffing his own for a moment, "I've things to see to, wounded to care for, that depot to set alight as soon as the negotiations are done. A hospital set up on the beach?"

Lewrie noted that one of his regiments was plodding back from the ridge, some of its rankers quickly bandaged and limping, supported by their mates, and some worse off being carried on stretchers.

"I will not keep you, sir," Lewrie said. "Oh, if your troops come back by here, or when they prepare the depot for destruction, you might warn them to keep clear of these guns. They might get hurt when they go bang for the last time."

"Hey? Oh, leave the French nothing, right!" Caruthers agreed. "Once again, my undying thanks for your timely aid, sir, and when we're all back at Messina, I'd admire to dine you and your officers in at my officers' mess."

"I'd be delighted to accept, sir," Lewrie told him, and after a last doffing of hats, Caruthers rode off.

"Praised highly in his reports, sir?" Lieutenant Grace asked. "My, that will be wonderful. We really *did* save their bacon."

"He'll spend more time praising himself," Lewrie said with his usual cynical outlook. "His sort do. And I won't hold my breath waiting to see any mention of our assistance. Ah, well. Let's get going on destroying these guns, then we can get back to the ship where things make sense."

"And we can scramble up the boarding nets one more time, sir?" Midshipman Chenery asked, tongue-in-cheek.

"Damn all Midshipmen's wit," Lewrie groused. "*You* can scramble up the boarding nets, if you've a mind, young sir. I mean to use the battens and man-ropes, like the weary man that I am."

As the flannel powder cartridges were piled under the carriages, Lewrie sat on an empty shell box, pulled his canteen round, and drank off at least a quarter of his cool tea, finding that the inadvertent admixture of ginger beer made an even more delightful beverage that he would insist upon in future.

The rain was still coming down and his hat and coat were getting soaked, so he reached into a side pocket for a handkerchief, but found a stub of his morning's sausage. And that tasted wonderful, too.

EPILOGUE

I say, Sir Alan, have you seen these?" Colonel Tarrant asked him as Lewrie made a courtesy call at the 94th Foot's encampment a few weeks later. He'd dropped by for tea, or something spiritous. "We've just gotten the latest London papers, and by the look of it, we, you and I, and the regiment, are suddenly rather famous!"

"What?" Lewrie said with a surprised start. "Famous?"

"Brigadier Caruthers's report of the landings at Locri and Siderno," Tarrant went on, handing him an untidy stack of newspapers.

"My word," Lewrie commented as he found the pages that Tarrant had folded over and circled with a pen. "He mentioned us?"

"Quite prominently," Tarrant assured him. "Well, only a short account of the 94th's skirmishing. He said we faced French troops, not Genoese, but as he said, we carried out our duties briskly and efficiently, and set the depot at Locri afire and got away without a man wounded.

"Now, his account of his own fight, well . . . ," Tarrant chuckled, pulling at his nose, "one *could* get the impression that the French had more troops, guns, and cavalry than what you told me they had when we sailed over to Messina for that mess supper, but, with none of his own artillery ashore, the lack of his third regiment with Siderno's harbour clogged, he gave you and your work with the captured howitzers a grand account. Your knowledge of fuses and explosive shells? The accuracy of your gunners, and the utter ruin of the French your ship's guns made? Yes, we are quite famous, For a time, at least."

"I wasn't sure he'd even mention us," Lewrie said, shaking his head in mild wonder as he read the newspaper accounts cribbed from the official report, and written in the best "By Jingo" bravado. "If the papers could get any more fawning, I'd begin t'think I'm part of the Second Coming, hah! What high-flown moonshine!"

"You haven't gotten your latest letters from home?" Tarrant asked as he poured them both a top-up of white wine.

"Nothing since last week," Lewrie said as he read on, thinking that his next batch of letters from home would be full of their perceptions of the news, delighted that Jessica would be over the moon to see her husband's name in print.

"Oh, by the by," Tarrant continued. "I've heard from the city fathers of Peterborough. They, and the gentry who paid to raise the regiment, are suddenly bursting with pride in our accomplishments . . . after years of benign neglect, as I complained to you. Everyone seems to love us, of a sudden. You may have to find us another couple of transports."

"Transports?" Lewrie said, coming up from his reading.

"The city, and the county, have decided to hold a whole round of subscription balls, patriotic assemblies, and recruiting celebrations," Tarrant boasted. "They've promised to raise at least two new companies, and enough volunteers to flesh out the six I have. Give it three or four months and I might be able to field a Grenadier Company, again, and a second Light Company, for a total of eight. I've found that soldiers best suited as skirmishers are more useful in our line of work than Line Companies. We will most definitely *not* try to fight Caruthers's style of battle. Not as long as I'm in command!"

"Well, that's grand, good for you, sir!" Lewrie said, truly glad for him, though where he would obtain two more troop transports, deemed armed transports, with large Navy crews, and the necessary number of sailors to man them, was beyond him at the moment.

And where's Captain Middleton when I need him, this *time?* Lewrie wondered; *Ships, crews, barges . . . boarding nets? So long as I never have t'use 'em again!*

"There's even a vague promise of finding us a proper barracks and establishment for a home station, with a training and recruiting cadre," Tarrant said with a shrug, as if he didn't quite believe it. "It will most-like turn out to be an abandoned brick works that I know of, way out in the country. If they *do* put a roof on it, I'd be damned surprised. Been crumbling to dust for years.

"Oh!" Tarrant exclaimed. "I've also heard from Horse Guards. I have been made substantive Leftenant-Colonel, and Gittings is now a substantive Major, not a Brevet."

"Now we'll have to celebrate *that*!" Lewrie declared. "My treat! We'll wet the two of you down, Navy fashion."

"It doesn't involve a sail in a boat, does it?" Tarrant asked, with a wary look.

"No no, nothing like that," Lewrie promised with a hearty laugh. "Though it does involve a lot of wine and brandy."

"So, how does it feel to be celebrated" Tarrant asked him.

"It feels . . . damned good," Lewrie decided. "It makes me feel . . . justified. Will you have a glass with me, sir?" he posed, lifting his wine to be tossed back in a toast.

Justified, indeed, Lewrie thought; *And all my detractors can buss my blind cheeks, leap to their feet, and kick furniture, 'cause they can't blight me, or destroy me.*

He began to chuckle, then laugh out loud, and a rather evil and satisfying laugh it was, too. But retribution must be savoured with mirthful delight.